OMEGA

The demonstrators, banner aloft, had marched into the Great Circle, trampling straight through the little Circles towards the Cauldron, chanting in unison: 'Goddess worship is Satan worship! Goddess worship is Satan worship! Goddess worship is Satan worship!'

Some of the older people not in the Dance were running forward, trying to stop them. But the demonstrators were young, clothed and booted, and swept the elderly skyclad bodies easily aside. The younger baby-minding fathers, like Dan, hesitated, torn between repelling the intruders and standing guard over their children. Moira grabbed at Dan's arm, restraining him; he shrugged helplessly and acquiesced.

But now the dancers had heard the chanting and had turned, incredulous anger in their faces. The demonstrators did not pause; they headed straight for the Sabbat Queen, who was clearly their target.

The chanting changed. 'Witch whore! Witch whore! Witch whore!'

Also in Arrow by Stewart Farrar

The Twelve Maidens
The Serpent of Lilith
The Dance of Blood
The Sword of Orley

OMEGA

Stewart Farrar

ARROW BOOKS

Arrow Books Limited
3 Fitzroy Square, London WIP 6JD

An imprint of the Hutchinson Publishing Group

London Melbourne Sydney Auckland
Wellington Johannesburg and agencies
throughout the world

First published by Arrow Books 1980
© Stewart Farrar 1980

Set in Intertype Plantin

Made and printed in Great Britain by
The Anchor Press Ltd,
Tiptree, Essex

ISBN 0 09 920700 1

In memory of our friend
DAVID BUCKINGHAM
who was in at the birth

PROLOGUE

It had been amazingly simple, the fur-clad engineer from Florida told himself, to turn the Earth into a huge electric battery, with terminals 12,700 kilometres apart, give or take a few. But it would have been one hell of a lot more comfortable for the terminal crews if Earth had arranged itself better, with land masses opposite land masses – instead of perversely (almost ingeniously, if you looked at the globe which some wit had made the decorative centrepiece of the Mess lobby) land opposite sea and sea opposite land.

Even worse, the more civilized the climate of any given hunk of land – Florida, for instance – the vaster, emptier and less hospitable was the stretch of ocean which diametrically opposed it.

Earth was a mean bitch, he decided, crunching his frosty way up Sunset Strip (all of four metres wide – there were too many witty guys around here) towards the Control Complex.

Why, for Christ's sake, did she have to balance the United States of America with nine million square kilometres of Indian Ocean – except for this Godforsaken strip of Antarctica, leased from Norway in Princess Astrid Land for uncountable dollars, just because it lay opposite equally Godforsaken Alaska?

It *was* economically feasible to drill terminals at sea, thousands of kilometres from nowhere, with floating platform control bases. But the shrinks had worked out that it was psychologically undesirable. Land bases permitted families, sport and cultural facilities and so on. The engineer from Florida was not impressed; he was unmarried, his sport was skin-diving and his taste in films was as diametrically opposite to that of the Entertainment Officer as Princess Astrid Land was to Alaska. He firmly believed that the reasons *were* economic, whatever Washington said and that the shrinks had merely been called in to justify them.

Governments were mean bastards, too.

It was all right for the British, with their terminals in New Zealand (ten degrees out didn't diminish the Mendoza Effect unacceptably), or the Chinese with their Chilean agreement, or even for the guys on the Siberian–Argentinian project (*somebody* must love Siberia). But the Americans, the Canadians, the Africans, the Indians, the Arabs, the Israelis – bloody Earth had sold them all short.

The engineer from Florida did not lack imagination. He could well envisage that, say, a Leningrad technician fretting in exile in the Andean foothills, or a geophysicist from Florence pining for the Ponte Vecchio in the lonely Chatham Islands, might be cursing his environment and Earth in roughly identical terms to his own. But that was little consolation. Fellow-feeling didn't bring home any closer.

The Mendoza Effect had been discovered in 1995 by one Dr Juan Jesus Mendoza, a native of Segovia working on a

United Nations water-drilling project in the Sahara. He was a laser technician; high-speed laser drilling was a comparatively new development then but the doctor was still too young to have been one of those who made his name in that development. The method called for subtle electronic controls and Mendoza, if at that time still unknown to the public, was nothing if not subtle.

He had been in charge of the monitoring and control of three test-drillings about 100 kilometres apart. These three drillings had not been directly for water, but for the location of the optimum water-drilling sites by an ingenious system of pulse-transmission and triangulation. Mendoza's immediate boss had had a theory that the system would work more reliably if the pulse-transmission electrodes were in the Moho, the boundary between the Earth's crust and mantle, some thirty-five kilometres down. Laser drilling made this quite feasible, the only major expense being just over 100 kilometres of insulated conductor-rod in screw-ended, ten-metre sections.

Once the three Moho electrodes were in place and activated, it had become clear that the boss's theory had been wrong and the expense unjustified; and since the project chief had had an axe poised for him already, the axe had been delightedly wielded and the miscalculator had been transferred elsewhere, leaving Mendoza in sole charge of the triple station.

It was in his lonely desert control hut in the middle of the triangle, some six weeks later, that Mendoza had noticed an odd symptom. He would have noticed it before, if all three lines had not been working faultlessly; but on this particular night a maintenance party was out hunting for a fault in the northerly line, so only the south-easterly and south-westerly electrodes were sending in their signals. Mendoza knew to a fraction how many milliamps were produced by the apparently permanent voltage difference between the two electrodes and this amperage was duly showing on his meters.

There had been no radio report from the maintenance party for a while. Bored, Mendoza had flicked a switch which sent a test-pulse along the faulty line. To his surprise, the needles on the two other ammeters had suddenly jerked to the end of the scales, taking several seconds to settle down again. Mendoza had frowned, and flicked the switch once more; the same thing had happened. Then he had noticed that the individual test switches were set to 'on' for all three lines, so he must have sent a test pulse along the working lines, too. He had tried reducing the strength of the test pulse; the answering jerks on the needles had become less violent but he had had to reduce the pulse almost to zero before the needles would remain within the scales.

On some irrational hunch which he could never afterwards fathom, Dr Juan Jesus Mendoza had then done the apparently pointless thing which was to make him famous and comfortably wealthy. He had sent out a test pulse of five times the standard strength.

Both test circuits had blown their fuses, simultaneously.

He had no means of knowing, of course, that his historic flick of the switch would lead within a decade to a very nearly complete depopulation of the Earth. Had he known, it is only fair to say that he would have abandoned all further experiments on the phenomenon without a qualm, and would have done everything he could to prevent anyone else noticing it; for Juan Jesus Mendoza was a good man as well as a clever one.

But without suspicion of danger, he had stared at the two dead needles for several minutes without moving, while he did some rapid sums in his head. For some unimaginable reason, a stimulus of thirty-two milliamps, applied to two Moho electrodes 84.7 kilometres apart – and reaching them, because of the different cable lengths, with a time difference of about nine microseconds – had produced a surge of current between them thousands of times larger than the stimulus. He did not understand the phenomenon but over the next few weeks he worked hard at it and it was during those weeks that he made the imaginative leap which revealed his genius.

When he was ready, he had invited the project chief to a private demonstration in which, by sending out alternate pulses from a small flashlamp battery along two of his Moho lines, at a sixty-cycle frequency, he received a feedback current that kept a two-kilowatt electric bowl fire glowing steadily at full strength. The project chief did not study the mathematics which were far above his head; but he could not ignore the electric fire and he knew enough about circuitry (and about Mendoza) to rule out fraud. So he had hastened to assume patronage of his gifted subordinate and had taken him higher.

The politics of the thing had proved tedious and it would be tedious to recount them. It is enough to say that a year later Mendoza got a UN grant to test his theory – which was that in the Mendoza Effect lay the possibility of a major alleviation of the world's power crisis.

His claim was simple, staggering, and well-documented, though the theory was a long way ahead of the Saharan evidence and only comprehensible to a few experts. With his two Saharan electrodes he had achieved a maximum output of 3.2 kilowatts. But (his theory said) given two pairs of Moho electrodes, each electrode being 117.3 kilometres from its partner, and the two pairs being separated by the diameter of the globe – and given a phased stimulus of a few kilowatts, synchronized by orbiting satellite, being fed to those four electrodes – the output from each pair would be of the order of several thousand megawatts.

The UN Secretary-General didn't understand it either and the experts he consulted contradicted each other. But he had a feeling about this serious young Spaniard; and anyway laser drilling was getting cheaper by the month. So he took a chance and pushed Project Mohowatt through the appropriate Committee.

On 15 March 1997 Dr Juan Jesus Mendoza ran his first test on the completed Mohowatt prototype, which had one station near Obidos in Brazil and the other near Manado in the Celebes. His input at each station was 150 kilowatts and his output at each was 4015 megawatts. Once the process was started, controlled feedback from the output supplied the necessary input.

The UN Secretary-General in person made a splendid speech at the inaugural demonstration to diplomats and the media. But Mendoza remembered better his chief engineer's comment afterwards: '*He* doesn't understand it? Hell, Juan, *I* don't understand it, and I built the thing for you! But this gizmo hauls itself up by its own bootstraps and if we don't watch that feedback like bloody hawks, it could blow the roof.'

Enlightened world opinion congratulated itself that the Mohowatt principle was UN-sponsored and so freely available to any nation wishing to exploit it. Practically all of them did, though some were at a disadvantage if thousands of fathoms of sea covered their globally opposite areas; but even they could console themselves with the knowledge that much cheaper power would soon be purchasable from not-too-distant neighbours, who would be undercutting each other to sell it to them.

By the turn of the century, over a hundred Mohowatt

couples were in operation round the globe, with as many more under construction.

There seemed to be only two snags – one economic, the other navigational; but both, everyone predicted, would soon be adjusted to. First, by the nature of the system, there were Mohowatt stations in isolated places with thousands of megawatts running to waste because output at the two ends of any couple was equal; so there was a certain amount of economic disturbance as new productive enterprises mushroomed in unsuitable areas. Second, magnetic compasses became unreliable without constant reference to the latest magnetic variation charts, which a hastily set up UN service had to publish monthly; somehow, the strange electrical events which were being provoked in the belly of Mother Earth were making her magnetic field unprecedentedly turbulent.

Still, these were small problems compared with the golden prospect of a twenty-first century of unlimited power – which pleased, among others, environmentalists who were unhappy about nuclear power stations and geologists with a gloomy eye on dwindling oil and coal deposits.

Professor Bernard Arklow, of the International Seismological Centre at Newbury, Berkshire, worried about neither of these. In fact he worried about very little, being completely wrapped up in his own subject; the standing joke among his more worldly wise colleagues was that old Arklow's ivory tower was the only known structure which would stand up even to his own beloved earthquakes.

He was all the more surprised, therefore, when the outer world impinged on him abruptly. He had been becoming increasingly excited by the implications of certain statistics, from the seismologists of the world, which it was his happy function to collate; and when the time came to prepare his annual departmental report for the year 2002–3, he felt ready to communicate his provisional conclusions, in his usual scholarly preamble to that report.

Translated into everyday language, those conclusion were that over the past year increasingly abnormal movements and correspondingly abnormal stresses had been arising in the handful of giant plates which composed the Earth's crust. These stresses would continue to build up, the Professor convincingly showed, and would produce seismic phenomena – in short, earthquakes – not only along the classic earthquake zones where the edges of the plates met but within the area of each plate itself.

When he had completed and submitted his report, the Professor sat back contentedly. He looked forward to its inclusion in the Centre's overall report and to the impact it would have on his fellow-specialists. They would be furious at not having realized it first, but on the facts, they would be obliged to admit he was right.

No one could have been more astonished than the Professor when, three days after the typescript had left his desk, he received a summons to Whitehall – from a very high personage indeed.

He returned to Newbury the following day looking, for once in his life, subdued.

PART ONE

Nemesis

1

'My dear General,' the Permanent Secretary said impatiently, 'it's no good looking to the Prime Minister. He hasn't the remotest idea of the seriousness of the situation. As long as the balance of payments is improving – which it is at the moment, for a combination of seasonal and one-off reasons – he can concentrate on the things that matter to him. Exploiting differences within his own Party to his own advantage, and scoring points off the Opposition.'

There was silence between the four of them for a while. Down Whitehall Big Ben boomed the three-quarters. As its echoes sank into the murmur of the traffic beyond the tall windows, General Mullard shook his head. 'It's a terrifying thought, Harley, that the Government of our country . . .'

Harley snorted. 'I am tempted to reply, with Shaw's Undershaft: "*I* am the Government of your country." Or to be more accurate, *we*. The Civil Service – and don't imagine for a moment that I speak only for the Treasury . . .'

'I don't,' the General said drily.

'Quite. The Civil Service, the Services, industry, and

the TUC. Of which we four — let's be frank about it — are the key minds in the key positions.'

'I doubt if ICI would agree with you about *me*,' Lord Stayne laughed.

'Come off it, Joe,' the TUC man said. 'ICI know the facts of life, whatever they *wish* they were. When you pipe, they dance — especially if I'm playing the drum. Same with the General here. He's not the top brass but he's the key brass. Thompson's a figurehead. No, Harley's right. So let's talk about realities.'

'Thank you, Sir Walter,' Harley nodded. 'And if — or rather, when — Situation Beehive arises, those realities will become even sharper.'

There was another brief silence, which General Mullard broke with the question: 'How long?'

'One month, six months — the seismologists can't be sure. They're all agreed that Professor Arklow's deductions are correct. The facts are no longer in dispute. Only the time factor is.'

'And the magnitude?'

'Only roughly predictable. But serious enough for the Official Secrets Act, with trimmings, to have been clapped on the Newbury staff as soon as the Professor set the cat among the pigeons.'

'Tricky, I'd have thought? The Centre is international.'

'Very tricky, in theory. But in practice we got rapid cooperation from other Governments. Once they read Arklow's report — even ahead of their own experts' confirmation — they were as concerned as we were not to create public panic. So foreigners attached to the Centre had their own Embassies down on them at the same time.' He smiled thinly. 'However cumbersome the diplomatic machine may appear, there *are* means of short-circuiting it when danger, and common interest, are self-evident.'

'I should hope so,' the General said, 'or my profession would be a lot busier. . . . By the way, what's being done about the theory that the Mohowatt stations are causing the crust disturbances?'

'Oh, for God's sake,' Lord Stayne snorted. 'Old wives' tales!'

'You're scarcely impartial, with millions invested in them,' the General pointed out. 'And Sir Walter has thousands of his members' jobs at stake.'

'All the same,' Harley told him, 'I agree with Stayne. There *is* no evidence to link the two. Only the kind of *post ergo propter* argument one expects from the more sensationally minded of our environmentalists – and fortunately Arklow's report is not available to them, or we'd have some real red herrings to deal with. . . . The remote possibility of some such link existing is being investigated, of course,' he continued blandly, 'but meanwhile it would be extremely premature, and highly disruptive, to envisage any modification of the Mohowatt programme. All the interested governments are agreed on this.'

'Oh, well. . . . But to get back to the earthquakes . . .'

'We prefer to call them "seismic abnormalities".'

The General gave a short bark of a laugh. 'As Sir Walter said – let's talk about realities, within these four walls.'

'Very well. Earthquakes.'

'Will Beehive stand up to them, I wonder? So deep underground?'

Lord Stayne said, 'Surely,' and Sir Walter humphed in agreement.

Harley inclined his head. 'They should know. After all, they built it, virtually – they and their predecessors. And on the best possible advice. . . . In fact, of course, the picture has changed with Arklow's evidence. Beehive is likely to suffer *some* damage. But remember, the code-name Beehive is an over-simplification. It's really a complex of hives, well dispersed over the country, with everything that matters reduplicated. As long as there's anything of Britain left to control, there'll be enough of Beehive left to take control of it when the worst is over and the time is ripe. . . . Which is why – I need hardly say this – you gentlemen must be continuously careful about the quality and preparedness of your key men at the regional hives.'

'You, too,' the General said pointedly.

'Of course.'

'Let's talk about *now*,' Sir Walter suggested. 'Operation Beehive's cut and dried, ready for when the balloon goes up. We can trust each other to go on improving our own aspects of it. So let's not waste time. The first week after Beehive Red will be the crunch. If Beehive can establish an authoritative image then, it'll keep it. The real problem's *now* – the one month, or six months or whatever, *before* the balloon. How to prepare people without letting them know they're being prepared.'

'You have put your finger,' Harley said, with slightly pompous approval, 'on the real purpose of this meeting.'

Sir Walter grinned sardonically. 'And in view of the Hitlerian overtone of the only possible solution – the one that's on all our minds – you'd be much happier if I, good old Walter Jennings, the golden voice of organized labour, were the one to name it.'

'Since you put it that way' – Harley's smile was unabashed – 'yes.'

'You old fox.'

The other three went on looking at Jennings, waiting.

Jennings shrugged. 'All right. I'll say it. We need a scapegoat. We need one urgently, to forestall any possibility that Mohowatt might become that scapegoat, which could be disastrous.'

'We need an identifiable category of *human* scapegoats,' Harley amplified. 'And there's one ready to hand, isn't there? The witchcraft movement.'

'It seems a shame,' the General said, with unexpected wistfulness. 'They're a harmless enough lot. Rather endearing, some of them.'

'Not all of them, by any means. And have you any alternative?' When the General shook his head, Harley went on: 'They're tailor-made for it, you must realize. They've been a really widespread and public movement for only about twenty years, since the 1980s. By now there are at least a quarter of a million of them – though one can only estimate, since they have no formal national organization. They've been part of the scenery long enough for everybody to know who most of them are – but they're new enough as a mass phenomenon, and bizarre enough by conventional standards, to make millions of people uneasy. *Very* uneasy. I know they've behaved themselves remarkably well, in public-order terms – there's been localized trouble from teenage elements at one or two of their Festivals, and not even that for some years. But under the surface their very existence touches on some terrifyingly atavistic emotions. Trigger those off . . .'

He left the sentence unfinished, hanging in the air.

After a while Lord Stayne said: 'This will require very careful planning if it's not to get out of hand.'

'That shouldn't be difficult.'

'What had you in mind? You've obviously given thought to it already.'

'A little curtain-raiser to test public response,' Harley said. 'A little – er – "spontaneous" provocation and over-reaction, to be followed up with some inspired comment in the media. And so on. . . . There isn't much time to waste, but fortunately they've a Festival coming up.'

Stayne nodded. 'The Midsummer Solstice.'

'Thank God Beltane's over,' Jennings said. 'It's got altogether too tangled up with May Day. And that I *might* have found embarrassing.'

'With regard to your "spontaneous" provocation, Harley,' General Mullard asked thoughtfully. 'How little is "little"?'

2

All over Bell Beacon the small fires were being lit and the scent of woodsmoke hung in the almost motionless air. Moira estimated that there must be at least a hundred covens spread out over the three-hectare plateau which sloped gently southwards from the northern summit. Not over the whole of it, of course; the space around the still unlit Great Fire in the centre had been left well clear for the Ring Dance; and besides, once *that* was ablaze, too close would be too hot.

The Beacon really was an ideal place for a Sabbat, Moira thought. The little plateau was almost perfectly flat, the short downland grass was like a lawn and there were no bushes or trees which might catch fire. The slope was too slight for even a candlestick to show a noticeable tilt, yet it was enough to give appropriate dignity to the summit itself, the northern hump a few metres across on which the Great Altar stood.

Bell Beacon rose a good hundred metres above the surrounding countryside, and from its summit in daylight one could look down not only on much of Buckinghamshire in which it stood, but eastwards into Middlesex and southwards across the Thames into Berkshire and Surrey. Yet except at the northern face, which ended the ridge, it was not precipitous and could easily be climbed on foot. On normal summer days cars would drive up here by the long slanting road, but not tonight. Ever since the Beacon had started to be used openly for the local mass Sabbats (Moira, twenty-seven now, had been brought to one of the earliest by her parents as a little girl) custom had established that cars be parked out of sight below Gresham Wood and the footpath used for the last half-kilometre. There were still latecomers winding up it now, in the twilight, and spreading out to find spaces for their own individual coven Circles, calling cheerful 'Blessed be!' greetings to friends as they threaded their way among the Circles already established.

Each Circle was marked by a ring of white cord laid on the grass, of a diameter still referred to by the traditional measure of nine feet but produced – as every efficient High Priestess knew by heart – by a circumferential cord of 8.62 metres. Most covens, like Moira's, kept a special 8.62-metre ring ready spliced for public Festivals. Since the Craft had become open and widespread (the historic Glastonbury Beltane of 1983 was generally accepted as the turning-point) many new conventions had evolved naturally. One of these was that it was selfish, and therefore bad manners, to have an individual Circle larger than nine feet at a mass Festival, however large your coven. In any case, covens which grew beyond the equally traditional thirteen-member maximum, without hiving off, were looked at askance by their neighbours and hints would be dropped; Craft opinion strongly favoured the small, personalized, autonomous group, feeling that oversize covens ran the risk of a change of nature.

Moira and Daniel's coven consisted of five; six if you included four-year-old Diana, who was here tonight, bouncing excitedly at Moira's side and squealing 'Blessed be!' to everyone who passed, friend or stranger. Rosemary and Greg, their next-door neighbours in Staines, had founded the coven with them three years earlier when Moira had decided that, as a wife and mother, it was time for her to hive off from her own mother's group – a decision for which, she knew, Daniel had been secretly eager, though too fond of his mother-in-law to urge it. Too bad that Sally, she of the large heart and the ironic tongue who was their neighbour on the other side, could not be here tonight; but Sally had to admit, regretfully, that at eighty-two, hilltop Sabbats were no longer for her. . . . It was a happy and close-knit coven, of which Moira as High Priestess was proud. Dan had joked once that it worked well because it had its own built-in representatives of the Triple Goddess: fairylike Rosemary as the Maid, tall Moira as the Mother and shrewd Sally as the Crone; and Moira had known that, like so many of Dan's jokes, it was meant seriously.

'Which side does the salt go, Mummy?' Diana interrupted her thoughts. 'I can't properly remember.'

'You should ask Rosemary that, darling. She's High Priestess tonight.'

'Why, Mummy? You're High Priestess really.'

'Because in a little while they'll light that big bonfire in the middle, and everybody'll go and dance round it. Except for very old people or people with little children who'll stay in their own Circles and watch. Daddy and I will stay with you but Rosemary and Greg will go and do our dancing for us. So it's their special night and *they're* being High Priestess and High Priest. It's only fair, isn't it?'

'Why can't I dance too? Then we could all go.'

'Next year, maybe. The dancing gets very fast, and you're a bit small for it yet.'

'But I can run like *mad*.'

'I know you can, darling. But next year you'll be a little taller and stronger.'

'Like the Goddess up there?'

'Not quite that tall,' Moira laughed, looking towards the Demeter-like figure of the Goddess which towered three metres high behind the Great Altar, the very last rays of the setting sun reddening its pure whiteness. It was unmistakably a Howard Frank creation; Frank was the Craft's most gifted sculptor and his work was much in demand, particularly the one-occasion polystyrene figures like this, of astonishing vitality, which he could shape in a day's working when the mood was on him. He never charged for Festival pieces but he never did more than three or four and he made his own decisions as to who should have them. This Midsummer Bell Beacon had been lucky.

'I'm glad it's warm,' Diana said. 'I don't like robes.'

'Me neither,' Moira agreed, enjoying the feel of the grass under her bare skin. This part of the Thames Valley was predominantly Gardnerian territory, and the Gardnerians (and their Alexandrian offshoots, though the two had tended to re-merge) had clung to their 'skyclad' tradition of ritual nudity even for public Festivals, weather permitting; so most of the covens on this mild Midsummer night were, like Moira and Dan's, skyclad. The individual Circle fires helped, of course; they had become an established part of the public Festival tradition, encouraged no doubt by the British climate. Moira could just remember the public controversy that had raged and quickly died away over those early skyclad Festivals. The police (in Warwickshire somewhere, wasn't it?) had made a much-headlined test case of one Midsummer Festival in 1985, arresting a dozen people and charging them with causing a breach of the peace. But since the peace, on that occasion, had only been disturbed by a handful of hecklers who (as the defence had delightedly proved) had travelled all the way from London for the purpose – and since nude bathing had been unofficially tolerated on many British beaches since the end of the 1970s – the bench had dismissed the charges. There had been no more arrests and few Festivals nowadays attracted more than a sprinkling of voyeurs, whom the covens ignored.

Here and there on the plateau Moira could make out robed covens, presumably Celtic Traditionals; but in these ecumenical days they would be as welcome as the rest. The Craft was too jealous of coven autonomy for anyone to try to impose uniformity. There had been one attempt, in 1989, to summon a National Convention for such a purpose. It had been heavily attended and the floor had defeated the conveners on every point, except for a few proposals to make voluntary communication between covens smoother – which meant little in practice because inter-coven links were and had remained mainly local and almost entirely spontaneous.

Ad hoc meetings of High Priestesses and High Priests in various areas provided what little organization was needed for public Festivals, which were the only occasion – eight a year – when large numbers of covens gathered together. Each Yule the same *ad hoc* caucus would choose the local Sabbat Maiden for the following year's eight Festivals. This choice was really a two-year appointment, because each Sabbat Maiden became the following year's Sabbat Queen, leader of the whole mass ritual. Her consort Priest needed no choosing; her own working partner automatically took the role.

Now the sun had set. It shouldn't be long before the

Queen, the Maiden and their Priests made their ceremonial appearance.

Moira, from habit, glanced around her own Circle to make sure that all was in order; then reminded herself that tonight was Rosemary's honour. North, east, south and west candles burned in the little glass lanterns kept for outdoor use. By the north candle, a picnic hamper with a cloth over it served as an altar, with the ritual tools and two more candle-lanterns arranged on the cloth. When the ritual part of the Sabbat was over, the ceremonial objects would be packed away and the altar-cloth folded, and the hamper would surrender its food and drink. Then the feast would begin, and the coming and going of friends. . . .

A hush falling on the plateau made Moira look up.

All eyes were turned to a small tent near the Great Altar – the only enclosed structure in the whole Great Circle. Moira's Circle was about twenty metres from the tent, so she could see clearly the two men who had emerged and now stood flanking the doorway, in the light of the many fires and candles and of the nearly full moon which was already bright.

She knew them both. Nigel Pickering from Cookham, robed in dark red, High Priest of Mary Andrews, this year's Sabbat Maiden. (Even though the covens were skyclad, custom laid down that the Four always at least began the Sabbat in ceremonial vestments.) Nigel, as the Maiden's Priest, would have little to do but escort her, he would come into his own next year. John Hassell from Chertsey, splendid in gold kilt and pectoral, High Priest and husband of Joy Hassell, the Sabbat Queen; Moira felt a tremor of excited pride, for John and Joy were close friends of theirs – in fact she and Dan had conducted their Handfasting and had a slightly parental feeling for them, even though the Hassells were barely their juniors.

Somebody struck a single brazen note on a big cymbal and the assembly stood, in their hundreds, facing the Great Altar. Diana whimpered to see and Dan lifted her on to his shoulders.

The Sabbat Queen appeared between the two Priests to a whisper of awed approval from the watchers. She certainly looked a representative of the Goddess, Moira thought lovingly. Stately in blue and silver, her long fair hair crowned with the crescent moon, moving with calm dignity barefoot on the grass while her sun-girt Priest fell into step beside her.

Then the Sabbat Maid, in a simple tunic of leaf green, her hair short, dark and curly, a complete contrast to the Queen. Again the brief whisper from the assembled covens, but this time, perhaps more simply affectionate, appropriate to the Maiden.

The Four made their way to the Great Altar where two huge candles were already alight, strong-flamed enough to burn without lanterns in this almost still air. The Maiden picked up a torch, lit it from one of the candle-flames and presented it to the High Priest. John held it aloft, pacing slowly to the piled oak branches in the centre clearing and then plunged it into the kindling at the foot of the pile.

Within seconds the Sabbat Fire blazed skywards, borne aloft by a roar of triumph from hundreds of throats. Moira hugged Daniel happily, and Diana, squealing anew, drummed her heels on his chest. That fire, Moira rejoiced, would be seen for miles, like it was in the old days, marking, honouring, reinforcing the cycle of the year. . . . This was really something to be part of, this reborn brotherhood; no grovelling self-abasement, no exploited hysteria – just this proud communal delight, this willing communion with the rhythms of nature, this joy before the Goddess.

She realized suddenly that she had drifted off into formless thought, into an involuntary firelit meditation, when she felt Daniel turning beside her. She pulled herself together, smiling; minutes must have passed. The solar High Priest was already in position behind the Great Altar, silhouetted and almost dwarfed against the white statue of the Goddess. The Sabbat Queen, sword in hand, was already on her way round the perimeter, casting the Great Circle, while the covens turned with her, each in its own little Circle. This took time, for the Great Circle was a good half-kilometre round but no one was impatient; everyone was mentally backing Joy, willing the 'meeting-place of love and joy and truth' into being.

Down the slanting road, perhaps a kilometre away, a motor-cycle revved up briefly. Moira felt and shared the flicker of annoyance around her; then silence fell again and the interruption was forgotten.

Now the Sabbat Queen was once more before the Altar, facing the High Priest across it. Her voice rang out in the night: 'Great One of Heaven, Power of the Sun, we invoke thee in thine ancient names – Michael, Balin, Arthur, Lugh, Herne; come again as of old into this thy land. Lift up thy shining spear of light to protect us. Put to flight the powers of darkness. Give us fair woodlands and green fields, blossoming orchards and ripening corn. Bring us to stand upon thy hill of vision, and show us the lovely realms of the Gods.'

She swept her hand towards him in the invoking Pentagram and he walked forward round the Altar to join her. The Maiden bowed before them and handed the High Priest a gilded lance. Together, the Four moved towards the central fire, halting before it at the big iron Cauldron which swung, full of water, from a flower-wreathed tripod. The High Priest held up the glittering lance, point downwards, and lowered it into the Cauldron, calling out in a voice resonant with authority: 'The Spear to the Cauldron, the Lance to the Grail, Spirit to Flesh, Man to Woman, Sun to Earth!'

The silence was absolute as he laid the lance on the ground beside the Cauldron. The Sabbat Queen, smiling, spread her arms wide and high, summoning the covens: 'Dance ye about the Cauldron of Cerridwen, the Goddess, and be ye blessed with the touch of this consecrated water; even as the Sun, the Lord of Life, ariseth in his strength in the sign of the Waters of Life.'

It was the signal; before her voice had ceased, the tide was moving inwards, hundreds of firelit bodies, laughing and calling to each other, weaving between the Circles like shore-foam around rocks, inwards, inwards to the central blaze, linking hands as they reached it, man to woman, woman to man; already the Ring Dance wheeled clockwise round the Midsummer Fire, High Priest, Maiden, and Maiden's Priest leading, till the inward tide ceased flowing and all were in the circling ring, and the head joined the tail, the High Priest catching the last woman's hand to close it. By the Cauldron the Sabbat Queen still stood, sprinkling water on the passing dancers with an aspergill of heather twigs. She had shed her robe and was one of them now, skyclad and laughing like the rest.

Only a scattering of old people and baby-minders were left in the honeycomb of coven Circles, gazing inwards at the dancers, identifying with them. Moira and Daniel squatted with Diana between them, their backs warmed by their own little fire which Dan had just replenished.

'Are you sure you don't want to join them, darling?' Moira asked him. 'I'll stay with Diana. We'll be all right.'

Dan said simply: 'Not without you,' in a voice that left no room for discussion. Moira nodded, glowing with love for him. Not alone. Never alone. . . .

'Who are those people, Daddy?'

'What people, love?'

'Over there.' The child pointed behind them, at the edge of the plateau and they turned to look.

'My God!' Dan said. 'Bloody cheek!'

There were perhaps thirty of them, in ordinary clothes, just outside the Great Circle, busy unfurling a banner between two poles; they must have crept up the western slope unnoticed while all eyes were turned inwards. As Dan and Moira watched the banner spread to its full length.

GODDESS WORSHIP IS SATAN WORSHIP

Moira clenched her fists in a moment of blind fury, then unclenched them, deliberately taking a deep breath before she spoke. 'Don't worry, Dan. The cops will move them. They don't like this kind of trouble.'

'Have you noticed something?' Dan said. 'There aren't any cops.'

Moira frowned, puzzled. She hadn't noticed it but it was true. The handful of police outside the Great Circle, amiable or bored, exchanging the odd joke or accepting the odd chicken-leg during the feast if the Sergeant wasn't looking, had become such an accepted part of the Festival scene that she simply hadn't thought about them; yet to-night, she realized, the only uniforms in sight were the usual St John's men and women around their ambulance, fifty metres along the ridge.

'But why?' Moira wondered.

'Perhaps they've decided it's not worth it. After all, they never have anything to do. . . . Jesus! They're coming in!'

The demonstrators, banner aloft, had marched into the Great Circle, trampling straight through the little Circles towards the Cauldron, chanting in unison: 'Goddess worship is Satan worship! Goddess worship is Satan worship! Goddess worship is Satan worship!'

Some of the older people not in the Dance were running forward, trying to stop them. But the demonstrators were young, clothed and booted, and swept the elderly skyclad bodies easily aside. The younger baby-minding fathers, like Dan, hesitated, torn between repelling the intruders and standing guard over their children. Moira grabbed at Dan's arm, restraining him; he shrugged helplessly and acquiesced.

But now the dancers had heard the chanting and had turned, incredulous anger in their faces. The demonstrators did not pause; they headed straight for the Sabbat Queen, who was clearly their target.

The chanting changed. 'Witch whore! Witch whore! Witch whore!'

That final blasphemy broke the Ring. The dancers swept down on the invaders, boots or no boots. The banner swayed and fell in a mass of clothed and unclothed bodies.

Diana was sobbing now. Moira hugged her fiercely, cried out: 'Dan! Look! The Altar!'

As she pointed, the white statue of the Goddess tottered and fell. More intruders, unnoticed till now, were tearing the fragile polystyrene into great lumps, scattering them about the smashed Altar.

Moira screamed.

It was then that the unbelievable happened. The ground beneath them, the whole of Bell Beacon, moved, throwing attackers and defenders alike off their feet. It only lasted for a few seconds, but in those seconds the hill groaned like a giant in pain. Then it was still.

There was a moment, after the turmoil, of silence, the silence of utter shock.

One of the demonstrators, a wild-eyed woman, was the

first on her feet. 'It's the wrath of God!' she yelled. 'The wrath of God, smiting the witches!'

Naked bodies sprang up to drag her down and the fight was on again; then, above the screaming and the shouting and the tears came the sound of the motor-cycles roaring up the long slanting road.

Moira and Dan stood stunned, no longer able to take it all in. Even Diana, clutched between them, was soundless and trembling.

The motor-cyclists, a dozen helmeted, visored, anonymous monsters, charged on to the plateau, sweeping into a circle round the mêlée, herding it inward towards the fire like armoured sheepdogs.

Dan shook Moira out of her paralysis, shouting at her over the din: 'Clothes! Quick!'

Suddenly and desperately active, Moira swept the little altar bare and tore open the hamper-lid, flinging out sweaters, jeans, plimsolls from underneath the pathetic provisions for the feast that would never be eaten. Rosemary and Greg ran up and joined them; how they had dodged through the cordon of bikes, Moira had no time to wonder.

Throwing clothes on to Diana and herself, she heard Greg shout to Daniel, 'Got to get the girls out of this!' Dan nodded, grimly.

Clothed, Greg started trying to pack the hamper, but Daniel waved him off it. 'Leave it – no time!' By unspoken instinct, the four of them grabbed the ritual tools in their hands and stuck their athames, the black-handled knives which are each witch's personal symbol, into their belts.

Then they were running, Diana held in Dan's arms.

The motor-cylists were tightening and loosening their ring, teasing the crowd inside it. The Cauldron lay beyond the ring, toppled and abandoned. Greg, in the lead, saw that that was the clearest path, and made for it. But as he reached it, he halted in his tracks, staring down.

Moira followed his look, and screamed again.

Naked and dead, the gilded iron Lance of Light impaling her belly, lay the Sabbat Queen, staring upwards; their lovely Joy, their friend.

Dan pulled Moira away, roughly. Through her tears, she saw John, berserk in his torn golden kilt, a burning log in his hand, leap crazily between two motor-cycles and run to his dead wife. Standing over her, he flung the log at the engine of a passing cycle.

Machine and rider burst into flame, colliding with the next, which swerved aside and then fell. The hemmed-in crowd saw, and copied; all at once the hunters became the hunted, trying to escape a shower of blazing missiles.

Dan almost swept Moira off her feet, hustling her over the edge of the plateau away from the horror.

There was one more earth tremor as the five of them stumbled down the path towards their car. But it was slight, and stunned by all that had happened, they barely noticed it.

3

It was obvious from the London papers (there were no Manchester or Glasgow editions all day, till power had been restored) that the geologists and seismologists either could not or would not explain what had happened; and even those who were brave enough not to take refuge in incomprehensible jargon, contradicted each other. The disturbance, whatever it was, must lie deep; because a chain of shocks that ran from Merseyside into Wales, and then obliquely across the Cotswolds and Chilterns to the North Downs, made no kind of sense in terms of surface structure; any well-educated layman could see that. In Scotland, of course, the tremor that smashed the canal locks all along the Great Glen, and caused serious fires in Fort William, Invergarry, Fort Augustus and Inverness, was more understandable. On the subject of that ruler-straight primordial fracture, the nature of which was clear from any child's atlas, the experts pontificated at length to cover their vagueness over the rest.

Reports from the continent were equally puzzling. Most dramatic was the breach in Holland's Ijsselmeer dyke, through which the North Sea was pouring to inundate thousands of hectares of hard-won polder. But this, geologically speaking, was a mere incident in the strange network of tremors that stretched from Portugal to the Caspian, and south-west (more conventionally) into the Balkans and Turkey.

Deaths in the circumstances were remarkably few, in Britain at least. Fourteen people had died and six were missing in the collapse of a Salford block of flats; nine had drowned in a capsized pleasure craft on Loch Linnhe; and five had been killed by an exploding gas-main at Reading. Apart from these, no single British incident (the first day's reports suggested) had killed more than two. The total ranged from sixty-seven in *The Times* to 103 in the *Sun*. The continental figures were higher, though still very tentative; but in the trauma of home disaster, foreign deaths were statistics not people.

Disaster it was, of course – all the headlines said so. But as the hours passed and the fires were doused and the telephone panic by anxious relatives had abated a little, the usual defence mechanisms began to work. Those with problems were busy coping with them, those unaffected were busy congratulating themselves and a kind of eerie calm seemed to prevail. It was helped by the quite uncharacteristic promptness and efficiency of the emergency relief services – which aroused the curiosity of some of the more observant citizens, though this curiosity was for some reason not reflected by the media.

The media also avoided reporting the fact that three of Britain's eight Mohowatt electrodes were out of action, their conductors having been fractured by the tremors at a considerable depth. Fortunately two of the couples were still working and recently redundant conventional power stations could be brought back into service (again with uncharacteristic speed), so the Central Electricity Generating Board did not find it necessary to be publicly specific about the damage.

Practically the only reference (and that one indirect) to Mohowatt was in the *Evening News*'s first leader in its 4.30 edition, which ran, after a platitudinous opening paragraph:

> As the overall picture becomes clearer, the feeling must be acknowledged that Mother Earth has issued a warning. Never before in history has an earthquake struck, simultaneously, across the face of Europe. Yet no single incident was truly catastrophic, on the scale of such classic disasters as San Francisco, Agadir, or Skopje.
>
> Why was the blow so widespread, yet so locally lenient? The experts cannot tell us. Whatever Mother Earth is up to, it is so deep in her womb that they fail to analyse it.
>
> We have done many strange things to her in recent years – some perhaps with too hasty greed and too scanty knowledge. Is this her rap over the knuckles, to brace us for the real disaster?
>
> If so, we must hope that our leaders and administrators are heeding her voice. She is not in the habit of warning twice.

The leader had disappeared from the 5.00 edition. Fleet Street rumour spoke of a phone call to the Editor from Downing Street and of the sudden relegation of a leader writer to the subs' desk.

The relegation, at least, was fact. The victim was a promising young journalist called George Barrett, who had only recently been given a chance to try leader-writing. Today, back on the desk as abruptly as he had left it, his first subbing chore was to tack a new head and intro on to the below-the-fold story on page 7: 'THREE DIE IN WITCH FESTIVAL RIOT'. PA tape said that a fourth – a seven-year-old boy – had died in hospital. A dead child (especially a naked one) always enlivened a story lead, the professional half of his mind observed, while acknowledging that the flaxen-haired beauty impaled with a golden spear (and also naked) would have to retain pride of place. One motor-cyclist burned to death and two others hospitalized, plus one clothed woman demonstrator dead from multiple injuries, made a good second par. He typed the new intro with practised speed, while the human half of his mind felt slightly sick. Unreligious himself, he rather liked the witches. . . . He told himself that on an ordinary day the story would have made the front page and possibly the splash. But this was no ordinary day. He wondered again why the Old Man had been so embarrassed about his demotion, wrapping it up with unconvincing flattery about the desk needing the best men in this crisis. Oh, well – easy come, easy go. He tossed the revised copy to the Chief Sub's tray, and reached for the next.

It was a phoned piece from their Bath stringer, reporting that the Cheddar caves had been closed to visitors, after the first morning tour had come up complaining of an irritant dust in the air of the lower chambers. The local Medical Officer of Health had ordered an inspection. Several of the party were in hospital with severe pulmonary symptoms.

The sub's professional instincts nudged at him, mysteriously. He frowned for a moment and then reached for the phone .

'But what's he *done*?' Betty Summers asked, helplessly aware that her voice was rising towards hysteria.

The taller policeman (at least, Betty supposed they were

39

policemen – she hadn't understood the identity cards they'd shown her) said soothingly: 'Your husband has done nothing, Mrs Summers. Please don't worry. Now why don't you just make yourself a cup of tea and we'll wait till he gets home?' His smile was bland, uninformative. 'You could make us one, too, if you like.'

'But . . .'

'Just relax, Mrs Summers.'

She straightened a table-runner, unnecessarily, her hand shaking. She didn't believe a word of his reassurance. Phil *must* have been up to something – and now it was catching up on him. He'd been so preoccupied lately, not himself at all. There'd been no secrets between them in four years of marriage, till recently; the last four or five months, perhaps. Then he'd taken to brooding to himself at the oddest times – or worse, being falsely cheerful. . . .

The phone rang and Betty jumped. She moved towards it but the second man reached it before her.

'Yes? . . . No, I'm afraid Mr and Mrs Summers are out this evening. . . . Just a friend. I'll tell them you rang.'

Betty had wanted to call out but she had caught the taller man's warning eye and had been too afraid. Now she managed to ask: 'Who was it?'

'Somebody called Trevor. I'm sorry, Mrs Summers. It has to be this way.'

'Has to be *what* way? Why can't you *tell* me?'

'When your husband comes. He shouldn't be long now, should he?'

'I . . .'

'How about that tea? I'm sure you'd feel better.'

Perhaps he's right, she thought, a little desperately. She went to the kitchen, fighting back the tears that were trying to break out. This wouldn't do. If Phil was in trouble, he'd need her support, her help, not a weeping wife making things more difficult. . . . If only . . .

She heard his key in the door, and Timmy's paws, scuffling at the woodwork as they always did. Oh, thank God. . . . Or was it going to be even worse, now?

Betty ran to the hall but the two men were there as soon as she was. Timmy rushed in ahead of Phil, his tail wagging furiously, and stopped and growled when he saw the two strangers. Phil stopped too, questioningly.

She went to him, managing to keep her poise somehow. 'Darling – I think these gentlemen are police.'

'No, Mr Summers. Not police. LB7.'

Phil seemed to pale a little. He said 'Oh', and shut the front door carefully. As soon as it was closed, the taller man showed Phil his identity card and then said: 'Beehive Amber, I'm afraid. Sorry about the short notice but you have an hour. I suggest you and your wife go and pack. You can explain to her now, of course.'

'*Pack?*' Betty croaked.

Phil put an arm round her. 'It's all right, darling. I wasn't allowed to tell even you. . . . Oh Christ, I suppose I should have expected it, after last night. . . . We're going away for a bit. An official job.'

'Are you a secret agent or something?' She felt ridiculous as soon as she'd said it.

Phil sighed. 'Nothing so dramatic. Only a ventilation engineer.' He made an attempt at a laugh. 'They tell me it's a privilege to be on the list. . . . Come on, I'll explain upstairs. Thank God I can get it off my chest at last.'

The taller man said: 'You didn't report the dog.'

'Nobody asked me,' Phil replied, looking suddenly alarmed. 'Christ, you don't have to . . .'

'We'll handle it.'

'Nobody asked me,' he repeated lamely.

'D'you imagine there's room for them down there? . . .

Go on, lad, or you'll upset Mrs Summers more.'

Phil patted Timmy's head, turning his face away. The shorter man coughed. Then Phil took his wife upstairs. The two men could hear their voices from the bedroom – hers high-pitched and bewildered, his rumbling on and on and on.

The shorter man picked up the phone and dialled a number. 'It's the only thing that gets me, when there's pets,' he complained over his shoulder. 'Why the hell don't they brief these people properly?'

Miss Angela Smith, at fifty-three the elder stateswoman of the Borough Treasurer's Department, thanked the post girl with a motherly smile. The girl had been very jittery since yesterday morning's news; the nearest earth tremor had been thirty or forty kilometres away (London had been quite unscathed) but you'd think her own house had fallen down. Oh well, not surprising when you knew the girl's neurotic mother, which Miss Smith did. As, indeed, she knew most of the borough.

Miss Smith flicked through the routine bulk of the post to see what she had to deal with herself. The perforated edge of a telex sheet caught her eye and she pulled it out; they had a way of being urgent – or if not urgent, at least from someone high enough for them to be treated as urgent.

She read it and pursed her lips in a silent whistle, an unladylike mannerism she was well aware of but could not cure.

After the address and priority coding, the text began: FOLLOWING TO BE TRANSFERRED TO FILE LB 0806 WEF. 26/6/04. CROWTHER 102 HOLLY MANSIONS E17. SUMMERS 43 MANOR CRESCENT E10. BERNSTEIN 97 BOUNDARY PLACE E10 . . .'

Eighteen names and addresses. Eighteen! There had never been more than two on a File LB 0806 instruction before.

File LB 0806 matters were always handled by Miss Smith, in liaison with the Borough Treasurer himself and with no one else. She had never been told the purpose of the drill; merely given it on a sheet which was to be kept locked in her desk and reminded her of her responsibilities under the Official Secrets Act which she had been required to sign.

But Miss Smith was not a fool.

The drill itself was uncomplicated (at least when there was only one name at a time) but it was a nuisance. First, inform the accounts department that until further notice rates demands were to be sent not to the ratepayer concerned but to Miss Smith's desk. Next, contact certain named officials at the local London Electricity Board, North Thames Gas, Thames Water Authority and East Telephone Area with the same instruction. Finally (and the cloak-and-dagger solemnity of this amused Miss Smith), go to the address concerned, where a note would be – always was – pinned to the front door, telling the milkman, newsagent and anyone else concerned not to make any more deliveries till further notice. This note would always name the dairy, the newsagent and so on, and since they were all on the same sheet, none of them would have removed it. Miss Smith, however, had to remove it and then go to each of the addresses and say that as a friend of Mr So-and-so she'd been asked to settle the outstanding account. She was going to look a right Charley, this time, she thought, turning up at (for instance) one of the three major dairies in the borough and claiming to be the personal friend of half a dozen customers who'd all gone on holiday without warning on the same day.

All the accounts and the retailers' receipts, Miss Smith would then address (personally sealing the envelope) to the Home Office, Department LB7. Payment always arrived by return of post and Miss Smith's final duty would be to reimburse the London Electricity Board and the others.

Miss Smith, as has been remarked, was not a fool. Nine ratepayers of the borough had so far disappeared into File LB 0806, over the past year, and so far none of them had returned home. But these homes, she had soon become aware, were also on a Metropolitan Police list for periodic checking to make sure no harm came to them, and the police had their own keys. She guessed that the Post Office had their instructions, too.

It was all so neat, so quiet. All the same, there had been whispers; and Miss Smith, who kept her ear to the ground, knew of worried relatives who had been visited by anonymous soothing officials, and who now wore a 'We could an if we would' air. It had also not escaped her attention that the names accumulating in File LB 0806 included a high proportion of technicians, as well as one nurse and one pest control officer.

And now eighteen of them in one day – immediately after a nation-wide chain of local disasters which some said were a portent of worse to come. Eighteen people, with their immediate families if any, from a single London borough.

Miss Smith had a strong instinct of survival and she had been thinking ahead for some time. She had converted all her savings into small valuables and rarities which she estimated had a good chance of retaining at least a barter price in any circumstances. She also kept £800 in notes stitched into the lining of an anorak. It was a pity about her pension, but . . .

She finished her day's work meticulously, and a busy day it was; none of the eighteen names was missed, though it cost the Council a lot in taxi fares, for which (and for the milk and newsagents' payments) she took care to reimburse herself from Petty-Cash immediately. She said good night to her colleagues in exactly her usual manner.

Then she caught a bus home, to her terraced house in Vicarage Road. She was as unobtrusive as possible about the final packing of her motor caravan which stood outside the front gate, but in fact there was little to do because she kept it always ready.

She rolled up a note to the milkman and put it in an empty bottle; the pound note pinned inside it would pay for this week's milk so far. No problems with the newsagent because she always bought her papers over the counter on her way to work. She checked again that the electricity and gas were turned off at the mains.

Everything ready. She picked up Ginger Lad under one arm, which started him purring. Thank God he hadn't been out courting, or she'd have had to wait for him. She'd never had the heart to have him doctored.

With her free hand, she put the milk bottle on the step and double-locked the front door. Then she climbed aboard.

She sat behind the wheel in a last moment of doubt, while Ginger Lad, quite undoubting, curled up on the seat beside her. Was she being too precipitate? It might be days, or it might be months. . . .

She braced herself. Days or months, she had no intention of being caught in a great city when *it* happened.

Miss Smith started the engine and drove off.

Suddenly she chuckled, remembering her secret parting joke. She had added her own name to File LB 0806. After all, the LEB might as well get its money.

'Your little "incident" rather missed the limelight, didn't it?' Jennings grinned.

There were times when Harley found his ironical manner exasperating but he was too aware of Jennings' quality, and of his importance to his own private plans, to react to it outwardly.

'We'll see,' he smiled back. 'Its coincidence with the earth tremors may turn out to be to our advantage in the end.'

The four of them were meeting in very different surroundings from those of their last conference. This, too, was Harley's office; but here were no tall Whitehall windows, only grey concrete walls hung with maps and charts; no Adam fireplace, only an extractor grille through which the conditioned air whispered steadily. One feature alone echoed the Whitehall room, an Aubusson carpet. A little out of place two hundred metres below Primrose Hill, Harley realized, but he was, after all, the Permanent Secretary.

As yet they were still on Beehive Amber so he spent about half his time here and half in Whitehall. In the unpublicized hierarchy which had been set up for Beehive, Harley was Chief Administrator of the London hive, responsible to the Prime Minister alone and senior to all the regional Chief Administrators. With Beehive Amber, only certain key personnel of the Beehive establishment – just over twenty per cent – were already in full-time residence; another five per cent, either because they were top officials like himself or because of the nature of their work, still commuted with Surface. The remaining three-quarters were on standby, awaiting Beehive Red. When Red was ordered, all would come below; only law enforcement units, intelligence agents and certain specialists need come and go from Beehive by one of the thirty-seven airlocked exits which were concealed all over London, or their equivalents around the regional hives. In the case of real surface chaos (the situation defined by various criteria in the Beehive directives as 'Category Five Disorganization') even these would be withdrawn; the airlocks would be steel-shuttered and Beehive would settle down, secure, fed, immune and disciplined, till Surface life was so weakened and demoralized that Beehive could send out its forces and take control. (Half a dozen secret exits would remain available whatever the situation, but these – which emerged in such places as a grocer's shabby garage in Camden Town and the up platform of Brixton underground station – were known only to Harley and to a handful of others, most of them in Intelligence Section.)

Beehive, sealed off, could survive on normal rations and full establishment for two years and seven months. Power supplies would never run out, coming as they did from fourteen well-dispersed and interchangeable submarine-type nuclear reactors.

When the time came for Beehive Red (it could be days, it could be months) individual orders would be impracticable. So would watertight security. 'Beehive Red' would be announced without explanation on television and radio; whereupon the remaining three-quarters would make for their designated entrances without further notice. According to plan, twenty-four hours should see virtually all of them underground, out of reach of alerted popular interference or sabotage. Martial law would then be declared. But that part of the plan had to remain elastic; there were too many imponderable factors.

Harley was allergic to imponderable factors and worked round the clock to minimize them.

One thing worried him constantly. Three-quarters of eighteen thousand people meant altogether too many possible leaks, even allowing for the fact that half of them were Servicemen who needed to know very little till their officers told them to move. And one or two of the more sensational continental newspapers had carried stories. . . . Most of Britain must have heard hints of Beehive, however distorted; and Beehive Amber must have spawned more hints which would fall on much more attentive ears in the aftermath of the earth tremors.

It was just as well, Harley thought, that the seismologists' reports were top secret (the real ones, of course, not the statements they were allowed to give to the media). These experts could not hide the inadequacy of their time-factor data but the secret reports showed their unanimous alarm. Harley had not only read the reports – he had cultivated the authors, with everything from flattery to alcohol. And with every day his conviction grew that Beehive Red was approaching rapidly.

With these thoughts, as ever, hovering about the threshold of his mind, Harley said: 'I'm sure I don't have to tell you that a scapegoat may at any moment become an urgent necessity.'

'You lost one of your men on Bell Beacon, didn't you?' General Mullard asked.

'Yes, that was unfortunate. One doesn't like identifiable bodies getting into the hands of unbriefed authorities. So was the death of the Hassell woman. We don't want to provide the witches with any martyrs, especially young and beautiful ones. But I think something can be made of Andrea Sutton, by way of compensation.'

'The leader of the banner lot?'

'Yes. I've seen the autopsy report. Multiple injuries – the burning motor-cycle ran over her and so did another that went out of control. But those injuries would be compatible with her already having been dead, considering how quickly it all happened.'

'I don't follow you.'

48

'Quite simple. There will be two witnesses at the inquest who will insist they saw a group of witches stab her in the heart, catch some of the blood in a bowl and run with it to their Great Altar.'

'Duty outweighing perjury,' Jennings murmured. Harley chose not to hear him.

'But the autopsy showed no stab wound?' the General asked.

'The rib-cage was crushed by the motor-cycle.'

'Any competent pathologist would still know.'

'Of course, but that doesn't matter. The suggestion will have been made and I can see to it that it is headlined. The pathologist's denial will be accepted by the coroner but ignored by the rumour-mongers. The blood-sacrifice theory will very quickly become "fact" – all the more effectively because it will be believed to have been officially suppressed. And fortunately, Andrea Sutton was President of the Anti-Pagan Crusade – a non-denominational group which has had little impact so far. . . . She wasn't an agent of ours, by the way, though she was manoeuvred into this demonstration by – er – appropriate influences.' He gave his thin smile. 'And further appropriate influences have arranged that her Vice-President and successor will be the main attraction on BBC 1's "Paul Grant Hour" the day after the inquest. He is Ben Stoddart, a quick-witted speaker of considerable personal magnetism. Grant himself has been briefed. . . . I think, gentlemen, that a sacrificed Andrea Sutton will prove a much more effective martyr than a mere naked blonde.'

4

It was not easy to return to normal but they did their best, for Diana's sake in particular. Mercifully, the child had not seen Joy's murdered body; her face had been buried in Dan's shoulder and he had managed to keep it there. But the uproar, the violence, the thunderous motor-cycles, inexplicably shattering a treat which she had been promised for weeks, had terrified her. She had been sick twice on the way home to Staines, and had whimpered herself to sleep in Moira's arms. Moira had knelt by the small bed, cradling and soothing her, till her knees ached.

When Diana had finally dozed off through sheer exhaustion, Moira had joined the other three downstairs. They had talked for a while, disjointedly, and then had set up an altar in the living room and cast a Circle. The familiar ritual had calmed them a little, and when they were ready they had sat facing inwards, instinctively drawing closer to each other, linking hands, woman, man, woman, man, striving to harmonize and activate the group mind which they had spent the past three years building up. (They missed old Sally, but all her lights had been out when they reached home and they had decided against waking her up with their terrible news.) When Moira had felt the power rising in them, she had begun to speak quietly, invoking an image of peace, conquering and transcending all disaster; then projecting it outwards, to the child upstairs, to bereaved John whose torment they could feel as though he were in the room with them, to Joy's astral consciousness brutally and prematurely torn from its lovely, and loved, physical vessel. . . . They had all felt drained but at least, for an hour, enfolded by the peace which they had invoked.

Moira had banished the Circle and they put on their clothes again, speaking little and softly. With the habitual exchange of kisses, Rosemary and Greg had bid them 'blessed be' and gone to their own home next door.

Moira had pressed herself close against Dan in their bed, needing the contact, clasping his hand to her breasts with her own. They had lain like that for a while, drawing on each other's strength; then her need for him had pervaded all her levels and she had turned in his arms, fondling him and moaning. She had been ready for him and he for her, and foreplay was, for once, forgotten; they had merged compulsively, with a swift and urgent climax, and had flung their arms wide as though to push away the terror with their passion.

As the tide ebbed, a half-remembered couplet had slipped unbidden into Moira's mind:

> And 'mid this tumult Kubla heard from far
> Ancestral voices prophesying war.

Dan had felt the tears suddenly on her cheeks and had held her close, murmuring to her wordlessly till they both slept.

Next morning, breakfast had been dominated unexpectedly by the eight o'clock radio news. Moira and Dan had listened to the headlines, wide-eyed; almost at once Rosemary and Greg, their coffee-mugs still in their hands, had run through the gap in the fence between their gardens, calling to them to switch on if they hadn't already. The four of them had stood round the set, stunned by the list of large and small disasters that had spanned Europe during the night. When it was over, Dan had switched off and they had stared at each other.

It had been Rosemary who finally broke the silence. 'For God's sake! Do you know – I'd *forgotten* that bloody earthquake! It was so much part of the whole thing that I'd *forgotten* it!'

So, it seemed, had they all. Now reminded and abruptly aware of the scale of it, they had all talked at once, trying to take it in, till Dan had noticed the clock. He had hurried off to his estate agency partnership, Greg to his motor repair shop, Rosemary to her till in the supermarket. Moira had been left suddenly alone; Diana was still asleep upstairs (let her sleep, poor mite) and Sally next door was not yet about.

On an impulse, she had gone to her Tarot pack, shuffled and cut the major arcana and the four aces, and dealt them in a Tree of Life layout:

The Hanged Man

Ace of Pentacles reversed	The Hermit reversed

Death

Justice
reversed

The Tower

The Moon reversed	The Devil

The Wheel of
Fortune
reversed

The Lovers

She had stared sombrely at the layout for a full ten minutes.
If that's how our world stands, she had told herself, last
night was only a beginning.

She had hardly dared to deal out the three qualifying
cards, but knowing that she must not baulk at them, she
had turned them face upwards firmly.

The High Priestess – the Chariot – the Star.

Moira had drawn a deep breath and then said out loud:
'So it's up to me, Lady, isn't it?'

Since then, a week had passed; a week of unnatural and
uneasy calm throughout Europe. There were riots in
Brussels, Athens, and Turin but in each of these places
there had already been some explosive local controversy
which natural disaster had merely detonated.

Where there had been damage, people were busy repairing it; where there had been none, they were busy discussing it. Opinions were bandied about and prophecies made,
from ostrich-like to apocalyptic. But in fact there was
nothing for the prophets to get their teeth into and everyone knew it. If there was real information available, the
authorities were keeping it to themselves.

The Prime Minister appeared on television and said
nothing with artfully homely eloquence.

In the Mackenzie household, Diana seemed to have forgotten Bell Beacon, though Moira and Dan watched her
carefully for any recurrence of distress. Sally next door
was splendid; she seemed to absorb the double shock of

the earthquake news and the Bell Beacon shambles like a soldier to whom catastrophe was commonplace and concentrated on keeping Diana amused and on seeing that Moira was left alone as little as possible when Dan was at work.

'Don't brood, pet,' she had told Moira firmly on the first day. 'Gets you nowhere. Joy's dead, may the Goddess rest her, and you can't bring her back. Out of our hands. Our job's the living. Damn it, I'm out of tea. Make me a pot, there's a good girl.'

Moira had laughed, helplessly, for the first time in many hours. Sally had smiled, with a shrewd eye on her – for signs of hysteria, Moira knew; and the knowledge helped her to keep a grip on herself.

As the days went by, their life appeared to regain its normal rhythms. But Moira had a strong sense of foreboding which she could not shake off; nor could she be certain in her own mind how much of that foreboding was personal, on behalf of her family and her coven, and how much of it was on a larger scale altogether.

One anxiety was already personal; Dan's business became suddenly slack. Two years earlier, Dan and his friend Steve Gilchrist had bought up a near-moribund estate agency, with its few clients and tenuous goodwill, and had set about reviving it. Steve had put up two-thirds of the capital, but Dan had been the one with the drive and the ability to get on with clients. They had done well so far and the office on the High Street had become bright and busy. But after the tremors, day by day more of the country properties on their lists were withdrawn from the market. In most cases only vague reasons or none were given, but one client at least was frank.

'If we get more quakes I'll feel a dam' sight safer out there in the woods,' he told Dan. 'And if things break down

and there's violence, who the hell wants to be in London?'
Dan, who for all his energy was perhaps too honest to be a
tycoon-class salesman, admitted that he had a point.

The partners knew that the trend was two-edged; prices
of the country places which did remain on offer would
rocket. But any benefit to them would be transient, because
if the alarm continued the market would soon dry up
altogether.

Moira thought about asking for her old job back, to bring
more money into the house if Dan's business met with prolonged difficulties. She had been a fashion buyer at
Debenhams, the big department store in Staines, and only
recently they had asked her if she would return, but she
and Dan were agreed that she should stay at home till
Diana started school. They might have to reconsider this
attitude if things got worse. She kept the thought in reserve
for the moment, however; only extreme pessimism would
make Dan accept it and she did not want to disturb him
until she felt it was absolutely necessary. Besides, her
intuition nagged at her with another thought: if things
really got worse, would their problems in fact be one of
money?

The implications of that disturbed her even more than
the state of Dan's business but she could not dismiss it.

In contrast to Dan, Greg was working overtime. He was
head mechanic in the workshop attached to a big filling-
station on the Kingston Road.

'You wouldn't believe it,' he told them on the Sunday
afternoon as they all sunbathed on the Bayneses' lawn. (In
the near-communal life that had evolved between them,
Greg and Rosemary had the bigger lawn, and Dan and
Moira the bigger vegetable garden, both families making
use of both.) 'All of a sudden everyone wants to be road-
worthy. You know how it is – not many people really get

their periodic maintenance done when the ten thousand comes up, or whatever. Now they're bringing 'em in *ahead* of time. They're queuing up for decokes and God knows what, even old bangers with holes in their coachwork, as long as the mechanics are sound. We can't get new tyres fast enough – or light bulbs, everyone wants a spare set. Petrol cans, too. And on the forecourt they've sold more road maps in a week than they usually do all year.'

'Road maps of where, as a matter of interest?' Dan asked.

'Yes, I'd wondered that, too – I checked up. East Anglia, the Pennines, central Wales, the Highlands – all the least populated areas, the ones people usually buy only to go on holiday. The town ones too, of course – lots of people just buy complete sets and be done with it. But the country ones are the hot cakes.'

'That figures,' Rosemary said. 'I was in Debenhams yesterday and you couldn't get near the camping department. I doubt if they've got a tent or a camp cooker left in the place.'

'I'm glad *we* have,' Moira said suddenly.

Her remarked seemed to hang challengingly in the air, but for now, at least, nobody commented on it.

Dan was determined to attend the Bell Beacon inquest, so Moira left Diana with Sally and accompanied him. She felt no particular urge to be there, herself; her sense of outrage had been all-consuming at the time, while Dan had been absorbed in necessary action. As the days had passed, she had tended to put the irrevocable behind her while he had mulled over his memories, weighing and classifying them, assembling a case in his mind with a growing sense of indignation. This was typical of each of them as Moira well knew. But she also knew that such complementary attitudes were part of the strength of their partnership and she made no attempt to upset the balance by persuading him to forget before he was ready – any more than he would have belittled her on-the-spot reaction.

The coroner's court was packed and although Dan and Moira arrived in good time they only just got in. The proceedings were long and unpleasant. For the first hour, Dan and Moira learned nothing which they had not seen themselves or already gleaned from the newspapers. The dead motor-cyclist was Terence Watt, twenty-nine, of Raynes Park, newsagent; a surprising age and background for a leather-clad trouble-seeker, perhaps, but otherwise unremarkable. The seven-year-old boy, Bobby Thornley, was the child of a couple from Woking, who were with their solicitor in court, looking pale and ill. John Hassell was beside them with his own solictor; his expressionless face had only softened once, as he caught Dan and Moira's eyes when they came in. Andrea Sutton, it appeared, only had relatives in Johannesburg, whom a third solicitor nominally represented, though he was in constant whispered discussion with a handsome man of about sixty who turned out to be Ben Stoddart, Vice-President of Andrea Sutton's Anti-Pagan Crusade.

There were no surprises to begin with, as a string of witnesses gave their various versions of the disturbance and a pathologist reported the causes of death. The latter amounted to massive haemorrhage in Joy's case, burning to death in Watt's and multiple injuries due to being run over in Andrea Sutton's and the boy's. Andrea Sutton had in fact been run over twice, and then hit by a falling machine; her rib-cage had been badly crushed.

The coroner impressed Moira; a shrewd man, quiet-spoken, but authoritative in spite of the deceptively casual way in which he put questions – as when he asked the senior police witness: 'Superintendent, why have none of the motor-cylists been brought before me?'

'I regret to report, sir, that we have been unable to trace them. Apart from the deceased Watt, there were eleven of them, as witnesses have told the court. Nine of them rode away after the disturbance, my officers were told when they reached the scene; and we do not even have descriptions of them since they all apparently wore crash helmets and visors.'

'I see. But two others were admitted to hospital, were they not?'

'Yes, sir. They were in adjacent beds in Slough General Hospital until approximately eleven o'clock the following morning, one being treated for burns on his hands, the other awaiting the results of an X-ray for a suspected fracture of the right humerus. They were the only patients in a four-bed ward and while they were unattended for about half an hour they seem to have dressed themselves and disappeared.'

'*Disappeared?*'

'Yes, sir. The Ward Sister is in court if you wish to question her.'

'But this is extraordinary, Superintendent. I may hear the Sister in due course but this is surely also a police matter. These two men were known to have taken an active part in a disturbance in which three people had already died. Why was there no police guard on them?'

The superintendent looked embarrassed. 'There appears to have been a breakdown of communication between the St John Ambulance, whose detachment transported them to hospital, and the police. The ambulance officer told the hospital casualty department that he had reported to us, via his own headquarters, but there is no record of the report having been received. We were unaware of the two men's admission till they had already discharged themselves – and it transpired that they had given false names and addresses on admission.'

' "Discharged themselves" strikes me as somewhat of a euphemism, in the circumstances. . . . And what about their machines? Presumably they had registration numbers?'

'One or two witnesses did note down the registration numbers, sir, and their reports tallied. But all twelve – including the burnt-out machine which is in our possession – proved to be carrying false number-plates. And the engine number of the one we do have had been filed off, too deep for radiography.'

'What about the two abandoned by the riders who were taken to hospital?'

'They were removed by persons unknown immediately after the disturbance, sir. It was an estimated half-hour between the riot ending and the first police car reaching the scene, I regret to say. Our switchboards were swamped with earth tremor reports and our cars were busy – but all the same, we could have been called to Bell Beacon earlier if the St John Ambulance radio had been working. The ambulance officer will tell you that he suspects it had been sabotaged.'

'Superintendent, your quite remarkable evidence does not seem to me to point to an act of spontaneous hooliganism. It points to a carefully organized plot.'

'One cannot escape that conclusion, sir, I agree.'

'And *I* may not be able to escape the conclusion that this inquest should be adjourned to allow for further police inquiries. . . . However, we shall at least continue until all the evidence which is so far available has been heard, before I decide whether an adjournment is advisable.'

'As the court pleases.'

'The court would also be pleased to know why no police were in attendance at this Festival. I understand that until this occasion, it has been the invariable practice for a suitable number of officers to be present.'

'My instructions were that since there had been no trouble at such events for many years, police presence was an unnecessary waste of manpower and should be discontinued – by our county force, at least.'

'And this was the first application of the new policy?'

'In Buckingham, yes, sir. I understand that other forces have continued the old practice.'

'An astonishingly unfortunate coincidence,' the coroner said quietly.

The superintendent reddened. 'I can only follow my instructions, sir.'

'Instructions from whom, in this case?'

The superintendent hesitated, then answered: 'From my Chief Constable, sir.'

'I see. . . . And were those instructions in accordance with your own judgement, as an experienced officer?'

'With respect, sir, I ask to be excused from answering that question.'

The coroner nodded several times, slowly, and the superintendent's face grew even redder.

The ambulance officer was next. He stuck firmly to his story that the ambulance radio had been sabotaged but he had no way of proving it. He also insisted that he had telephoned his HQ from the hospital, reporting the two casualties and requesting that his report be passed on to the police.

When the next witness was called, Moira hissed to Dan: 'Good God! Him!'

'What about him?'

'Mike Wharton. Renegade.'

'Black?'

'He hasn't got the guts. Just a rat.'

'Don't recognize him.'

'Shush. Tell you later.'

Andrea Sutton's solicitor was on his feet. 'I must apologize, sir, for asking the court to hear this witness, Mr Michael Wharton, virtually without notice. Mr Wharton came to me about twenty minutes before the court convened, with such an extraordinary story that had there been more time I would have accompanied him straight to the police, because it has a direct bearing on the murder of Miss Sutton.'

'Do not anticipate the verdict of this court, Mr James.'

'I was about to add, sir – "if murder it was, as Mr Wharton alleges".'

'I see. And Mr Wharton is a stranger, who came to you completely out of the blue?'

'I had not met him before, sir, personally, but I knew of him. He is a well-known and respected figure in the witchcraft movement . . .'

('Like hell!' Moira muttered.)

'. . . who has contributed many articles to the movement's periodicals. Recognizing him and knowing his standing within his own field, I knew his story could not be lightly dismissed. I saw no alternative, in view of the time factor, but to bring him before you, sir.'

The coroner studied the witness. 'Mr Wharton – before I hear what you have to say, I would like to ask one thing. If you have vital evidence on the death of Miss Sutton, why did you not go straight to the police with it? Why have you waited till now?'

Wharton peered back at him through tinted glasses, under carefully groomed black hair. 'I was afraid, sir. These people . . .'

'Which people?'

'The black element in the Craft, sir.'

' "Black" in this context of witchcraft and magic meaning malignant?'

'Yes, sir. And ruthless. I was afraid of what they might do if I told what I saw. I am still afraid, but . . . I felt, this morning, that if I didn't speak now it would be too late.'

'You are safe here,' the coroner told him, 'and if you do have cause to be afraid once you leave this court, the police will arrange for your protection. The court takes a very serious view of the intimidation of witnesses. I shall be better able to form a conclusion about that when I have heard your evidence.'

('Which'll be a load of lies,' Moira whispered.)

('Let's hear him, at least,' Dan whispered back, judicious as always.)

To begin with, Wharton's evidence differed little from everyone else's, or from Moira and Dan's memory. He said that he had been in a Circle in the direct path of the Crusade demonstrators, who had reached it just about the time when the dancers had converged on them and tried to stop them. He himself had offered no violence; he had merely attempted to argue with the leading demonstrators, who had included Miss Sutton, but they had gone on chanting and would have pushed him aside. But at that moment he had been caught between attackers and defenders near the Cauldron.

'I fell over, sir – most of us did, the demonstrators and the others, all mixed up together in a heap of people. Some were fighting, some trying to tear up the banner, and some – like me – just trying to break free. One is pretty vulnerable with no clothes on. . . . But I was trapped under two or three people. Miss Sutton was about three metres away from me – she was on the ground, too, pinned down by the crowd. One man was hitting at her face, and she was protecting it with her hands. . . . Then the earth tremor came and more people fell on top of me – I thought my back would break and I could hardly breathe. Then Miss Sutton managed to get to her feet and yelled out about the wrath of God smiting the witches. She was dragged down again, and then the fighting started again – only harder, as though the tremor had rattled people. I was still trapped. Then I saw two people – a man and a woman – pushing their way through the crowd towards Miss Sutton. They went down on their hands and knees as they reached her. They were skyclad – naked, that is – and he was carrying an athame and she a copper bowl. An athame is a witch's ritual black-handled knife, sir.'

The coroner nodded. 'Did you recognize these two people?'

'No, sir. Their backs were to me and they both had long hair falling forward, the way they were moving. His was black and hers light brown. I never saw his face and I only got a glimpse of hers in profile – round, with a big mouth and small nose. I'd say they were both about thirty. He was thin, a little tall as far as I could judge. She was on the plump side but small-breasted.' He paused.

'Go on, Mr Wharton.'

'By then, sir, Miss Sutton was still pinned down by the crowd, but no one was paying attention to her, if you understand me. The man and woman wriggled between a lot of legs till they reached her, and then. . . . It was horrible, sir. He pulled up her sweater and stabbed her in the ribs with his athame. I think I screamed – but there was so much noise and screaming no one would have heard. She must have died almost at once, there was so much blood. And the woman was catching as much of it as she could in the copper bowl. . . . Then someone fell in front of me and I couldn't see them any more. The crowd moved and I managed to get up. The man and woman had gone. I looked around, I think I must have called out something, but no one listened – then I saw them running towards the Great Altar. She was holding the bowl up high as though she were carrying an offering, and he was running beside her holding his athame up like a salute. Four other people had joined them – two men and two women, like an escort. . . . I never saw them reach the Altar; I was knocked over again. The Altar had been smashed up by then and the statue. I suppose they intended to pour the blood over it, as a sacrifice to avenge the sacrilege. . . .'

'Do not suppose, Mr Wharton. Confine yourself to what you saw and heard.'

'Yes, sir. Actually I didn't see any more of them, because it was then that the motor-cyclists arrived and the crowd scattered. I managed to get outside the ring of cycles before it closed. I saw one of them run over Miss Sutton's body. . . . I knew there was nothing I could do so I found my clothes and escaped down the hill to my car.'

'Being too afraid to inform the police,' the coroner said.

'Yes, sir, I was. I'm not proud of it but I've seen what these people can do.'

The coroner looked at him inscrutably for a moment, and then asked: 'The man's athame, Mr Wharton. Would you please describe it?'

'An ordinary sheath-knife, sir. About a twelve- or fifteen-centimetre blade. You know, sharp along one edge and thick along the other.'

Appalled and furious, Moira was gripping Dan's arm, unable even to whisper. She saw that one or two reporters were hurrying out of the press box. She was so angry that she hardly heard the coroner's questions, clarifying points in Wharton's story. Her attention was dragged back by a sudden cry of 'It's true!' from a woman who had jumped to her feet from the witnesses' seats.

The coroner restored order, and then asked: 'Miss Chalmers, isn't it?'

The woman, a frightened-looking creature with mousey hair, nodded as though she had lost her voice.

'Do I understand that you wish to add to, or amend, the evidence you gave earlier?'

Now the words came in a flood. 'Yes, sir, I do. I was afraid, like him. He's right about what they can do. . . . But I saw those two stab Miss Sutton and her collecting the blood. Just like he said. It was awful . . .'

'Can you describe them?'

'No more than *he* did, sir. It was all that hair. . . . Then I saw them running, and I *did* follow them, not too close, they still had their backs to me. And he's right, they *did* pour the blood on the ground, in front of where the Altar had been smashed up. I'm afraid I just turned and ran. . . .'

('Oh, God,' Moira breathed. 'Dan, this *stinks*. But it'll stick! People'll *believe* it!')

('I hope you're wrong, love.')

The coroner, at least, was not credulous. After he had questioned Miss Chalmers, he recalled the pathologist.

'Doctor, when you examined the body of Miss Sutton, did you find any evidence of a knife wound?'

'No, sir, I did not.'

'You gave evidence that the rib-cage was badly crushed. Is it possible that this damage could have concealed the fact that she had been stabbed, by such a weapon as Mr Wharton has described, deeply enough to cause the kind of bleeding he described?'

'No, sir. The wound would still have been detectable to a careful examination.'

'Which you carried out in this case?'

'Of course, sir. When a cadaver has suffered multiple injuries, one always bears in mind that those injuries may conceal an earlier and significant injury. One is therefore particularly careful to search for such evidence.'

'Thank you, Doctor.'

Andrea Sutton's solicitor rose immediately. 'Doctor – in addition to being run over twice, Miss Sutton's body had also been hit by a falling motor-cycle, had it not?'

'That is so, yes.'

'And would not that machine have sharp projections?'

'Yes. There were several lacerations from such projections, but mostly on the legs and pelvis, across which the machine fell. There was one such wound in the chest, which would appear to have been inflicted by the clutch lever on the left handlebar. It had penerated to about six centimetres.'

'You say "would appear to have been".'

'The machine is not available for examination. I was being careful to distinguish between deduction and hard fact.'

'I put it to you, Doctor, that the wound which you *deduce* was caused by a clutch lever could equally well have been caused by a sheath-knife.'

'It could not. The wound would be different.'

'And that difference could be detected after the rib-cage had been badly crushed?'

'This wound was in a part of the chest which was otherwise comparatively undamaged.'

'Ah. Then in the *more* damaged parts, the evidence would be more doubtful.'

'Not at all. It would merely require more careful examination – which, as I have said, I carried out. There was no knife-wound in the chest.'

'I suggest, Doctor, that you are being over-confident.'

'And I strongly resent that suggestion.'

The solicitor sat down, smiling.

The coroner lifted his hand to still the murmur that ran round the court. 'It is clear to me that further police investigation is necessary in this case, before a proper verdict can be arrived at. Among the aspects calling for investigation . . .' (he looked steadily at Wharton and then at Miss Chalmers) '. . . is the possibility that perjury has been committed. Superintendent, you will please speak with me in my office after the court has risen. This inquest stands adjourned *sine die.*'

'Sally, I've never been so angry in my life,' Moira said. 'God *knows* what Mike Wharton and that Chalmers woman are up to. But I didn't believe a bloody word of it.'

'Nor did the coroner,' Dan snorted. 'He made that pretty clear.'

'What frightens me is that I don't think they *expected* him to believe it. All that was for Joe Public.'

'I hope Joe Public isn't that stupid,' Dan said.

Sally asked drily: 'Do you want to bet?'

'Oh, I know but . . . All right, people will read it but they'll also read that the coroner practically called them liars.'

'Do you want to bet on that, too?'

They were interrupted by the sound of the evening paper falling on the front doormat. Dan went to fetch it. Moira and Sally heard him pick it up but his footsteps halted halfway down the hall.

'Come on,' Sally called. 'Let's know the worst.'

Dan came in and threw the paper down in front of them. The banner headline read: 'BLOOD SACRIFICE AT WITCH RIOT? *Inquest Adjourned for Probe*'.

They read the story through together. The main emphasis was on Wharton's and Miss Chalmers' evidence and on the solicitor's attack on the pathologist's evidence. The coroner's remarks on possible perjury were not quoted.

'The next stage,' Moira said bitterly, 'will be the bricks through our windows.'

5

Come Devil or Doomsday, Miss Smith was enjoying herself. It was high summer; she, the caravan, and Ginger Lad were all three in excellent health, and she was quite content to be a directionless nomad for a while. The crisis would erupt soon enough – of that she was still sure – but until she could see the shape of it, she was making no definite plan. It was enough to be mobile and free, and out of town.

She followed the news carefully on the radio and on her little fifteen-centimetre television and bought a different newspaper each day in the hope of getting a cross-section of what was being thought and said; though she had a growing feeling that the media were not being frank. There was no formal censorship as yet but a lifetime in local government had given Miss Smith a sensitive nose for the symptoms of back-door pressures and Establishment manipulation and that nose told her that such influences were increasingly active.

But sniffing the political wind was only a minor part of Miss Smith's new way of life. What she enjoyed most was exercising and perfecting her ability to live off the land.

She was quite skilled at it already; she had been an enthusiastic camper since she was a girl. Then, it had been a bicycle and a tent. In her twenties she had graduated to a Lambretta scooter, and in due course to her first motor caravan. With characteristic thoroughness, she had taught herself how to maintain it. Within a year she could, and did, dismantle and reassemble the engine. Her present caravan was her fourth and most luxurious; she had bought it brand-new two years ago, when her father had died and left her a few thousand in life insurance.

Camping and caravanning had become an addiction with her, as she cheerfully admitted. A boyfriend had once persuaded her to join him in a package-tour holiday in Greece; the boyfriend had been satisfactory, but the confinement of hotel life had been less so. Her eyes had always been on the olive-studded hills and the emptier beaches, while his had been on the bars and the concrete swimming pools. She had liked him but she had been only briefly upset when six months later he had transferred his affections to a night-club hostess in Chelsea.

The following year she had gone alone, in her caravan, to those same hills and beaches; her love affair with the man had been consummated, but her love affair with Greece had not and she had been aware of the frustration all winter. She had driven home to London happy and she had never taken another hotel holiday.

In nearly forty years of camping, Miss Smith had learned a good deal. She knew what she could eat from the fields and hedgerows and what she could not; when she toured abroad – as she had done in places as far apart as Finland and Morocco – part of the fun was seeing how much of the same lore she could acquire locally. It tickled her pride that she could identify at least three High Atlas cacti which would enhance a *couscous* and two Arctic mosses which gave a unique flavour to soups. Such knowledge was gratifying but of course exotic; the British Isles were her real field of study and she could do well for herself anywhere from the Fens to the Burren, from the Hampshire woods to the Sutherland glens. She could light and maintain a fire in a snowstorm. She could pick herbs to staunch bleeding, soothe headaches or ease constipation. She was an accomplished (and so far uncaught) poacher; she owned a licensed .22 rifle but she could hunt silently when discretion dictated. She disliked snares but had taught herself to use them and she had even had passable success with a catapult.

She did not object on principle to technical aids; her methane cooker was a beauty and she had a well-equipped medical cupboard; but she was wary of becoming dependent on them. She liked to feel she could manage if the gas gave out or the drugs could not be bought. Her little caravan library was strictly practical: road atlases, *Culpeper's Complete Herbal*, *Black's Medical Dictionary*, the caravan workshop manual and so on.

When Miss Smith had driven out of London into Epping Forest a week ago, she was only doing what she had done on more summer weekends than she could count (winter ones, too, come to that). But this time, from the start, the feeling was different. It was one thing to set off on a holiday of two or three days or weeks, knowing that the little house in Vicarage Road lay at the end of it, that minor extravagances were permissible, that whatever was used up could be replaced. It was quite another to accept that this was no holiday but the start of a new life-style, an open-ended journey that might never lead back to Vicarage Road. There were moments, in those first few days, when she asked herself if she was crazy. But her instinct told her otherwise, and in any case it was not Miss Smith's habit to brood on a decision once taken. So she slipped quite naturally into altered ways of thinking.

She must be careful with money, but not miserly because she might as well make the best use of it while it retained its value; and if she was right about the approaching crisis, the time might come when it was so much waste paper. She must reckon on becoming immobile when petrol disappeared from the pumps; but a full tank, and the jerrycans padlocked on her roof-rack, would take her almost a thousand kilometres, so she topped up the tank regularly. She kept on thinking of simple things that might run out. For example, it would be a pity to be reduced to stick-rubbing through lack of lighter flints. . . . So at the next tobacconist's she bought a dozen packets which should last for years as she was a non-smoker, and four lighter-gas canisters. (She had two lighters, which had belonged to her father; it was not till weeks later that she discovered that one could buy flintless lighters, which annoyed her; such a *silly* thing not to know.)

She busied herself with such thoughts and preparations but she saw no reason to be tense or solemn about them. While petrol could be freely bought, she was determined to have fun wandering.

She had kept moving in short daily hops, circling London to pick up the Thames above Reading, and then on to Savernake Forest, Avebury, Frome and the Mendips. Her westward move was not entirely planless. For one thing, she felt that before too long she should be basing herself somewhere in the Pennine area, because if petrol suddenly became unobtainable, the nearer she was to the centre of the island the more scope would her thousand-kilometre reserve give her; the wider the geographical choice one had, once the crisis took shape, the better. So she wanted to visit some of her favourite southern places before she settled down.

But a particular reason was that she wanted to go and see her only living relative, a young cousin who was a nurse in a hospital a few miles inland from Weston-super-Mare. Eileen was a sensible girl and Miss Smith felt that she, if no one else, should know what her eccentric middle-aged relative was up to.

It would be pleasant, Miss Smith thought as she came into Compton Martin, to go through Cheddar Gorge instead of taking the direct road. On this impulse, she swung south-west to cross the spine of the Mendips by the B 3371. It was a hot morning and Miss Smith sang to herself as the van climbed. She had happy memories of the Gorge and she wondered why she hadn't thought of this detour in the first place.

She might even put off visiting Eileen till tomorrow and spend the night near Cheddar. Yes, why not? She hadn't been down the Caves for years. . . .

She reached the junction with the B 3135 and saw the road block. It was manned by half a dozen soldiers and a sergeant was signalling to her to stop.

Miss Smith pulled up, puzzled.

The sergeant asked politely: 'Where are you heading, ma'am?'

'Down the Gorge to Cheddar.'

'I'm sorry, ma'am – the Gorge is closed. You'll have to turn here and circle round through Draycott.'

'Oh, what a pity. Why?'

'A rock fall, after the tremors. It'll take some time to clear.'

'Well, I hope it's not near the Caves. You can reach them from the Cheddar end, I hope?'

'I'm afraid you can't, ma'am. The Caves are closed to the public. Routine precaution.'

The phrase 'routine precaution' aroused Miss Smith's suspicion at once. That old cliché. . . . She said with deliberate innocence: 'Someone might have put up a warning notice at the crossroads back there, to save people wasting time.'

'I'll suggest it to my officer, ma'am,' the sergeant replied. Somehow Miss Smith felt that that was a cliché, too. She did not know why, but she sensed that the Gorge was being kept closed with the minimum of publicity. . . . No, I'm being a suspicious old woman.

She smiled at the sergeant, and said, 'I think I'll turn back, then, and go on to Weston. No point in going to Cheddar if I can't see the Caves.'

The sergeant nodded and stepped aside. Miss Smith reversed into the fork, and swung round the way she had come, giving the sergeant a friendly wave as she left. He saluted her expressionlessly.

Am I being a suspicious old woman? she asked herself as she drove downhill again. Soldiers don't man road blocks. Police do. . . . Though if there's been tremor damage round here (had the Mendips been mentioned? – she couldn't remember) perhaps the police are overworked and the Army's been giving a hand. Forget it. Enjoy the day.

But the question-mark stayed in the back of her mind all the way to Eileen's hospital.

She left the van in the car park and walked over to the main entrance. A red-haired young nurse grinned at her cheerfully from the admissions counter; Miss Smith had been going to enquire at the porter's lodge, but it was empty, so she crossed over to the nurse.

'Good morning. I wonder if I could see Nurse Eileen Roberts?'

'Eileen? Ooh, dear, you're out of luck. She's one of the ones who've been whipped off to the Banwell Emergency Unit.'

'Oh, that's a pity,' Miss Smith said for the second time this morning.

'Right nuisance to us, too, love. Five they've taken, and a doctor, and we're short-staffed already. . . .'

'Nurse!' The sister had emerged suddenly from the door behind the counter, and her tone was sharp. 'I'll attend to this lady. You can go for your lunch-break.'

The nurse flushed and scuttled away.

'Yes?' the sister asked abruptly.

'I was asking for my cousin, Nurse Eileen Roberts. But I understand she's away.'

'I'm afraid so. She's been lent to another hospital.'

'At Banwell?'

'The nurse was misinformed. Nurse Roberts went to Weston, yesterday, but she was due for two weeks' holiday first. So it'll be no use asking for her there for another fortnight.'

Miss Smith said 'Thank you, Sister' and left. When she was back in the van she looked at Ginger Lad curled up in his usual place on the passenger seat. 'You know what, my friend? There's something very odd going on. That sister was lying. And so was the sergeant, back there.'

Ginger Lad yawned.

'You're probably right,' Miss Smith told him. 'All the same, we're going to Banwell to have a look-see.'

She remembered passing through Banwell three or four kilometres back; just as well, because she had not known the name and if it hadn't been fresh in her visual memory she might not have caught what the nurse had said. As she drove towards it again, she wondered what she should do. She was obstinately determined to see Eileen, quite apart from the fact that her curiosity (an active element in Miss Smith's make-up) had been aroused. But her experience with the sister warned her that there might be snags to simply asking for Banwell Emergency Unit. Miss Smith was not at all sure what she was up against, but she felt wary.

On the other hand, the young nurse *had* told her that Eileen was at Banwell Emergency Unit. Maybe she shouldn't have but that wasn't Miss Smith's fault. And Eileen *was* her cousin, which gave her every excuse for asking for her. . . .

She decided to risk it.

As she came to the outskirts of Banwell, she kept her eyes open for a suitable pedestrian – preferably someone a little naïve and unsuspicious. She picked on a housewifely woman of about forty and pulled up beside her.

'Excuse me. Can you direct me to the Banwell Emergency Unit?'

The woman had smiled when Miss Smith leaned through the window to speak to her, but now the smile faded. She looked at Miss Smith nervously.

'You'd better ask at the police station,' she said, and turned away.

Miss Smith sat there for a moment, thinking. She decided she did not want to ask at the police station. She did not want her name noted down in the station book. Obviously, to ask for the Emergency Unit made one suspect; and if, somewhere along the official wires, that suspicion linked up with the disappearance of a local government officer and an unauthorized entry in File LB o8o6. . . . She was beginning to regret that little joke.

Oh well. One more 'innocent' try. She drove up to the post office and parked.

From the medical cupboard she took a cardboard carton

of penicillin tablets which she had somewhat unofficially acquired as useful stores; it was still in its hospital wrapping. That would do. She could carry it into the post office and say she had orders to deliver it in person to the Unit; it might work, and if it didn't, she could say she was going on to the police station.

But Miss Smith was saved the trouble of finding out. As she opened the door of the van, a nurse walked out of the post office.

Miss Smith called, 'Eileen!'

The nurse spun round, startled. She gasped, 'Angie!' and then looked quickly up and down the street. No one was looking their way. Miss Smith jumped back into the van and opened the passenger door from inside.

'Move over, Ginger Lad. We've got a visitor.'

Eileen said, 'Drive straight on, Angie,' as soon as she was seated.

Miss Smith did as she was told, asking, 'Where are we going?'

'Towards the Unit, as long as anyone can see us. But not *to* it. . . . How the hell did you find me? We're supposed to be top secret. We can't write or phone anyone.'

'Never mind that now – tell you later. What were you doing in the town, then?'

'Official errand. But if I'd tried to use the phone, the post office would have stopped me. They're under orders, too. . . . Turn up here. We can keep out of sight for a while and talk.'

Miss Smith chose a spot to park and then turned and looked at her cousin. My God, she thought, she's been through the mill. . . . Eileen Roberts was a pretty girl; twenty-three, with a sturdy little figure, a sunny face, rather high-coloured and framed with black curls. But now the face was pale and drawn and the curls seemed to have lost their sheen. And the eyes . . .

'Can you tell me?' Miss Smith asked gently.

'I don't know how much has leaked out,' Eileen said. 'Do you know anything about what's going on round here?'

'Only that the Gorge is closed. I was turned back by an Army road block, of all things. I smelt a rat then. I went on to look you up at the hospital and a little nurse let slip you were at Banwell Emergency Unit, before a sister came and shut her up. The sister tried to put me off your scent with some yarn about your being on holiday.'

'The Gorge is closed, all right – and the Cave entrances sealed off with God knows how many tons of concrete. Ever since the first tour came up the day after the tremors. Those people are at the Unit, Angie. And a few others who caught it from fissures in the ground before those were sealed, too.'

'Caught *what*?'

'The Dust. . . . That's what they call it but it's so fine it's more like a vapour. At least, that's how the . . . the patients described it, while they still could. . . . First day, they were treated as acute bronchitis cases. Matron told me one story did reach a London evening paper but they rang back for more details and by that time the clamps were on. So it never appeared.'

She broke off, and was silent for some time before Miss Smith realized she was crying. Just sitting there, trembling, while the tears ran down her cheeks.

Miss Smith put an arm round her and Eileen clutched at her, sobbing now. 'Call myself a nurse! But oh, Angie – it's awful. . . .'

'There now, love.'

Eileen sat determinedly upright and managed to regain control of herself. 'But then, I'm not a nurse. I'm a bloody jailer. We all are. . . . No, listen – I'll try to tell you. It *starts off* like acute bronchitis, but after a day that clears and they're breathing normally. For another couple of days they're just weak, like fever cases recovering. Then it starts. Out of the blue, fits of violence, lasting only a minute or two and then passing. The first patients smashed furniture and windows and one broke a nurse's arm – after that we were prepared for it. They get steadily worse till the fits are continuous. By about the fifth day, they're wild animals. They don't seem to be in pain – just stark, staring mad – and *violent*. In strait-jackets, round the clock. It takes two of us to feed one patient – a male nurse to hold him and a female nurse to spoon it into him. Or her. Otherwise the feeder may get bitten. One girl was; it fractured two of her fingers.' Eileen laughed, harshly. 'They gave her an anti-rabies course, to be on the safe side. But it doesn't seem to be infectious, or contagious. And that's about all we *do* know. . . . We've got experts with strings of letters after their names as long as your arm, up there at the Unit. They've been running tests and Christ knows what, and they haven't a *clue*. It's a week now since the first ones went mad and all we've learned so far is how not to get ourselves hurt. . . . Angie, I wouldn't confess this to anyone else, but. . . . Look, I'm a nurse. I've got my reasonable share of compassion; you must have in my job or it gets impossible. But these. . . . They're so awful, so far away from being human, I can't even feel *sorry* for them. I'm afraid of them and I *hate* them. I hate them for not being human and for keeping me away from being a nurse. . . . I said I was a jailer but I'm not even that. I'm a keeper of wild beasts which haven't even got the nobility of *real* beasts. . . . I know some of the others feel the same. One day soon, one of us is going to kill one of them. And what that would trigger off, I daren't think. . . . Angie, it's like the end of my world.'

'Oh, my God,' Miss Smith said.

'I might *just* be able to ride it out,' Eileen went on, 'if I thought that it. . . . Angie, I discovered something two days ago, by accident. One of the doctors let it drop without realizing what he'd said. He'd only just joined us, and he was discussing a symptom with another doctor – and he said "We found at Corwen it only occurs in the women". He'd forgotten I was in the room and I slipped out. . . . You see what it means? Corwen's in North Wales, isn't it? – and *that* was on the tremor line. So this isn't the only place. . . . Angie, *what the hell are we sitting on top of?* And what happens if that little earthquake was only a starter?'

Miss Smith thought for a moment, and then asked: 'Eileen, are you being *useful* there? In any way, as a nurse?'

'In *no* way. My job could be done far better by an all-in wrestler.'

'Are you prepared to desert, then?'

'*What?*'

'Drive away with me. Now.'

'Angie, I'm a *nurse*!'

'Precisely. And in normal times that means taking orders – though even then, you can give notice. I'm just asking you to leave without notice, because the way things are developing, I think your knowledge is going to be valuable to real people *not* wild animals beyond help. And I think you may find yourself having to use it on your own initiative without a nation-wide organization to work in and take orders from. . . . I was a public servant, too. But I smelt the way the wind was blowing and prepared accordingly. This caravan's a carefully planned survival base, if that doesn't sound too melodramatic. . . . I'm not on holiday,

Eileen. I walked out last week, without telling anybody. That's why I came looking for you; I'm all the family you've got, for what I'm worth, so I thought you'd a right to know what I was up to. . . . I made my decision but since I started out I've wondered sometimes if I was *over*-dramatizing. Not any more, I don't. Not since I heard your story. . . . There's room for you.' She waved at the two bunks behind them.

'But, Angie – we'd never get away with it. Did you say you were my cousin, at the hospital?'

'Yes.'

'Then if I disappear, the same day, from a top-secret place . . . By this time tomorrow all the police in Britain would be on the look-out for this caravan.'

'I said the caravan was *planned*. I have back there the number plates, registration book, and tax disc to next March of a bashed-in van of the same make which I bought for £50 in notes from a scrap dealer. I didn't give my name and he didn't ask for it. It would just go, and I drove it on to the Corporation dump of a borough which I happen to know doesn't bother to check up on dumped wrecks. There are some advantages to being a well-informed Council employee. . . . We'll change the plates and disc today, and we'll be OK for anything short of a chassis number examination. And by this time tomorrow we could be in the Lake District or somewhere.'

'Angie, you're an old crook.' Miss Smith could see that her cousin was brightening already.

'A survivor has to be, within reason. And I blush to admit to one more James Bond touch; I've got a couple of wigs in one of those drawers, and your head's about the same size as mine. How d'you fancy yourself as a blonde? . . . I'd better find it for you right away. And a sweater and slacks, though you'll have to pull the waist in a few inches. Have to get you out of that uniform *now*.'

'You've made up your mind about it, haven't you?'

'Yes.'

Eileen said: 'I can change on the floor while you drive. Let's get moving.'

They found a wood a few miles away towards Chew Magna where they changed the plates, and Eileen made a slightly more satisfactory job of re-clothing herself by moving the buttons on a wrap-around skirt of Miss Smiths. By mid-afternoon they were in Cheltenham, where Miss Smith insisted that Eileen bought herself some clothes in her own size ('Get a bikini and some shorts and a couple of sun-tops too, love – we ought to look and behave like holidaymakers'), and by taking it in turns to drive, before sunset they reached a quiet river-bank in Northamptonshire where they settled to cook a meal and spend the night.

Over a tin of pineapple (and how long would *they* be available?) Miss Smith casually switched to BBC 1 on the little television. The chronically surprised face of Paul Grant was asking: 'But are you seriously suggesting, Mr Stoddart, that the earth tremors were an expression of the wrath of God against resurgent paganism?'

Ben Stoddart's voice was as charming and reasonable as his smile. 'I wouldn't dream of suggesting any such thing. God works in mysterious ways and it's not for me to attempt to oversimplify them.'

'Isn't your slogan "Goddess worship is Satan worship" an oversimplification?'

'Essentially, no; it puts truth in a nutshell – and it concerns human activity, not Divine. One may – indeed one should – be categorical about human error. But one must bow to the mystery of God's intervention and accept that it *is* a mystery.'

'A mystery which may, or may not, include earth tremors to punish witches – and to punish the rest of us for tolerating them?'

'Let us put it this way, Paul. Andrea Sutton's last words, before she was martyred on Bell Beacon – or worse than martyred, if the blood sacrifice account by two independent witnesses is substantiated . . .'

'That is *sub judice*, so we can't discuss it,' Grant interrupted.

'Of course, of course. Please ignore my remark about blood sacrifice. But our dear friend Andrea's last words were: "It's the wrath of God, smiting the witches!" Now whatever the geologists may say (and heaven knows they say little that is comprehensible), it may be that millions of people will feel that, *in extremis*, Andrea expressed a profound *spiritual* truth. And millions may wonder if those words should go unheeded . . .'

Miss Smith reached out and turned him off. 'I can't stand that man,' she told Eileen. 'Unctuous, dangerous bastard. They're the worst rabble-rousers, the smooth and reasonable ones.'

'Are you a witch, Angie?'

'Me? I'm nothing in particular. Agnostic, I suppose. I just loath heresy-hunters. And at a time like this, they're dynamite.'

'Or a damp squib. He'll be forgotten in a week.'

'Maybe . . . Are *you* a witch?'

'I went to one of their festivals once, at Glastonbury – a friend invited me.' She laughed. 'I took off my clothes and danced round the bonfire with the rest. Tell you the truth, I thoroughly enjoyed myself. Not just the dancing – the ritual too. I think they've got something. . . . I've been meaning to look into it a bit more but I've been too busy yet.'

They took their cups of tea and sat on the river-bank as the stars came out. Eileen leaned back against a tree-trunk and sighed happily.

'Thank you for bringing me with you, Angie. I couldn't have taken *that* much longer.'

'Quite right too. . . . Glad to have you along, love. So's Ginger Lad – look.'

Ginger Lad had strolled across from the van to butt his head against Eileen's hand, demanding to be stroked. She laughed and rubbed behind his ears while he snaked his neck ecstatically.

'Where shall we find ourselves tomorrow, Ginger Lad?'

6

Philip Summers had always loved his wife, but in the first week or two after Beehive Amber he found himself falling in love with her. The experience took him completely by surprise – or rather, Betty's changed persona did, illuminating the busy bewilderment of their new existence. He was almost afraid to tell her, lest the spell be broken.

Most people would have described Betty Summers at thirty-one as a typical middle-class suburban housewife. Philip's mother, who was a self-conscious aesthete, did in fact call her that, though only to her husband ('I *ask* you, Charles – ducks on the wall!') and to chosen intimates, for she had given up Philip as lost when he insisted on studying engineering instead of the sculpture for which he had some limited talent. To be fair to Philip's mother, Betty had looked the part. Neat but unexciting figure, neat but unexciting clothes, soft mouse-coloured hair and regular features in an unmemorable face. Still, Philip had seemed contented in their neat but unexciting home, and at least Betty had the saving grace that she was studying with the televised Open University – though a geography degree was hardly an 'in' ambition. Philip's mother had shrugged and left them to it.

Philip had indeed been contented, until the shadow of Beehive had entered their lives – a secret which he had kept from her, as instructed, for he was a meticulous man. He enjoyed his work as a ventilation engineer; he made good money; Betty was a good cook and a welcoming if quiet bedmate. Their life together was pleasant, unturbulent and planned. When Betty had her degree, they would try for two children; her interest in the degree was purely amateur. And so on, milestone by modest milestone – had it not been for Beehive.

Beehive, as a secret, had been a worm in their bud. As a realized fact, it had a surprising effect on Betty Summers.

During their hasty packing, she had been stunned, querulous and tearful, lapsing into silence as the two men drove them to the designated Beehive entrance off Essex Road. Philip, watching her anxiously, believed that she was hardly aware of the three-kilometre subterranean journey by electric shuttle-car to the Centre. It was not until the door closed behind them on their four-metre-square cubicle in Centre Married Quarters that her eyes came to life.

Philip held a privileged position by accident. He had been enlisted for the London Beehive as one of five Area Ventilation Officers, under his own chief, who had been recruited earlier as Senior VO for the central governmental hub under Primrose Hill. Then, a month before Beehive Amber, his chief had been seriously injured in a car smash – and from his hospital bed (to Philip's surprise, for he was not the oldest in service) had nominated Philip as his replacement. So Philip, though a mere engineer, was to work cheek-by-jowl with Cabinet ministers, senior civil servants, generals and other elevated figures; to sit as a suitably respectful adviser on various key committees; and even (which amused Philip inexplicably) to undertake personally in the Royal Apartments the routine ventilation maintenance which in other places was left to his thoroughly competent Area staff of three technicians. He had, in addition, to supervise his colleagues in the other four Areas; so he expected to be fully occupied.

There were personal fringe benefits from being SVO. He and his wife would use the Senior Central Mess, only one degree less exalted than the Ministerial Mess (already nicknamed 'the Athenaeum'). Theoretically, all Beehive rations were identical, but one could not escape the fact that the Senior Central Mess kitchen was run by the head chef of Claridges. Again, the SVO's cubicle in Centre Married Quarters was forty centimetres wider and longer than those of his Area colleagues.

Suddenly alone with Betty in their air-conditioned concrete cell, Philip had it on the tip of his tongue to make a joke about those extra forty centimetres to coax her out of her silence. But he saw the look on her face and kept silent himself.

It was a strange, bright-eyed, secret look.

Still unspeaking, Betty gazed around: at the recessed bed with the storage cupboards over and under it, the fold-back table between bench seats, the tiny snacks-only kitchenette corner (communal feeding had to be the rule), the built-in wardrobe, the handbasin unit (showers and toilets communal, too), the two compact armchairs, the wall-mounted television screen and radio with their channel-selector switches, the telephone whose closeness to the bed seemed to emphasize that privacy was strictly provisional, the ever-whispering extractor grill . . . More like a ship's cabin than a room.

Betty turned to her husband and kissed him, suddenly and briefly, without smiling. 'Well, darling, this is it. Put those suitcases on the bed, and let's get cracking.'

He asked, tentatively: 'Are you all right, love?'

Then she did smile. Her face seemed to him, in some indefinable way, both harder and warmer than he had ever seen it before.

'Yes, Phil, I'm all right. Are you?'

'If you are. I've been . . . lonely, since I knew about this.'

'I know.'

They unpacked, Betty briskly dictating where things were to go. When the suitcases were empty, Philip took them away to Baggage Store. He returned a few minutes later to find Betty hanging a poster on the only available wall space, its string tied to the extractor grill. He realized that she had been carrying it in the car, rolled up, though he had been too preoccupied to ask what it was. Now he saw. It had hung on the landing at home; a reproduction of one of the Zodiac paintings by Johfra – the Virgo sign in which both their birthdays fell. Its central figure was a winged, half-naked woman, carrying a stem of barley in one hand and a flame-enclosing crystal egg in the other. Behind her were tilled fields and an open sky, which Philip did under-stand; the whole picture was framed with many symbols which he did not. On the woman's face was a secret smile that was somehow akin to the new look on Betty's.

He nodded and said 'Good'; he did not know what else to say, because the winged figure transformed the cubicle. He felt at once disturbed and comforted.

'The kettle's on,' Betty said. 'Will a sandwich do, or do you want to go to the Mess?'

'Not tonight. A sandwich'll be fine. I don't want to see anyone but you, right now.'

'Second thoughts, to hell with the kettle. Can you buy a bottle of wine from that Mess of yours?'

'Oh, I'm sure. Want me to try?'

'Yes, but don't be long.'

'Ten minutes.'

He came back with the bottle to find Betty in a négligée, with her hair brushed loose and shining and her make-up renewed. When he had poured the wine, she clinked glasses with him and then held hers towards the winged figure on the wall. 'Here's to us – and to Her. Whatever happens.'

'Whatever happens,' he echoed, and they drank.

Philip could never remember, afterwards, what they talked about during that strange supper; much of it was like the symbols around the winged Virgo, numinous but only half comprehended. What he did remember was that for the first time in their marriage, instead of him making love to her, she made love to him.

Philip, next morning, had no time for self-analysis. He was more than fully occupied at once. He had to arrange a rota for his three maintenance men; organize his corner of the office which he shared with his power, water and sewage opposite numbers; make himself known (and agreeable) to the head of the Typing Pool (fed by Claridges' chef he might be but he still did not rate an individual secretary); make a fuss about indented stores which had still not arrived – and at the same time to try to get Area North organized, by telephone and a flying visit by shuttle-car, because its AVO had been on holiday when Beehive Amber was ordered and had not yet reported in; so the Area was in charge of its senior maintenance man, who was brilliant with equipment but out of his depth with administration. Philip managed to cope reasonably well but he had to skip lunch and he reached 'home' just after six, exhausted.

Betty had been busy, too. She had found her way around ('After all, darling, geography's my subject'), investigated the Mess, the shop and the other services, bought various oddments to domesticate their cubicle ('No flowers, I'm afraid'), lunched with a couple of other wives and even found time to watch her Open University lecture on TV. She had also, thank God, stocked a little drinks cupboard and she had a whisky poured almost as soon as Philip came in the door.

They watched the BBC TV news together. There was, of course, no mention of Beehive Amber. Much of the news was taken up with the aftermath of the earth tremors. The tremors had never been far from Philip's mind all day – both because (although no official statement had been made to them) he and everyone he had spoken to took it for granted that the tremors had directly led to the Beehive Amber order, and because he was professionally anxious. If there were more tremors, ventilation, sewage and water would be among the most vulnerable aspects of Beehive and everyone in his shared office knew it. He had discovered that the reason why some of his stores had still not arrived was that they had been diverted to the Birmingham and Bristol hives – both of which were on the tremor lines. His sewage colleague had the same problem, and both of them had tried to phone their Bristol and Birmingham opposite numbers but had been told by the switchboard that 'until the Amber intake phase is complete' inter-hive communication was confined to Ministerial level. The sewage man had commented drily: 'Well, Phil – I guess down here lesson number one is to learn when to stop asking questions.' Philip had agreed, uneasily.

Something about the tone of the BBC news added to his unease. It was too smooth, too reassuring. Even compared with yesterday's newspapers, there was too little about actual damage and too much about confident officials. Yesterday there had been estimates of the number dead or injured and Philip had expected more authoritative figures today, but the question of numbers was ignored. Overseas news, too, devoted more minutes to reporting that the

Western Hemisphere was unaffected than to amplifying yesterday's information from Europe – with the exception of heartening shots of the speed and ingenuity with which the Dutch were repairing the Ijsselmeer dyke. One new significant item did emerge: Russia had cancelled all Intourist visits from abroad for the time being 'for meteorological reasons' – a characteristically obscure explanation but couched in terms of uncharacteristically courteous apology for the inconvenience.

The Soviet announcement meshed in Philip's mind with the recall of an incident that had puzzled him during the day. He had been passing the offices of the Chief Administrator – the Great God Harley himself – when a group came out who were obviously VIPs, from the deference with which they were being escorted. Two of them had been conversing earnestly in Russian and two others, though silent, looked Chinese. He had wondered to himself: 'Diplomats? – surely not' . . . because an emphatic part of his pre-Beehive briefing had been that he should be constantly on the watch for the slightest hint of Eastern espionage sniffing at Beehive, and report even his most improbable suspicions at once. Had the situation now changed? Were national establishments becoming a world establishment, closing its ranks in the face of a common danger? Were Western diplomats now conferring in the Beehives that doubtless existed under Moscow and Peking? . . . If so, the situation was far worse than even Beehive personnel were being told.

He glanced across at his wife, who was watching the TV screen intently. He had no idea at all what thoughts were passing through her mind. Ever since they had walked in that door, last night, her eyes had looked more alive. . . . No, he told himself immediately, that was absurd. Betty had never lacked life or warmth; she was an introvert, certainly, but a calm and loving one with a gentle but refreshing sense of humour. Something *had* changed in her, though, in the past twenty-four hours. The only way he could express it to himself, in his own technician's terms, was that her voltage had been stepped up. . . . It could not be that she *liked* it here. She had loved their home and looked after it devotedly and she had been torn out of it at one hour's notice with nothing but two suitcases and a rolled-up poster; yet after that almost cataleptically silent journey, not only had she not mentioned it – she had shown no signs of grieving over it, and puzzled by her though he was, Philip felt he would have known if she had been.

Could it be, he wondered suddenly, that under her suburban exterior (and Philip was well of his mother's view of her) there lurked the unexpressed potential of a pioneer wife? She was intelligent, she must know that their future was unpredictable, that even this concrete cell offered only a provisional security, beyond which lay . . . what? Had the sudden challenge (more than sudden – traumatic, surely) resonated some chord in her of which even she had been unaware until now?

Or *had* she been unaware? He asked himself a question which he realized he had always taken for granted; why was she studying for a geography degree, of all things, working hard at it too, even though she had no plans to earn her living by it? The unfulfilled pioneer again, urged to conquer and understand the round world, even if only from her suburban armchair?

He knew that only time would give him understanding.

Betty was still watching the screen, apparently unconscious of his scrutiny. Her legs were draped over one arm of her chair, her hands clasped round her knees, her head relaxedly erect.

Another novel thought came into Philip's mind, on the heels of the others; my wife is beautiful.

He turned his attention back to the news, inexplicably shy about being caught watching her.

Next morning he made his scheduled weekly inspection of the ventilation system of the Royal Apartments. During the Amber phase, he had been told, the Family would only be sleeping in Beehive; presumably their daytime presence on Surface would be a necessary part of the pretence of normality, until Beehive Red abandoned that pretence. So during the day the Apartments were manned only by a skeleton staff, presided over by a gentleman whose official appointment Philip did not know, but whom he heard addressed as Sir Wilfred. Admittance to the Apartments was through a military guardroom, manned today by the Coldstreams (in functional battledress – Philip had half expected the ceremonial scarlet) whose officer carefully checked Philip's fingerprinted identity card against a list of 'Technical Personnel – Authorized Access'. Behind the guardroom, two sentries stood rigid but watchful in front of an elevator door; Philip knew, because it was on his ventilation charts, that the elevator rose in two stages to the Palace, the stages being separated by a steel-shuttered airlock.

Philip had rather disliked having to wear battledress himself – the dark green of Technical Services, with the shoulder tabs of Civilian Officer Grade Two – but today he decided he was glad of it. Life and work in Beehive was going to be as compact, crowded, and busy as that of its natural namesake, and with as rigid a division of functions; indeed, individual and function would merge, so it would save a lot of time if one were seen to be what one was. . . .
He deliberately tried to suppress his natural aversion to

regimentation; here he was and he might as well make the best of it.

He set about checking the air-conditioning methodically – it was the first time he had seen it but his task was made easier by the fact that his own firm had installed it, so equipment and system were thoroughly familiar. He discovered a slight malfunction of the thermostat in the bedroom of one of the Princesses; correcting it took about twenty minutes and the chambermaid who had been hovering warily got bored after a while and left him alone. On the dressing-table Philip noticed a vase of about two dozen roses, the first flowers he had seen in Beehive; down here, they would obviously be a rare luxury. . . . His hand moved ahead of his thought and he was shocked to find himself committing his first conscious theft since he was a sweet-pilfering schoolboy; but the single bloom was inside his battledress blouse before he could stop himself and the bunch as quickly rearranged to hide the gap.

On his way out through the guardroom, later, he was gripped with a sudden terror that outgoing 'Technical Personnel' might be searched; but he was passed straight through, and his outbreak of sweat cooled on him in the safety of the corridor.

He was able to get to Married Quarters in time to collect Betty for a Mess lunch, and he did not dare to take the rose from its hiding place until he was inside their cubicle. He presented the slightly crushed bloom to her with a smile that was as much relief as gallantry. For a moment Betty was speechless, her bright-eyed control wavering; then she said with a quiver in her voice 'That's lovely, darling' and turned her back to put the rose in a tumbler of water. It stayed on the little shelf which served her as a dressing-table for days, until long after it was shrivelled and dead.

'But I don't *want* to be in bloody Beehive,' the tall girl said. 'I'm an American citizen . . .'

'What's that got to do with it?' Her bureau chief was beginning to sound exasperated. 'You're an Associated Press correspondent, is what matters as of now.'

'With a duty to tell the folks back home what's happening – right?'

'Right. And Beehive is where it's happening.'

'Oh, come off it, Gene. This is where the handouts are, is all. Down here, the AP bureau could be run by any high-school kid who could write his own name.'

'Thank – you – Tonia – Lynd.'

Tonia grinned, suddenly. 'Sorry. Eugene Macallister, genius diplomat-quizzer, *plus* one high-school kid. . . . Honestly, Gene, you know the score as well as I do. Till after Beehive Red, we can't even admit publicly that Beehive *exists*, let alone that it's operating already. And nobody down here's going to say *anything*. . . . Even if somebody did, by mistake, old Blue Pencil next door would kill it. Censorship, for God's sake! Anybody'd think this was Moscow.'

'Necessary censorship, honey. You got to admit that.'

'Oh, sure, it's necessary. So's a crutch, if you've got a broken leg. But my legs ain't broken, and I want to go walkabout.'

'Metaphor Minnie, at it again. . . . Look, Tonia, I know Vox Pop's your thing – and sure, you're feeling frustrated. But Beehive Red could happen any day and when it does I want you right here. *Until* then I want you right here because it'll take both of us to nose out even what news there is.'

'Take it in turn to say "thank you kindly" for the handouts?' Tonia snorted. 'What news there is, is up there on Surface. This witch-hunt thing, for instance . . .'

'What witch-hunt thing?'

'Actual, not metaphorical.'

'Oh, the nutters. . . . No one's hunting them, as far as I can see.'

'Didn't you read the inquest report on that Beacon Hill shindig?'

Gene shrugged. 'A local riot got out of hand. What's so special about that? Untypical, I'll agree. These screwy festivals of theirs are usually pretty quiet. This one happened to blow up, is all.'

'Did you *read* it, Gene?'

'Sure. Some demonstrators busted in, the nutters reacted, the party got violent, a kid was run over, somebody stuck a spear in the boss-woman and in revenge a few of the nutters blood-sacrificed a demonstrator. All very dramatic, for a one-off story, and singularly nasty. But a freak phenomenon – could happen any time with these religious jamborees. Not *significant*.'

Tonia nodded. 'I thought so. You read the story as published, not the full PA tape.'

'So?'

'I *did* read the tape. Local riot getting out of hand, my ass. That demo was *planned*, like a military operation. And as for the "blood sacrifice" – that yarn came from two witnesses only and the coroner as good as called them liars. Which did *not* get into the papers.'

'Tonia, honey,' Gene sighed, 'you've got a good nose for telling you when something stinks. None better. And sure, you could be right. But here and now, history's being made – and as journalists, we've got to get our priorities right, keep a sense of proportion, you know? Any ordinary time, you could chase this wild goose of yours *and* get some good copy out of it. But in the context of Beehive Amber – potentially the biggest story of our lifetime – that witch riot's nothing. *Nothing*. And you and I haven't got time for nothings.'

Tonia looked stubborn. 'I don't think it's nothing. My nose, that you're so flattering about, tells me the Beacon Hill attack was *planned*. Planned right here in Beehive – or topside in Whitehall. Act One of a deliberate diversion. And the curtain-raiser to Act Two was that Ben Stoddart man on the "Paul Grant Hour", on BBC.'

'Didn't see it.'

'I *did*. . . . You talk about "the context of Beehive Amber". Know what, Gene? I think, *in* that context, this Government was up to something on Beacon Hill. And I want to know what and why.'

Gene began flipping through a pile of copy on his desk. He said casually: 'Keep an eye on it, then.'

Two years of working under Gene Macallister had taught her the danger signals, the lowering of the shutters, but she persisted. 'Topside, Gene. If I'm right, that's where the story is. Get me a Surface pass, huh?'

He did not look up. 'Sorry, honey. No.'

'Please, Gene.'

He laid his palm flat on the top sheet of copy, deliberately; danger signal number two. '*No*, Tonia. In words of one syllable – we have Beehive accreditation and I will *not* have you endangering it by stirring up mud against the Government or by letting yourself appear to champion the witches.'

'Even if what my nose tells me is right?'

'For Chrissake, even *more* so if you're right! If the Department of Dirty Tricks, for its own good reasons, wants to make a scapegoat of the witches – and *you* start throwing spanners in the works – the Department of Dirty Tricks could have us out of here in no time flat. *Persona non* bloody *grata*, and no reasons would have to be given. *You* know that.'

'In the context of Beehive Amber,' Tonia said tonelessly.

'Or even Beehive Red, any day now! That's what it's all *about*, Tonia. AP has a job to do here and AP is you and me and no one else. If we lost our Beehive status, AP would be unrepresented in Britain, as good as.'

Tonia said nothing. Gene seemed to take her silence as acquiescence, and after a while he continued with the paternal air which always infuriated her: 'One other thing to remember. AP correspondents do not identify themselves, in either the public or the official mind, with screwballs. So if you have any private sympathies with those naked pagans and their subversive ideas, for God's sake – and AP's – *keep* 'em private.'

Tonia, who had no particular feelings about the witches one way or the other, could not resist asking: 'Subversive of what?'

'Christianity, decency, Western civilization – you name it,' Gene said impatiently. 'And I'll tell you something. If they *are* being set up as scapegoats, they've asked for it.'

'Nero must have found the early Christians equally convenient.'

'Now you're just being smart. Run along and let me work, there's a good girl. Go and watch "News at Ten". One of us ought to.'

Tonia went, her lips pursed. Out in the corridor she laughed to herself, suddenly: perhaps it was just as well Beehive doors didn't lend themselves to slamming.

'News at Ten', my ass.

Brenda Pavitt locked the last card-index drawer and straightened up, flexing her shoulders and stretching. It had been a long and tiring day but she was happy. As Chief

Librarian of London Beehive, she had been commuting with Surface for the past year, building up the remarkable collection of books, documents and microfilms which now surrounded her; and it had been the kind of assignment librarians dream about. A staggering budget and a virtually free hand. She had had, of course, to request, collate and cater for departmental requirements – but these had been in amplification, not restriction, of her own judgement. Realistically, she admitted to herself that being the Chief Administrator's mistress had helped a lot; Reggie Harley had cut several corners for her and smoothed several paths. But she did not feel in the least guilty about it. She had never taken advantage of their relationship for her personal gain (she considered herself too well paid to need it), but the Library was something different; for that, she would exploit God himself. And Reggie had indulged her.

But Brenda was a librarian by vocation as well as by appointment, and once the Library had come as near to comprehensive perfection as Brenda could make it, she had found herself fretting over its virgin quietness and longing for the consummation of readers. Now at last, with Beehive Amber, the consummation was beginning; the coming and going of faces, the vague or precise requests, the telephoned queries, the appeals for help from less knowledgeable assistants, and Brenda felt fulfilled. She and her system had stood up well to the first rush, with very few teething troubles. Come Beehive Red, and they would be able to cope. She knew that now.

She took a last unnecessary look around, said good-bye to the night duty girl, and left the Library to walk the hundred metres of corridor to her cubicle. Another favour from Reggie; her home-cell was not in Bachelor Quarters, half a kilometre away, but was one of the privileged few which were close to their occupants' workplaces. Also, of course, easier for Reggie to visit discreetly. Their affair was hardly secret any more, after six years, but one still went through the motions.

He was already there when she let herself in, sprawled in the armchair and talking to someone on the phone. He waved his free hand at her and continued his conversation. 'Very well, Professor. I get the picture. Your admirable tuition is turning me into quite a knowledgeable seismologist myself.' Smooth little laugh. 'I cannot stress too clearly that what we must have *at once* is any hint of the process accelerating. . . . Yes, quite. . . . I very much appreciate your daily written reports and *please* continue to phone me with your elucidations of them – they are most enlightening. But if you notice *any* symptoms of a change in the pattern – even if it's merely, shall we say, a hunch on your part, and your hunches, Professor, are worth a dozen lesser men's calculations – please don't wait till evening to tell me. Use the priority number at any hour of the day or night and speak to me personally. . . .'

As she poured herself a drink and renewed the one at Harley's elbow, Brenda reprimanded herself for her initial flash of resentment. She was only too glad for Reggie to have his own key, of course – he had had one on Surface, after all – but this leaving of her cubicle telephone number at the switchboard galled her. On Surface, Reggie's housekeeper (a friend of hers, fortunately) had come between them and urgent calls; she would simply phone the message to Brenda's flat and Reggie would ring the caller back. That arrangement had been acceptably personal. But now, she was sourly aware, anyone on the 'priority number' list could ring them up in the middle of an orgasm. . . . Still, she was also aware that Professor Arklow, for instance, might at any time be the bearer of news on which instant decisions, even the fate of nations, depended. Beehive was not Chelsea. Don't be a spoiled child, Brenda.

She gave vent to her self-reproach by kissing him extra warmly as he laid down the phone.

'Brenda, my dear. A good day?'

'Tiring but rewarding. My Library is actually being *used*.' She did not ask about Reggie's day; she had learned very early in their relationship that any such initiative on her part was taboo. Her function was to be a good listener once *he* had decided when, and how much, to talk about his work. Her comments were expected to be sympathetic but non-committal unless he actually asked her opinion. He did sometimes ask it: she knew he did not undervalue her intelligence but he had a devious set of criteria for defining the areas in which he should avail himself of it. She could talk about her own work as much she liked – it seemed to relax him, and to begin with she had believed he had welcomed it merely as a soothing noise until she discovered how shrewd his occasional comments were.

On the whole, she found him soothing, too. She had never wanted to marry him; she had in fact refused his one proposal, years back, and neither of them had mentioned it again. Marriage, for her, would have been too total. Their present relationship, with its well-defined if unspoken agreement on the areas of intimacy or independence, seemed to suit them both. Even their sex-life was similarly sub-divided. Harley, wiry and grey and well groomed as he appeared, was a surprisingly efficient lover; erotically, he could play her like a violin, as she could him; but they left each other's souls alone, so to speak. He had never called her anything more than 'my dear', and she had confined herself to 'Reggie', in or out of bed. And that, Brenda told herself, was the way she liked it. They gratified each other physically and they relaxed each other mentally. More than that would be a mutually unwelcome intrusion.

She was about to ask him if he had eaten, when the phone rang. Harley picked it up and said 'Yes?'

Brenda said 'Damn' but under her breath.

Harley went on: 'Of course, Chandler. Be on hand yourself, will you? You know what data he's likely to ask for. The Cabinet Office? Right.'

He rang off and stood. 'Dreadfully sorry, my dear. The Prime Minister – probably half the night. . . . The man's a fool, Brenda.'

Invitation to comment, she knew. 'It won't help your work down here, will it – being right in his pocket all the time?'

Harley smiled. 'It will be a question of who is in whose pocket. The – er – "democratic process" is a Surface plant. I doubt if it will take root in Beehive soil. . . . Have you ever studied a real beehive, Brenda? It is a highly efficient community, unhampered by pretence.'

'And you,' Brenda risked, 'propose to be Queen Bee?'

His eyes were inscrutable and she wondered if she had overstepped the mark. But he merely asked pleasantly enough: 'Did I say that?' and laughed.

After he had gone, she shivered, unaccountably.

7

'I thought those two were going to be pinched for perjury,' Dan said, dropping the *Guardian*.

'Which two?' Moira asked absently.

'Wharton and the whatsername woman – Chalmers. At the Bell Beacon inquest.'

'Oh . . .' Moira dragged her attention away from the book she was reading and asked: 'Can you be sure they haven't?'

'The *Guardian* wouldn't miss a thing like that. They reported the inquest – badly, for them, but they *did* report it. So they'd report any follow-up.'

'The papers haven't been exactly themselves recently,' Moira said. 'Not even your sea-green incorruptible *Guardian*.'

'Yes, but . . .' Dan plunged in, then hesitated, his battle-ready shoulders slumping. 'I wish I could say you were wrong, love,' he admitted finally.

Moira dropped her book on to her lap and stared through the open French windows at the bright little garden. 'Me too. . . . Something's going to happen, Dan, and soon – but what *is* it? More earthquakes? A full-scale witch-hunt?'

'Both?' Dan wondered, and when she did not reply, he went on: 'What do your cards say?'

She smiled, a little ruefully. 'That shows how worried you are.'

He looked surprised. 'But, Moira – you know how I trust your Tarot readings. You're bang on, time and again. I'm always asking you – I don't wait till I'm worried!'

'I know you don't, darling. But this time you have. You've been dying to ask me for days – but you've been afraid to. Not like you at all. Which means *you* feel it, too.'

'Of course I bloody feel it.'

'Then why don't *you* read the cards? You're as good as I am, if you'd let yourself be. If you'd trust yourself.'

It was Dan's turn to smile. 'Stop changing the subject. You haven't answered me.'

She was silent for what seemed to him a long time. Then she said 'Yes, I've read them. And they frighten me even worse. . . . Darkness and evil and I can't see the shape of it.'

'Why didn't you tell me?'

'Because you looking cheerful and confident keeps *me* going. Sometimes I don't want to disturb it.'

Dan shook his head; this was an old argument. 'If you're depressed, I want to know – and why. Me being falsely cheerful's no help.'

'Darling, you're never falsely cheerful. My own personal St George – you never lose heart even when you can *see* the dragon and it's ten times bigger than you are.'

'More fool me, probably,' he said, but looked pleased. 'And you're still changing the subject.'

'No I'm not. Right now neither of us can see the dragon. But it's there, all right.'

Dan had the familiar look in his eye which told her he was about to try cutting through the metaphors to the facts; but the point was never reached, because Rosemary suddenly appeared in the French windows, backlit by the sun.

'Hi, there,' Moira said. 'Come in and cheer us up. We're feeling low.'

Rosemary joined them, dropping into an armchair. 'That makes three of us. So *I* won't be much help.'

'On an afternoon like this too. . . . Hey, what are you home for anyway? I thought this was your Saturday on.'

'It was,' Rosemary said. 'I've been sacked.'

They stared at her, unbelieving. Rosemary, now twenty-four, had been a cashier at the biggest supermarket in the High Street ever since she left school at eighteen. Even to Moira, who was her closest friend, her daytime personality seemed a part of the place; Moira always shopped there and always brought her trolley to Rosemary's till, even if it had the longest queue. Somehow, it was impossible to visualize the supermarket without her. *Sacked?*

'What did you do?' Dan asked, as bewildered as Moira. 'Shoot the manager?'

'I didn't do anything.'

'What, then?'

'Would you believe – *redundancy*?'

Dan said, 'Oh, balls.'

'You may think so. I may think so. But that's what it says in my polite letter of dismissal, which was handed to me an hour ago with the exact amount of redundancy pay called for under the union agreement.' Her ironic calm was belied by the angry flush on her cheeks. 'Want to see it?'

'But – weren't you showing the ropes to a new girl, only last week?' Moira demanded.

'I was.'

'Oh, Rosemary! What the hell goes on?'

'Someone else went, too. We were called into old Jepson's

office together. . . . . Gilly Stevens, from delicatessen. Odd, don't you think, that Gilly and I were the only two known witches on the staff?'

There was a pause and then Dan said quietly: 'Oh, Jesus.'

Rosemary laughed. 'The old devil slipped up on one thing, though. He forgot to ask for our staff discount cards back. So we went straight out and loaded ourselves up with enough shopping for a week, paid for it on discount at Claire's till, and *then* trundled our trolleys to Jepson's office and handed in our cards. He'd have whipped the lot back if he could – you could see his nasty little brain working – but he knew it was too late and it was his fault.' She sighed. 'At least I can soften the blow to Greg by giving him a slap-up dinner, cheap. Want to join us?'

As July wore on, Moira and Dan began to realize that the 'redundancy' of Rosemary was not an isolated phenomenon. The widely believed version of what had happened on Bell Beacon had had more impact than had at first appeared; and there was still no news of perjury charges against Wharton and Miss Chalmers, or of a resumption of the inquest. Ben Stoddart and his Anti-Pagan Crusade were not allowing the issue to die. Few people had heard of the Crusade before Bell Beacon but now it seemed to be getting almost daily publicity – and, as Dan observed, to be immune to the *sub judice* laws. Little by little the blood-sacrifice story was becoming established 'fact', and if few people openly maintained the theory that the earth tremors had been the judgement of God on the witches and on those who tolerated them, there were signs that it was seeping into current folklore.

Anti-pagan feeling was becoming a public issue. Between the two committed viewpoints – the witches themselves and the Crusade – mass opinion, habitually either tolerant or indifferent, was beginning to polarize.

'People are still nervous about the earth tremors,' was Greg's opinion, 'but they don't understand them and they don't know if they're coming again – so they work out their nervousness on something they think they do understand. Us. Bell Beacon happened at a bad time. Gave 'em something to get their teeth into when they were frightened. Just our bad luck, that it happened when it did.'

'I'm beginning to think it's more than that,' Dan said.

'What do you mean?'

'I don't *know*. There's something stage-managed about it, Greg. I'm not sure whether it was planned though or just a coincidence the powers-that-be latched on to. . . . Look at the media, since the tremors. There's an unreal feeling about them – too smooth altogether. There are things they're not telling us, I'm bloody sure of it. . . . *Something's* going on and I wish I knew what it was.'

Dan's worrying had a personal element as well. The property market had remained paralysed by uncertainty, and the few country places still for sale were fetching very high prices; so although Dan and his partner Steve Gilchrist were partly cushioned against the financial effects of the slack market by higher commissions on the sales they did handle, in fact they had little work to do. Habitually, Dan was the outside man, the meeter of clients, while Steve stayed in the office watching over the legal chores. But in the last week or two their roles had tended to become reversed. Dan knew that Steve was quietly arranging things that way without openly referring to the change and that he was embarrassed about it. For the sake of the business, the known witch was being kept out of sight. . . . Steve had also avoided commenting on the fact that two properties which had been withdrawn from their list had reappeared on another agency's, and his very silence implied that he knew, or had guessed, the reason. Steve and Dan were friends, but how much of this would it take to break up their partnership?

Worry was one thing and could be openly voiced at home. Fear of actual violence was another, and although none of them had spoken of it since the first days after Bell Beacon, Moira knew it was in the back of all their minds. At their weekly Circles, she noticed that they were all especially careful in drawing the curtains, lest a careless chink should reveal the telltale arrangement of candles around the room; and each time she ritually cast the Circle she could feel the more-than-usual concentration of the others behind her willing its psychic ramparts into being. Till now, little Diana had sometimes been present in the Circle and sometimes not, according to the hour and her own wishes; now she was always included and the Circles began on time to allow for it.

When the violence did begin, it was not near home; but Moira witnessed it none the less. About once a fortnight, she was in the habit of leaving Diana with old Sally and going up to London for a few hours, shopping for things she could not get in Staines. She always made a point of visiting Atlantis Books, near the British Museum. Though it was not large, for a couple of generations Atlantis had been the best occult bookshop in the capital and it had a reputation for friendliness. Even occasional customers seemed to be remembered and recognized when they came again. Moira, being a regular, loved the place, with its ceiling-high shelves of new and second-hand books, its central display of latest issues and the little corner barricade of magazines behind which sat whatever member of the owning family happened to be on duty.

Today it was a round smiling young woman of the latest generation of that family, who said 'Hullo, Moira!' as soon as she walked in. 'Nice timing. We've just got the new Liz St George in. You'll be wanting it.'

Moira took the volume the girl held out and leafed through it. 'I think that woman's immortal. One a year, since before I was born.'

'Oh, more than one, some years. . . . Yes, she is. She was in here yesterday, like a laughing tornado. . . .' Atlantis was not only a bookshop, it was a clearing-house for personal news. Few people knew whether the family were witches, Golden Dawn magicians, spiritualists, or of any other occult persuasion; they had a natural gift for ecumenism, so everybody talked to them and listened to them. The girl went on exchanging news with Moira while Moira browsed.

She bought two books and a magazine, and was still lingering and chatting when the fire-bomb was flung through the door. Moira ducked instinctively as it flew past her and burst into flame at the back of the little shop, behind the central display. They both screamed in disbelief and shock, but the very speed with which the fire took hold jerked them into action. The girl cried, 'Take the till!' as she grabbed the phone and dialled 999 for the fire brigade. Moira swept the till off the cash table and took some seconds to open the door inwards with the awkward load in her arms; whoever had thrown the bomb had slammed it shut afterwards. By the time she had got the till across the narrow street to the opposite pavement, the girl had run to join her.

Already it was too late to save anything else. Whatever the bomb had been made of, it engulfed the whole shop in less than a minute. They stood watching helplessly among the fast-growing crowd, while tears of rage and grief poured down the girl's face.

Nobody had seen the attacker, although two policemen were on the spot almost at once asking for witnesses, so no one was ever charged with the crime. Of the entire stock, fourteen undamaged and just over a hundred slightly damaged volumes were salvaged. The rest was a dead loss.

Gregory said: 'I think we ought to be ready to take to the woods,' and for a while nobody in the candlelit Circle spoke.

It was the quiet time after the ritual, when they all sat on the floor around the chalice of wine for a while, relaxed, savouring both the wine and the comfort of the still unbanished Circle. Diana had fallen asleep, her small head cradled against old Sally's ample naked belly; they had all been keeping their voices low so as not to waken her, and somehow the very quietness of Greg's pronouncement loaded it with drama.

Dan eventually broke the silence with a cautious: 'Let's not panic, Greg. It may just be a passing phase.'

'You don't believe that any more than I do,' Greg told him. 'And I didn't say we should rush off right now. I said we should be *ready*. For when the balloon goes up, if it does. Come the crunch, it'd be too late to pack, we'd have to *go*. Not even stand and fight, with Sally and Di to think of.'

'I'm not senile yet,' said Sally predictably.

Equally predictably, Dan insisted, 'Cut the metaphors, Greg – what balloon – what crunch?'

'All right, Devil's Advocate, I'll tell you. Another earthquake, maybe a much worse one. *Real* panic and an anti-witch explosion. We're being set up for it, whether deliberately or not. And it wouldn't be just books they'd be burning. They'd be burning *us*.'

Diana stirred in her sleep, murmuring, and Rosemary said, 'Careful, Greg. Small ears.'

They were silent again, but all the faces turned towards Moira, sitting cross-legged with her back to the altar. She drew herself up instinctively, knowing that it was always like this while they were in the Circle. Dan and Greg would state the facts as they saw them, checked and balanced by contributions from Rosemary and Sally, and when they were ready, they would lay the problem at her feet. Not as Moira Mackenzie, wife and friend, alone; but as High Priestess, into whom, with the 'drawing down of the Moon' early in the ritual, the Goddess had been invoked, as channel, as oracle, as pythoness.

'Greg is right,' she said.

Dan asked immediately: 'What had you in mind, Greg?'

'We're lucky,' Greg said, 'we've both got garages. We can keep the cars loaded up without attracting attention. Your station wagon's ideal, but our Beetle's too small. There's a Bedford van in the workshop the owner wants to flog – I can trade the Beetle in for that. It's in good nick, I overhauled it myself. We're OK for camping equipment – Sally could have the blow-up igloo tent and the rest of us the big frame jobs. Use the van as kitchen . . .'

'Rosemary and I will stock up rations,' Sally interrupted. 'Moira can see to Di's needs, medical stuff, and so on. You boys can see to tools, gas cylinders, weapons and that.'

How calm she is, Moira thought.

'Did you say weapons?' Rosemary asked, a little shakily.

'Don't be daft, girl. Of course I said weapons.'

'But . . .'

'Leave that to us,' Dan said. 'Think of rabbits and pheasants if it makes you easier. . . . Should we pack a sewing machine?'

'Mine's the lightest,' Moira said.

'OK then. Now, about currency . . .'

The practical debate became almost eager, and Moira (High Priestess or not) was suddenly overtaken by a moment of terror. She managed to conceal it, because she recognized it for what it was: the acknowledgement, at last, of the spectre they had all been suppressing. They *had* all been telling themselves that the earth tremors were a freak phenomenon, that the witch-hunt was a passing madness; they had paid lip-service to the sense of growing crisis but they had not really let themselves believe it. Even she, with the clear warnings which her Tarot readings had unlocked from the storehouse of her intuition, had been running away from their implications. Now the barriers were down. It had only taken Greg's proposal, and her own *ex cathedra* endorsement of it, for pretence to evaporate. . . . They could be on the brink of disaster. Homes, friendships, the protection of law, the certainty of recognizable tomorrows, could all be snatched from them. They must be ready. The truth had been faced; now, in an avalanche of acceptance, they could talk of cars, tents, sewing machines – and weapons.

Moira's moment of terror ebbed. She was aware of the altar at her back, and of her own function; she straightened her spine proudly, throwing her hair backwards, hollowing her stomach, jutting her breasts, grasping her spread knees firmly in each hand.

Dan caught her eye and sent her a private smile. He always knew.

Some news of anti-witch violence did get into the media but they suspected that more was going on than was being reported. A neighbouring coven in Woking had a window broken and two parked cars burned during a Circle, and a friend of Greg's who was a High Priest in Liverpool wrote that his teenage daughter had been waylaid in a back street by an unknown but obviously purposeful gang who shaved her head and painted 'WITCH' on her scalp with gentian violet. Neither of these incidents made even the local press – probably, Dan suggested, because they might create sympathy for the victims. Reporting seemed selective and mostly confined to clashes where the witches had fought back, so that doubt could be cast on who had provoked whom.

Some liberal opinion did make itself heard, condemning the violence, but even this current of feeling could, it seemed, be exploited. It so happened that a parliamentary by-election was to be held on 20 July in the constituency which included Bell Beacon and an Independent candidate, Quentin White, who had been standing on a rather vague combination of local issues, came out with a new demand – that public pagan festivals be made illegal, in the interests of civic order. White had been expected, indeed, had himself expected, to lose his deposit, but local revulsion at the Bell Beacon shambles was given a new outlet by his switched campaign, and his meetings, which had drawn handfuls, were now attracting hundreds. The constituency bordered on Staines, and Moira's group watched the campaign apprehensively.

'He can't get in, though, surely,' Dan said. 'This ban-the-Festivals thing of his – it's too bloody woolly. He doesn't say *how* it could be made law. Probably unconstitutional, in any case.'

'Come off it, Dan,' Greg protested. 'Voters aren't legalistic, they go for causes. And there's no such thing as the British Constitution. If an Act of Parliament says Tuesday is Wednesday, that's the law. The Constitution's only all the laws in force as of now, added together. And a State of Emergency could suspend even that.'

'You're over-simplifying . . .'

'Sure I am and so's Quentin White. So will the voters, come polling day. I don't like it, mate.'

None of them liked it, and they liked it even less as the days went by. Parliament, the Prime Minister announced, was being recalled from its summer recess to debate an Emergency Powers Bill. This, he explained, would be merely a contingency measure to enable the Cabinet to act without delay in the event of any further natural disaster. Once passed, it would be held in reserve, only to be put into force by Order in Council, 'if and when a national emergency should make it necessary'. With his gift for making circumlocution sound earthily forthright, the Prime Minister managed to convey the simultaneous impression that earth tremors could strike again at any moment and that there was nothing at all to worry about.

On the face of it, they all agreed, there was nothing about the Emergency Powers Bill to which any reasonable person could object. It was the Government's clear duty to be fully prepared to deal with the effects of any future earth tremors, and with the localized wreckage of the Midsummer tremors still to be seen, no one could pretend that the danger did not exist. But they could not help noticing that the Prime Minister had avoided too precise a definition of 'national emergency'. Once the Bill became an Act, it could be an all-purpose weapon.

None the less, the Bill was necessary and everybody knew it, so it had the nation's support. It did, however, create a climate favourable to firm government, and even in many minds (whether consciously or not) to the authorities' cutting red tape, taking short cuts and not being too squeamish about traditional liberties. So the effect on the by-election was marked; after the Prime Minister's statement, Quentin White had to begin hiring larger halls for his campaign meetings and the funds seemed to be forth-coming.

It was at this strategic moment that Ben Stoddart step-ped in. Two days after the statement, Stoddart publicly threw the whole weight of his Anti-Pagan Crusade behind White's candidature. Two days after that, he appeared with White on the same platform. The meeting was packed out and had nation-wide TV coverage. There was little trouble from hecklers, both because the rest of the audience was hostile to the few who raised their voices and because two coachloads of visibly tough young Crusader arrived at the hall an hour in advance 'to give a hand with the stewarding'.

Next morning the 'stewards' were still in the constit-uency and reported for duty to White's committee rooms. They were sent out canvassing and within days the nick-name 'stormtroopers' was being bandied about – not always, as Dan sourly observed, with disapproval.

Only once did the unspoken threat of their presence manifest in actual violence. A fiery young man who was well known locally as an active witch heckled persistently at one of the open-air Crusader meetings and was set upon by the stewards. The hospital had to put five stitches in his left cheek and four dangerously high inside his right thigh. Ben Stoddart issued a public reprimand to the stewards for 'over-enthusiasm' – a reprimand so mild that it was virtually an endorsement. After that there was no more trouble from hecklers.

The by-election remained national news, a focus for the whole anti-witch controversy. One side-effect was to intro-duce controversy, for the first time, into the Emergency Powers debate in the Commons. A group of members who had already declared their support for White's campaign introduced an amendment which would empower the Government to ban public religious gatherings of a pagan nature. The amendment, legally imprecise, was patently unacceptable as it stood, and the Government was able to secure its withdrawal by pointing out that the Bill in any case would give them all the necessary powers to forbid gatherings of any category that seemed undesirable in the context of any given crisis; but the tone of the debate had already changed. A small minority of MPs of various parties now began to voice criticisms of the Bill, on the grounds that the powers it gave would be open to abuse. What had looked like a quick and easy passage suddenly became hotly argued. The Government were worried; they had no doubt of a majority, but the debate was prolonging itself and they had hoped to avoid the imposing of a guillotine which would be psychologically regrettable.

On 24 July, Quentin White was returned with a 1832 majority over his nearest opponent in a four-cornered fight. The Liberal candidate lost his deposit. While the other two had hedged, he had been the only one to condemn the witch-hunt unequivocally. An hour after the result was declared, all his front windows were smashed.

Felicity Holroyd was not a brave woman. Barely one metre fifty-five tall, and very thin, she had to rely on quick wits and a sense of humour to control her classes; even so she had to put up with a certain amount of what her more awe-inspiring colleagues would have called gross impertinence. Her small face with it unnaturally large eyes gave her an air of vulnerability which simply invited teasing. What saved her from complete indiscipline was her gift of communicating her passionate love of her subject – English literature – to the most unpromising children. It might take her five minutes to get a class settled and reasonably quiet; but once launched, she held them, till the bell surprised them and her. She had had a chance, a year or two back, of a post with a distinguished grammar school in the South, but to her friends' surprise she had preferred to stay with very run-of-the-mill Wolverhampton comprehensive where she had started teaching nine years earlier. 'Any fool can stuff Shakespeare into a bright kid's head,' she had explained. 'But get *these* semi-literate telly-addicts enjoying him and life's worth while.'

That she had a remarkable proportion of them enjoying him – and enjoying many others from Austen to Yeats – she knew from the gratifying exam results; but more personally, for her, from her daily hour at the desk of the school library. The library was in her charge, and no one knew better than she who borrowed what and what they said about it when they brought it back.

But this evening she sat at that desk in a white rage, glad for once that a fine hot evening had thinned out her customers. Her anger was as much against herself as against the headmaster. She remembered the interview that afternoon with shame. She had stammered a protest, it was true; and given a few minutes she might have pulled herself together and made that protest a reasoned one. But the headmaster's phone had rung even as he brushed the protest aside and she had been left standing there, not knowing what to do, while he became involved in what was obviously going to be a long conversation. After a while he had put his hand over the mouthpiece, given her a quick lofty smile, said, 'See to it, will you, Felicity?', and returned to his conversation without waiting for an answer or even looking for her reaction.

And she (*oh, you bloody coward*) had stood for another second or two indecisively, before walking out and shutting the door behind her, the list in her hand. It lay on the desk before her now. *All works by T. C. Lethbridge, Gerald*

Gardner, C. G. Leland, C. A. Burland, Doreen Valiente, Israel Regardie ...

'Miss?'

She forced her attention to the boy standing waiting at the desk; she had not even noticed him arrive. 'Sorry, Don, I was dreaming. . . . What is it?'

The lanky sixth-former put a book on the desk. 'I brought back *The Sea Priestess* – I didn't quite get all of it but it was terrific. Have we got the other one, *Moon Magic*? . . . Claire say it's not quite as good but I'd like to read it anyway.'

Felicity answered before thinking: 'By all means – I agree with Claire, actually, but if you liked *The Sea Priestess* it's still . . .' She broke off, suddenly realizing.

'Miss – you all right?'

The irrelevant thought came to her, unreasonably inflaming her anger: *He couldn't even take the trouble to put them in alphabetical order.* . . . She picked up the list, so fiercely that she almost tore it. 'I'm sorry, Don. You can't have *Moon Magic*. Or anything else by Dion Fortune.'

'But, miss – why?'

Claire Evans joined Don, drawn away from her shelf-browsing by the unwonted sharpness in the teacher's tone. Felicity looked up at them. Don, Claire, the inseparables – two of her favourites; she had been midwife to their blossoming minds, their probing intelligence; even indirectly to their love.

'Are you two busy for an hour?'

Surprised by the question, they glanced at each other and said, 'No, miss,' together.

Felicity knew she was breaking the rules by involving them in her own anger against the headmaster but she could not help herself. 'You see this list? It contains all the authors the headmaster considers to be dangerously pagan-oriented. I've go to remove them all from the school library shelves and lock them in a cupboard. I suppose I'm lucky I haven't got to make a bonfire of them in the playground. . . . Will you give me a hand?'

They stared at her and then they stared at the list.

'Miss Holroyd – you can't do it!'

'Are you asking me to disobey the head, Claire?'

'I . . .' The girl changed her tack, asking suddenly: 'Miss, are *you* a pagan?'

'I'm a Quaker.'

'I don't know much about Quakers, but I know you, miss. And I know what you've always told us. People got a right to say what they believe and write about it – and we ought to look at 'em all, an' then decide what *we* believe. Not have anyone *tell* us what to believe or think. Right?'

Felicity sighed. 'Right.'

Don held out the list to her and asked almost shyly: 'Well?'

Claire followed up immediately with: 'You want us to *help* you with that thing?'

There was a long moment while anger, love, and professional habit struggled within Felicity Holroyd. Then something broke. She took the list calmly from the boy's fingers and tore it in two. 'Will you please take a note to the head for me? It won't take me a minute to write it.'

'You're not resigning, are you?'

The alarm in Claire's eyes strengthened her, overcoming the instant of panic her decision had sparked in her. 'No, Claire. I'm going to lock myself in this library and refuse to budge. And I'm not removing a single book. You can tell the others – Miss Holroyd's staging a protest sit-in.'

'We'll stay here with you!'

'You will not. Thanks for offering but no. A sit-in's one thing – inciting pupils to join it's another. Put me in the wrong straight away. Just take the note for me – and remember you don't know what's in it if he asks you.'

Claire hesitated, then nodded. 'All right. But while you're writing it, I'm going to get you some sandwiches and a bottle of coke. Two or *three* bottles. No point in making it a hunger-strike.'

'And a sleeping bag,' Don said. 'Don't lock up till we're back, will you?'

'I don't like it, Mr Barker,' the police sergeant said. 'There must be about a hundred and fifty kids out there picketing and another hundred blocking the corridor to the library. We've tried reasoning with them but they just start chanting and drown us. The library door's very solid and she's got heavy steel filing cabinets jammed against it – we can see that through the window. The windows are all steel-barred, too. What is this place, Fort Knox?'

'My predecessor put them in, during the vandalism wave in the eighties,' the headmaster told him. 'Look, Sergeant, I want that woman *out*. She's been there all last night and this morning. I gave her an ultimatum for eight o'clock this morning to come out or be dismissed. She said she would stay there till my instructions about the books were withdrawn. There was no question of that, of course, so at eight-fifteen I told her she was dismissed and pushed her formal letter of dismissal under the door. That was while I could still *reach* the door. A few minutes later the pupils started arriving – with *banners*, Sergeant! The whole thing's a conspiracy. She must have told them what she was going to do and they got ready for this – this outrage, overnight.'

'You're their headmaster, sir. Surely they'd listen to you before they'd listen to the police?'

'Do you think I haven't tried, damn it? And my staff? – or most of them, anyway. I strongly suspect that one or two of the other teachers are in sympathy with her though none of them have said so to my face. . . . First I reasoned with the pickets, and all they said was, "Sorry, sir, but we think Miss Holroyd's right." They simply refused to move. So then I threatened them. I had no alternative.'

'Threatened them with what exactly, sir?'

'With *you*, Sergeant. I told them they had one hour to clear the corridor and the playground and assemble in their classrooms. After that I would call in the police to clear them.'

'Did *any* obey you?'

The headmaster snorted. 'About a dozen. Out of two or three hundred. So, you see, my threat has to be made good. Otherwise we face total breakdown of discipline – how permanent, God alone knows.'

'Have you called on parents for help?'

'Sergeant, this is a working weekday and our pupils come from an area of about forty square kilometres. . . . I've managed to contact a few and get them here. One father persuaded his son to go home and that's all.' The headmaster frowned nervously. 'Another unfortunate factor – Miss Holroyd is popular with parents. . . . One husband and wife arrived together and told me flatly that if Miss Holroyd had felt driven to this extraordinary action there must be something wrong with *my* attitude. They refused to help. In fact, they smiled and waved at the children in the playground on the way out – and the children cheered them. It was intolerable.'

The sergeant seemed to be about to ask something, and then to think better of it. After a moment or two he said, 'Look, Mr Barker, you're asking me to take my men and clear a way through those kids – boys *and* girls – by force, and then to smash down the door, or do the same thing from outside and cut through the window-bars. And then to bring their heroine out under arrest, right through the middle of them. The mood they're in, we'd have little chance of doing all that without kids getting hurt. If you ask me, *no* chance. . . . Why don't we just play it cool? Keep my lads in sight and let the kids wonder what we mean to do. By this evening, they'll start being hungry and bored. . . .'

'Sergeant, there are reporters outside. They've been pestering me all morning. Television news have been on the phone – BBC *and* ITN – and if this thing isn't cleared up pretty dam' quick there'll be cameras in the street. And you think those youngsters will drift away through *boredom*?'

The sergeant said, expressionlessly: 'I think I'd better call in my superiors, sir.'

'Yes,' the headmaster told him. 'I think you'd better.'

Few newly elected Members of Parliament can have had such heaven-sent material for a maiden speech as Quentin White. House of Commons etiquette decrees that maiden speeches be received with special sympathy and tolerance whether one agrees with them or not, but in the present climate of the House White commanded even closer attention than that laid down by parliamentary good manners.

Virtually every member, of course, had read the *Evening News* edition which White brandished in his hand as he spoke, and those who had not were hurriedly scanning copies borrowed from their neighbours.

The page 1 splash read:

SCHOOL BLAZE ENDS LIBRARY LOCK-OUT
15 children, 27 others injured

Six children were hospitalized with bone fractures, nine with lesser injuries, and five policemen and 22 adult civilians were also admitted following the rioting and arson which climaxed Wolverhampton school-teacher Felicity Holroyd's protest lock-out this afternoon.

The fire, which broke out in or near the school library minutes before police cut through a steel-barred window to arrest Miss Holroyd, was still raging an hour later. Firemen's work was hampered by the crowd of anxious parents, escaping children, and onlookers – some vociferously protesting for or against Miss Holroyd – who packed the narrow streets around the school.

Miss Holroyd was arrested on a charge of causing a breach of the peace, and a police spokesman said other charges might be preferred against her when the incident had been fully investigated.

Twelve adult demonstrators and twenty-three children had been arrested at the time of going to press.

Cause of the fire and the exact point of outbreak were still unknown, and the police spokesman refused to speculate. He agreed, however, that in addition to aggravating panic, the fire had incited some demonstrators to shout that Miss Holroyd had started it, and others to insist that it was the work of a provocateur. From this, street fighting had broken out.

Miss Holroyd locked herself in the library at about 5.30 pm yesterday in protest against the headmaster's order to remove certain pagan-oriented books from the shelves.

'She did it quite without warning,' headmaster William Barker told our reporter. 'She did not even ask me to reconsider my order – merely barricaded herself in and sent one of the pupils to me with a note.

'Next morning, hundreds of pupils set up a mass picket-line, with banners and placards already prepared. Miss Holroyd had clearly incited these children, for whom she shared responsibility, into deliberate, organized rebellion against authority.

'And for what? In an attempt to keep morally poisonous material on the library shelves. . . .'

Quentin White made the most of it.

'The tip of the iceberg, Mr Speaker. Or should I say the crack in the sewer? For while honourable members debate whether or not to give His Majesty's Government the powers it seeks, the bearers of moral infection are busy below the surface, gnawing at the fabric of our civilization. Because one headmaster was on the watch, and took action, the underground menace – at one point only – took fright and struck. The result? Physical damage, certainly – to an important school and to the bodies of innocent children and adults. But who can calculate the moral and psychological damage?

'More important, Mr Speaker – I have already emphasized that this has happened *at one point only*, where the spark of one man's integrity and one woman's breach of professional ethics – to say the very least – have detonated an explosion. Who can calculate the extent of the danger which is still concealed, still undetonated? At what point could local disaster erupt into national disaster?

'I believe, sir, that the answer stares honourable members in the face. The moral threat could erupt uncontrollably, if we suffered just one more natural calamity like the wave of earth tremors from which we have barely recovered. The experts cannot assure us that it will not happen. They cannot even assure us that the next earthquake would not be incalculably worse.

'If that should happen – and happen without warning – His Majesty's Government will be fighting on two fronts. Against physical disruption on an unheard-of scale – and against the spiritual saboteurs who would seize on that disruption with eagerness.

'Mr Speaker, new as I am to this Mother of Parliaments, I urge honourable members to waste no time in arming His Majesty's Government with the powers that it must have, *before* the crisis which may break upon us any day, any hour. . . .'

For the Prime Minister to rise, seeking the Speaker's eyes, in the middle of a maiden speech was so unthinkable that a tremor of astonishment ran through the House. Quentin White, quick-witted but still unsure of procedure, bowed towards the Premier and sat down in mid-sentence.

'Mr Speaker,' the Prime Minister said, 'I must apologize to the honourable member, and to the House, for what must appear to be a quite unprecedented breach of courtesy. But I am sure the whole House, including the honourable and eloquent gentleman I was obliged to interrupt – with your permission, sir – will wish to be informed immediately of the news item which has just been handed to me. . . . The whole of North America, and the northern part of South America, has in the past half-hour suffered widespread earth tremors of uneven distribution and varying intensity. Information is still incomplete, of course, but the Associated Press describe the disaster as being similar to, and at least as destructive as, that which recently affected Europe and parts of Asia.'

As the Premier sat down again, Quentin White made no attempt to continue his speech; he knew he had no need.

Under cover of the general commotion, the Premier whispered to the Chancellor of the Exchequer: 'Bertie, we're home and dry.'

An hour later, the Commons passed the Emergency Powers Bill by 652 votes to eleven.

8

The American media being less compact and amenable to control than the British, the cables that flowed into AP's Beehive office in the first hour or two after the Western Hemisphere tremors were uninhibited. Eugene and Tonia's job was purely newsgathering for the New York office; the AP tape service to British customers was still put out by the Fleet Street bureau, but all that bureau's inflow and outflow was duplicated by teleprinters in the Beehive office, to keep it fully in the picture. Fortunately, some humane colleague in New York had found time to check with the London staff's next-of-kin, and to cable reassurance as replies came in; so within half an hour of the news breaking, Eugene and Tonia received a service message MACALLISTER AND LYND FAMILIES OKAY HOMES UNDAMAGED, which at least made the trauma of national disaster slightly less personal. Only slightly; homes might be undamaged but *home* had been shaken to its foundations; families might be safe, but friends? – hundreds of them, from coast to coast? . . . Even Gene, normally a model of lofty composure, was pale and trembling, and Tonia doubted if she looked any better. Having nothing to do but read made it worse for them; what British news there was seemed, for the moment, confined to Surface.

The pattern of the incoming reports increased their frustration. The uninhibited phase did not last and unfortunately it coincided with the period when the information was provisional, confused and incomplete. As soon as hard facts and figures began to emerge, Tonia's professional instincts told her that the security blanket was beginning to operate. The trend towards clarity was suddenly reversed and imposed vagueness replaced mere unavoidable uncertainty.

Nevertheless, some kind of overall picture had materialized. As in Europe, the tremors seemed partly related to natural features and partly and mysteriously unrelated. A major quake had hit the Colorado River all the way from the Gulf of California through the Grand Canyon and up into Utah; early cables quoted unconfirmed reports of serious damage to the great dams but these were not referred to again. Another tremor line, apparently less serious, ran up the Snake River valley from about Pocatello right into the Blue Mountains. The Dakotas, Nebraska, Kansas, Oklahoma and Arkansas reported a confusing pattern of minor tremors with only localized damage. Chicago, Detroit and the Great Lakes seemed unaffected, but from the Adirondacks to Maine and across the Canadian border to the St Lawrence, damage was heavier but still localized. Quebec was hit and hard news continued to arrive direct from Canada for some time after the States security clamp-down; initial estimates spoke of thirty dead in Quebec and twelve in Montreal, though northwards and westwards of that, Canada – and Alaska – were apparently unaffected.

Down the Atlantic seaboard from Boston to Georgia,

everywhere east of the Appalachians seemed to have escaped entirely; but from Florida all the way round the Gulf of Mexico and the Caribbean the emphasis was on freak tides and flooding. One AP cable, about earth tremor reports from Nicaragua and Costa Rica, stopped in the middle of a folio; the teleprinter was silent for fifteen seconds, then suddenly clattered out: CANCEL FOREGOING PARA, without explanation. Later, on the Lloyds' teleprinter, Tonia spotted PANAMA CANAL CLOSED ALL TRAFFIC FURTHER NOTICE – also without explanation, and no reference to the Canal appeared on the AP tape. Nor were the Mohowatt stations mentioned at any time.

Early reports which included northern South America in the outbreak of tremors were said to have been premature and based on nervous misreading of local seismographs when the scale of the North American phenomenon was first realized. Beyond Venezuela, the coastal flooding rapidly died out, and although Colombia and Ecuador reported a few mountain landslides, only faint echoes of the disaster seemed to have been felt south of the equator.

Gene and Tonia kept an eye on the Reuter and UP tapes but they added nothing of significance. There was some British official reaction on the PA printer, but it was mostly formal sympathy, unoriginal and unmemorable.

'It'll be tomorrow morning the fun starts,' Gene predicted sombrely. 'When the Stock Exchange opens.'

Tonia, who for all her extraversion always had difficulty in articulating the deep love she felt for her own country, realized with a spasm of anger that she could not care less about the Stock Exchange or even Wall Street. What about 'Frisco and LA? – neither of them had been mentioned. What about the little farm in Maine where . . .

Tonia Lynd said nothing but went on ripping off folios and adding them to the clip-boards.

In the closed garage, Rosemary and Sally were going through kitchen equipment choosing a basic set from the three households' stock. Gregory and Dan had already done the same with the tools and were arguing whether precious space should be taken up with power-tools when the availability of power would be highly doubtful. Dan was against it but Greg was reasoning that the country was full of mobile generators and in the event of complete breakdown they might be able to commandeer one.

'And if we did, think of the hours a few power tools would save.'

'What'd be the use of a generator if there wasn't any fuel for it?'

'We might be able to hitch it to a waterfall.'

'Oh, for Christ's sake . . .'

Moira, with Diana's enthusiastic but unhelpful help, was packing clothes. The boys had installed a zip-up plastic wardrobe in the van with a tallboy beside it; as they had good tents, they had abandoned all ideas of leaving sleeping-space in the vehicles in favour of maximum storage. One side of the van was wardrobe, drawers and built-in wooden shelves; the other, kitchen, with water-tank, sink, cooker and food storage. Bedding, tools and more clothing and footwear were in the station wagon. Greg had fitted both vehicles with roof racks for tents, petrol cans and a second spare wheel each. The van's roof rack created a problem; loaded, it would not clear the garage door. So they had its load stacked ready at the back of the garage, where it could be stowed quickly in the van's central gangway when the move seemed imminent; they had practised the loading drill and got it down to one minute and forty seconds. Once clear of danger, they could stop and transfer the load to the roof, leaving the gangway free.

Sally and Rosemary had been stocking with milk and perishable foods daily, removing them for consumption next day and re-stocking, so that they would always at least start off with something fresh.

The problem of weapons had led to their first deliberate theft. They had one legal gun already, because Dan was a member of a pistol club and owned a licensed .22 target pistol; scarcely lethal except at short range, but accurate, and Dan was a good shot. But they were determined that each vehicle should be armed somehow and Greg came up with an answer, though he said nothing to the others till he had achieved it. One of his regular customers at the service station was a big-mouthed character who boasted too much of his prowess as a poacher, and of what he would like to do to the witches – not knowing, fortunately, that Greg was one. The man was a bachelor living alone in a cottage out beyond Addlestone, and Greg had no difficulty in discovering his drinking habits.

Next time he started his usual Friday-night session at the Swan by Staines Bridge, Greg quickly and expertly immobilized the man's car, drove to the cottage, broke in without a qualm, and soon discovered the double-barrelled folding .410 shotgun he kept under the bed, of all obvious places. Boxes of cartridges were beside it and Greg removed the lot.

When he got home and showed the others his loot, Rosemary was only briefly shocked, and the rest not at all. 'I'd put our safety before that bastard's pot,' declared Sally, who knew the man from her days as a barmaid; Sally had been many things in her long life. Shotgun and ammunition were hidden in the van within reach of the driver's seat and nothing more was said, but all of them knew that with this uncharacteristic act and its acceptance they had crossed a kind of Rubicon. War had not yet been declared, but mobilization was in full swing. Would-be survivors could no longer afford illusions.

'Have we got a knife-sharpener?' Rosemary was now asking. 'These things are going to have to last.'

'The boys have an oilstone with the tools,' Sally said. 'I saw it. . . . Can-openers . . . bottle-openers . . . Where's Moira's garlic press? She'd be lost without it.'

'We might not be able to get garlic.'

'Easy to grow. Plant it on the shortest day and lift it on the longest. Remind me to save some outside cloves of it to plant. . . . Oh, here's the press. . . .' Sally raised her voice suddenly. 'Hey, everybody – we never thought of vegetable seeds!'

'None in the shops this time of the year,' Dan called back.

'Yes, there are. Little place up by the station – whole rack of 'em, covered with dust from the spring. You know, sort of shop that never clears out anything. I'll get a few quids' worth tomorrow. Won't take up any room.'

So it had gone on for days – selecting, remembering, reassuring. Diana had been told they were getting ready for a camping holiday and Moira couldn't help feeling that it had something of that atmosphere; which seemed an almost frivolous reaction to a two-pronged threat, natural and human, whose scale and degree of horror none of them could as yet foresee. To be actually enjoying the fun of equipping their little survival convoy of two vehicles and six people was surely unrealistic, irresponsible. . . . And yet she knew it wasn't like that at all. The 'fun' was relief at having something practical to do and do together, in the face of the faceless; and the horror was never far below the surface. Dan had a new briskness, a new light in his eye, as their preparations went ahead; even an extra (and Moira had to admit, exciting) verve about his love-making; it was as though the prospect of a bedouin existence had sharpened his masculinity – and perhaps her own femaleness, too? She found it hard to judge. . . . And yet there were times when he cried out in his sleep, grinding his teeth and tensing his muscles, and Moira would cradle him in her arms, crooning to him as she would to Diana, till he relaxed again. He had no conscious memory of these experiences when he awoke, because Moira would have known if he was deliberately hiding them – quite apart from her ever-alert sensitivity to his moods. Like most witches they took a keen interest in their own dreams and had the habit of exchanging them as soon as they were both awake. They still did so, as unreservedly as ever, and she knew Dan was not censoring his; he was simply unaware that the intensity behind them had surfaced as muscular and vocal reactions which they had never done before except when he was ill.

She did not tell him because he would have worried, but she spoke of it to Rosemary. Rosemary smiled and said 'Greg, too'.

The five of them were all together when the Prime Minister made his television statement of 29 July. They had taken to reading and watching the news with close attention because if they did have to 'take to the woods', speed of reaction to events might well make the difference between success and failure, and the last few days, with the American tremors and the passing of the Emergency Powers Bill, had made them even more watchful. For such things they had been prepared, but what had shocked them was the Commons' almost panic reaction to the Wolver-hampton affair and the ease with which the Emergency Powers debate inside and outside Parliament – originally and reasonably concerned with the possibility of further earth tremors – had become confused with the anti-witch hysteria. The Bill had received the Royal Assent that morning, and the day after tomorrow was August Eve, the witch festival of Lughnasadh; so they listened to the Premier with foreboding.

He began with the predictable platitudes about the grave times through which this nation 'and, indeed, the world' was passing, the British tradition of standing together in the face of (unspecified) danger, and the need for calm. After a few confused and homespun references to Agincourt, the Armada and our grandparents' defiance of the Blitz, he suddenly came to the point.

'At such a time, nothing must be allowed to happen which could provoke public disorder or conflict. You will remember that when the unpredictable calamity of the earth tremors hit this country five weeks ago, it coincided with the grave and fatal events on Bell Beacon, the full nature of which is still being investigated. Now I am not one of those who would go the whole way with people who claim that what happened on Bell Beacon was Divine retribution; but His Majesty's Government would be failing in its duty if it did not recognize that such a view is widely and sincerely held, and that the public conscience has been aroused – even among those who would not go so far – by these unashamedly pagan celebrations in our midst. Freedom of worship, even when it takes bizarre forms, is of course one of the cornerstones of British liberty. But this cannot include the freedom to offend and provoke, especially at times of national crisis; if that is allowed, freedom itself is in danger.

'And this, my friends, *is* a time of national crisis. Our American cousins – an old-fashioned phrase, I know, but when natural disaster strikes, all the world is kin – our

American cousins have just been through what *we* went through at Midsummer, and it could happen to us again, at any moment. It is to be ready for such a blow that the people's representatives have, almost unanimously, entrusted His Majesty's Government with emergency powers – which that Government must therefore be prepared to exercise in the public interest.

'Most of you are aware that in two days' time the small minority of witches all over Britain would, according to their peculiar calendar, be publicly celebrating the next of their seasonal festivals. It is the Government's view – which I am sure the great majority of you will share – that to allow such public gatherings, in the present situation, would lead inevitably to conflict and casualties and possibly to further loss of life.

'An Order in Council has therefore been made, under the Emergency Powers Act, forbidding them. The full text of the Order is being published in tomorrow morning's newspapers. In simple terms, what it amounts to is this. All public religious gatherings and all private religious meetings of more than six persons, are banned with effect from midnight tonight, with the exception of those held under the chairmanship of an ordained clergyman of one of the Christian churches, or of one of the equivalent functionaries of the Jewish, Moslem or Sikh religions. A list of the authorized denominations is included in the Order.

'Responsible worshippers – that is to say, followers of the traditional religions of the several communities of which this country is composed – will thus be able to pursue their devotions and hold their services entirely as normal. I am sure everyone will wish this to be so; I have already pointed out that we are in a crisis situation and the solace of genuine religious belief and practice is a pillar of strength and a contribution to stability in such times.

'But let this be clearly understood: no breach of the Order will be tolerated. The police have been instructed to arrest anyone committing such a breach – and they will *not* be granted bail pending the hearing of their cases; the Order specifically prohibits it.

'To make sure that the purposes of the Order are fully achieved, the police have been empowered to take into preventive custody, on the written authority of a Justice of the Peace, any persons who they have reason to believe may be about to commit a breach of the Order. To ensure the least possible infringement of the liberty of the subject, such persons must be brought before a magistrates' court within seventy-two hours and given an opportunity to obtain their release by giving an undertaking to keep the peace. Anyone breaking that undertaking will be liable to re-arrest and imprisonment.

'A few critics – I think very few – may call this Order an unjustifiably harsh one. But I am confident that the great majority of my fellow-citizens, remembering the tragedy of Bell Beacon, the recent serious disorder at a school in Wolverhampton and many disturbing local incidents in between – the great majority of you will support the Order wholeheartedly.

'Good night and God bless you.'

In the special television studio in Beehive which had been designed as a facsimile of one end of the Cabinet Room at No 10 Downing Street (for obvious reasons of public reassurance) the red light went out, and the Premier asked Harley, who had been standing beside the camera: 'How was it, Reggie?'

'Excellent, Prime Minister. Very effective.'

The Premier waited till Harley had joined him, and then said in an undertone: 'I'm still not altogether convinced in my own mind that I shouldn't have combined it with a statement on the Dust and the vinegar masks.'

Harley cast a frown towards the camera crew but they were already respectfully out of earshot. 'Premature, sir, believe me,' he said, even more quietly. 'As it was, you had the country in the palm of your hand. Any more might have upset the balance and panicked them. The public can only absorb one idea at a time. I'm sure your wide political experience . . .'

'Oh, you're right, of course, Reggie. It's just that if we leave the vinegar-mask announcement *too* late and there's a really extensive outbreak of the Dust . . .'

'It was only Cheddar, Corwen and Whitehaven last time. And we were able to act promptly, seal it off and isolate the victims without publicity. We have no reason to believe it would be any worse the next time.'

'We've no reason to believe or disbelieve *anything* about the next time, in spite of your experts,' the Premier pointed out glumly. 'They know dam' all, and so do we.'

'Very little, it's true. All the more reason for not making premature announcements.'

'The Americans had the Dust worse than we did, remember.'

'But localized, too. *And* they were able to contain it just as effectively as we did. Besides, sir – the President has personally decided there will be no announcement as yet. We wouldn't want any failure of coordination with the White House, would we?'

It was the Premier's tender spot and they both knew it.

'Of course not, Reggie. You're quite right. We'll wait for – er – the right moment.'

In the numb days that had followed Joy's murder on Bell Beacon, John Hassell's coven had been his only comfort.

They had rallied round him to the best of their ability and he in turn had done his best to give them leadership. In his heart, he wished it were still the old coven, which he and Joy had had the year before; the closeness of *that* unit had been built into a real group mind which he could have done with now. But around Yule, they had been faced with the sudden inrush of new recruits which most established covens experience from time to time, often without any apparent special cause. The recruits had all seemed promising material and Joy and John had not felt justified in turning them away, so they had dealt with the situation in the traditional manner, by hiving-off. Their two best couples had been set up with their own covens, and each of the three groups had taken a proportion of the old and the new blood. It had worked smoothly with few problems, but it had meant that by Midsummer, Joy and John's group, like the other two, had still been in the process of integrating itself as an entity. Most of its members, though enthusiastic, were still inexperienced.

The Maiden, Karen Morley, had been one of the earliest members of the old coven, and of her dedication, knowledge and psychic power there could be no doubt. She thought, worked, slept, ate and drank the Craft all round the clock. Joy had found her too obsessional to be quite natural and had tried to make her understand that a witch must be first and foremost a human being: 'Dost thou think, because thou art virtuous, there shall be no more cakes and ale?' she had quoted at her, and Karen had laughed dutifully but done little to change her ways. One result had been the strange one that Karen, a second-degree witch for two years now and on the face of it well qualified for her third degree, was still without a regular working partner. Her intensity had frightened too many men off and her indifference to any kind of social life had prevented the development of any partnership by the normal process of mutual liking laying the foundations of magical collaboration. That struck Joy and John as a pity on purely human grounds, because Karen was undeniably attractive with the long black hair and the slightly oriental eyes which had earned her the nickname, even among witches, of 'witchy Karen'.

When the other groups had hived off, Joy had kept Karen with her and appointed her Maiden – virtually assistant High Priestess – of the residual coven, where she and John could keep an eye on her. With Joy's death, Karen had been the only possible choice as High Priestess; she had taken over with energetic efficiency but surprising tact, handling John with a gentleness that had never been evident in her before. (One slightly astringent member remarked privately to her husband, 'Karen's not such a fool as we thought,' but her comment remained private.)

On the evening of 30 July, the whole coven – eight members in all – gathered at John's house to discuss the Premier's statement.

Grace Peebles, one of the original members with a congenital streak of nostalgia (John, while he could still be light-hearted, had often teased her with being an 'Old Gardnerian Holy-Writter'), was riding her favourite hobbyhorse. 'The whole thing's our own fault. Wicca should never have gone public. It started with Alex Sanders and it's got worse ever since. The old Craft was never like that – which is why it survived for centuries.'

'The old Craft *when*?' John asked wearily, no teasing in his voice now. 'During the seventeenth century? Of course it wasn't – you kept it secret or you ended on the gallows. Two thousand years ago? Of course it was – the festivals involved everybody. The last twenty years, Wicca hasn't deliberately *gone* public. It *became* public because thousands were turning to it naturally and no one was persecuting it. The Craft adjusts itself to the situation, not to any rigid pattern.'

'We've got some adjusting to do now, that's for sure,' Bill Lazenby said. 'For a start – what are we doing tomorrow, for Lughnasadh? Even if we hold it indoors, we're still an illegal religious gathering of more than six people. Do we cancel it? Or split into two fours? Or say, to hell with them – and get together with Anna's and Jean's?'

Karen said calmly: 'To hell with them. . . . John?'

John was silent for a moment, and then said: 'Yes. We hold our Festival. And with Anna's and Jean's covens, if they're willing. The place near Virginia Water – we've never been disturbed there before, and it's in thick woodland a good kilometre from the road. . . . If anyone wants to stay away, I won't criticize them.'

Nobody did and they began discussing whether to phone Anna and Jean or to send messengers. The matter was never resolved, because a sharp, imperative knocking on the front door silenced them.

Karen was the first to gather her wits. 'Bill, Penelope – upstairs, quick. That'll make us six. Legal, if this is what it sounds like.'

Thirty seconds later, John opened the front door.

'Mr John Hassell?'

'Yes.'

'We are police officers. We must ask you to accompany us to the station.'

John glanced at the man's warrant card, and asked: 'Are you arresting me – and if so, on what charge?'

'Preventive custody, sir, under the new Order in Council. Here is the magistrate's warrant.'

'So you have reason to believe I'm planning to contravene the Order? You're quite wrong, I assure you.'

'I can't comment on that, sir; my superiors applied for the warrant, and it is merely my duty to implement it. But you have the right to make a statement to the court within . . .'

'I know my rights, officer. I've read the Order with great care.'

'Shall we keep it quiet and friendly, then?'

'By all means. Come inside and I'll pack a few things – for seventy-two hours.'

'As you say, sir.' When they were in the hall and the door was shut, the officer said awkwardly: 'Off the record, Mr Hassell, I'm sorry about this. I know what happened to your wife and if it had been up to me I'd have left you in peace. But that's how it is. I've got my job to do.'

John gave him a brittle, bright-eyed look. 'I know, officer. But cheer up. I'm sure you'll have far worse jobs to do before this is over.'

The policeman compressed his lips and did not answer. He glanced towards the sitting-room door, which was ajar and showed light from inside, but after a moment's hesitation deliberately turned his back on it.

'I'll get my things,' John said.

When John and the policemen had left, Karen closed the sitting-room door and stood with her back to the fireplace, looking down at the coven.

'Now,' she told them. 'We have a lot to talk about.'

Just how many High Priests and High Priestesses were taken into preventive custody that night the witchcraft movement never knew because no figures were published – in fact, although the police swoop was nation-wide and carefully simultaneous, the media only reported it indirectly and piecemeal. But within the movement the news spread like wildfire and no one was in any doubt that the arrests ran into several hundreds, or that the police knew exactly whom to take. In each area which was in the habit of holding collective Festivals, the year's Sabbat Queen, the Sabbat Maiden, and their respective Priests, were put under lock and key without a single exception; two who happened to be in hospital were placed under police guard and their substitutes who had been chosen to officiate at Lughnasadh were arrested as well. These seemed to make up the bulk of the arrests, though a handful of other key figures who might have been expected to step into the breach were also taken in. Officially, preventive custody was not 'arrest' but that was what everybody called it.

The effect on the witchcraft movement, already shaken by sudden and unheralded harassment after a generation of tolerance, was traumatic. In general covens withdrew into their shells; some celebrated Lughnasadh in groups of not more than six, others took a chance with full covens behind thick curtains, a few disappeared into woods or empty heathland with carefully screened candle-lanterns. Nobody risked the usual large-scale collective Sabbat, except one in Suffolk, one in Cornwall, and one – astonishingly – on Primrose Hill in London. These, to the bafflement of the police, were not in breach of the Order, because in each case a local clergyman (the Suffolk one a Catholic priest), his conscience outraged by the Order, had offered himself as official chairman of the gathering and been gladly accepted. Large contingents of police, arriving hurriedly at the three locations to break up the assembled witches and arrest the ringleaders, found everything legally in order, and themselves in the curious position of having to protect the witches against angry hecklers who wanted to take the law into their own hands. Next morning, three very indignant bishops had the culprits on their respective carpets, and the Archbishops of Canterbury and Westminster demanded a joint meeting with the Prime Minister to devise a means of plugging the loophole in the Order immediately, lest any other of the more turbulent progressives in their own flocks might get the same idea. The Prime Minister was only too willing, and called in the President of the Methodist Conference and the Chief Rabbi as well. Within hours, an amendment to the Order was laid down that if, in the opinion of the police, a significant number attending any religious meeting were not genuinely of the denomination of the official chairman, that meeting constituted a breach of the Order. The progressives were even more outraged, quoting the Bible, the Koran and the Buddha with what might have been devastating effect if anyone had been listening; but few were and the loophole was plugged.

The Crusaders were not interested in legal niceties; they were out in force in search of Lughnasadh coven meetings and were unconcerned whether or not these exceeded the permitted number of six. How many curtained windows, up and down the country, which might conceal candlelight the Crusaders smashed that night, not even they bothered to count; and if quite a few of the curtains merely hid innocent people watching television, that was just too bad. (From then on, television-watchers developed the habit of leaving their curtains open.) In scattered areas the 'stormtroopers' succeeded in tracking down open-air Sabbats in what their celebrants had hoped were sufficiently isolated hiding places. All in all, according to the confidential report which reached Harley's desk in Beehive next day, 137 people were arrested for contravening the Order and twenty-eight under various headings from breach of the peace to grievous bodily harm. Of the three GBH arrests, only one had been an attacking Crusader; he had been unfortunate enough to be witnessed in action by a policeman with old-fashioned ideas about the beating-up of women.

The figure of twenty-eight was low in relation to the number known to have been treated in hospital as a result of Lughnasadh incidents; this was eighty-five, of whom nineteen had been admitted; the condition of four of them was serious. The contrast was due to the fact that almost all the casualties occurred in Crusader attacks on Sabbats before the police arrived – if they arrived. In general, police and Crusaders had not pounced on the same targets; or (so the witches believed) on finding the others already there, had turned back. Another reason for the few arrests for violence was that only a small minority of witches resisted the police, so it was simpler – and publicly more effective – to arrest them for defying the Order in Council.

'Nobody actually dead,' Sir Walter Jennings, who was with Harley when the report reached him, commented drily. 'Just as well. Martyrs are so inconvenient. The Hassell woman would have been bad enough, if she and Andrea Sutton hadn't cancelled each other out.'

'I understand Ben Stoddart has pointed out the danger to his people,' Harley said. 'Their discipline is remarkable considering the recruitment explosion the Crusade has undergone in the past five weeks. We must thank Stoddart's charisma for that – he sees to it that all the, er, stormtroopers have met him personally at least once, and his local leaders are hand-picked. Barring accidents, they will not go so far as to kill anyone.'

'For the present.'

'I am talking of the present, naturally.'

Jennings thought for a moment, and then said: 'One thing puzzles me slightly. All the clashes seem to be between Crusaders and witches. Isn't that over-simplifying? Other pagan and occult fraternities beside the witches celebrate the eight Festivals. Have none of them been involved? And are *all* the attackers Crusader stormtroops? What about the spontaneous public resentment you had in mind? Hasn't it happened?'

'To your first question – yes, of course other occultists are involved; but most of them are either more académic than the witches or more private. I can assure you that my – that is, *the* Intelligence arm is keeping a close watch on them. Remember, the Order relates to "religious" meetings. It's up to us to decide whether a fraternity is "religious" – the Home Secretary has that power. If we need to move against one of them, he has merely to define it as religious in an instruction to the police and it becomes subject to the Order in Council. But at this stage, I would remind you, we are concerned with creating an *identifiable* scapegoat, with a single, simple label. And that label is "the witches".'

'Fair enough. And my second question – the Crusaders?'

'So far, yes, eighty or ninety per cent of the actual *aggression* against the witches has been by the Crusaders, or at least under their on-the-spot leadership. But more and more the public are, so to speak, cheering them from the sidelines. And the amount of non-violent pressure on the witches – ostracism, deprival of business, redundancy dismissals and so on – that is gathering momentum.'

'There's still one aspect that needs strengthening,' Jennings said. 'It's all very well having a scapegoat but a scapegoat for what? The idea was to link them in the public mind, whether consciously or subconsciously, with the earth tremors. Now let's be honest – only the lunatic fringe will actually *believe* the witches are responsible for them. But we *can* create an irrational conditioned reflex about it so that when the real disaster comes, and Beehive Red and all it entails – as much as possible of the public anger is diverted from Beehive which they can't get at anyway, towards the witches whom they *can* get at. They won't even stop to think why.'

'That is obviously our aim.'

'But are we achieving it? The witches are being set up as Public Enemy No 1 – with some success, I'll grant you. But what about the associative link "witches/earthquake"? How's *that* coming along?'

'I'm glad you asked,' Harley replied with a touch of smugness. 'When you leave here, take a look at your evening paper. And this evening, at the television news commentaries.'

Jennings glanced at him sharply. 'Come on, Harley. You look too pleased with yourself. What've you been up to?'

'I have arranged for an accidental lapse of security. One of Professor Arklow's daily seismological reports has been leaked to the press.'

'For Christ's sake! Not the *real* one?'

'The real one.'

'But, Harley, what the hell . . . There aren't two hundred people in Britain who know what we're really sitting on – perhaps a thousand more who could make an educated guess. Let the public know what's building up before we're safely into Beehive Red, and you're asking for panic and worse!'

'I said *one* of Arklow's reports. To know what's building up, one has to study them in sequence. A single day's report is frightening enough, but it *could* represent a peak in activity – perhaps the worst day since Midsummer. We shall see to it that it is so interpreted on the media, by well-briefed experts. Tonight, the Government will refuse to comment on the leak. Tomorrow, it will reluctantly admit that the report was genuine. What will *not* be revealed is that it is typical of the whole period since Midsummer – merely a single point on a steadily rising graph.' Harley smiled. 'The leaked report is the one for the twenty-four hours ending 0600 hours this morning. In other words, for the period during which thousands of witches, legally or illegally, were celebrating the Lughnasadh Sabbat. And to underline the message, tomorrow's papers will carry extensive coverage of the charges against the 137 who were arrested for celebrating it illegally. Most of the sentences, too – over half of them have been in front of magistrates' courts today. With the point made that hundreds more must have broken the law and not been caught – not to mention the thousands who just kept within it, with the legal maximum gathering of six. Do you begin to get the picture?'

Jennings whistled. 'A gift on a golden platter for the Wrath of God school.'

'And a subliminal injection of unease for the rest. . . . Are you happier now about your association link?'

Tonia Lynd looked up from the morning papers spread on her desk and said: 'Gene, there's something phoney about this whole business.'

'You mean the leak?'

'Yes. I can smell a deliberate "leak" when it's under my nose and so can you. And this one's too damn convenient.'

'Oh, God, Tonia – are you on to that witch-hunt thing again? . . . Look, if by sheer coincidence a bad night on the seismographs happens to coincide with the broomstick jamboree, it's a bonus for the Government's propaganda. Do you *blame* them for cashing in?'

'Short answer – yes, but let's not go into that. I just don't believe it's coincidence. . . . Gene, what do you and I know about these seismo reports?'

'Damn all and quite right too. All we can guess is that something pretty nasty's on its way, which is why Beehive Amber was ordered. Come Beehive Red; and we'll know it's any day now. Of *course* the public don't know the score or all hell'd break loose.'

'Then why was that one day's report leaked?'

'I've already agreed with you – because it was convenient. An extra nasty rumble down under, happening to coincide with the witches' shindig. Jackpot.'

'But *was* it extra nasty – or just average on the curve of increasing nastiness?'

'For God's sake, what's the difference? We should worry, down here!'

'Oh, no difference, I guess. I just wish to hell I *weren't* down here.'

'What are you – suicidal? Be your age, Tonia.'

Tonia shrugged and said no more. A minute or two later she was aware of Gene watching her, assessing her. She shuddered inwardly; his eyes seemed cold, alien, almost reptilian. They were no longer the eyes of the Gene Macallister she had worked with – and for all his limitations liked – for two years. Tonia decided she must be very, very careful.

At first, Betty Summers had found it hard to adjust to the total blackness of their Beehive cell when they went to bed and switched the light off. At home there had always been the friendly neon glow of London's night sky filtering through the curtains, with now and then a moon fighting splendidly to outshine it. True, she had liked even better the velvet nights of their occasional deep-country holidays – star-dusted, moon-etched, or merely making a subtle difference between the grey square of window and the greyer walls. But always *something*, however faintly discernible, to give reality to the world around her. Here there was nothing; darkness made even more absolute by the multicoloured scintillae, the writhing tapestry, of her

148

own optic nerves. Reality was Philip beside her, their two bodies, the bedding where it touched their skin; only her mind, not her senses, could put out tendrils to what lay beyond. The solitary tiny message still reaching her from that outer world – the whisper of the air-conditioning – even that was strangely personal because it was the one thing in Beehive that was Philip's responsibility. Their isolation was complete.

But as the days and nights passed she had first come to terms with it and then found herself welcoming it. She had, instinctively, little trust in their concrete fortress, no affinity with the dimly apprehended thinking of those who ruled it and no certainty of what lay ahead. All she had was a fierce, new-found determination to survive if survival were even slenderly possible – and her love for Philip around which that determination orbited. And so she learned to draw strength from their nightly cocoon of blackness; it fed in her an almost mystic sense of invulnerability. She was intelligent enough to realize it might be illusory – but wise enough, too, to cherish it as a spirtual armour which equipped them better to achieve survival.

Intuitively, their pillow-talk was always whispered. Betty had wondered, in this security-ridden complex, whether the living quarters were bugged; but Philip, whose work entitled him to detailed plans of the structure and was giving him a daily more intimate practical knowledge of it, assured her that they were not. All the same, she felt driven to reinforce her cocoon-image by whispering and Philip, without remarking on it, followed her lead.

Tonight, her arm across him and her chin in his shoulder, she murmured: 'What's wrong, Phil? You're fretting about something.'

'Not really.'

'Come on, darling.'

He paused, then: 'Oh, just this seismological report thing. It's a con trick, Betty. I'm one of the people who has to see them every day, remember. That one yesterday – I'm damn sure it was deliberately leaked out of context to stir things up against the witches.'

'That figures. The whole witch-hunt's been a con trick, darling.'

Philip was surprised. 'How do you know?'

'Of course it has. And it's working down here, too.'

'I haven't heard people talking about it, all that much.'

'Probably not. The people *you* meet all day are as busy as you are. None of you has much time for anything but shop.'

'We have some social life – in the Mess and that, with the wives around.'

'Wives are different when you're *not* around. The rules of the game change.'

'I didn't think you mixed with them much on your own. In fact, I've been worrying about your being lonely.'

'Open University keeps me quite busy. I'm catching up on my studies with no house to look after.'

'All the same, don't leave yourself without any friends.'

It was Betty's turn to pause before she said: 'It's my own choice, darling. I don't exactly get on with them.'

'Why not? You got on with all sorts of neighbours at home.'

'That was *before*.'

'Before what?'

'What we were talking about. When I said it was working down here.'

'The witch-hunt? Oh, but surely that's not *all* they talk about. And you're not a witch!'

'No, darling, I'm not a witch. But neither will I sip scotch with the girls while we howl for the witches' scalps.

I won't even pay lip-service to intolerance – and in the past few days it's reached the stage where even saying nothing won't get you by. You join in or you're ostracized. In words of one syllable, my darling – I won't, so I am.'

'Oh, God, love – I didn't realize!'

'I didn't tell you because you had plenty on your plate – and I'm happy when you're here and busy studying when you're not. But since you're worrying about the same thing from a different angle, we might as well compare notes.'

'The bitches,' Philip muttered.

'Oh, don't blame them too much – they're just swimming with the tide and worrying about their place in the pecking order. If you want to get angry, think about the people who started the tide and are keeping it going.'

'I work for them, unfortunately.'

'Now don't *you* start feeling guilty. All you do is feed 'em clean air.'

'Which is more than they deserve.'

'Probably,' she laughed.

It struck Philip that Betty laughing in a whisper was irresistibly sexy, and he began kissing her. She responded and they were swept away by a sudden mutual passion, neither having to woo the other, both plunging simultaneously into a little tornado of longing and gratification that left them exhausted and silent, clinging to each other in the blackness.

As they were drifting into sleep, Betty said unexpectedly: 'We'll make out, darling. We'll get through this thing.'

'But how?'

'I don't know,' Betty told him. 'Yet.'

Miss Smith and Eileen had managed for a while, in spite of everything, to make the most of their holiday. Petrol could still be bought, the weather was fine, and although the news did nothing to calm their forebodings, there seemed to be no reason for them as yet to go to ground or even to take up their prudently planned position near the geographical centre of the island. So they had continued to wander, visiting favourite places, swimming, sun-bathing, and (Miss Smith's unspoken aim) restoring the shocked Eileen to something resembling normality. Eileen was certainly much better; she smiled more, her dark curls were springy again and the contrast between her browning body and her white bikini-protected triangles was almost Mediterranean. To only one thing was she neurotically vulnerable – any mention of man-inflicted violent death; about that she had none of a nurse's stoicism but betrayed immediate distress, however academic the discussion or however distant the news. It was as though, Miss Smith thought, she was still haunted by the chasm which had opened at her feet during her time at the Banwell Emer-gency Unit – the dread that 'One day soon, one of us is going to kill one of them'. She had never repeated that confession, though she did not avoid discussion of the Unit and its significance. Miss Smith sensed that buried inside her, thrust impulsively below the threshold of awareness, was the unfaceable knowledge that 'us' had included her-self, Eileen. One day, Miss Smith knew, that guilt would have to be exorcised; but not yet – and meanwhile any-thing that approached its defences produced the telltale distress. Even the one occasion when Miss Smith got out her .22 and shot a rabbit for dinner had plunged Eileen into a trembling silence and for all her operating-theatre experience she had had to go for a walk while Miss Smith skinned it, though she had regained control of herself sufficiently to eat it once it was cooked and thus less recognizable. Miss Smith decided hunting could wait till it became really necessary.

But today there had been no cloud on Eileen's cheerfulness. They had spent the morning on a hot beach near Aldeburgh in Suffolk, had lazed over a midday Guinness on the lawn of a pub near Wickham Market, and were now heading further inland in the direction of Stowmarket by little winding back lanes.

They did not see the young woman till they were almost on her; she had been hidden by a corner, and as they rounded it Miss Smith jammed on her brakes. The woman jerked her head round defensively and for a moment they simply stared at her, not believing what they saw.

She was about twenty-five, stark naked and riding a broomstick. She had no choice; it was jammed high between her legs and roped tightly to her thighs, and her wrists were tied securely to the front end of the handle; the twigs of the besom projected behind her rump. Across the back of her shoulders had been scrawled the one word 'WITCH' in black paint. She had a swelling black eye, dried tearmarks in the dust on her cheeks, blistered and bleeding feet and her fair skin showed angry red patches of developing sunburn.

Miss Smith and Eileen came to their senses simultaneously and jumped into the road, running towards her. She gave a little cry of fright, nearly stumbling as she backed into the grass verge, but then hesitated as she realized they were women alone.

Incoherent noises of reassurance tumbled from Miss Smith's lips as she struggled vainly to untie the girl's wrists. Eileen cried, 'I'll get a knife,' and ran back to the caravan. The girl, once she realized she was safe with them, seemed in spite of her pain to be trying to hold herself erect, and there was a look of stubborn pride on her bruised face which brought a lump into Miss Smith's throat.

'Take it easy, now, love,' Miss Smith said gruffly. 'We'll see to you.'

'I'm glad you came,' the girl told her. 'It was . . .'

'Don't try to tell us yet. Wait till you're in the caravan.'

Eileen was back and cutting at the cords, the girl gritting her teeth as the strands came away from the raw weals they had bitten into her flesh. With the rope binding her thighs to the broomstick Eileen had to be very gentle, for it was obvious the girl had walked – or hobbled – for some distance in that state; nor, Eileen diagnosed sickly, was that all that had been done to her.

The broomstick removed and thrown into the hedge, they supported her to the caravan. Eileen spread a blanket and sheet on one of the bunks, and the girl had to lie on it face downwards because her back was too painful.

'I'm a nurse,' Eileen told her, 'and before we do anything you're getting a bit of first aid. . . . I'm Eileen and this is Angela. What's your name?'

'May Groombridge. I live in Coddenham, a couple of kilometres ahead. I was trying to get there.'

'How far had you come already?'

'About the same. Bit more, perhaps.'

'Good God! Want to tell us what happened?'

'Oh, I'll tell you – but . . .' For the first time she seemed embarrassed. 'Before that, just in case it's not too late – I mean, you're a nurse . . . Have you got anything – well, contraceptive?'

Miss Smith had to admire her cousin's professional calm. 'How long ago was it?'

'An hour – I don't know, exactly. Hard to judge time – like when you're drunk, sort of.'

'I know.'

Eileen did the best she could in the circumstances, and then treated and bandaged her patient's other injuries.

May bore it all very well and managed to sit up and be clothed in a towelling robe. By then Miss Smith had made some hot tea.

'Do you feel ready to go home now? Will there be anybody there?'

'My husband – Jimmy – he won't be back till six. No one else. But there's neighbours. Good friends – I can bring one of them in. Witches, like me.' Again the note of pride. 'Most of Coddenham is, now. I guess that's why they picked on us.'

'They?'

'I don't know who they were. Six of them – they came in a van, rather like yours. Had a drink in the pub and then wandered round the village for an hour or so. Didn't speak to anybody or smile or anything, just watched; it was creepy. . . . I had to go out of the village a way, I had a message for one of the farms, so I got on my bike – and soon as I was out of sight of the houses, they caught up with me. Must've been waiting for one of us to be alone. Clever, they were. Strong, too, else I might've got away – but six of 'em . . . Anyway, they chucked my bike in a field and took me up to an old empty barn back there.' She broke off for a moment, her control wavering.

'Don't push yourself,' Eileen warned her. 'You've been marvellous – but you'd better know, the shock will probably hit you later. So take it easy.'

'I know it will – I ain't no fool. . . . Anyway, they gagged me and tied me up, and four of them had me. The fellow who seemed in charge, he just seemed to get a kick out of watching, and the other one, he looked a queer to me. . . . It sounds silly but do you know the awful thing? None of 'em hardly *spoke*, except every now and then one of 'em would say "Witch!", horribly, like spitting it. . . . Then when they'd done, they tied me to the broomstick, like you saw, and put me in their van, and dropped me in this road where there's no farms or anything near and said to enjoy my walk home.'

Miss Smith let out her breath which she realized she had been holding. 'Right, love. First stop, the police. Then home.'

May Groombridge snorted. 'Police? You're joking. They took Sergeant Wells away from the village just after Midsummer and put a new man in who's got no time for witches an' says that's why he was sent here, 'cos we're a hotbed. Very fond of that word, hotbed, he is.'

'Oh, surely – over *this* . . .'

This time the snort was a bitter laugh. 'You weren't the first car that came by me, you know. There was one other – *him*, in his lovely clean panda. He looked me straight in the eye – and then up and down, nice and slow. Then he drove on.'

Miss Smith turned to her cousin. 'Eileen – I think the holiday's over.'

Eileen was right about the shock. May maintained her unnatural poise until after they had taken her to her cottage and fetched the neighbour she asked for, a motherly woman who seemed reassuringly capable. Then, clinging to her, May screamed and screamed and went on screaming. It was a heavily sedated wife they handed over to Jimmy Groombridge, hastily summoned by phone from his work in Ipswich.

Jimmy, though white with rage, was collected enough to be grateful for Eileen's professional presence, especially as the village doctor was still out on his rounds. Eileen guessed that the very fact of May's collapse helped him to keep his head for both of them.

Eileen offered to stay till the doctor came and they were

glad to have her; Jimmy was probably as frightened as he was angry, because he pressed Eileen for full details of May's condition. Eileen gave them, adding the warning that the contraceptive douche she had administered would have been too late to be more than a hope. Fortunately Jimmy was able to reinforce the hope with a precise knowledge of May's menstrual cycle and Eileen confirmed that the time was 'safe' in theory at least.

With Jimmy back, May rallied, and drugged though she was she would not rest till she had told him the whole story. Eileen was puzzled by the purposefulness of the telling; it seemed more than the natural urge many wives would have felt in the circumstances – more as though May knew her husband needed the facts for action. It troubled Eileen, especially when May described the policeman's deliberate callousness amounting to complicity. She wondered if Jimmy – who was a big man – would rush up to the policeman's house and exact revenge, which would be understandable but would only land him in prison when his wife needed him most. But Jimmy merely went on listening and holding May's hand, though his other fist clenched till the knuckles cracked.

May had barely finished when the doctor arrived. He examined her, thanked Eileen and approved her treatment, and promised to look in again later in the evening about nine o'clock. He was obviously a friend, and Eileen wondered if he, too, was a witch; she could not help noticing that he never mentioned the police, not even to ask if they had been informed. Witch or not, he must know the local situation – and it seemed that May had not been exaggerating.

After the doctor had left, May asked slowly but clearly: 'Eileen – Angela – you've been right good, an' I'm grateful. Would you do just one other thing – please?'

They both said 'Of course'.

May went on: 'Just sit with me for an hour or two. Jimmy an' our friends, they got a job to do.'

They looked at Jimmy, surprised, and Eileen asked: 'You're not going to do anything stupid, are you? I mean, of course we'll stay, if May wants – but it's *you* May will be needing over the next days and weeks, and you wouldn't be much help to her in jail would you?'

Jimmy looked her in the eyes and told her: 'I know that, don't you fret. The job's right there beyond that wall, in the next cottage. You need me, you bang twice on the wall, an' I'll be here in no time. But don't you bang unless that's real urgent. That job shouldn't rightly be disturbed in the middle, see?'

Eileen didn't see but she caught May's pleading look and nodded to Jimmy. Jimmy leaned over and kissed his wife, taking her face in both his large hands. Then he said, 'Thank you both,' and was gone.

Over the next twenty minutes they saw, through the window, at least a dozen men and women arrive at the next-door cottage. May appeared to be asleep, so they could do nothing but wait and wonder. No more people came next door and for a while there was silence. Then their ears picked up what sounded like a low, rhythmic murmur from a number of voices, more like a vocal drum-beat than a chant. After a gradual crescendo, it stopped dead; they thought they could hear movements and the clink of metal against metal; then again silence.

May opened her eyes and smiled. 'He'll be back now.'

Miss Smith asked, 'How do you know?', but May did not answer.

A minute later Jimmy walked in and said pleasantly: 'I reckon you'd like something to eat now, wouldn't you? Mrs Wainwright next door, she's cooking for all of us. Half an hour, she says. How'd you like to try May's elderberry wine, while you're waiting? That's middlin' good.'

While they drank May's elderberry which Miss Smith pronounced more than middling good, Jimmy apologized for not having spare beds but said they were welcome to put their caravan in the field on the other side of the cottage as it was getting a bit late for them to move on tonight.

May had brightened a lot and even joked about not being allowed wine on top of the sedatives she'd had. By the time Mrs Wainwright produced her substantial meal, they were chatting happily about safe subjects – Miss Smith in particular enjoying herself exchanging country lore with Jimmy.

It was nearly ten before the doctor came back.

'Sorry I was held up,' he said as he timed May's pulse. 'I got called to the sergeant's house – you know, the new fellow. Heart attack. No apparent cause – he was sitting down watching telly at the time. I had to get an ambulance to whip him off to Ipswich General. Reckon *he* won't be back on duty for a month or two at least – and then they'll probably give him a desk job. . . . Well, young lady, I'm very pleased with you. Picking up nicely. What you need now's a good night's sleep and I'll be round to see you in the morning. Here's some calamine for that sunburn and a couple of knock-me-out pills to take when you're ready to settle down.'

On the way out, he turned and said casually: 'I wonder if they'll send old Sergeant Wells back? Everyone was sorry to see him go. Knew our ways, that man did.'

When he had gone, Jimmy and May gave each other a secret smile. Eileen and Miss Smith said nothing because neither of them knew what to say.

Next morning was a Saturday, so Jimmy was off work without having to ask for it. The doctor, though still pleased with May, told her to stay in bed, so Miss Smith and Eileen said good-bye to her indoors.

As Jimmy walked with them to the caravan, Eileen asked suddenly: 'Jimmy, do you trust me?'

Jimmy grinned. 'That's a damn fool question after all you done for May.'

'Right then, listen to me. If the earthquakes come back, watch out for a kind of mist or Dust that comes up out of cracks in the ground. It's absolutely deadly. But you can protect yourself by breathing through gauze soaked in vinegar, while the Dust's visible and for at least a couple of hours afterwards. *Please* believe that I know what I'm talking about. See that everyone you care for has gauze and vinegar handy *from now on*. But don't say who told you.'

'You haven't told many people about it, have you?' Jimmy asked, looking at her shrewdly.

'No. I worked for a while, after the Midsummer quakes, at a place where they were investigating the Dust, and that was about the only thing they'd found out about it by the time I left. And every time I tell someone, I'm leaving a clue which could put *them* on my trail.'

'Then I *am* grateful. We'll remember.'

They climbed in, waved to him, and set off for the Midlands.

9

Moira jumped involuntarily when the knock on the front door came just before midnight on 2 August. Dan went to the bay window and peered through a chink in the curtains.

'It's all right, love. It's John Hassell and Karen.'

Moira let out a sigh of relief and hurried to the hall with Dan to welcome them. The last few days had tautened her nerves. Since they were a small coven, compact in their three adjoining houses and not publicly active, they had not so far been molested at home. This was a quiet, mainly middle-class area of Staines which might be expected to lag behind less inhibited places in open violence and they had always got on well with most of their immediate neighbours. But the signs were already there, in the eyes that were beginning to avoid theirs and in the whisperings just out of earshot. Besides, it was clear from their phone talks with other witches (the phone hardly stopped ringing these days) that the Crusaders were becoming more methodical in their intimidation, as though they were building up local lists and working their way through them. Their commonest tactic so far was the brick through the window, though there had been many street attacks on individuals, several of them brutal and none of them reaching the newspapers or, apparently, leading to arrests; and one house in Kettering and at least four cars had been burned.

One policeman friend who was himself a witch had, riskily, phoned Moira and told her what he knew was happening in the Metropolitan force at least. All ranks had been told, though only verbally, 'not to interfere if possible in sectarian disputes', as the formula went. It had soon become clear that 'if possible' meant in practice 'except where a witch can plausibly be charged with an offence' and that any arrest of Crusaders would be frowned on. The order had aroused a good deal of resentment among the more conscientious officers but any who tried to ignore it found themselves promptly disciplined, directly or indirectly. At one police station in Lambeth everyone from the superintendent downwards had stood together on the issue and for a few days had been able to keep the local Crusaders under control. Within a week, all of them down to the rank of sergeant had been transferred elsewhere and the station restaffed under a notorious martinet.

This call, disturbing as it was, had had the effect of strengthening Dan and Moira in their determination. They had had their moments of doubt as they checked and rechecked their vehicle stores; sometimes they had wondered what on earth they were doing, contemplating the abandonment of homes and jobs in the face of what might be a passing hysteria. But their instincts told them the hysteria was not passing but planned, and their police friend's call had confirmed it. As for jobs – Rosemary's had already gone, Dan's was becoming impossible, and even Greg's employer at the service station was beginning to talk vaguely of 'reorganization'. Dan, aware of his partner Steve's growing worry and embarrassment, had openly raised the question of Steve buying him out. Steve's rejection of the idea had been hasty and not very coherent and Dan was sure it could not last. They had been friends for a long time but the business was patently suffering from Dan's known presence. It had reached the stage now where their typist was bringing him paperwork to do at home and even this was becoming increasingly nominal.

And beneath all this, there was the certainty – indefinable but growing – that the Midsummer earth tremors were only a curtain-raiser. No, they were right to prepare for flight and they knew it. They found themselves spending more and more time studying maps.

They were both glad and shocked to see John. They had not met him since the inquest, and although they had expected to find him badly hit by Joy's death, they found the contrast between the bitterness in his eyes and his unnaturally controlled voice disturbing. In the hall, he received Moira's kiss and Dan's handshake with a flash of the old warmth but it was quickly veiled.

They kissed Karen too, as was Wiccan custom, and Moira led them into the sitting-room while Dan went to fetch Greg, Rosemary and Sally, who were all still up.

'When did they let you out, John?'

'This morning. Mary Andrews and Nigel Pickering were in the same nick and we were all brought in front of the bench together at ten o'clock. We expected to get a chance to protest about being arrested and to plead our case, but all we got was a lecture from the beak – a warning to behave ourselves and give no trouble. Then he dismissed us before we could even open our mouths.'

'Yes,' Moira said, 'it seems to have been the same all over. One or two of the others have phoned. Looks like the drill was cut and dried.'

'What else did you expect?' Karen asked.

'Oh, I don't know – a bit of local variation, I suppose. Magistrates have the reputation of being pretty individual.'

Karen said 'Huh!' and at that point the others came in. Greetings exchanged, they all sat down and looked at John expectantly; he had the air of one about to deliver a statement.

'You all know, I suppose, that Karen has taken over as High Priestess,' he told them almost stiffly. 'Sonia Forde has been appointed Maiden in her place.'

'Good choice,' Moira said, looking at Karen with deliberate friendliness. 'Sonia should be a big help to you.' She had known Joy's uneasiness about Karen and had shared it, but the poor girl's in a difficult situation, she told herself, and it's up to me to show support – for John's sake if nothing else.

'Yes, she is,' Karen said.

John went on: 'We came to ask what *you* are planning to do, in the present situation.'

'Keeping our cars packed ready for a camping holiday at a moment's notice,' Dan said.

'So are we, except that we're not waiting for notice. We're getting out the day after tomorrow, during the small hours. Our coven and Anna and Joe Fenton's. Nineteen of us altogether. We've got a place recce'd in Savernake Forest. Will you come with us?'

There was a moment's silence. The others look at John with immediate interest but a warning bell seemed to ring in Moira's mind.

'What about Jean and Fred Thomas?' she asked. 'They were your oldest members, before you all hived off. Aren't they taking theirs with you?'

'No, I'm afraid not,' John said. 'They think we're being premature.'

Dan, who for all his logicality could still surprise Moira

164

with his sudden shafts of intuition, shook his head. 'There's more to it than that, John – isn't there? More than just being premature?'

John did not seem put out. 'Yes, Dan, there's more to it than that. Jean and Fred don't agree with our plan of campaign and their coven support them – all except one, Harry Earley. He's opted to come with us, so Jean's let him transfer.'

'What plan of campaign?'

'Dan, all of you . . . We have to face it – this is war. The powers that be are out to destroy the Craft. We can't let them.'

'Of course we can't,' Greg put in. 'Why d'you think we're getting ready to take to the woods, too? Self-bloody-preservation. Not just as people but as witches.'

'But *how* as witches?' John asked, with sudden vehemence. 'The other side are using every weapon they can lay their hands on. And so should we.'

'What you mean is,' old Sally said, 'that you're going to work black.'

Karen laughed. 'If you like to call it that. Yes.'

'What do *you* call it?'

'As Greg just said. Self-bloody-preservation. Which of us is pure white, anyway? Aren't we all various shades of grey?'

'Of course we are – we're human. But most of us are grey trying to get whiter; grey trying to get black is something else again.' Sally did not often make speeches but once she got the bit between her teeth she did not pull any punches. 'You know the law of the Craft as well as I do: "An' it harm none, do what you will." Set out to harm people – worst of all, to use psychic power to harm them – and you're on the long slippery slope. You're heading for self-destruction.'

'Even when the people you're fighting are evil?' John asked.

'Good God, John – you're a High Priest, and you're talking as if you were initiated yesterday! You've seen what happens to people who turn black. They get away with it for a while, then sooner or later they crash. And only the Lords of Karma know how many lives it takes 'em to climb out of what they've done to *themselves*, never mind other people.'

'In ordinary times, Sally, I'd agree with you all the way. But this is *war*. In war you shoot to kill – you have to. In peacetime it'd be murder. In war it's survival – not just yours, but the people you're protecting.'

Dan came back into the argument. 'We've got other weapons, John. If somebody's doing evil, we can work magically to bind him – and it *does* work, you know that. *Attacking* him magically's different.'

'Can you honestly say you never would?' John asked.

'Oh Christ, of course I can't – like Sally says, we're human, and I can get angry like the next bloke. Look, John – say you'd known who it was had killed Joy and you'd used all your powers to hit at him – d'you think I'd have blamed you? I'd probably have helped if you'd asked me and there was no other way of getting at him. Maybe we'd have been wrong but we're not saints yet. I know if anyone harmed Moira, I'd lash out first and ask questions afterwards. But that's personal – and if you get too pernickety about how you defend people you love, could be you're piling up other sorts of Karma instead. But unless I'm mistaking you, what you're proposing is calculated, wholesale, *impersonal* black magic against opponents of the Craft in general. And that's different.'

John had not yet said as much in words but Moira knew Dan was not mistaking him; still less was he mistaking

Karen. And it was Karen who answered.

'It is *not* different,' she said, and her dark eyes were burning with intensity. '*They're* being calculating, wholesale and impersonal, and in everything but magic they're stronger than we are. We must be the same – with the weapon's *we* are strong in. Otherwise we go under.'

'I don't believe it.'

Karen laughed. 'I expect there were some who said that in the Burning Time. And they'd be the first to die.'

'I'd rather die clean,' Dan said, too quickly and dramatically. Karen pounced on the opening he'd given her.

'And watch Moira die clean, too? And Diana, and Sally, and Rosemary?'

Dan darkened with anger and Moira stepped in. 'Let's cool the melodrama. John – Karen – I'm sorry, we can't go with you. We'll survive, but *that*'s not our way.'

There was silence again. John looked round them all; they could see the pleading behind the hard bitterness in his eyes but everyone was with Moira. There was no pleading in Karen's eyes, only a hint of triumph. She stood up, with a kind of sensuous arrogance.

'Come on, John. We're wasting our time.'

She made for the hall and after a moment's hesitation John followed her. Moira and Dan went with them.

At the front door, John turned. 'Even if you can't join us – you won't let anyone know about it being Savernake Forest, will you?'

'Oh, *John*!' Moira said, her voice full of reproach.

John sighed. 'Blessed be, you two.'

'Blessed be. And *please* – think again . . .'

But John shook his head and Karen smiled unashamedly in Moira's face. Then they were gone.

10

For about ten days Britain was suspended in what looked, on the surface at least, like an uneasy calm. Sporadic attacks on witches continued but at least they did not seem to be intensifying and no more major incidents or burned houses were reported, either on the media or on Moira's telephone. The Crusade was recruiting fast. Ben Stoddart and Quentin White had become national figures, and the organization had launched its own weekly paper, *The Hammer*. Street corner and door-to-door sales of the paper were obviously absorbing some of the energies which might have gone to smashing windows, but *The Hammer* was also providing a new focus around which the Crusaders could build both their public presence and their intelligence network. It was clear that any respite was only temporary while the Crusade absorbed the influx of recruits and consolidated itself. The paper was a clever mixture of religious, intellectual, and sensationalist appeal, and its main strength was that it went virtually unanswered. Press, radio and television were becoming more and more reluctant to give any prominence to liberal viewpoints. *The Times* and the *Guardian* still retained some semblance of balance but as

Dan sourly remarked: 'When it comes to building up mass hysteria, it's the populars that matter. Get *them* in action and you can let the posh dailies do the fig-leaf job. They're just preaching to the converted and bloody few of them at that. It's the "don't knows" who swing the balance – and "don't knows" don't read long sentences.'

'But how have the Government got the media doing as they're told so quickly?' Moira wondered. 'It's not natural – this is still England. They can't twist everybody's arm at once.'

'It must be *something* to do with the earthquakes,' Dan said. 'The establishment knows more than we do, that's obvious. And they're blackmailing the top brass of the media with it.'

If Dan had known more about Beehive than the vague rumours that were circulating, he could have answered Moira's question; and answered it precisely if he could have eavesdropped on the excellent lunch to which Harley was at that very moment entertaining the editor of the *Daily Mirror* in Beehive's Ministerial Mess. The *Mirror* had not, in Harley's view, been quite as understanding of the Government's attitude lately as he might have wished. Over the *truite Jurassienne* Harley was making it clear that for the editor ('and your charming wife, of course, my dear fellow') a safe berth underground once Beehive Red was ordered would be dependent upon such understanding.

The editor was a very experienced journalist but physically unheroic, and he loved his wife; and after all (he told himself) only a *minor* shift of emphasis was being asked for. . . . The *Mirror* toed the line.

Of all this, Dan and Moira knew nothing. But they were in fact better informed than most of the public of the situation up and down the country because they were coming to be, informally and unexpectedly, a link in a growing

Wiccan telephone network. They really owed this, indirectly, to Moira's parents who were now over twelve thousand kilometres away. Although Dan and Moira had not yet been publicly prominent in the witchcraft movement and had only been running their own small coven for three years, her parents had been very active and well-known; and so, since she was a child, everyone had also known Moira. Her father and mother had retired to New Zealand the year before to live with Moira's only brother (for which Moira, in the last weeks, had come to be grateful), and she seemed to have inherited their wide circle of contacts. Now, as these realized that she and Dan were still unmolested and contactable, they were coming more and more to use them as an information-exchange centre.

'I shall miss it when we take off,' Moira said. 'It's comforting to get *some* news at least – even if the news itself isn't very comforting. If you see what I mean.'

Dan did, and told her: 'We mustn't make any notes but let's try to remember as much as we can about all these people – where they were when we last heard and so on. If things break down, it might be very useful to have all that tucked inside our heads.'

Moira agreed, and from then on whichever of them took a call repeated all the details to the other while it was still fresh.

But Moira's was not the only network. Karen Morley, too, had her friends and she was a capable organizer.

Dr Stanley Friell, of the Banwell Emergency Unit, was a chemist not a physician. He had been attached to the Unit very early, as soon as its importance was realized, for although he was not yet thirty he was one of the most ingenious brains in his field. It was he who achieved the only success the Unit had been able to record so far – the discovery that the Dust, a complex and baffling assembly of organic molecules at least two of which were hitherto unknown, owed their disastrous interaction once they were absorbed into the human bloodstream to an alkaline catalyst which always accompanied them. Without this catalyst, they were harmless and the bloodstream broke them down almost at once. A simple gauze filter soaked in a mild acid – vinegar being ideal – neutralized the catalyst; so a breathing mask which anyone could make at home gave complete protection against the Dust. This information – and, indeed, the very existence of the Dust – had not yet been revealed to the public.

Dr Friell was indifferent to the public, for he was an élitist to the marrow of his bones. His passion, on which he had written one or two brilliant if esoteric monographs, was the history of occult chemistry up to and including the Middle Ages. He had made up, and tried out on himself, every known recipe for the hallucinogenic 'flying ointment' of the old witches; had experimented with the 'sacred mushroom' *amanita muscaria* and others less well documented; and had clarified several uncertainties about the drugs and poisons believed to have been used by sorcery's blacker brethren. He had an iron constitution and a will to match, so he emerged unscathed and unaddicted from his carefully controlled trials of the drugs and hallucinogens, and the poisons he tested only on laboratory rats.

At first, his interest had been purely pharmaceutical but his researches into the strange world of the men and women who had once used these substances had brought him into contact with some of their modern counterparts, both reputable and disreputable, and he had been fascinated. He had toyed (though with him even 'toying' was an energetic and methodical process) with ritual magic of the Golden

Dawn variety, rapidly attaining the grade of ③ = 8
Practicus in an easily overawed lodge. But although he
was impressed by the system he found the ritual practice
somewhat anaemic and transferred to one of the wholeheartedly sexual splinter groups of the Ordo Templi
Orientis, where he had progressed to 7° Mystic Templar
by the time he was summoned to Banwell. At the same
time, out of curiosity, he had got himself initiated into an
ex-Gardnerian coven of witches who had 'gone black';
privately he considered them ignorant dabblers but he
maintained friendly contact with them as potentially useful. At least two of them he knew to be psychotic and he
was very interested in the psychic power of insanity. He
was a natural sensitive and had worked to develop the gift,
and he could hardly help being aware of the psychic
dynamite which lurked in the Banwell incurables.

As one of the top researchers at the Unit, Dr Friell belonged to the handful of staff who were necessarily permitted to come and go while the ordinary doctors, nurses,
and domestics were confined to the premises (a restriction
which had been even more rigorously enforced since the
disappearance of Nurse Eileen Roberts). Early in August
he had to drive to London for consultation with a particular
specialist, and having an evening to spare after his meeting
he spent it, discreetly covering his tracks, with the High
Priestess and High Priest of the 'black' coven. It was from
them that he learned a very interesting piece of information
and was armed with a map reference and a password.

He lay awake in his hotel that night thinking carefully,
re-examining and developing the seed of an idea which
had been with him for the past two or three weeks. Next
morning he started back to Banwell – by way of Savernake
Forest. In the end he reached the Unit a day later than
he had originally intended, tingling with well-concealed

excitement. He was too senior for anyone to ask him why he was late.

Ben Stoddart was, yet again, a guest on BBC's 'Paul Grant Hour'. The producer, high in his gallery, flicked his eye morosely back and forth across the bank of monitor-screens which faced him, remembering the morning's conference where he had suggested that Stoddart was being over-exposed. His chief had answered smoothly: 'We all know you have the interests of your programme at heart but don't rock the boat, there's a good chap,' – and the matter had been closed.

The producer disliked everything Stoddart stood for, and hated the man himself even more because he could not deny he made for very gripping television.

'Jack – a bit tighter on that profile,' he ordered into his microphone and saw Stoddart's head grow larger in No 2 camera's monitor. Fascinated, he watched the handsome lips moving.

When the unthinkable happened it took the producer no more than a couple of seconds to realize that although Stoddart was still speaking, the sound had gone silent. He turned his head quickly to the soundproof window on his right beyond which the sound booth lay and saw that Bernie had already reacted, so he issued no order, knowing that Bernie would trace and correct the fault all the quicker without interruption. Then, suddenly, over the visual of Stoddart still mouthing unaware, a strange voice broke out: *'The Angels of Lucifer have condemned Ben Stoddart to death! The Angels of Lucifer . . .'*

The producer and Bernie had pounced on their buttons in the same instant and that was as far as the voice got, but it was done, it was said, the pirate voice had already given its message to God knew how many millions from Land's

End to John o'Groats. On the floor, of course, Ben Stoddart and Paul Grant still talked and smiled, having heard nothing; and the cameramen, though they must have picked it up on their gallery-fed earphones, did not waver. The producer handed over to his assistant, phoned the security men, and ran through to Bernie's booth.

They soon found the loop of tape, still running on a machine in an empty sound-editing cubicle, and the ingenious re-wiring which had made the interruption possible. They also found the time-switch which had triggered the device and which could have been set minutes or hours earlier. None of this highly professional sabotage bore any fingerprints, and although everybody who could possibly have committed it was grilled for hours, the culprit was never identified.

Although the pirate broadcast was made in the middle of a BBC programme – at 9.43 pm, to be exact – ITN had a beat on its news coverage, to the BBC's chagrin. Seventeen minutes were quite enough for ITN to be able to lead 'News at Ten' with the story, whereas BBC 1's main news had already gone out at 9.00, and BBC 2's was not due till 10.40. BBC, of course, was able to hold on to Ben Stoddart for interview, but ITN smartly grabbed Quentin White and had him in their House of Commons interviewing studio by 10.03.

'How seriously do you think this threat should be taken, Mr White?' the ITN man asked.

'Very seriously indeed. The so-called Angels of Lucifer . . .'

'Had you ever heard of them before?'

'Nobody has, to my knowledge. But the very name proclaims their allegiance – and who else but witches would threaten the life of Ben Stoddart, their staunchest opponent?

The rats are at bay and they are showing their true colours. Rats always do when they are cornered. They have been cornered by the vigilance and courage of the Anti-Pagan Crusade, by the aroused conscience of the British public and by the prompt measures of the Government.'

'If they are, as you say, cornered – may they not be bluffing?'

'It would be most dangerous to assume that. These people are ruthless, and they have secret supporters in key positions. The very way they issued their threat proves that. You're a television man; am I not right in saying the interruption must have been an inside job – and a technically difficult one at that?'

'Yes to both questions,' the ITN man said, resisting the temptation to rub salt in the BBC's wounds, and went on: 'If the threat is serious, what is its nature? A physical one or a black magic one?' He felt a little foolish asking it, but White had asked him to during their brief preparation and he had to admit it was attention-grabbing.

White, who had had no television experience before his election campaign but had quickly absorbed Stoddart's coaching, turned from facing the interviewer to gaze dramatically into the camera lens which had the red light over it.

'Let no one be in any *doubt* about the nature of the threat,' he declared, separating the syllables as though he were handing out gold coin by coin. 'No *physical* assassin can reach Ben Stoddart – he is too well protected by his friends who know that since Midsummer he has incurred the vicious enmity of evil men and women. But these men and women have their own chosen weapons. For two or three centuries now, it has been fashionable to dismiss as a fairy-tale the old belief that one could sell one's soul to the devil in exchange for power in this world. I am not so sure that it can any longer be so dismissed. In the last decades, science itself has come to realize that the human mind has unsuspected latent abilities, to which it has attached modern-sounding labels such as telekinesis, ESP, the psi-factor and so on. I believe that the witches have been laughing behind the scientists' backs – for these new labels merely hide timeless *facts*, which the witches have known about, and used, since before written history. They have trained and developed these abilities in themselves as an athlete trains his muscles – and just like the athlete, *because* of that deliberate training they can, in their chosen field, achieve results which ordinary people cannot. And as for selling their souls to the devil – the phrase may be outdated, but the thing which it expresses is *not*. By deliberately abandoning all restraints of morality, humanity and compassion, these men and women avail themselves of the incalculable powers of darkness – the evil powers which those God-given restraints, in all decent humans, keep in check. And if *that* is not selling your soul to the devil in exchange for power – what *is*? I ask you, my friends – what *is*? . . . The Angels of Lucifer – and what a revealing name they have chosen! – the Angels of Lucifer are not threatening Ben Stoddart with the bullet or the knife. They are threatening him with those very powers for which they *have* sold their souls to Satan. . . . Whether each of you, listening to me in the security of your own homes, can believe they are capable of carrying out that threat, is up to you to decide. But *I* believe that Ben Stoddart *is* in grave danger because here on earth he stands in the front rank of the hosts of God, and he is the declared target of God's enemies. So I ask you – all of you, whatever your beliefs – to fortify this great and saintly man with your prayers.'

The Angels of Lucifer were the splash in every single morning paper (and a few hours later were big news in America, too, for Gene Macallister and Tonia Lynd had been busy all night). The pirate broadcast was news that could not be censored, because millions had heard it, so almost in relief the media went to town on the story. Quentin White's statement was quoted in full and set up the tone of editorial debate; he had shifted the emphasis, within minutes of the pirate broadcast, away from the threat of physical assassination to that of 'the powers of darkness' and there it stayed. It made much more dramatic reading and listening anyway, and the big question – 'Can they do it?' – could be expanded to fill as many column inches, or minutes of air time, as any editor or producer could wish. Everybody from the Archbishops of Canterbury ('yes'), Westminster ('yes' qualified) and York ('no') to the Professor of Parapsychological Studies at King's College, London ('five decades of clinical experiment have established beyond reasonable doubt . . .') and the Astronomer Royal ('telekinesis does not exist') was willing and eager to be quoted at length. Jungian psychologists clashed with Freudian, vicars with their own curates, and Mods with Rockers (the 1960s idiom was enjoying a mushroom revival among the trendier young this summer; it had begun to peter out, but Mods' 'no' and Rockers' 'yes' gave it a new lease of life). Fleet Street astrologers contradicted each other as usual.

Ben Stoddart, after a quick consultation with Quentin White before he had to appear on the BBC 2 news, had agreed that gallant defiance was the appropriate image for him especially after White's remark about 'the front rank of the hosts of God'; so Stoddart, while being careful not to contradict his colleague on the question of the reality of the powers of darkness, told his BBC viewers that he doubted whether 'these people could raise enough magical power to fry an egg' and challenged them to do their worst. His statement was printed next morning alongside White's, and most of the picture editors reinforced them with White looking like Savonarola and Stoddart looking like St George.

In Beehive, Harley needed to do nothing except sit back and smile. 'How about your associative links now, Sir Walter?' he asked Jennings triumphantly. 'These Angels of Lucifer have played right into our hands. They've branded every witch in Britain as a potential black-magic murderer.'

'Poor sods,' Sir Walter said. 'If you could take a referendum among witches today, ninety-eight per cent of them would condemn the Angels of Lucifer by every rule in their book. You do know that, don't you?'

'Of course I do – but the public doesn't.' He chuckled. 'And all achieved by one five-second pirate broadcast. Marvellous, isn't it?'

Sir Walter looked at him thoughtfully. 'You didn't set it up yourself by any chance, did you?'

'No, I didn't. But if I'd thought of it, I might have done.'

Sir Walter said nothing; he still wasn't altogether sure.

Five people, at least, were sure. Moira and Dan's coven had not heard the original pirate broadcast, but the BBC, having the tape in their possession, had naturally re-run it as part of their 10.40 news report. The coven, listening, had gasped simultaneously. They all recognized the voice as that of Bill Lazenby, a member of John Hassell's coven. He had never been publicly active so his voice was unlikely to be on file anywhere; but to the few who knew him, it was unmistakable.

'Oh, God,' Rosemary had cried. 'So they really meant

it! It's that bitch Karen. What's she done to John – to *all* of them?'

'John was a ripe plum after Joy was murdered,' Sally said. 'Someone a lot less clever than Karen could have made him go black. And Karen *is* clever. She won him over and swept the rest along with them.'

'All the same, I never expected *this* – an all-out public attack, so soon. . . . *Have* they the power?'

They all looked at Moira, who said: 'Frankly, I don't know. She *is* powerful – and harnessing John's bitterness – plus all the others. . . . They might do it.'

'I know it sounds crazy,' Rosemary said, 'but since we know where the attack's coming from – shouldn't *we* work to protect Stoddart?'

'*Him?*' Dan snorted.

'I know what Rosemary means,' Greg put in more calmly. 'Ben Stoddart's a bastard, of course – but *if* they managed to kill him, think of the repercussions. The Crusaders would go berserk.'

They thought, they discussed, but as usual it was Moira who had the final say. 'Greg's got a good point but I'm afraid we'll have to stay clear of it. One of these days – I'm sorry, dreadfully sorry, but it's true – one of these days we're going to have to fight John and Karen head on. They've put themselves beyond the pale and Gods knows what they'll let loose. But when we do, we've got to win – and that means all the allies we can get. This isn't the time. We must wait for it – and meantime, no skirmishes with them. At the moment, we're too vulnerable. Karen's highly clairvoyant and she'd pick us up at once and turn on us. Right now we've got other things to concentrate on. Ben Stoddart must look after himself.'

Dr Friell knew the outlines of the plan and many of the

details – after all, he had suggested it in the first place and had provided all the inside information the Angels would need. The only thing he did not know was the timing of the raid; it had not been possible to finalize the date or the hour during their discussions in Savernake Forest, and they had agreed that any more communication between the Angels and Friell, once he had returned to Banwell, would be unwise. They had not even been certain, then, how the public threat to Stoddart's life would be made. John Hassell had merely said he had 'an idea about that' – an idea which had apparently borne fruit as the pirate broadcast. The threat *had* been made and all Stanley Friell could do was wait for the raid which might come any day, any hour. . . . It was always possible, he realized, that the Angels of Lucifer did not entirely trust him; he doubted if that slant-eyed vixen Karen, who was clearly the driving force of the group, trusted anyone. Friell didn't resent it. Mistrust was sound procedure in guerilla operations. Outside the Savernake Forest group, Friell was the only one who knew the part the Banwell Emergency Unit was to play or even that it entered into the picture at all. They were right to be wary of him; if they had not been, he would have thought them naïve and feared for the success of the plan.

As it was, he had confidence in their ability to carry out the practical side of the plan; there were by now about thirty witches in their group, most of them young and determined and fit-looking. One of them, a little older, was an ex-Sergeant of the Royal Marines and he had been organizing and training the others from the moment they arrived in the Forest. It was clear that John and Karen did not intend their group to survive on magical weapons only.

Yet as far as the Banwell raid was concerned, it was the

magical operation that mattered; the military operation was merely to make it possible. And about the magical success Friell had no doubts whatever. He was satisfied, from his studies and his own experience, that psychic attack worked given sufficient emotional force and a capable directing will. He knew what a psychic volcano smouldered at Banwell and he knew that Karen and John had the nerve and the knowledge to harness and direct it. It *could not* fail . . . and he, Stanley Friell, was both instigator and observer in an experiment few psychic researchers would ever have the possibility – let alone the courage and freedom from scruple – to conduct or even contemplate.

He was tense with anticipation and his tension was aggravated by the impossibility of knowing when the action would be launched. Being a sensitive, he felt the tension as an increasing static charge, a potential which must be released – and he released it in a very practical manner, by responding at last to the silent invitation which his assistant, Nurse Parker, had been directing at him ever since she was allocated to him and which he had so far been too preoccupied to bother with. Jenny Parker had an average figure and a rather plain, unsmiling little face, so the temptation had not been great. But when he did take her to bed, with the minimum of preparatory gallantry and nothing more in mind than the release of tension, he found to his surprise and pleasure that she was a dedicated sensualist of considerable ingenuity and stamina, as impersonally hungry as he himself. They suited each other very well and in Friell's bedroom they took advantage of the fact in periodic fierce encounters whose intensity no one could have inferred from their professional relationship.

They were, in fact, about to be so engaged when the raid came, just after 8 pm four days after the pirate broadcast. Jenny had begun to undress, stripping to the waist first because she knew he liked that, to see her topless and loose-haired above her uniform skirt. Friell had come behind her while her arms were raised to unpin her hair and had squeezed her breasts in his two hands almost to the point of pain – which *he* knew *she* liked. It was at that instant that they heard a commotion in the corridor outside and momentarily froze. Then the door burst open, the lock splintering, and one of the Angels of Lucifer was covering them with a Lüger. Friell recognized him even through his stocking-mask and he knew the boy knew him, too; though as planned neither gave it away, and Friell shouted 'What the hell?' at him in suitably convincing anger. At the same time he could not help noticing Jenny's reaction; she clasped her hands to her breasts as most women would when intruded upon, but over *his* hands which she squeezed even more fiercely to herself – while her face, which Friell could see in the mirror, stared in fascinated excitement at the gun.

The man said 'Outside!' and the brief tableau dissolved. Jenny reached for her blouse which she had thrown on the bed, but the man stepped forward and pointed the gun at her face. 'I said *outside*. There's no time for that. Move!'

The next moment they were herded along the corridor to the landing, where the man handed them over to a woman with a shotgun, who stood guard over the half-dozen staff who had already been driven from their rooms. It was obvious that none of them had been allowed any time, though only one – a middle-aged woman doctor in a wet bathrobe, with bare feet – was in anything like Jenny's state of *déshabillé*. The Angels were ignoring the babble of protests and clearing the corridor with speed and efficiency. Jenny had not uttered a word since the door burst open but the glint of excitement was still there in her eyes and she seemed indifferent to the fact that she was naked to the waist. The detached scientist in Friell observed her reactions curiously.

He was still wondering about it when the entire roll-call of the Unit – twenty-nine staff and twenty-six strait-jacketed patients – had been herded into the staff dining-room. Of the Angels of Lucifer, ten men and four women were in evidence, all armed. Friell could not see John and Karen. Again, the same swift efficiency; the Unit had once been a school and this room the gymnasium – and all four-teen patients had been tied to the wall-bars which lined one end of the room. The male nurses had been ordered, at gun-point, to tie them there as they were brought in, and in fact had obeyed quickly, since all twenty-six were never taken out of their rooms at once and would have been too much for the staff to control, even in strait-jackets.

Some of the patients were quiet for the moment, glanc-ing around with bright ferrety eyes; several rolled and swayed as far as the ropes allowed, making a high keening noise. Two, just out of reach of each other's teeth, were straining and snapping – and at any moment at least three or four of them would be uttering a stream of words, at anything from a croak to a shout, without coherence but somehow conjuring up wild and terrible images.

At either end of the line, the staff were bunched under guard, some still protesting, some pale and terrified. With everyone in place, four of the guards cleared the room in front of the patients, sliding chairs and tables quickly out of the way. In the middle, about three metres apart, they stood two squat butane cylinders with open-ended burners on them, which they lit. Two roaring tongues of flame, each a metre or more high, shot up from the burners and illu-mined the room with an infernal brightness, made more eerie when the Angels turned the electric lights off.

Almost quicker than the bewildered prisoners could take

it in, the stage was set; a two-metre-high head-and-shoulders caricature of Ben Stoddart hung from the bars on the opposite wall; a table slid below it as an altar on which a skull grinned beside a live and terrified hare in a wire-fronted cat-basket; one of the Angels squatting over a bongo drum and building up an insistent, inescapable rhythm. . . . Then Karen and John dancing.

They seemed to appear from nowhere, weaving in and out around the roaring flames and each other, their glistening skin naked except for barbaric ornaments – slowly at first, but rapidly building their tempo in time with the drum. Also in time with the drum, the rest of the Angels had begun to chant: 'Kill Ben Stoddart! Kill Ben Stoddart! Kill Ben Stoddart!', directing their chanting at the patients who, entranced by the flames and the drum and the erotic dance, were already beginning to pick it up, to join in. 'Kill Ben Stoddart! Kill Ben Stoddart!' – twenty-six people, incurably insane, suddenly becoming a choir of united purpose, simple and terrible: 'Kill Ben Stoddart! Kill Ben Stoddart!'

Most of the staff stood appalled and speechless but one or two of the nurses were weeping uncontrollably. Stanley Friell observed, feeling the avalanche of psychic power building and building. Suddenly, beside him, her bare arms and shoulders and breasts dripping with sweat, Nurse Jenny Parker began to shake like a dervish; then she, too, was crying out 'Kill Ben Stoddart! Kill Ben Stoddart!'

Even Stanley Friell gasped.

For a moment, such was the intensity of the shouting and the dance, Friell thought John and Karen would couple in wild ritual orgasm before their eyes. But at the moment when no other outcome seemed possible they leaped together at the altar and John dragged the struggling hare out of its basket and Karen seized a knife. They both screamed in unison: 'Kill Ben Stoddart!' as Karen slashed the hare's throat and John flung the blood direct from the pulsing, severed neck across Ben Stoddart's picture.

The screaming seemed to reach an unbearable pitch; Friell could no longer tell if his own voice was a part of it. The detached observer was swept away and he saw in a flame-lit dream the picture of Stoddart being ripped to pieces by the talons of two demonic figures, a dancing man and a dancing woman whom he barely knew.

A blow came down on the back of his skull, and the split second of awareness that remained to him was filled with the thought, 'Oblivion will be a relief!'

'Hey, love – what's the matter?' The man put his beer down on the wall, the better to attend to the dishevelled and breathless young nurse who had cannoned into him. 'Take it easy, now . . .'

The girl gasped 'Police, police', clinging to him for support. One of the half dozen people who had been drinking outside the pub called urgently through the saloon-bar door: 'Mike, ring the cops, quick' – which of course brought everybody out to see what was happening. The nurse, exhausted anyway by her two-kilometre run from the Unit, was pouring out her story in near-hysteria to a growing crowd. If she had not been so obviously and genuinely terrified, it would have been an incredible tale; the commando raid, the cut telephone lines, the staff herded at gunpoint, the roped mad patients, the wild flame-lit dance, the crescendo of murderous chanting, the blood sacrifice . . . 'They said they were the Angels of Lucifer,' she sobbed, 'and they've gone, you'll never catch them now, half an hour ago – they kidnapped Dr Friell and Nurse Parker, took them with 'em – and the mess they left, and getting the patients back, it was awful – couldn't get help, no phone, and they'd done something to all the cars – I ran . . .'

She broke down at last into wordless tears, just as a police car arrived and whisked her away. But by then the bare bones of the story, and the loaded words 'Angels of Lucifer', had been heard not only by thirty or forty villagers but also by eight London-bound and five Bristol-bound motorists.

Moira had been on edge since early evening; that something was brewing – something evil and specific – she was certain. She had a feeling that it had to do with John and Karen, but she could not be sure whether this feeling was clairvoyance or guesswork. Putting Diana to bed kept her attention off it for a while because the child was particularly lively and talkative tonight, but as soon as she had settled down Moira found herself brooding again. Dan was not there to talk to about it; he had an evening appointment with one of the few clients who had become more, not less, friendly towards him since the discrimination against witches had begun to be felt, and he would not be back till about nine. She knew Rosemary and Greg were eating, and that Sally probably was, so she did not like to disturb them.

She turned on the television for company. BBC 1 offered a Western, and BBC 2 a discussion on schizophrenia, neither of which tempted her at the moment. ITV had a series comedy, undemanding and cheerful; she left it on, giving it half her attention while she prepared a meal for Dan.

At about half past eight, without warning, she felt a brief wave of vertigo and gasped to herself, automatically throwing up her psychic defences. She knew she had picked up something which had the flavour of malignancy, of black magic – not directed at her, but sensed by her because of its intensity and because she had some personal link with its source. *It's got to be John and Karen*, she told herself, sombrely. She sat down, closed her eyes, and cast deliberate mental circles around Diana and Dan. She relaxed a little – the peak of whatever-it-was seemed to have passed – but she was still uneasy.

At ten to nine Dan came home; she ran to greet him, smiling with relief. They returned to the living-room together just as the continuity announcer broke into the comedy with a news flash:

'The headquarters of the Anti-Pagan Crusade announced a few minutes ago that their president, Mr Ben Stoddart, died suddenly at about 8.30 this evening. The cause of death is still uncertain but he had been protected by a bodyguard of Crusaders ever since the recent threat by the so-called Angels of Lucifer and they insist that physical attack can be ruled out. That is the end of the news flash.'

Stanley Friell drifted back into consciousness, his head throbbing. He was lying on a narrow mattress on the floor of a closed van, and to judge by its high and steady speed the van was on a motorway. One of the Angel women was squatting beside him, watching him, and as soon as he opened his eyes she called 'Karen!' and clambered forward.

A few seconds later Karen was looking down at him. 'How do you feel?'

'Not too bad, in the circumstances. Did you *have* to slug me?'

'Sorry about that but we couldn't leave you there, you know. We're ninety-nine per cent certain you're reliable but we couldn't afford the one per cent. You knew too much. And at the speed we had to get out, there was no time to argue. Slugging was quicker.'

Friell nodded, carefully. 'Don't blame you. I'd have done the same. . . . Anyhow, the Unit's become a dead end for me. I think I'd rather join you.' He rolled sideways to ease his limbs and caught sight of Jenny Parker, still unconscious and wrapped in a blanket, on the other side of the van. 'Good God! You brought *her*, too?'

Karen smiled. '(A), as a consolation prize for you since we'd kidnapped you! and (B), because her reaction to the ritual suggests she's promising material for the Angels of Lucifer.'

'Fair enough. . . . I wonder how Ben Stoddart's feeling now?'

'Oh, it's been on the radio already. You're not joining amateurs, Stanley. Ben Stoddart is dead.'

Stoddart's death gave Harley his first opportunity to test the 'sensitive news' system which he had devised in consultation with the experts of BBC News and ITN. Each of the latter had a small news studio in Beehive, with a hand-picked staff, in close touch with Harley's own office. The moment a news story was classified as 'sensitive', its handling was transferred to the Beehive studios – whose output could be integrated with those of the Surface studios during news bulletins in the same way as that of OB vans or of the Parliamentary interview studios.

A hunch made Harley rule that Stoddart's death was 'sensitive', and he was glad later. At first, the death itself; the almost immediate official confirmation by doctors and police that neither violence nor poisoning had killed him; the 'spontaneous' demonstrations in Parliament Square by crowds chanting 'Ban the witches!' and worse (illegally, since Parliament was sitting but with little police interference); Quentin White's impassioned speech in the House demanding 'in the name of our martyred friend' that, pending legislation, a more stringent Order in Council be made declaring the professing or practising of witchcraft illegal – all these could have been suitably handled by BBC and ITN on Surface without Harley's guidance. But when the first hint of the Banwell Emergency Unit raid came in, Harley knew he had been right.

He told BBC and ITN to hold the Banwell story till the news was harder and a suitably guarded version of it could be released. Within half an hour, he had received a concise police report, and spoken to the Unit chief (a personal appointee of his own) on the telephone. Ten minutes later, he let the BBC and ITN loose on the story in all its lurid detail – with the only provisos that the Unit was to be described as 'a small isolation hospital for the specialized treatment of violent mental patients', no mention was to be made of the Dust or of any connection between the Unit and the earth tremors, and no one was to be interviewed on camera except the Unit chief and the local police superintendent.

For apart from the Dust, there was no need to censor the story. The Angels of Lucifer had carried out their threat in a way bizarre enough to turn the witch-hunt into a stampede. Harley had merely to sit back and watch.

The Order in Council which Quentin White was demanding had in fact already been prepared, and tonight was psychologically the ideal moment to impose it. So at 10.30, half an hour after the Banwell story had hit a public already stunned by the death of Ben Stoddart, the Prime Minister announced that as from midnight, the new Order in Council made the practice, profession or promotion of witchcraft illegal. Penalties ranged from a minimum fine of £10 to a maximum prison sentence of two years. Certain

periodicals were prohibited by name and the Home Secretary was empowered to add to the list.

As soon as Ben Stoddart's death was announced, Moira and
Dan knew the time had come. Rosemary, Greg, and Sally
agreed with them at once. Dan and Greg stowed the roof-
rack load in the van's central gangway, while the women
made hot soup for the thermos flasks and other last-minute
comforts; there seemed no minute-by-minute urgency.
But the report of the Banwell raid changed their minds
about that; Moira hurried upstairs to dress Diana, if possible without waking her too much. The child was a little
querulous and confused at first, but fortunately soon
decided it was a surprise game and cooperated, happily if
sleepily.

Moira nearly had her ready when Rosemary ran upstairs. 'Got to go *now*, love. There's a small crowd gathering on the corner of the road – can't see much from this
end but they could be after *us*.'

They hurried down together, Moira carrying Diana. Both
vehicles were still in their garages; Sally was already in the
car back seat and Dan behind the steering wheel. 'Keep Di
on your lap,' he told her as she climbed in. 'No time to
tuck her in behind. . . . Greg's going first, because the van's
bigger and heavier in case we have to scatter the crowd.
The moment we see him go, I follow. Right? You can
start the engine while I open the door.'

He got out and stood with his hand on the already-
unlatched garage door, which was of the up-and-over type,
while he watched through the window towards Greg's
garage. In the waiting silence, Moira suddenly heard the
noise of the crowd. The corner was over a hundred metres
away but they must be beginning to move nearer. . . .

Greg's door crashed upwards, quickly followed by Dan's,

and Moira had the engine running before Dan jumped in beside her. She held Diana tightly as the car surged and swung to fit in behind the van. She could see the crowd reacting, spreading across the road to challenge them; see Greg's momentary hesitation, and then his sudden acceleration as he drove full tilt at the mob. She wanted to shout encouragement, *It's them or us, Greg,* but she must not distract Dan, who was matching Greg's speed and might have to react quickly. In seconds they were ploughing through, people scattering to left and right – she didn't think anyone stayed long enough to be hit but she couldn't be sure. . . . Faces, shouts of anger, the glint of a flaming torch, the rattle of flung stones on the roof, Diana screaming. . . . Then they were away, free, circling round behind the estate to join the by-pass.

She had thought Diana's scream was of fright but now she was able to look at her. A stone must have found the open window because her forehead was bleeding and she was whimpering in Moira's arms, trying (as she usually did when she was hurt) not to cry. Moira said, 'Di's hit but keep going,' and started cleaning the wound with a tissue while she soothed her. Diana attempted a smile and said, '*Horrid* people.'

'Yes, darling, horrid. But they can't catch us now. . . . She's all right, Dan. . . . Hold still, my love, while I stick a little plaster on it.'

They drove in silence for a while, out into the country, skirting Heathrow; they had agreed not to stop till they were well into the Chilterns and certain none of the mob had jumped into cars and followed.

Dan glanced down at Diana to make sure she had fallen asleep and said at last: 'I wonder when we'll be back.'

Sally leaned forward, her forearms on the tops of their seats, her head between theirs. 'I didn't tell you before, my loves, because of little ears. But *I* could see our houses as we came round the back road. That lot weren't carrying torches for nothing, you know. Our places were well alight already. . . . Sorry, dears, but it's *got* to be forward, 'cos there's nowhere to go back to.'

11

They drove for about an hour before Greg pulled into a lonely woodland verge beyond Great Missenden, where they loaded the van roof-rack to clear the central gangway for domestic use. Rosemary made toast to go with the hot soup and they stood around sipping and nibbling and saying little. Now that the planned-for crisis had overtaken them, they all admitted to a sense of unreality; even the burning of their homes seemed a fact from another existence, and the brief drama of their escape a fictional episode. Too much had happened in a few hours; erstwhile friends had dragged witchcraft's name into the mire, psychic murder had triggered off mob violence, their religion and Craft had been declared criminal and now they were nomads in a land with too little open space where nomads might breathe. It was nearly midnight on a still August night, with nothing familiar around them but a van and a car crammed with all they possessed. Their minds needed a rest before they could take it all in. At this moment, all they felt (and they felt it unanimously) was the need to see tomorrow's dawn in a new landscape, a long way from the treachery of friends and the ashes of their homes. Physical distance seemed to have spiritual meaning; let them seize that distance and they would feel strong.

They decided to make for the Welsh mountains – a choice they had more or less finalized over the past week – but to reach them overnight, instead of taking the two or three days they had envisaged. There could be night-time violence in the big cities in reaction to the day's events, so they agreed upon as rural a route as possible, via Princes Risborough, Bicester, Chipping Norton, Evesham, Worcester (the biggest town on their route, but it could be by-passed, and it would be well into the small hours), Ludlow and Welshpool – in which area they could explore more slowly for somewhere to settle, at least temporarily. But tonight's objective was the Welsh Border and a reasonably secure spot for a few hours' rest and consideration.

They agreed to stop every hour to stretch legs and change drivers. Sally did not drive but by taking charge of Diana on the back seat with her, she could free Dan and Moira for alternate hours of dozing and driving.

They washed up the mugs and set off, the car taking its turn in the lead.

'All these practical arrangements may sound petty, the way things are,' Dan said to Moira as he settled back in the passenger seat. 'But you know what, darling missus? They help us keep sane.'

Moira smiled and let in the clutch, suddenly warmed by his use of their private-language title. 'That's right, darling mister,' she told him. 'Now you go to sleep and let me drive in peace.'

Eileen had not slept well. Last evening's news had depressed and confused her. Since their Suffolk experience a few days earlier, she and Angela had not knowingly met any more witches but had found themselves identifying with them more and more. They had liked the Coddenham group, shared their fury over the rape and humiliation of May Groombridge, and felt no unease about what had happened to the callous policeman – whether or not it was a coincidence. But the Angels of Lucifer and the death (again, coincidence or not) of Ben Stoddart, were a very different matter. The 'small isolation hospital' where the savage ritual had been enacted had not been named nor its location given, but Dr Friell and Nurse Parker *had* been named and their violent kidnapping reported, so Eileen had no doubt that the 'hospital' was the Banwell Emergency Unit. The knowledge had let loose a flood of conflicting emotions – reawakened guilt, outrage on behalf of former friends, curiosity (which she felt to be morbid but could not banish) about the actual details, paralysed inability to decide whether Ben Stoddart really had died from psychic attack or from auto-suggestion. . . . Angela Smith had had to work very hard to soothe her young cousin and had lain anxiously awake till about two in the morning listening to her tossing and muttering in her sleep.

Eileen woke suddenly just after sunrise. She thought at first Angie had spoken and looked across at the other bunk, but Angie was still unconscious. Then the voice came again and Eileen realized it was outside the caravan. Two or three voices, men and women, and the clink and shuffle of move-ment. She must finally have exhausted herself into really deep sleep, she decided, because the layby had been empty except for themselves and she had been unaware of any other vehicles arriving.

A young child whimpered in pain and a worried woman's voice said: 'Dan, we'll have to get her to a doctor.' The man's reply was indistinguishable but the tone was equally worried.

Eileen unzipped her sleeping bag, pulled on slacks and

sweater, and opened the caravan door and looked out.

'Did someone mention a doctor? I'm a nurse, if I can be any help.'

The young couple looked round, at first startled, then relieved; they seemed tired and nervous. '*Could* you have a look at her?' the mother said. 'We'd be very grateful. We . . .' She broke off and lifted a little girl about four years old out of their heavily loaded station wagon. 'She had a bump on the head last night and it seemed all right – but I think she's a little feverish now.'

Eileen gave her attention to the child but was still aware of the atmosphere of nervousness; another couple had emerged from the second vehicle – a big Bedford van – and an elderly woman was hovering watchfully beside the car.

Angie had come out of their own caravan and on an impulse Eileen said: 'There's only the two of us.' She felt the strangers begin to relax. 'What's your name?' she asked the little girl.

'Diana.'

'Mine's Eileen and I'm going to see if I can make that bump better.'

'Some horrid people threw stones at us.'

Tension again. Eileen was getting impatient with it, wanting to concentrate on Diana, when Angie took the problem out of her hands. 'Look, everybody – if you're on the run, relax – so are we. And if you're witches, we don't give a damn; we're not bloody Crusaders. So while Eileen looks at the kid, why don't we all organize breakfast?'

The sun was well up by the time they had exchanged their stories. They had all been a little wary at first but as they got the measure of each other they became increasingly frank. A communal feast of bacon, eggs, toast, tea and coffee, plus Eileen's reassurance that there was nothing wrong with Diana that her professional dressing and a few hours' proper sleep wouldn't put right, encouraged mutual confidence.

'Tell you the truth,' Eileen admitted, 'it's done me good to meet you lot. I'd always rather liked the witches but last night's news made me wonder just how many of them *could* be evil. . . . You see, that place they raided – I used to work there, I know all about it and that made it sort of personal. . . . I was pretty upset. But I can't imagine *you* being evil, somehow. So you've restored my belief that people like the Angels of Lucifer aren't typical witches. I'd like to think that *you* are.'

Moira smiled. 'Thanks. . . . We're not saints, you know – and God knows what we may have to do to survive if things get worse. But we won't "go black", if you know what we mean by that.'

'I think I do. . . . *Did* the Angels of Lucifer kill Ben Stoddart – by black magic, I mean?'

Moira did not feel ready, yet, to say that they knew the identity of the Angels, so she countered with: 'Do *you* believe it's possible?'

Eileen paused, then said 'A couple of weeks ago I'd have doubted it. But this would make *two* coincidences, so I'm not sure any longer.'

'Two coincidences?'

Eileen told them the story of May Groombridge and the witches of Coddenham. 'That policeman deserved what he got – but *if* they did it – and I know they believe they did, and I think I do too. . . . If they did it, they've only put him where he can't do any harm for a while. And after what he had done to May, that very day, I suppose they were pretty restrained. But *killing* someone, deliberately and impersonally . . .' She shuddered. 'No. That's different.'

'Quite apart from the morals of the thing, it was damn stupid,' Angie said briskly. 'All it did was make things worse for the rest of you. Like getting *your* houses burned. . . . What are your plans, now?'

'Immediately?' Dan replied. 'Find somewhere isolated to rest up for a day or two. After that, with any luck, find somewhere where we can stay put. . . . Something worse than Orders in Council's on the way. Some kind of breakdown – probably to do with these earthquakes and from what you were saying, you know more about that than we do. Whatever it is, we don't know if we can survive – but we're going to have a bloody good try.'

'And the Welsh mountains seemed a good place to do it,' Greg added.

'Why d'you think *we* are here?' Angie asked. 'Same guesswork and same reasoning – *and* same "bloody good try". So why don't we join forces? . . . No, don't answer right now – talk it over among yourselves. Eileen and I will, too – after all, I haven't asked her yet. Just my own idea but there's a lot to be said for it. Pooled resources give us a better chance. More people means division of labour, less wasted effort. Communal cooking and so on. Easier look-out roster, if it becomes necessary. *We* can contribute one trained nurse, and – if I may say so – one highly experienced camper; been my hobby all my life. *You* can contribute – among other things, I'm sure – two strong-armed men, one of 'em a professional mechanic. . . .'

'And the liability of one eighty-year-old woman and one four-year-old child,' Sally pointed out.

'For Christ's sake,' Angie told her, 'a survival group's got to be a human family – a representative sample, if you like, something *worth* preserving in terms of human balance. You and little Di help to make it that. You're assets, not liabilities.'

Moira's mind had been made up before Angie had even put her suggestion, which she had sensed was coming; but with that last remark, she knew Angie had the others as well. She smiled and asked: 'Does anyone really *want* to talk it over privately?'

There was an immediate chorus of 'No', and Dan went on: 'It's a marvellous idea and it'll obviously improve our chances. We'll probably spit at each other sometimes but that's "human balance" too, isn't it?'

'Right, then,' Angie said. 'Practicalities; any of you know this area?'

'Where are we now, exactly? Our map-reading was getting a bit bleary-eyed. A few kilometres west of Llanfyllin, aren't we?'

'That's right.'

'Rosemary and I toured around here a year or two back,' Greg said. 'We seemed to remember some promising Forestry Commission land ahead, just south of Lake Vyrnwy. Thirty or forty square kilometres of it, by the map, nice and mountainous but with little valleys and streams and that, and it looks as if there might be clear patches hidden away here and there, where we could plant vegetables, if we stayed. And forestry plantations are marvellous to disappear into if you're attacked. . . . All guesswork from map-reading, though. We visited Lake Vyrnwy on that tour but we didn't explore the forestry bits.'

Angie nodded. 'We had the same idea though I don't know it personally either. I think the plantations have been extended in the past few years which'll make it even better. Dyfnant Forest, it's called. Shall we take a look, when you've rested a bit?'

'I don't know about the others,' Moira said, 'but that

breakfast's set me up – *and* meeting you. I *feel* rested. Sally and Di could sleep on the way. . . .'

'Like hell I'll sleep,' Sally protested. 'I want to be in on this. I snored most of the night, didn't I?'

Dyfnant Forest was dark, silent and reassuring, hugging the Afon Vyrnwy and Afon Cownwy rivers between precipitous ridges, and spreading out westwards into equally lofty but more gently sloping mountains. The little convoy wound upwards through a village called New Dyfnant, which Angie (comparing a recent map and an old gazetteer) decided must have been built about 1990. From there the road became a logging lane which they followed for four or five kilometres until they rounded a shoulder of the valley and suddenly found themselves in a little clearing, perhaps six hectares of natural meadow along the edge of which ran a trout-promising stream. It formed a perfect cul-de-sac, because the far end was a cliff with a waterfall tumbling down it; at the near end, where they had stopped, the logging lane elbowed sharply right to hairpin back up the mountainside above the way they had come. The stream lay to the left of the clearing, with steep and broken mountains rising from it – not quite cliff but too rough for plantation, so that a mixture of deciduous trees grew wild. The slope up from the right of the clearing was a little gentler and thick with ordered ranks of Norway spruce, their Christmas-tree fingers pointing to the sky.

Spontaneously, they all switched off their engines and climbed out to look.

'It looks so right,' Sally said after a few seconds, 'I'm almost suspicious of it.'

'Whatever for?' Angie demanded. 'It *is* right. Couldn't be better. What do you think, boys?'

'Looks good to me – provided that meadow's not boggy or liable to flooding,' Dan said.

'Not on your life – I know bog when I see it. And the stream'd have to rise a good metre and a half to top those banks. . . . Look, the meadow slopes up to the right a little, too. Sort of flat shelf along the edge of the trees – make a good camp site.'

'No reason why we shouldn't camp here for a day or two, anyway,' Greg said. 'We can recce the place while we rest up.'

Diana had been asleep when the convoy stopped but now she suddenly said from behind them. 'Yes, do let's recce the place. It's ever so pretty.'

Everybody laughed and Angie asked: 'And what does "recce the place" mean, young lady?'

'Put the tents on it, of course.'

'Orders is orders,' Dan said. 'Come on, let's get cracking.'

They drove carefully along the edge of the trees for a couple of hundred metres, watching the surface but it remained good. Then they reached a feature that had been invisible from the logging lane – a re-entrant in the forest, a little bay in the tree-line, that curved back in an approximate semicircle embracing about a hectare.

'Even better,' Greg said. 'Can't be seen from the lane. But I wonder why it's not planted?'

Examination of the ground answered him. The floor of the re-entrant was thin soil on a flat bed of rock which extended out into the edge of the meadow to form the shelf Angie had noticed; a freak of stratification unsuitable for tree-planting but ideal for a camp-site. They parked the vehicles by the trees at the mid-point of the semicircle and erected the two big frame-tents and the inflatable igloo tent, in front of them at either side, to form a C-shaped, inward-facing laager. The sun was higher now, the shadow of the opposite mountain moving away across the meadow like an ebbing tide. Dan and Greg went to erect the screen for the chemical closet, just out of sight in the trees, while the women furnished the tents, unpacked stores from a big plastic dustbin so that it could be used for rubbish, spread bedding to air, began to plan the midday meal and generally 'made the place like home' as Rosemary put it. Moira noticed, without comment but with a lifting of the spirit, that there was no hint of nostalgia in Rosemary's remark and that everyone – including herself – took it quite naturally. This isolated and beautiful spot had achieved, for the moment at least, what they had instinctively looked for; an immediate change of scene so complete that Staines, the witch-hunt, their burning homes, seemed distant and unreal. She noticed, too, that nobody had switched on the radio, or Angie's television, to keep track of the news – a rest, too, from that.

A shot rang out in the woods and they all froze in what they were doing, the talk and laughter cut off.

Dan and Greg ran back and fetched the pistol and the shotgun and stood looking around, wary and silent. Angie appeared in the door of her caravan, with the .22 rifle in her hands.

'For heaven's sake,' Sally cried. 'It's somebody hunting. What are we all scared of?'

They all relaxed a little. Sally was obviously right and the startling report became natural in retrospect.

'Lot of townies, aren't we?' Rosemary laughed, a little nervously.

Dan said: 'All the same, we might as well start as we mean to go on. Weapons handy but out of sight – and one of us always close to them. Angie, are you a good shot?'

'Very good,' Angie told him calmly, patting her telescopic sight.

'Right – stay in your caravan; you're our armed guard for the first stint. And at night, we'll always have one sentry awake – two hours each, on a roster.'

Nobody argued. Moira felt her stomach tighten and realized it was only partly fear; there was an element of excitement in it – an atavistic tingling of the nerves. *This is no holiday, this is the tribe and the tribe must survive – we must learn the ways. . . .*

More cautiously, they all went back to work – except for Angie, shadowed and watchful in her caravan. After a while they began talking again, in low voices.

'Listen!' Greg snapped suddenly.

They all heard the footsteps for a second or two before the young man stepped out of the forest edge. He had a double-barrelled twelve-bore, broken open, in the crook of his arm and he carried the body of a grey squirrel in his other hand.

'Hullo!' he called cheerfully, and came towards them.

Nobody spoke for a moment as he approached. He looked from one to the other, smiled a little shyly, and laid the twelve-bore on the trestle table they had set up in the middle of the laager. The gesture was so deliberately peaceful that it broke the spell.

'Hullo,' Dan said. 'Sorry if we seemed nervous. Are you Forestry?'

'That's right. My name's Peter O'Malley. Don't apologize – a lot of people are feeling a bit nervous at the moment.'

'We've just got a kettle boiling,' Moira said. 'Would you like some tea or coffee? We're making both . . . Or there's a can of beer.'

'Coffee'd be fine, if there's some going.'

He looked in his middle twenties, lean and black-bearded, about a metre seventy-five tall; his jeans, tee-shirt, bush-jacket and soft boots suited his unself-conscious Celtic good looks. More of a young poet than a forestry worker, Moira thought, and then wondered why she had thought of it as a contradiction.

'Why did you shoot that squirrel?' Eileen asked unexpectedly and there was an edge to her voice that made Moira wonder.

'My job, I'm afraid, or part of it,' Peter O'Malley told her. 'I'm not responsible for the timber, directly, though I keep my eyes open for anything wrong, of course, just like the others. . . . No, I work for the Forestry Commission but my job's ecology. Animal population census, protecting rare species, watching for disease and so on. Culling, where necessary. Like this little chap. There's been a bit of a population explosion of grey squirrels in Dyfnant Forest this year and they're destructive buggers.'

'Like man,' Eileen said.

'Yes, like man. But you can try to teach man, or even put him in jail or fine him if he won't learn. You can't with grey squirrels, can you?' He flashed his shy attractive smile at her.

Eileen looked a little ashamed of herself and said: 'Sorry, I was rude. I hate killing things, that's all.'

'Do you think I don't? But if protecting the other species means I've got to cut my grey squirrel population by thirty per cent, then I do it – and if it makes you feel any better, I never wound 'em, I shoot 'em dead, first time.'

'Actually, we're just cooking up lunch,' Moira interrupted to save both of them further embarrassment. 'Why don't you join us? After all, it's your forest.'

Peter grinned his thanks. 'You know, I think I'll take you up on that. I get tired of cooking for myself.'

'And of your own company? It must be lonely up here sometimes.'

'Oh, I don't mind that. But yes, it's nice to see people now and again. Often I don't for a couple of weeks or more at a time.'

'Not even your own colleagues?' Dan asked.

'Not around here much, this summer. There's no planting or felling going on in this section right now. Nearest is two, three kilometres away – and even that's finished for the year. They're felling still below New Dyfnant.'

'Is that out of your territory?'

'Oh, no – I cover the whole forest. But I base myself in one section each year, study that intensively and just keep an eye on the rest. I've got my trailer about a kilometre away, back there off the logging road you came up. I'm your nearest neighbour.' Again the smile. 'In fact, your only neighbour, till the village.'

Dan asked 'Is it all right if we camp here?' He asked it naturally, but Moira knew his question was less casual than he made it sound.

'Sure, as far as I'm concerned. People do sometimes, though you're the only ones this summer. Just don't light a fire within about fifty metres of the trees or at all if there's much of a wind. And never leave it unattended.'

'We'll be disciplined, I promise you.'

Peter hesitated, and then asked: 'How long are you here for?'

'Oh . . . we hadn't decided. A while, anyway.'

The young ecologist looked from face to face, shrewdly. 'Even up here, I listen to the news. I've been kind of expecting someone like you.'

'Like us?'

'Shall we say – people who can guess which way things are going? . . . Oh, don't worry. I . . .' He seemed shy again. 'Well, ecologists don't like mass hysteria. And I'm constitutionally inclined to mind my own business. . . .

Look, if anyone does come up here – and once in a blue moon they do – tell 'em Peter O'Malley said you could camp here. I'm in well with my boss so you'll be all right.'

'You're a pal,' Dan told him, and Moira, on an impulse, leaned over and gave him a quick hug.

Peter cleared his throat awkwardly but looked pleased. 'Got to earn my lunch, haven't I?'

They all laughed and got on with preparing it.

Later, when he was briefly alone with Dan, Peter said: 'I may be talking out of turn and I'm not asking questions – but if things *do* break down . . . That meadow there and the stream . . . Well, the stream's full of trout – and the meadow's lovely soil. Should grow vegetables well.'

Dan was silent for a moment. 'We do happen to be well-stocked up with seeds – just in case, you know. And we've got rods and tackle. . . . The seeds can wait for a bit, while we see how the cat jumps. But we might as well get the rods out. I'm very fond of trout.'

'Are your guns licensed?'

'What guns?'

Peter just grinned. 'Forget I asked. But there's plenty of rabbit . . . Only one thing – there's a pair of peregrine falcon nesting over the cliff up there. It's their second season and there haven't been peregrine in Dyfnant Forest since 1987. Disturb them, and I'll be after your scalp, in person.'

It was Dan's turn to grin. 'Show me exactly where and we'll put their patch out of bounds. If any of our lot go near them, *I'll* have their scalps – never mind you.'

'Loner I may be,' Peter said. 'But people like you I can do with as neighbours. Look after those seeds, won't you?'

They all slept for two or three hours during the afternoon, except for Angie and Eileen, who had spent the night before in their own bunks and did not need extra rest.

When they got up again, they found Angie and Eileen had been collecting firewood, of which there was plenty lying around without any necessity of cutting. The weather was very warm for August but they lit a fire in the evening, well clear of the trees. Greg took a spade and stripped a couple of square metres of topsoil off the rock to make a hearth-pit, edging it with stones. There they cooked their evening meal. They had, between them, a good stock of gas cylinders for their camp cookers and planned to buy more. However it would obviously be wise to hoard these as much as possible for quick boiling of water and bad-weather cooking, so they agreed that camp-fire cooking would be the general rule. Tonight's meal was, deliciously, grilled trout. Dan and Rosemary were both good fly-fishers and two of their assortment of rods were suitable, so at about five o'clock they had taken them to the stream and quickly proved Peter right about it; by half past six they had the necessary eight fish – 'though I doubt if we'll be so lucky when they get wise to us,' Dan said. 'They must have been undisturbed since God knows when.' Rosemary had caught five of the eight and was understandably cocky.

Diana had sulked a little because she had been shooed back to camp after five minutes of running up and down the banks screaming with delight, making success unlikely and casting hazardous, but had forgotten about it when Sally recruited her to help build the fire.

The meal over, they sat around the fire as the light faded, sharing a litre of red wine Angie had bought the day before ('Sorry it isn't hock') and slipping into a half-serious debate on what they should agree to call their meals, to avoid confusion.

'English is a daft language that way,' Sally complained. 'Lunch at midday and dinner in the evening is middle-class; dinner at midday is working-class, and in the evening it may be tea or supper according to where you live. French is much more sensible – everyone knows what you mean by "déjeuner" and "dîner". And German *says* what they are "Mittagessen" and "Abendessen".'

'Oh, but English is more complicated than that,' Dan said. 'It's not *just* a class thing. A London working man'll talk of "dinner" and "tea" at work and at home, but if he takes his wife to a restaurant he'll call it "lunch" and "dinner".'

'Period differences, too,' Angie pointed out. 'Dinner has shifted about, over the centuries. . . . But it's always tended to be the *main* meal. So since it looks as though our main meal's going to be in the evening, when work's over and we've all settled down – I suggest we call that dinner and the midday one lunch. Sorry if it sounds middle-class but at least we'll understand each other.'

'I don't mind being thought bourgeois,' Greg conceded, 'as long as I get a solid working-class breakfast.'

'Who are you kidding?' Eileen asked. 'My father was a railway porter, so I reckon that makes me working-class. And *my* breakfast's a cup of coffee and a biscuit.'

'It wasn't this morning.'

'That was a special occasion.'

'Couple of months of this sort of life,' Dan said, 'and we'll *all* be wanting a real breakfast.'

With mock solemnity he put it to the vote, and Angie's suggested nomenclature was duly adopted. Moira found herself strangely pleased by the apparently trivial exchange, if only because everybody had so easily entered into the fun of it; the ability to share such nonsense cemented the tribe. . . . Come on now, she told herself, don't get so analytical! But the feeling remained.

The time came to put Diana to bed, in her little inner

'room' of the tent. She put up a show of reluctance but in fact could hardly keep her eyes open, and Dan, who had a way with bedtime stories, managed to settle her down and she was fast asleep with the story half told. Dan and Moira rejoined the others round the fire; a contented silence had fallen on them all and a bright first-quarter moon was transforming mountain, forest and meadow.

After a while, Rosemary said quietly: 'What a night for a Circle.'

'We're not all witches, now,' Moira said. 'We'll have to hold our Circles when we're not putting Angie and Eileen out.'

'You do your own thing as and when you want to, my dears,' Angie told them. 'You want to dance round the fire, or something, you do it. I'll go and baby-mind Diana – and Eileen can read a book or knit a sock or whatever.'

They protested politely but Angie firmly withdrew, taking Eileen with her. Eileen disappeared into the caravan and Angie settled down in a camp-chair by Moira and Dan's tent where she could hear if Diana woke. Ginger Lad (who had spent the day exploring and approving the camp site) climbed into her lap and purred.

She watched, with half-sleepy interest, while the two young couples and the old woman set up their Circle with the fire as its centre, some fifty paces from where she sat. Tightly packed as their vehicles had been, they obviously regarded their ritual equipment as essential baggage, for Dan fetched a hamper from the car and took from it various objects including a cloth which he used to transform the hamper into an altar, placing it to the north, which lay towards the tents and the forest of spruce. They stood three candle-lanterns around the Circle at the east, south, and west points and three more on the altar with other things which Angie could not distinguish at that distance, except for a chalice and an incense-burner and a couple of bowls. A light sword flashed firelight as Moira laid it at the foot of the altar. When everything was ready, the four younger ones took off all their clothes. Angie wondered if old Sally would too, and was amused to hear snatches of an exchange between her and Moira in which Sally wanted to strip – which, Angie inferred, she always did indoors – but Moira forbade it. Sally appeared to grumble, briefly, but remained clothed. Youngster or not, Moira's authority as High Priestess was obviously accepted.

Moira picked up the sword and began to walk clockwise round the Circle.

'O thou Circle; be thou a meeting-place of love and joy and truth, a shield against all wickedness and evil. . . .'

Moira's voice came clearly to her in the still air but after a while Angie stopped listening to the words themselves, finding herself caught up in the magical atmosphere of the scene and the dignified intimacy of the ritual. It was almost as though the mountains and the forest had moved imperceptibly inwards, watching and uniting with the focal fire and the young and old bodies that moved around it. The coven had linked hands now – not in a full ring, because the five of them could not quite reach each other round the fire, but in a circling chain with Moira at its head, chanting in quiet chorus:

> *'Eko, Eko, Azarak,*
> *Eko, Eko, Zamilak,*
> *Eko, Eko, Cernunnos,*
> *Eko, Eko, Aradia . . .'*

Then Angie saw two things, simultaneously; Eileen walking naked from the caravan towards the Circle, and Peter

O'Malley watching, motionless, from the edge of the forest. Moira saw Eileen coming and smiled, breaking away from the circling group to pick up the sword and sweep it anti-clockwise over a part of the perimeter as though opening an invisible door. Eileen ran through it, Moira closed the 'door' with a clockwise sweep, and Eileen was circling with the rest.

Angie looked across at Peter, wondering what he would do.

'By all the power of land and sea,
By all the might of moon and sun . . .'

Unhurriedly, Peter took off his clothes and laid them by the forest edge. Then he, too, walked across to the Circle like a young bearded Pan, and waited outside it. Moira was still smiling, and picked up her sword again to admit him as she had Eileen.

Seven of them were enough to encircle the fire and the ring closed.

Angie was spellbound; the circling bodies, moon- and fire-lit, seemed like nature-spirits, as much creatures of earth, air, fire and water as the wild landscape within which they moved. She wondered how long it would be before she, too, was irresistibly drawn in. The thought scared her a little and she drew back from it, but the magic still held her. The chanting became wordless, one with the distant rushing of the waterfall, the crackling of the fire and the secretive forest-sounds.

It was almost a shock when Moira spoke, her words unmistakably human again. She had halted before the altar with her arms raised, a tall fire-bronzed nymph about to call on the powers that created her, while the others ranged themselves behind her, suddenly still after their ring-dance.

Moira's voice was not loud but it seemed to flow through Angie and past her into the depths and heights of the forest and into nameless regions beyond.

'O Great Mother, thou who are called in this land Cerridwen of the rich earth and Arianrhod of the infinite sky, hear us! Let us be at peace in this place, at one with thy creatures and at one with thy mysteries. Nourish us at thy cauldron of abundance and immortality, O Cerridwen; teach us thy heavenly wisdom, O Arianrhod of the Silver Wheel. We invoke thee to aid us and we invoke thy consort, the Horned God of the Forest, to protect us and strengthen us; for we are all your creatures, we of the Craft and our friends also; and into your hands, our Mother and our Father, we place ourselves. Hear us, and grant that we may hear you. So mote it be!'

'*So mote it be!*'

Wide-eyed, Angie saw, but could not believe, that the High Priestess and her followers stood within a sphere of pale, shimmering violet that domed above them and completed itself (she knew but could not see) in the dark rock beneath them. And from forest and mountain came a deep sigh of acceptance, a wind that was not a wind, limitless yet living; it embraced the sphere and all within it, sweeping over Angie too, leaving her breathless and blind. She lost herself in that living wind for a time that had no measure.

Then, slowly, the moonlit landscape took on form around her once more. How long she had been entranced she could not tell, but Moira and the others stood around her now, clothed and smiling and human.

Moira asked without anxiety: 'Are you all right, Angie?'

'Yes . . . yes, I'm all right. What did you *do* then?'

'*I* didn't do it. It's there all the time. We just spoke to it – or to Her and Him, rather.'

Angie had no words.

Peter stood on the edge of the group and said: 'Thank you, all of you. I'll be off home now. Good night.'

They chorused 'Good night, Peter,' and he waved and left.

'I think it's time for bed,' Moira said.

12

As August moved towards September, the little group settled in and established a routine. In one sense they were in a difficult position; if what they all spoke of as 'the breakdown' (without being sure quite what it meant, but sharing the premonition) had already happened, they would have done many things such as starting to cultivate the meadow, even cutting timber to build winter shelters; but until then, they had at least to appear to be camping holiday-makers. Peter's permission would suffice if one of his Forestry Commission superiors came their way but if they had obviously made any move towards permanent settle-ment, they would land Peter himself in trouble for having allowed it.

They could, however, stockpile supplies, and Peter, now thoroughly in their confidence, helped in two ways. He showed them a logging road which bypassed New Dyfnant, so that they could come and go without drawing attention to their continuing presence; it was a good five kilometres longer but worth it. And he showed them a cave in the spruce forest, a few minutes from the camp but invisible to anyone who did not know the plantation intimately, where stores could be hidden. It was too irregularly shaped to be considered as living quarters, but for dry storage it was ideal, and from every shopping sortie they brought back more things to put in it: gas cylinders, potatoes by the sack, polythene sheeting, extra bedding, clothing, canned food, petrol whenever they could buy jerrycans, though these were becoming very scarce. . . . They had second thoughts about storing petrol in the cave and began burying the jerrycans instead.

Money, strangely enough in the circumstances, was no problem yet; they had hundreds of pounds with them in actual cash and Dan, Moira, and Greg had banker's cards, though they were reluctant to use them locally in case they were on any official 'wanted' list and their bank accounts were being watched for clues to their whereabouts – unlikely as yet but not impossible. But there was no point in hoarding money which might suddenly become worthless so they pooled it, and trusted whoever went on shopping sorties to spend it wisely. Buying gas cylinders without handing in empties, for example, was a highly expensive way of stock-piling gas, but they agreed it was worth doing. Greg, nosing round a dealer's yard in Welshpool, came home proudly with a second-hand rotovator and an even more second-hand chain-saw, which he had picked up very cheaply and was confident he could put in working order; these would be worth their weight in gold to get a per-manent settlement started and gave an additional incentive to stockpiling petrol – so they took to emptying the jerry-cans into more easily obtainable polythene containers, technically illegal for petrol storage but quite usable if sealed and buried with suitable care and well dispersed. He also bought a drum of twin-core flex and a lot of twelve-volt bulbs, an almost-new car alternator and various bits of junk out of which he planned, when the time came, to build a waterfall-driven battery-charger so that the camp could have wired lighting.

Eileen's needs, as camp medical officer, received particular attention; she drew up lists of stores and of reference books, which they bought for her as quickly as they could.

The shopping sorties were made daily, on a careful plan. Several towns within an hour's journey were visited, but never twice running, and as far as possible by different people. The one thing they did not want was for their faces to become familiar anywhere locally. They all agreed that Angie and Eileen who had both deserted security-classified jobs were better kept entirely out of sight (in addition to which, Eileen the nurse was too precious to risk) so they stayed in camp. So did Sally (though protesting) because of her age, and Diana because she did not understand enough to guard her tongue in front of strangers. This – apart from Peter, who helped a lot during his own shopping trips – reduced the shoppers to Dan and Moira, Greg and Rosemary. There was no real need for them to go in couples, but they did because they were determined to sink or swim together. If they ran into trouble, they preferred to do it as a pair, rather than face the unbearable possibility of one of them failing to return and the other being left both ignorant of his or her fate and helpless to do anything about it. In Dan and Moira's case, this meant a further distress – the possibility of not returning to Diana; but at least Di had grown up with Greg and Rosemary all her life and if anything happened to her parents they would treat her as their own and Di's own distress would be softened. All the same, Greg and Rosemary insisted on taking the bigger share of the trips and confining Dan and Moira to what Greg called 'the town-frequency requirement'.

Their insistence, voiced round the camp fire one evening while they were discussing the next day's work, brought into the open for the first time the question of leadership – and surprisingly, it was Eileen who put it into words. Dan was sticking out for an equal sharing of the shopping sorties when Eileen entered the argument.

'I think Greg's right,' she said, 'for another reason, too. An army doesn't put its generals at risk, if it's got any sense.'

'What do you mean?' Dan asked, a little startled.

'Well, let's face it – we've organized ourselves more or less spontaneously so far. But Dan and Moira have been the real leaders.'

Dan and Moira both protested but Eileen went on: 'You have, you know. Greg's the clever one with material things, making things work, knowing where to dig and that. Sally and Angie talk common sense at us when the rest of us get things out of proportion. Rosemary's a genius at turning a field and a pile of luggage into a home and making it *feel* like one. Me, all right, I'm camp MO. But whether we're witches or not, Moira's our High Priestess and whatever power it is that makes a priestess, she's got it and we need it. And Dan – he's sort of captain of the ship. He sees what to do while the rest of us are still wondering. And *I* think he's right oftener than the rest of us – and in an emergency he'd be right *quicker*. . . . We're a sort of family already, not a dictatorship. But there are going to *be* emergencies and I think we should agree, now, who to look to when somebody's got to take charge. . . . We can always talk things out round the fire and tell him if we think he's wrong afterwards. But I vote we elect Dan our Captain and Moira our Priestess. And because we need them, we don't let them risk their necks more than they have to.'

It was a very long speech for Eileen and Moira had the feeling she had been preparing it in her mind for days. When she stopped, everyone started speaking at once, and all in her support. Before they knew where they were, Dan and Moira were elected.

They both expressed their thanks, with more embarassment than they usually experienced. It was not till some minutes afterwards that Moira realized that Peter, unobtrusively companionable on the fringe as he so often was these evenings, had not opened his mouth.

'What do *you* think, Peter?' she asked.

'Me? Well, it's not my business, really; it's for you to settle. But Eileen's right, of course.'

Somehow, his quiet but unequivocal endorsement meant a iot to Moira. It meant a lot to Eileen, too, she knew; it had not escaped her notice that Eileen was always following Peter with her eyes and averting them quickly when he looked her way.

Eileen had made one other precise contribution to the group, in the first twenty-four hours. She had told them about the Dust and the vinegar masks, and taken daily care to see that gauze and vinegar were on hand and that everyone knew where they were; and she had included Peter in her insistence, as soon as they got to know him. Typically, Greg had introduced technical improvements; on his first shopping sortie he had bought a dozen cheap rubber hot water-bottles and a supply of cotton wool, and had designed simple but efficient vinegar masks from them, tailor-cut to fit each face snugly – including a little one for Diana. They were held on by straps and left both hands free.

Among the routine drills which Dan instituted was a roster for listening to every radio news bulletin – and (once Greg had rigged an aerial to get at least some sort of reception in this mountain-ringed valley) the TV bulletins on Angie's little set as well. The news they found almost unrelievingly depressing. Anti-witch riots were reported from somewhere almost every day and although the figures were always vague, it was obvious that more witches were being arrested than rioters – and many others were being arrested on charges of 'practising', several of them people known personally to Moira and Dan. The Crusaders were as active as ever, though no successor to Ben Stoddart had been publicly named; Quentin White remained their public spokesman and was on radio and television two or three times a week.

Of the possibility of further earth tremors there was no mention at all; nor – to Eileen's growing concern – of the Dust or the vinegar masks. As the days went by, the lunatics of Banwell began to haunt her dreams again, more and more. The absence of any announcement became an obsession with her and she tended to hover round the radio at news-time whether it was her duty-turn or not.

'*Why* aren't they telling people?' she cried at the camp-fire meeting one night. 'Does it mean the earthquake danger's past? Or does it mean they know just when it's going to happen and they're going to give instructions a day or two beforehand to cut down the panic?'

'I wish I could believe either of those things,' Dan told her. 'But I can't. I think they're gambling on time – and they don't want to divert people's attention from the witch-hunt.'

'Oh, God. If you'd *seen* those people at the Unit . . . If they keep putting it off, it could be too late – there might be millions like that!'

'I know, love. But there's nothing *you* can do, is there?'

'There is something,' Peter said suddenly. 'Not much, I know – but it'd make *me* feel better, and Eileen too, I think. I could take her down to New Dyfnant and she could tell the people there.'

The suggestion was so unexpected that nobody spoke for a moment. Peter went on: 'I know what you're thinking –

you're trying not to draw attention to yourselves. But I'd better tell you, there are rumours in the village that there's a group of witches up here in the Forest.'

'Peeping Toms?' Greg asked, worried.

'Could be – I haven't been able to pin it down. When I heard the rumour first, I said there'd been a bunch of campers but that they were behaving themselves and doing no harm. It didn't stop the rumours. . . . Don't worry, they're not the rioting kind. Good solid chapel-goers, every one of them. But *if* there were another earthquake and the country went really hysterical about the witches being responsible – well, I wouldn't swear it couldn't infect them too. . . . But say you'd given them a warning about the Dust beforehand and later on an official announcement proved you were right and had been trying to help them – they couldn't help thinking of you as friends, could they?'

'It's the hell of a risk,' Dan said. 'I see your point – but supposing someone reported that Eileen had told them? We'd have high-level fuzz on us like a ton of bricks.'

Peter shook his head. 'I know these people – you don't. And they know me. If I got them to promise not to reveal the source, they wouldn't. Welsh mountain villages can be very secretive, if they want to. Especially if they think it's to their advantage . . . Hell, I *like* them, they're my friends and I want them protected – I'll admit that. But I think I can look at them dispassionately, as well.'

Dan hesitated. 'It's up to Eileen, whether *she* thinks it's too much of a risk.'

'Oh no, it isn't just up to me,' Eileen said. 'We'll all have to agree what to do, one way or the other. If we *all* say yes, I'll go.'

The four men and one woman gathered in the Manse parlour looked very Welsh and rather formidable to Eileen.

She knew Peter had selected them as the key figures of New Dyfnant and she trusted his judgement; but she could not help reacting apprehensively when she saw that one of them was a uniformed constable. However, he was the only one who smiled at her when they were introduced which eased her apprehension a little.

As was almost inevitable in any group of Welsh villagers, two of them had the same name. One, the village council chairman and publican, she found was known as Dai Morgan Forest Inn; the other was the constable, Dai Morgan Police. The Methodist minister was present, the Rev. John Phillips; the village GP, Dr Hugh Owen, seventy if he was a day, but keen-eyed; and a wiry little woman in her forties, Bronwen Jones, who owned the village shop and had already (Eileen discovered later) outlived two husbands. (The second, so the local joke ran, had 'died in childbirth' from the shock of fathering Bronwen's only son.)

Peter startled Eileen by introducing her as Nurse Mary Brown and telling them immediately that that was not her real name. But it taught her that he knew his audience; he himself was obviously known and respected and his use of mystery as an opening gambit went down well – except perhaps with the Rev. Phillips who pursed his lips a little. Peter must have noticed this, for he addressed himself to the minister at once.

'I'll tell *you* her real name privately, Mr Phillips, if you wish, as trustee for the others, so to speak. I'm only trying to protect her because she's come here at considerable risk to herself, out of a simple desire to help the village and very possibly save lives. . . . She's a real nurse, though – I'm sure a few questions from Dr Owen will confirm that if you have any doubts. Until a few weeks ago, she was working in an official job connected with certain after-effects of the earth tremors. That job taught her things which are still being kept secret – things about very simple precautions which could protect people against some very terrible and quite incurable afflictions which would almost certainly be widespread if the earth tremors came back. Nurse Brown has had a very painful struggle with her conscience. She feels strongly that the danger *and* the precautions should be made public – and that to keep them secret, when the earth tremors might strike again at any moment, is an utterly immoral act on the part of the London government.'

Eileen had to admire his careful choice of words; barely perceptible nods confirmed that to brand the 'foreign' capital as immoral struck the right note.

'There's only one thing,' Peter went on. 'Nurse Brown feels duty-bound to pass on her knowledge at least to the people around her. But the law would certainly say otherwise. If the fact that she had spoken out reached the authorities, she would be tracked down and arrested. I think it's very brave of her to come here at all with nothing to gain from it personally and everything to lose. So if she is to tell you what she knows, I am asking you all – and that includes you, Dai Police, in spite of your uniform – to give us your solemn word that you will tell nobody where or how you learned it. To pass the knowledge she gives you on to your people, of course – that's why she's here. But never the *source* of it.'

Eileen could read nothing in their faces during the half-minute silence which followed. Finally Dai Forest Inn asked abruptly: 'Are you a witch, Nurse Brown or whatever your name is?'

In for a penny, in for a pound. 'No, I'm not,' Eileen told him. 'But I've never met any bad ones and I think the persecution of them is un-Christian.'

'Real witch, my mother was,' Dai Police said. 'None of

this "Eko, Eko, Azarak" business, or running around in her pelt. But no harm in the other ones I've found.'

'A thorn in the flesh of the Almighty your mother was, God rest her soul all the same,' Dai Forest Inn snorted, adding darkly: 'Wizards that peep and mutter!'

'I think you overestimate the sensitivity of the Almighty's skin,' the doctor commented. 'Unorthodox Myfanwy Morgan may have been, but I've known times when her herbs succeeded after my pills had failed, and very humiliating it was to me. God will remember her good deeds, eh, John Phillips?'

'It is not for man to anticipate the judgement of the Lord,' the minister replied.

Dai Forest Inn snorted again. 'Now there's cowardly, for a preacher! Have the courage of your convictions, man, and quote to us Exodus XXII, verse 18!'

'About not suffering a witch to live?' the doctor said. 'A mistranslation, many authorities maintain. The Hebrew word means "poisoner", not "witch", they say.'

'Also, since I have been accused of cowardice,' the minister put in, 'I must point out that the new dispensation of the Gospels abrogated certain of the harsher rulings of the Old Testament.'

Bronwen Jones threw up her hands. 'Men! Theological nit-picking they indulge in, when what we are here for is to decide whether this poor girl shall be allowed to help us, out of the goodness of her heart, or be carried off to London in handcuffs for her pains. Ashamed of yourselves, you should be.' She smiled at Eileen. 'Do not pay any attention to them, fach. Disputatious they may be but honourable they are too. If they give you their word, they will keep it.'

'Goes without saying,' Dai Forest Inn protested. 'What is under debate is whether we can honourably *give* our word – not whether we should keep it, once given. The latter is taken for granted. Now I would like to ask the young lady . . .'

Bronwen Jones interrupted him in Welsh. Eileen did not understand a word of it but it went on for at least a minute and was plainly sarcastic and to the point. It made Dai Police smile, the doctor laugh out loud, the minister clear his throat, and Dai Forest Inn blush. Eileen looked to Peter, but he shrugged helplessly.

When she had apparently completed the demolition of Dai Forest Inn, Bronwen turned back to Eileen and said in English: 'Settled it is, then. I give you my word, nurse fach, and so do the others. Let them say so themselves.'

They did, one by one; and Eileen told them about the Dust, the madness it caused, and the simple gauze-and-vinegar masks that would give protection.

When she had finished there was another brief silence. Then the doctor astonished her by asking: 'We've given our word, so don't be afraid. But was it Corwen Emergency Unit you were at?'

'No – I knew about Corwen but I was at another of the same kind. In fact, I only heard about Corwen by accident, when a doctor was transferred from there; I don't know how many others there are. . . . Why, doctor – have you been to the Corwen unit?'

Dr Owen shook his head. 'No one's allowed inside the place. But a colleague of mine at Bala – they whipped away a couple of his bronchitis patients, local people, and he's never seen them since and can't find out about them. It was a couple of days after the tremors. . . . Bears out your story, I must say; not that I disbelieved you, but . . . Oh, my God, what a terrible thing.'

'Nurse Brown . . .' the minister began.

'Roberts,' Eileen corrected him. 'Eileen Roberts.'

He nodded. 'I'm glad you trust us. I would say, on

behalf of this community, that we are deeply grateful to you. We shall see that everyone in the village follows your advice and you may rest secure that your confidence will not be betrayed.'

They all thanked her and there was no doubting their sincerity. Dai Police added that as for her friends in the Forest (about whom he apparently knew more than he had said) he personally would do all he could to see they were left in peace.

'And as for *me*,' Bronwen Jones said, 'I'll see the shop has all the vinegar and gauze anyone will need.' She paused, and then committed herself to the ultimate sacrifice. 'Sell it at cost price, I will.'

An immediate effect of Peter and Eileen's mission to New Dyfnant was that the Forest group became a little less wary of the outside world or at least of their immediate neighbours. A cautious visit by Greg, Rosemary, Eileen and Peter to the Forest Inn one lunchtime showed that they had nothing to fear from the villagers, who somehow managed to imply friendliness while studiously behaving as though they (with the exception of Peter, of course) were strangers passing through for the day. On the afternoon of the following day, Dan and Moira went shopping at Bronwen Jones's little store. Peter was not with them, and although Bronwen passed no comment she gave them all her attention, and after they had paid for their purchases, gave them a bar of chocolate 'for the little girl' – who was not with them either and had not been mentioned. They thanked her and she just smiled and said, 'My Trevor, he'll be about the same age. A beloved exasperation a child, innit?' – and left them to serve the next customer.

Warmed by the encounter, Dan and Moira allowed themselves the relaxation of a drive round the shore road of Lake

Vyrnwy which Greg and Rosemary had told them was beautiful. An artificially-created reservoir almost eight kilometres long, the lake ran from north-west to south-east between steep mountains, the dam at its lower end lying about three kilometres north of New Dyfnant. Another village, Llanwddyn, was in the river valley just downstream of the dam, and they knew from Peter that the people there had been in a very nervous state since the earth tremor. If another worse shock were to breach the dam, Llanwddyn would inevitably be badly hit, possibly destroyed. New Dyfnant was spared that fear at least, being well into the edge of the Forest and a good fifty metres higher than the lake surface. Dan and Moira took the minor road on the New Dyfnant side of the river, avoiding Llanwddyn.

They drove past the dam and followed the south-western shore which lay in the shadow of the mountains while the opposite bank, seven or eight hundred metres across the water, was bathed in sunlight, its reflection cats-pawed by little breezes and punctuated here and there by rings expanding and fading where a fish had jumped. 'Brown trout and rainbow trout,' said Dan, who as usual had done his homework.

'Greg's right,' Moira said. 'This is a beautiful part of the country. If we have to be gypsies, I'm glad we chose here.'

'Yes.'

They drove in silence for a few minutes and then stopped to admire a waterfall feathering and bouncing down the mountain. They were not the only visitors; an elderly cyclist squatted by the roadside gazing up at it, his cycle and rucksack on the ground beside him. They called a cheerful 'Good afternoon' to him, and would have passed on to walk up to the fall but something about the man's laboured gesture of acknowledgement made Moira turn back. The man smiled up at her almost apologetically. Moira noticed his collar.

'Are you all right, father?' she asked.

'Just a bit tired, my dear, that's all. I've cycled rather longer than I should have done today, I think. When the sun shines like this, it's all too easy to forget one is not a young man any more. . . . I'll be fine again when I've rested.'

'I don't think you will,' Moira told him, and turned to call 'Dan! Isn't there a thermometer in the first-aid kit?'

The old priest protested feebly but accepted the thermometer which Dan put under his tongue and stayed obediently silent till it was taken out again.

'Thirty-eight point six,' Dan read. 'Father, we're putting that bike of yours in the car and driving you to the doctor in New Dyfnant.'

'But I'm sure I'll . . .'

'No argument, now. You're ill.'

The priest sighed and said half to himself: 'Back to the habitations of men. God help me, that's what I was running from.'

Moira sat down beside him. 'What do you mean, father?'

'Take no notice of me, my dear, I'm a foolish old man. And a cowardly one, I think. . . . At the moment – and may God forgive me for saying it – I am weary of towns and villages and the stupidity and cruelty of men.' He craned his neck back and looked wistfully up at the mountain. ' "I will lift up mine eyes unto the hills, from whence cometh my help" . . . Perhaps you're right and I am ill. I must certainly sound a bit delirious. I'm very grateful for your help and if it's not taking you out of your way, it would be very good of you to drop me off at a doctor's.'

They put his machine on the roof-rack and him and his pack in the car and turned around to go back to New

Dyfnant. But Moira, who had taken the driving seat, paused with her hand on the ignition key, her intuition nagging at her. She took her hand away again and asked: 'What did you mean, exactly, father? Were you planning to be a hermit?'

'For a while, my dear, yes – I was planning to do just that. To escape to these forests, as I used to do thirty or forty years ago for my holidays when I was a young curate, away from the clamour of men. I've always found it easier to hear God's voice when man isn't trying to interrupt. . . . But it looks as though God has other plans for me.'

'Perhaps not, after all . . . Look, father – we're camping up in Dyfnant Forest, eight of us altogether. One of us is a trained nurse. We could take you back with us and she could look at you. If *she* says you must see a doctor, well, that'll be it, I'm afraid; we'll have to take you to the village. But if she says you'll be all right, why don't you be our guest for a while? We have a little spare tent and you could sleep warm and dry.' She smiled back at him. 'Be a hermit in the forest but with square meals and a fire to sit by in the evenings.'

The old priest gazed at her, speechless, and she went on: 'There's just one thing you ought to know, though. We've run away from the cruelty of man, too. Six of the eight of us – including us two – are witches. I hope you don't mind.'

To her surprise, he almost laughed. 'Witches. How very appropriate! In two ways, actually.'

'Oh?'

'The first way: do you know the parable of the Good Samaritan?'

'Of course.'

'But do you realize the *point* of it? Very few people do, I find. . . . Our Lord always spoke directly to his hearers in language they would understand; he spoke as a fisherman

to fishermen, as a peasant to peasants, as a priest to priests.
. . . And to his audience the striking thing about that
particular parable would be that the Samaritan was a
heretic – a religious untouchable. It would be almost shock-
ing to them – that the one who rescued the afflicted way-
farer and showed his compassion and love was a *heretic*. . . .
You see what I mean by "appropriate"?'

Dan smiled. 'A bit greener than the road from Jerusalem
to Jericho – but I take your point. . . . Come on, darling,
let's get him home. The poor man's shivering.'

Moira started up and asked as she drove: 'What was
your other reason for saying it was appropriate, father?'

The priest sighed. 'That is a longer and sadder story,
I'm afraid. May I save it for that fireside you spoke of?'

Eileen's ruling was that Father Byrne need not see a doctor
unless he failed to improve in the next day or two; but she
vetoed the tent because the site was subject to morning
ground-mist. She and Angie would have moved out of their
caravan and bedded down with the others, to give the
patient a more suitable bunk; but Peter, arriving as the
matter was being discussed, vetoed that in turn. Father
Byrne would sleep in his trailer and he would borrow the
little tent for himself. The old priest tried to argue with
all of them that he was being a nuisance but was firmly
overruled.

'There's nothing in the parable about the man *arguing*
with the Samaritan,' Moira told him, 'so stick to the text.'
Father Byrne was overcome with laughter till he had to be
patted on the back and the matter was settled.

An hour or two later, full of hot dinner and cocooned in
blankets on a camp-chair by the fire, he told them his story.
He had been for many years a parish priest in Liverpool,
and although he spoke modestly of it, they could imagine

that he had been a devout and hard-working one. He had had no more than the usual problems and crises of urban priesthood until the last few weeks because until then his views had not clashed with those of his parishioners. But with the explosion of the witch-hunt, everything had changed.

'Don't misunderstand me,' he said. 'I believe that witch-craft is a mistaken creed. Many good people follow it – and I have no doubt at all that that includes you, my new friends. I believe that in spite of your goodness, you have strayed from the truth. But that is for *you* to decide – and I believe, equally profoundly, that it is against God's law to try to impose a decision on you by legislation, perse-cution, mob violence or the burning of homes. Such methods have been tried again and again over the centuries and they have achieved nothing but the corruption of the persecutors. When this new persecution began, I stood up in my pulpit and condemned it.' He gave a diffident half-smile. 'I can be very vehement when I believe that I am right – perhaps too vehement for wisdom.

'At any rate, I am afraid that a majority of my flock dis-agreed with me. The Crusade stormtroopers – and I used that word in my sermon – are very active in our parish, and I made it clear that Christian or not, they were far worse than the witches because they were motivated by intoler-ance and hatred; and in my experience the witches are not so motivated.' He half-smiled again. 'Maybe that was over-stating it; there are wicked witches just as there are wicked Christians. But in *our* parish, certainly at the time, it was the Crusaders who were guilty of intolerance and hatred – and quite a number of them were members of my congre-gation. As their priest, I had no choice but to say so.'

The smile had disappeared now. He said, wearily: 'I was mobbed outside my own church.'

There was silence around the camp-fire for a while. Then Rosemary asked: 'Did they hurt you?'

'Physically? Oh, nothing much; it was not *that* . . . My curate – and it is not for me to judge him, he is young and fiery, as I was myself once – he disagreed with me, root and branch. To him, the witches were Antichrist, to be stamped out . . . He went to the bishop. And I am afraid the bishop supported him. He told me, in so many words, to watch my tongue.' Father Byrne sighed. 'And so I did, though with difficulty; I believe in obedience though not to the exclusion of all else. . . . I even kept quiet after this latest Order in Council when witchcraft was made illegal. As if you can make conscience illegal! . . . But I could not evade my own conscience indefinitely. A man came to me for confession . . . I could not tell you, of course, in the ordinary way – but he made it public himself. I knew he was a Crusader and had been out at night smashing windows, and worse, and I knew he had every intention of doing so again. I had to refuse him absolution because he was frankly, even blatantly, unrepentant. . . . My curate took him to the bishop who gave him absolution himself and suspended me from my parochial duties. He put my curate in temporary charge of the parish.'

'I don't know the rules of your Church,' Dan said. 'But couldn't you have gone to the archbishop?'

Father Byrne shook his head. 'Whether I could or not hardly matters. The man I'd refused to absolve told the whole story, in public, from a Crusader platform. The audience went straight to the presbytery and smashed up all my belongings. They left the curate's alone. . . . I was out at the time, fortunately, perhaps. When I came home and saw what had happened, I went into my church and prayed for guidance. And the mountains called me – by God's will,

I humbly believe. . . . That was two nights ago. And here I am, my Samaritan friends.'

'*Le cuidiú Dé*,' Peter said quietly. '*Fáilte romhat!*'

The old man's eyes lit up. '*An bhfuil tú o Éireann freisin?*'

'*Táim.*'

'Holy Mother, it seems a thousand years since I heard my native language! . . . Kerry, I'd say?'

'Right, father. I was born in Kenmare. And I recognized your Galway accent as soon as I met you.'

'And if that's not a fitting-exit-line,' Eileen laughed, 'I don't know what is. Take him off to bed, Peter. Nurse's orders.'

Moira and Dan sat in their tent-mouth in the moonlight, long after everyone else was asleep. Neither of them had spoken for quite a while when Dan asked: 'What on earth *are* we gathering together here, darling missus?'

'The Goddess alone knows,' Moira answered him. 'And that's not being pious. I mean it.'

13

'For God's sake, Harley,' Jennings said, 'Beehive Red will be any day now. Which means your experts believe the big quake is any day after *that*. And the big quake means the Dust . . .'

'We don't know that, Sir Walter,' Harley told him. 'The Dust may have been an isolated phenomenon. Several of those same experts believe it was.'

'Isolated? In twenty or thirty places all over Europe, rather more in the States and Canada and however many in Russian and China?'

'So it is suggested. That the Dust was released by the first, untypical, disturbances of the Earth's crust, under pressures which were thus dissipated. Further disturbances will not release more, because although they are expected to be more violent, the pockets of Dust have already been breached.'

'Bullshit. A more violent quake might breach deeper and bigger pockets.'

'Are you a geologist, Sir Walter?'

'No, I'm bloody not. But I know bluff and floundering when I see it. And your experts are guessing. God knows what the next quake may let loose – because I'm sure they don't. Nor you.'

'I will admit that we are having to work on probabilities. And that involves taking calculated risks.'

'With other people's lives? Millions of *my* members – or had you forgotten I'm General Secretary of the Trades Union Congress, in this cosy little power-drunk cabal we've got down here?'

Harley paled with anger. Jennings was notoriously blunt, but 'power-drunk' was overstepping the mark. 'I have not forgotten,' he said icily. 'The Beehive administration – the effective Government of United Kingdom – is the guardian of the *long-term* interests of the people. And they include your members.'

'When men like you start talking about "the people",' Sir Walter snorted, 'I don't know whether to laugh or throw up. I'm cynical enough, God knows, or I wouldn't be *in* your bloody cabal. But you, Harley – you take the cake . . . I wouldn't have reached General Secretary and a flipping knighthood if I hadn't known from way back that people have to be manipulated. But manipulation's one thing – and gambling on their lives is another.'

'I don't see . . .'

'Come off it, of course you see. If your experts are wrong and the Dust gets loose on a big scale – tens of millions of your "people" could go incurably mad, and all because you wouldn't make an announcement about the vinegar masks. . . . Long-term interests, eh?'

'Really, my dear chap – you're talking wildly. "Tens of millions!" The total of incurable inmates of the Emergency Units, since the Midsummer tremors, has been one hundred and three.'

'The total of *inmates*. They're all incurable.'

'Still only a hundred and three. All located, rounded

234

up and isolated, with remarkable efficiency. And next time, even if there should be another Dust outbreak – which, as I said, is regarded as unlikely – our people will be prepared and will isolate the victims with even greater speed. . . . In the present crisis, Sir Walter, we must face the hard fact that the possibility of two or three hundred Dust casualties is less important than the panic and disruption that could be caused by the announcement you ask for.'

'If it *is* only two or three hundred.'

'The considered opinion of my experts – who are not so stupid as you appear to think – is that there will be fewer than that and probably none at all.'

'A moment ago,' Sir Walter pointed out, 'you said "several" of your experts held that view. Are you now saying it's all of them?'

'The ones I find most convincing.'

'But they could be wrong.'

'I repeat – we are having to work on probabilities.'

The TUC man was on his feet now, pacing about Harley's office. 'And *you* have the final decision on those probabilities? . . . Two or three months ago, you seemed to regard the four of us – you, me, Stayne, and General Mullard – as the power behind the throne, the real deciders. "The key minds in the key positions", I think your phrase was. Is it now reduced to *you*?'

'By no means. But somebody has to make the on-the-spot judgements.'

'Involving millions of people? . . . All right, I'm on the spot too, right now. Where are Stayne and the General? What do they think about it?'

'Lord Stayne is at the Glasgow Beehive, conferring with his shipyard people. The General is fully occupied with the Army's preparations for Beehive Red.'

'I repeat – what do they think about delaying the announcement on vinegar masks?'

'In a day or two, they should both be available for a meeting. You can ask them then.'

'Unless Beehive Red intervenes, when they'll be too busy.'

Harley shrugged without speaking. Sir Walter leaned his knuckles on the front of Harley's desk and stared at him with the eyes that had quelled more than one rebellious Congress.

'Do you know what, Reggie boy? I think you regard us as useful yes-men – just like our precious Prime Minister. Well, watch it. I'll work with you, because I think your original idea about "key minds" was a sound one. But *minds*, not bloody string-puppets. You're not God, you know. And I can still pull a few strings myself.'

With that, he left the office. Harley sat for several minutes, his lips pursed. 'Reggie boy', indeed! . . . He had a prudent respect for ability and a shrewd gift for recruiting and exploiting it, but buried deeper within him was an ancestral contempt for the common herd – and Jennings was of that herd, for all his brilliance, his success, his knighthood. It only took one phrase of calculated disrespect to trigger off Harley's atavistic hatred in full flood. He allowed himself to wallow in it for a while and then took himself in hand. This would not do, he could not afford emotional reactions. He would have to watch himself.

And watch Sir Walter Jennings, even more carefully.

If Philip had not noticed the bruises, he doubted whether Betty would have told him. Last night she had (he now realized) deliberately dimmed the light before they went to bed and had undressed and climbed in beside him without turning her back. He had been very tired after a long and physically active day's work and must have fallen asleep at once, but he had wakened briefly once or twice during the night to find her restless, wriggling and rearranging herself as she sometimes did when she had indigestion. He had asked her if she was all right but she had only murmured wordlessly as though she were still asleep.

This morning, when the alarm clock buzzed, she was still heavily unconscious. Philip got up and made tea, dressing while the kettle boiled and then took a cup to her; she liked to be wakened for her tea if she had outslept him. He put the cup beside the bed and, as his habit was, pulled back the covers to wake her by kissing her between the shoulder-blades.

It was then he saw the marks.

With an involuntary gasp, he pulled the bedclothes down further. From shoulders to buttocks, she was marked with blue-black stripes as though she had been thrashed with a heavy cane.

She awoke and turned quickly to face him.

'Who did it?' he demanded. 'Who did that to you?'

'Oh, darling – I hoped you wouldn't see. . . .'

'Of course I'd see! Those bruises'll last for days. Who did it?'

She sat up in bed and reached for her cup of tea. 'I don't know, Phil. I could make a few guesses but what's the point? It doesn't matter who the actual ones were.'

'It damn well matters to *me*!'

'I know, darling. Of course it does. But if you went to Security and complained, what would it achieve? I couldn't *prove* who did it and I'd only be drawing more attention to myself for nothing. Security don't like witch-lovers any better than the ones who beat me up do.'

'Is that what they called you?'

'That's what they called me. . . . It was my own fault,

237

really. I was in the Mess for morning coffee and all the wives' gang were there – about a dozen of them, gloating over the papers, talking their usual nonsense. They'd almost stopped picking on me about the witches recently but this time a couple of them kept goading me. And in the end I'm afraid I lost my temper and told them what mugs they were being, how I thought the whole campaign had been deliberately whipped up and so on. I know – it was simply asking for trouble. . . . Anyway, I walked out and went to the shops. I was carrying a couple of full bags when I came out, otherwise they wouldn't have been able to jump me so easily. . . . It was in that corridor by the baggage store – they must have known that was the quietest place on my way home. . . . Anyhow, they pounced on me out of a doorway and one of them had a gag stuffed in my mouth before I could yell out. There were four of them and they all had scarves over their faces – not that I had time to look at them properly, they shoved a bag or something over my head and dragged me inside the door. . . . Then three of them held me while the other beat me – it felt like a whippy sort of rod or something. . . . They kept saying "witch-lover" at me, sort of croaking as though they were disguising their voices.' Betty gave a strained little laugh. 'All rather melodramatic, really – almost silly, except that they bloody well hurt. I think I almost fainted. . . . Then all of a sudden they dropped me on the floor and ran off. . . . I pulled myself together and came home. I was glad, for once, you didn't come back for lunch.'

'Christ, darling – you *must* know who they were! Tell me and I'll find a way, without Security . . .'

'You will *not*, darling man. It's over – and I'll just make sure I don't go down empty corridors in future. Now – out of the way and I'll get breakfast. I'm hungry if you're not.'

Philip was silent while she set the table and put slices

in the toaster. He took a longer time than usual to shave, struggling to control his anger and think calmly. When he had finished Betty was already seated. He came and sat opposite her, taking both her hands in his.

Involuntarily, he dropped his voice to the whisper they were accustomed to use on their pillow.

'Betty, my love – we're getting out of here.'

She simply said 'Yes' and the matter was settled.

Arranging their escape was less easy than deciding upon it. Philip could get a Surface pass at any time; he had merely to claim that a ventilation intake needed inspection and his chief, the Director of Structural Services, would sign a pass for him. But a pass for Betty was another matter. Beehive personnel who had no official reason for going to Surface were not allowed to leave except in special circumstances – the dangerous illness of an immediate relative, for example – and then only with a Security escort.

There was one possibility and it was a risky one. The first step in it, Philip achieved within two days. He applied at the appropriate office for a Surface pass for an inspection trip and while he was there noticed from which drawer the blank pass was taken and where the rubber stamp was kept. He also remarked to the clerk who dealt with him that the office air-conditioning extractor was unduly noisy, and promised to come back after his inspection trip to take a look at it. He then went to his chief for his signature on the pass and paid his visit to Surface for a quite unnecessary examination of a roof-top intake near Mornington Crescent.

When he got back, he made his promised inspection of the office extractor, which took half an hour because he removed the grille to do it. Cleaning the grille did reduce the noise, so the clerk was quite unsuspicious – and quite unaware, too, that during one of his frequent trips into the next office, Philip had stolen and stamped three blank passes.

So far, so good. Philip was confident he could make a satisfactory forgery of his chief's signature on each of the passes. Meanwhile, Betty was busy altering Philip's spare uniform to fit herself, and sewing 'Maintenance' shoulder-flashes to it. There were women maintenance workers; no difficulty there.

It was the actual passing of the exit-guard that would be dangerous. Betty would be carrying equipment as Philip's assistant and her forged pass would bear a fictitious name. The exit-guard would have no reason to suspect them – unless it happened to be someone who had seen them together as man and wife. To minimize this possibility, they planned to use one of the outlying exits several kilometres from anywhere that Betty had visited. Philip did a reconnaissance, and found an empty room half a kilometre from the exit. There Betty could change, having brought her uniform bundled up in a shopping bag.

If the guard did suspect, he might ask for Betty's identity card; then, of course, they would be in trouble because Philip had found no way of obtaining a blank identity card and would not have been able to put a plasticated colour photograph of Betty on it if he had. But assuming they got past the guard, a pass that tallied with her identity card might be useful on Surface; hence the third stolen pass which Philip made out in her real name.

All was ready at last. There was no point in waiting, so they fixed their escape for the next morning.

On his last afternoon, Philip was busy – of which he was glad; having professional problems to think about kept him from getting nervous. He had to dismantle a filter that was giving trouble with the help of one of his men because it was an awkwardly placed job. They were almost enjoying swearing at the thing and wrestling with it. It had been installed by Philip's own firm and his assistant had worked for their biggest rival, which gave the assistant an excuse for some cheerfully disrespectful sarcasm – to which Philip, equally cheerfully, replied in kind.

Absorbed in their work and their cross-talk, they both jumped and almost dropped a heavy casing-panel when a nearby loudspeaker suddenly bellowed, in their ears:

'*Attention, all personnel. Attention, all personnel. Beehive Red has been ordered. I say again, Beehive Red has been ordered. All personnel with special duties to perform on the ordering of Beehive Red will proceed to them immediately. All other personnel will continue with their normal duties. The following security measures will be observed as from now: exit-guards will double-check all Surface passes that are presented to them, by telephoning the officers who signed them for confirmation that the Surface visits concerned are still essential. Without such confirmation, no holders of Surface passes will be permitted to leave Beehive. I say again . . .*'

Talking far into the night, Philip and Betty still whispered from habit though they were growing hoarse with the effort.

'All that bloody work,' Philip said bitterly, after a couple of hours' discussion had got them nowhere. 'Theft, forgery and hours of bloody sewing. All for nothing. . . . For Christ's sake, I can't sleep. Want some coffee – or a scotch?'

'It had better be coffee. I'd like to get stinking drunk but it wouldn't help.'

Philip turned on the light and got out of bed, stumbling wearily and crossly about the cubicle, burning his fingers on the kettle and swearing. They nursed their cups, sitting side by side on the bed.

'What a future,' Philip said at last. 'Me spending all day clambering about air-ducts, and you trying not to get beaten up, till the big quake comes. And *then*, God knows. Beehive *should* stand up to it but there's no telling.'

'Climbing about air-ducts,' Betty repeated, suddenly thoughtful.

Philip looked at her, puzzled. 'Keep me occupied, at least.'

'No, it's just . . . Darling – how big are those air-ducts?'

'The trunk ones – quite big. Anything from sixty centimetres to a metre seventy-five.'

'All the way to Surface?'

He caught her meaning, suddenly, and said 'Jesus!'

'Well?'

'Hang on a moment – let me think . . . Oh, God, it'd be crazy.'

'Crazier than staying here?'

'Darling, it could take *hours*. . . . I'd have to work it out on my charts, of course – there'd be fans to bypass, filters to get through – it'd be murder. You'd never make it.'

'Could *you*?'

'I guess so – probably – but what good's that?'

'If you could, *I* could. I'm slimmer than you and I'm pretty tough.'

Philip was silent for quite a while before he said: 'We might just make it. You know what, darling? We might just make it.'

Betty took his empty cup from his hands. 'Right, then. Now perhaps we can sleep. And tomorrow, you get studying your charts.'

Two days later, they were ready.

The climb would be very hard work but possible. Even the vertical shafts would be easy to climb because the large ones they would be using were fitted with inspection-ladders. The problems would arise at the filters and fan-installations, of which there were several on the route Philip had planned. Some of the filters could be dismantled and replaced behind them, and all but one of the fans could be bypassed. But however they climbed, there were three places where they would have to emerge from inspection trap-doors into a corridor, and re-enter the duct through another trapdoor on the other side of the obstruction. They could have saved a lot of time by going directly via lift and corridor to the third of these open stretches, but that was ruled out because it could only be reached through areas for which Betty would have needed a special Security pass.

There was only one way to brave the open stretches; Betty must wear her maintenance uniform, and hope not to be seen – or at least not recognized – at those three perilous points.

They could take practically nothing with them apart from their anti-Dust respirators (compulsory at all times, in any case), all the money they had, and such small objects as they could stuff into their pockets. And, of course, the tools in the regulation maintenance kits they both carried – in Betty's case, as part of her disguise.

They debated whether it would be better to make their attempt during the day, or at night. Beehive corridors were swarming with the thousands of new arrivals brought in by the Beehive Red order, during the day; this would make busy maintenance workers less noticeable but on the other hand daytime meant a bigger danger of running into some-one who knew Betty. In the end, they decided that four o'clock in the morning was the least risky time. Very few people would be about and anyone they did meet would surely accept that they were engaged in urgent work on the ventilation system; Philip was, after all, the official judge of that urgency.

Leaving their cubicle was a nervous business. Betty was still in her ordinary clothes, with her uniform in the shopping-bag. If they met anyone they knew, they could have been at a private party – but that shopping bag looked odd, they felt, and they were both very conscious of it. In the event, they met no one in the kilometre walk to the trap-door they needed to start at, but there were still a few anxious minutes while Betty hid in a doorway till Philip had the trap open. They listened and she ran across. As soon as she was up the ladder a couple of metres out of his way, Philip came in after her and secured the trap-door behind them. Fortunately, they could be operated from both sides.

They climbed, against a steady and over-warm downdraught, for about a hundred metres till they reached a horizontal section of the duct. There, awkwardly in a sixty-centimetre space, Betty changed into her uniform – putting her other clothes in the shopping bag which had come with them till they found a suitable place to dump it.

They reached a filter, which took ten minutes to dismantle and replace – ten dirty and choking minutes, for the filter was excessively clogged. Philip caught himself making a mental note to find out why before he remembered that it was no longer his concern.

Just beyond the filter, they came to the first of their three danger-spots. A fan-installation had to be passed by emerging into a dozen metres of public corridor.

'Stay out of sight till I tell you,' Philip whispered, 'and for God's sake keep that torch out.'

He unfastened the trap-door and peered out. The corridor was empty, so he climbed through, propping the trap cover on the floor. Then he walked to the second trap-door and began to unfasten it.

Footsteps.

His heart in his mouth, Philip forced himself to carry on naturally. A man rounded the corner and stopped, looking at him. He wore the police-blue of Security.

'Hullo,' Philip said, without stopping his work.

'Hullo . . . What are you up to, sir?'

'Bloody temperature fluctuations on Level Three. Director got me out of bed. There's something clogging a filter somewhere.'

'Tough. . . . I'd better look at your ID, sir. Routine, you know. But everything's tightened up, since Beehive Red.'

'Sure.' Philip presented his card which not only identified him by name and photograph (a pity) but also gave his status of Senior Ventilation Officer (thank heaven). 'Hadn't the heart to get one of the lads up. They'd only just come off.'

'Thank you, sir.' The Security man gave him back his card and strolled on along the corridor to the other trapdoor. To Philip's horror, he stuck his head inside and pointed his torch about. After a few seconds he pulled his head out again, said chattily 'Never seen inside the ventilation – big, isn't it?', and moved away round the next corner.

Hardly believing their luck, Philip lowered the trap cover to the floor and hurried back to the first trap. When the Security man's footsteps were sufficiently faint, he called softly along the shaft: 'Betty? OK. Hurry.'

She slithered along the duct and joined him. He pointed to the second trap, and without a word she sprinted to it and disappeared.

When both trap-doors were back in place and he was beside her inside the duct, he whispered: 'How come he didn't see you?'

'Because I heard you talking and got back round the bend, stupid.'

'I love you,' he said, fervently.

Danger point number two passed without incident; nobody came near, and they were out and in again quickly. There followed a long and tiring climb, with several more filters to dismantle and replace, and a nerve-racking squeeze past a whirling fan whose bypass door was not really supposed to be opened unless the fan was switched off at the control room. Philip hoped the duty man was not awake enough to notice the temporary drop in air pressure which must be registering on one of his dials.

At last, a mere hundred metres from Surface, they reached danger point number three, the last and worst.

'Now let's recap the drill,' Philip whispered before he began unfastening the door. 'There's a good half-minute walk between this and the other door, so we can't do it like the first two. We have to play this for real, with you as my assistant. Out of this trap and re-close it; then walk naturally to the other one and open it, together. OK?'

'OK.'

He unfastened the trap and climbed out; no one in sight, no footsteps to be heard. He beckoned to Betty and she jumped down beside him. She was very quick with her fingers and working together they had the trap-door re-fastened in seconds.

'Now,' he said, 'Quick but not too quick.'

The first corner; no one. The second corner; no one.

They reached the trap-door and started to release the fastenings, two on each side. Philip had both his open while Betty was still struggling with the second.

'This one's jammed, Phil.'

'Hell!'

He took over and found she was right. It took him a

spanner and three minutes' effort to get it free. Hastily, they lowered the cover to the floor – so absorbed that they were unaware of the woman's presence till she spoke.

'Treasure-hunting, this time of night?'

They both spun round and Philip knew at once that in their surprise they had over-reacted. He managed a grin, and said: 'God, you made me jump, creeping up on us like that. . . . No, blockage-hunting . . .' He repeated the story he had told the Security man, hoping he sounded natural. Betty was behind him, so he could not see her, but he had more faith in her acting ability than in his own.

He had an uncomfortable feeling he had seen this woman before. She wore the shoulder-flashes of the Press Corps; looked, and in her single remark had sounded, American; about thirty-five, short strong fair hair, shrewd grey eyes that watched him. He finished his story, hesitated and then turned to Betty.

'Well, we'd better get in there, if we're ever going to find it.'

Betty moved towards the trap, picking up her maintenance kit and respirator haversack.

'Find what?' the American asked, too casually. 'Surface?'

'I told you . . .'

'And I didn't believe a word of it.' She had picked up the shopping bag before Betty could reach it and pulled out the obviously civilian sweater. 'To coin a phrase – that's no maintenance lady, that's your wife. I've seen you both in the Mess.'

Philip would never have dreamed Betty could move so fast. She was on the American woman like lightning, the edge of her hand slashing at her neck. But the woman was fast, too; she dodged just in time and they grappled. The American was saying 'Hold it, hold it!' as she defended herself, and it was only the fact that she did not shout that made Philip hesitate to use the spanner that was still in his hand. The hesitation was only momentary – he would *have* to use it – but it was long enough for the American to gasp 'For Chrissake – I'm on your side!'

Betty jumped back, watching the other warily.

'In here – quick,' the American said, and threw open a cubicle door across the corridor. For some reason they did as she said and found themselves in what was obviously her own room. She turned and faced them. 'Tonia Lynd, Associated Press correspondent. I know you' – to Betty – 'you're the one they've been calling witch-lover. My job to keep my ear to the ground. So you want out. Me too but my Chief won't give me an exit pass. My Press card will do once I *am* out. So can I come with you up that chimney? Because that's sure as hell where you're going and sure as hell *I'm* not going to snitch on you.'

Betty said 'Yes' while Philip was still gathering his wits. 'I'd feel safer not leaving you behind, just in case you're lying. Get your respirator, money, anything else you need that'll go in your pocket. But no luggage. Come on, then – there's no time to hang around.'

Philip could hardly remember, afterwards, the rest of the climb. All that remained vividly in his mind was the three of them – himself, his wife, and the American stranger – standing at last beside the concealed air intake on the roof of a Stoke Newington factory, breathing the fresh air and gazing out dumbly at the London dawn.

14

'Why are there no buses – or queues at the stops?' Philip
wondered when they had made their way out into the main
road. 'There should be, even this early.'

'Don't you know?' Tonia replied. 'They called a strike,
late last night. They're demanding Dust respirators for all
bus crews.'

Philip halted in his tracks and stared at her. 'Dust
respirators? But how did they know?'

'Holy Moses! Didn't you get the Prime Minister's TV
statement?'

'We didn't watch TV at all last night, or turn on the
radio. We were too busy getting ready.'

'I guess you would be, yes . . . Eight-thirty, it was. He
gave a warning about this Dust that might come up out of
the ground if there were any more tremors. Said you could
protect yourself against it by breathing through gauze
soaked in vinegar. . . . Walter Jennings, the TUC man,
spoke after him. He called on the unions to cooperate –
several factories are going over to producing proper respirators on a crash programme. Meanwhile there's enough
to equip the essential services. . . . That's what the bus

249

strike's all about. They found they weren't on the essential services list.'

They started walking again, towards the Walthamstow Marshes. The Summers' home lay in Leyton, on the other side, and they planned to pick up and stock their car before getting out of London. Tonia, planless after her unpremeditated escape from Beehive, asked if she could go along along with them till she had thought out what to do next.

'Stick with us till you're out of London anyway,' Philip advised her. 'You don't want to be caught in town if there *is* a Dust outbreak. . . . Did the Premier say what the Dust did?'

'Only that it was poisonous.'

'That's putting it mildly. I think I'm one of the few hundred who do know, because of my job. . . . Get the Dust in your lungs and it drives you incurably insane.'

'Jesus!'

'Thank God they *have* given the warning. At least people can get their hands on vinegar and gauze now. . . . If there'd been a Dust outbreak before that, in somewhere like London – within three days, it'd be a city of homicidal maniacs. . . . The Government's known about the vinegar-mask thing for a couple of months. I never could understand why they sat on it.'

'If you ask me,' Tonia said, 'Big Chief Harley was *still* sitting on it. He was away from Beehive last night. I wanted an interview with him for AP – he's been very polite to us, so far – and I managed to waylay him when he got back around midnight. He bit my head off and pushed past me, with a face like the wrath of God. . . . D'you know what? *I* think Jennings talked the Prime Minister into making his broadcast while Harley's back was turned. Only a guess, but it figures.'

'Do you notice something?' Betty said suddenly. 'People don't like these uniforms. They resent us.'

She was right. The steadily thickening early-morning crowds, walking to work through the busless streets, were eyeing them as they passed and the hostility could not be mistaken. Beehive was no longer a secret, that was plain – and somehow Beehive uniforms were recognized.

'I think,' Philip said, 'it would be a good idea if we tried some quieter back-streets. Everyone must know what these respirator haversacks are. We could easily be mugged for them.'

They cut across towards Mount Pleasant Hill. Philip knew there was a footbridge over the River Lea at the bottom of it which would enable them to cross the Marshes without using the Lea Bridge Road bottleneck. One other thing they had noticed; queues were already forming outside shops which would not be open for another hour or two. 'By the middle of the morning, there won't be a bottle of vinegar in any of them,' Philip predicted. 'And after that I wonder what the black-market price will be?'

As they climbed the footbridge over the Lea, they could see Lea Bridge Road a couple of hundred metres to their right. At this time of the morning, the bulk of the traffic should have been westwards towards Central London, but it was unmistakably eastwards. Lea Bridge Road was one of the principal arteries leading out to Epping Forest and the open country of East Anglia. If the eastward flow was building up already, at just after seven in the morning – then the exodus had started. Not a panic as yet, because the flow was moving steadily at a good forty to fifty kilometres per hour. But what would happen when the jam was nose-to-tail, alternately stopping and crawling? How long would tempers stand the strain? . . . Philip was glad they lived on the other side of the two-kilometre-long bottleneck, which was the only road across the Marshes for at least three kilometres north and south. On the Leyton side there were dozens of quiet side-roads which could be taken towards the Forest and Philip knew them like the palm of his hand.

Visiting home, even long enough to fetch and park the car, was dangerous enough, though he doubted if there could be a police call out for him and Betty yet. Staying there (quite apart from their determination to be out of town as soon as possible) would be out of the question; Beehive, he knew, took very prompt action against defectors and by this afternoon at the latest the local police would be alerted.

'Which way now?' Betty asked. 'We can't cross the Canal. It's either Lea Bridge Road or the railway.'

The Canal ran parallel to the Lea river, two or three hundred metres ahead. Crossing it by the road bridge would be almost direct but Philip thought it was better to avoid it. They swung north across the playing fields towards the railway bridge a kilometre away.

After a minute or so, Tonia stopped, her head on one side. 'Did you hear that?'

'Hear what?'

'And feel it. A sort of rumble.'

'Train coming, perhaps?'

'No – I . . .'

Even as she spoke, the great shock-wave threw them off their feet. If they all screamed, the sound was lost immediately in a vast thunder of noise. A fissure suddenly appeared in the ground beside them, widening and shooting out lengthwise as they scrambled away from it. 'Keep together, for God's sake!' Philip yelled. They were still on all fours, unable to stand on the jerking, groaning earth. How long it lasted, they never knew; ten seconds, half a

minute . . . They were too overwhelmed with impressions –
the railway bridge ahead of them twisting and tilting like
soft wax, the crash of falling buildings on each skyline, the
terrible metallic clatter of endless multiple pile-ups on Lea
Bridge Road . . . the deadly grey mist seeping up through
the nearby fissure and Tonia crying out 'Respirators –
quick!' . . .

They fumbled with the black rubber muzzles, holding
their breath while they pulled them over their mouths.
Now we're marked game, Philip thought dizzily – *the law
of the jungle.*

They gazed at each other, stunned by what had happened. It was some seconds before they realized that the
world around them was, briefly, almost silent.

And after the silence the screams began. Screams mounting and multiplying from the carnage on the roads; screams,
more distant, from the shattered bricks and concrete ahead
and behind, where the still-living were trapped and
maimed, and the lucky (lucky?) uninjured struggling to
free them. *In three days they'll be mad. . . .* Philip thrust
the thought away in horror.

'The river – look!'

The two women turned at his mask-muffled voice and
looked. Behind them, surging and tumbling, the River Lea
had burst its banks and was rising inexorably towards them.

They took to their heels, watching for fissures as they
ran. Philip led them obliquely northwards, in a race to
reach the twisted railway bridge before the flood did. They
made it with water lapping about their ankles and scrambled
to immediate safety among the ruined girders. Below them,
by some freak, the Canal bed had drained dry. A giant,
Dust-spewing fissure diagonally across it was a possible
reason but already the floodwaters were cascading over the
wall as though trying to refill it. They whole thing was a

Titan's beach-game, transforming in minutes a landscape that had been familiar to Philip since he was a boy.

He tore his eyes away from it and examined their position as coolly as he could.

The bridge was an X-shaped one on two levels, the Clapton–Walthamstow line crossing above the Tottenham–Stratford one and at right angles to it, each at forty-five degrees to the Canal. Both were now a single mass of wreckage, but the south-easterly line, towards Lea Bridge station and Stratford, looked walkable, and protected by the Canal bed from the floods; the water still seemed to be disappearing into the great fissure. It lay in the direction they wanted to go, so they climbed over the wreckage and followed it.

On the way, they kept their eyes open for weapons. They found a solid iron bar, the rusting front fork from a bicycle and a heavy shovel; with these in their hands, they felt safer. Philip worried about the bridge at Lea Bridge station, where the line passed under the crowded holocaust of a road; would they still be able to get through? The station itself was a relic, long closed down, but . . .

The bridge, when they reached it, had collapsed, but there was still a jagged tunnel of daylight to one side. They approached it carefully, hiding in the empty station, for there were people shouting and running above and still the wails of pain and helpless terror from the injured and the trapped. Once through the gap they ran – not merely to escape the crowds but because to their immediate left the gasworks were burning fiercely and there might be more explosions at any moment.

Their house was in Church Lane, a few hundred metres away across Leyton Marshes recreation ground and through Marsh Lane. It was not until they were in Marsh Lane itself that they came face to face with trouble.

Four youths saw them and one yelled out: 'Bloody Beehivers! Get 'em! Get their masks!'

The four rushed them together – the leader holding a knife as though he knew how to use it. Philip did not wait but made straight for the leader, swinging his iron bar, to put the women behind him. The leader slashed, jabbed, and dodged and once nearly reached him; then a full swing from Philip's bar caught his arm, probably breaking it. He fell to his knees, squealing, and Philip swung the bar again, down on to the youth's skull, feeling the bone shatter.

Philip spun round; Betty had already half-blinded one attacker with a jab from her bicycle-fork and Tonia was wielding her shovel like a battle-axe, holding the other two at bay. Philip disabled one with a blow to the knee and the survivor backed away, wild-eyed.

Philip shouted, 'That's enough – run!' The survivor made no attempt to follow.

Five minutes later they were inside their house, changing hurriedly into civilian clothes – including what Betty could find to fit Tonia. The back wall of the house had fallen away, bringing half the first floor with it, and there was not a window left unbroken. Fortunately the car was still in the lock-up shed round the back and undamaged. They loaded clothes, bedding, tinned food, tools into the car with little time for careful selection and within half an hour they were away, picking a hazardous route along ruined back-streets, eyes open for fissures, back-tracking often, the smell of burning houses in their nostrils, and all the time the crying and wailing, now mostly pitiful rather than terrified. They saw many people but were mainly ignored now that they were out of uniform. They had wrapped scarves round their heads to hide the official respirators – which did not look strange, because everyone who had been able to get hold of vinegar, and many who had not, had muffled their faces in one way or another.

Nobody mentioned the fight in Marsh Lane until they had been travelling a couple of hours and were well out into the Forest near Theydon Bois. Then Philip said dully, through the muffle of his respirator: 'I killed one of them, you know.'

'If you hadn't,' Betty said, 'they'd probably have got our respirators, and then we'd *all seven* have gone mad. Because it was too late for them – they'd already breathed it. Don't brood on it, darling. I put an eye out, too – and killing him would have been kinder, in the long run.'

'And we may have to again,' Tonia put in. 'I don't like it, either – I've never killed anyone, though I damn nearly did back there. But we didn't set this up – and if we're going to survive, there may be other times when it's them or us. Especially when God knows how many people start going crazy. Because if one in ten was ready with a vinegar mask by this morning, I'm a Dutchman.'

Philip nodded and then asked: 'Well, girls – we got out, somehow, and just in time. What do we do now?'

'Find somewhere lonely, fast,' Betty said. 'In *less* than three days. Then hide, hide, hide.'

The thunder of the mountains was majestic, terrifying.

Moira and Dan were on breakfast duty that morning. Dan had put up the trestle table in the middle of the laager, with the camp-chairs around it, and was laying out mugs, plates and cutlery. Moira, having brewed tea in the huge canteen pot Greg had picked up on one of his shopping sorties, was boiling eggs and toasting bread, at the canvas-screened cooker. She was thinking that before September was out they would have to devise a more sheltered kitchen area. Diana, beside her, was carefully unwrapping a half-kilo of butter, talking to it as she did so. Moira could hear

Rosemary singing in her tent as she got dressed and Greg teasing her. Angie and Eileen, in the open door of their caravan, were listening to the tail end of the seven o'clock radio news; it was Angie's news-monitoring day and Eileen always listened anyway – though since the Premier's announcement last night, she need not listen so anxiously. Thank heaven *that* worry's over, Moira thought; now all Britain knows about the vinegar masks . . .

Then the first tremor came and she gasped dropping an egg.

Diana had felt it, too, and asked 'Mummy?' anxiously. Moira snatched her up, instinctively moving away from the cooker. It was just as well she did because a second later there was another, worse tremor, which tumbled the boiling pan of water on to the ground where they had been standing.

Eileen called out: 'Respirators, everybody! Respirators!'

Moira ran to their tent, carrying Diana; Dan arrived a pace behind. Moira was saying hurriedly to Diana: 'Now, darling, this is the time we talked about. We'll all be all right but we *all* have to wear our respirators till Eileen says we can take them off . . .'

'I remember, Mummy. Because the air might make us sick.'

'Very sick, darling. So we'll keep them on and be safe – right?'

Dan was soaking the vinegar-pads with quick, pre-measured amounts and securing them into the masks. They put Diana's on together and had just donned their own when the real quake came.

They clung together, gasping, for what seemed like many seconds while the earth shook beneath them, again and again, and the mountains roared in pain.

Then the shaking was over and the earth was still. But

the thunder of the mountains went on, monstrous echoes flung back and forth as though the Gods bellowed their anger. Diana was crying, the little sound strange and piteous in the rubber mask, while they hugged and rocked her.

At last, into the horizons of infinity, the echoes faded and died.

Cautiously, they stood up, and walked outside.

Nothing in the immediate neighbourhood seemed to have been damaged. The mountains, the trees, the cliff, the waterfall – all looked as they had before, even the tents still stood. Only a few things like the boiling saucepan, two of the camp-chairs and some crockery from the table, had been disrupted. On the meadow the five goats – a billy and four nannies – which New Dyfnant had presented to them tugged and called, careering round on the ends of their tethering-ropes. Of Ginger Lad there was no sign. Every bird in the forest was clamouring and flocks of them wheeled and zigzagged above the valley as if they no longer trusted the earth.

The radio had gone dead. With remarkable calmness – having assured herself that everyone was all right – Angie explored the tuning dial. Nothing on any British, Irish, or French wavelength, all of which she could normally pick up; a Spanish broadcast broke off even as she listened to it; and one German station was babbling away a stream of words which she did not understand but which sounded hysterical. Here and there the clicking whistle of Morse, otherwise nothing.

My God, Angie thought – it's big. Bloody big.

The seven of them gathered together, instinctively well out in the open. They had only just begun to talk, to get their breath back, when Peter's Land-Rover shot round the corner and across the grass to join them, with Peter at the wheel and Father Byrne beside him, both wearing their respirators.

'We're all right but there's damage further down,' Peter told them. 'A big landslide from the Moel Achles ridge – and there's a fissure right down one side of it, with the Dust pouring out. And the wind's this way. We'd better keep these things on till the air in the fissure's clear. . . . Look, do you mind if I tow the trailer round later and we join your camp? I think we'd better be all together.'

They all agreed, of course. While they were talking about it, Peter suddenly cocked his head, listening. They all fell silent. Above the sound of the river they could pick out a deeper, more distant roar.

Rosemary said: 'Oh, please, no – not more earthquakes!'

Peter shook his head. 'No, not a steady noise like that. . . . I'm afraid there's only one thing it can be. Billions of tonnes of water rushing down the Vyrnwy valley – and taking Llanwddyn with it. The dam must have gone.'

It had been a dreadful morning in New Dyfnant. About a quarter of the houses were uninhabitable and few of the rest had escaped some sort of damage; six people were dead, and twenty or thirty – Dr Owen had lost count – sufficiently injured to be incapacitated. The doctor had got around as best he could (a Y-shaped fissure had divided the village into three areas between which cars could not cross) and Dai Forest Inn had turned his saloon bar into a field hospital. Fortunately, everybody seemed to have got his vinegar mask on in time, the uninjured helping the injured; but the Dust had hit the village within minutes and only time would tell if anyone had breathed it. There was one grim exception: Tom Jenkins, an isolated smallholder who had been scornful of Eileen's warning until last night's official announcement and had run-white-faced to the village in search of vinegar twenty minutes after the earthquake struck. Bronwen had supplied him and had summoned Dai Police urgently. Dai had promply locked Tom up; there seemed nothing else to do. He had promised Tom to send the doctor to him but Tom's terrified acquiescence had shown he had little faith in anything that could be done for him now.

Bronwen's shop, by some miracle, had suffered no more damage than broken windows. She had opened up immediately after the quake, pausing only to mask little Trevor and herself, and had served everybody who came whether or not they had money with them. She imposed her own hastily devised rationing system, having no idea when, or if, she would be able to re-stock. Some things, such as gas cylinders and kerosene, she refused to part with at all; the rationing of those might well have to be organized on a community basis. Jack Llewellyn, who ran the garage, was following a similar principle, allowing petrol only to the doctor, Dai Police, the minister and anyone else he decided was obliged to be mobile in the public interest. Electricity had failed immediately, of course, so Jack had to pump manually. He wondered if he would come to regret that his grandfather had changed the Llewellyns' hereditary craft from blacksmith to mechanic.

In all the frenzied activity, the vinegar masks were a great nuisance, hampering movement and producing sore mouths and noses after the first half-hour, but there was no alternative. The Dust was still visible till about ten o'clock, after which a quick reconnaissance showed no trace of it, either from the village fissures or from the bigger one on nearby Moel Achles. Remembering Eileen's two-hour safety margin, Dai Police extended it to two and a half, and passed the word round that the chapel bell would be rung as an all-clear when the masks could be put aside. The

Council had, years ago, installed a siren to give warning of forest fires, the village being surrounded by timber plantations on three sides; it had never had to be used but now it would serve as an alarm if the Dust reappeared.

Overshadowing all New Dyfnant's self-help was the terrible knowledge of what had happened to Llanwddyn. The Vyrnwy river valley, only a kilometre or two downhill from New Dyfnant, was a roaring torrent, full of tumbling wreckage, uprooted trees, dead cattle, smashed cars and the occasional human body. By about ten o'clock, a widening fringe of littered mud showed that the first unimaginable rush from the burst dam was abating. The people of New Dyfnant, almost to a man, had relatives or friends in Llanwddyn or in houses scattered along the valley but there was no way of discovering their fate until the flood was a great deal lower which might be several days. Most of them, if they had survived at all and had been able to reach their vinegar masks, would have escaped the effect of the Dust, for New Dyfnant had spread the word as best they could to their neighbours. But the valley homes had been decimated and the survivors must be tragically few.

With telephones dead and roads flooded or fissured, New Dyfnant still had one almost bizarre point of contact with a few voices in the outside world. Geraint Lloyd, the schoolmaster, was an enthusiastic radio ham, and by common consent he was delegated to stay with his battery-powered equipment and find out what he could. It was little enough. National broadcasting systems throughout Europe seemed to have ceased altogether; Geraint picked up a whisper or two from farther afield but nothing comprehensible – the ether was wild with static beyond his experience. Some police and fire services were still on the air but were obviously doing whatever they could on a strictly local basis. National coordination, for the time being at least, seemed

261

paralysed. Nowhere – at least within the limited range of police-car and similar transmitters – had escaped the disaster, that was clear. Those voices which spoke through respirators were unmistakable and sounded helpless, those without were understandably preoccupied with reporting and avoiding Dust outbreaks.

When he had gathered all he could from these frequencies (he made no attempt to speak to them – what was the point?), Geraint turned his attention to his fellow-hams. He managed Morse contact with three British, two Irish, a Pole, two Frenchmen, a Romanian and a Moroccan – and briefly, during a lull in the static, with a ham in New Jersey. Quite a list in the circumstances, but all of them were obviously doing what he himself was – using their suddenly precious hobby to build up as wide a picture as possible. So their exchanges were brief before they passed on to look for another piece in the jigsaw puzzle.

There was no escaping it; the overall picture was cataclysmic. Everywhere that Geraint spoke to had suffered only marginally more or less than New Dyfnant. One thing he did learn; that Dublin, Bucharest and Warsaw had given the vinegar-mask warning in time for it to be useful, unlike London. (Belfast had done so too, within hours of Dublin – that would have been politically obligatory, Geraint realized, whatever London did. In any case, the two parts of Ireland had developed an increasing *de facto* federalism since the détente of the 1980s.)

His equipment was indeed going to be precious in the months to come. Only one problem; how was he going to recharge his batteries, if mains electricity became a thing of the past?

Brenda Pavitt saw both more, and less, of Reggie Harley as Beehive isolated itself from Surface. Less, in that he was busier, and could rarely spend an uninterrupted evening hour with her. More, in that he now came to her every night, however late he was working or however early he must be up. His need for her was self-centred and never expressed in words, but it was compulsive and Brenda, responding to it, came nearer to loving him in these days and nights than she ever had. She found herself becoming a little afraid of him. Within Beehive, he was moving rapidly into the position of a despot. Nobody called him the Chief Administrator any longer – simply the Chief; and nobody (Brenda sensed) doubted that if it came to a show-down of any kind, the Army under General Mullard was behind him, not to mention Security, which was his own creation and officered by his own appointees.

Brenda, increasingly his intimate sounding-board – though she knew his frankness even with her was selective – had more clues than most to the deviousness of which he was capable. She had been aware for some time that he was cultivating Professor Arklow to the point where he was better informed on the seismological probabilities than the Prime Minister and Cabinet – and she strongly suspected that it was due to Reggie's manoeuvring that Cabinet Ministers had been well dispersed around the regional Hives at the time when the earthquake struck. With the notoriously weak Premier thus isolated, it had been easy for Reggie to persuade him that national cohesion was best served by leaving his Ministers in the other Hives as his 'representatives', and so the Premier was even more firmly under Reggie's thumb.

Then there was the affair of Sir Walter Jennings. Brenda had never seen Reggie so angry as he had been that night, when Jennings had persuaded the Premier to make the vinegar-mask broadcast during his absence. (The US President, who had been hovering on the brink of it himself, agreed after a brief telephone conference to make his announcement simultaneously.) But Jennings, in his padded cell in Beehive's hospital, would never throw another spanner into anybody's works. He had been on Surface on the morning of the earthquake, trying to settle the London busmen's strike and he must have breathed Dust because three days later he was insane beyond all help. Beehive rumour was that his respirator had been faulty. In the whole of the Beehive staff there had been only three victims of 'faulty respirators', and Brenda knew better than to comment on the fact that the other two had also been individuals whom Reggie had found inconvenient. . . . She was personally sorry about Jennings; he had been a regular and intelligent user of her library and she had liked him. But her loyalty was to Reggie and quite apart from her emotional involvement, she was realistic enough to know that survival in Beehive balanced on a knife-edge of loyalties.

It was almost funny, she thought, how Reggie's increasingly open behaviour as oriental despot was nowhere more sultan-like than in his attitude to her. She was his mistress, and far from going through the motions of hiding it, he was now treating her as such in public and expecting everyone to accord her the appropriate respect. It was a measure of the awe in which he was held that people had caught on quickly. She was beginning to understand how Madame Pompadour must have felt.

At some of his manoeuvres, she could only guess, though shrewdly. But as far as facts were concerned, Reggie kept her better informed than most of the Beehive department heads. On the whole, they were given facts on a 'need-to-know' basis; only Reggie, his chosen lieutenants and Brenda had a complete picture. It was, apparently, part of her function as mistress to share his burden of knowledge. He seemed almost impatient to keep her up to date.

His midnight summing-up of that first terrible day had been typical – as concise as though he had been dictating it to a secretary.

'London Beehive's practically undamaged; we've lost about two thousand square metres under Hampstead Heath – but only twelve people killed there, it was still thinly occupied – and a few corridors will have to be reconstructed. About the same at Edinburgh and Norwich, though Norwich is pretty small. Birmingham and Bristol have been virtually wiped out. Cardiff, Manchester, Leeds, Carlisle and Glasgow have all survived and will continue to be operational but they've all lost a third to a half of their personnel. . . . On the whole, satisfactory. We were prepared for worse. Beehive, as the governing machinery of this country, has come through the earthquake and has isolated itself from Surface, except for the necessary Intelligence contacts. Our provisional estimate is that this isolation will be maintained for a year to eighteen months. By then, conditions on Surface will have stabilized themselves on a primitive level. Meanwhile Beehive will have been observing, planning, and training its personnel to a high pitch of efficiency. When we emerge, we will be able to take complete and virtually immediate control.

'We might have to modify this programme, of course, in the light of any unexpected foreign developments. This can't be predicted at all accurately till we have a fuller international picture. But all the major powers are in close touch by radio satellite and it looks as though the British picture is typical. Certainly the United States, the Soviet Union, China, and the principal European states have paralleled our experience today, in general – though the Western Hemisphere was hit an hour or two after us. The chief difference has been between urban concentrations and rural areas – both of which we have in Britain, of course.

'As for the foreign equivalents of our Beehive – these have come through pretty well, as far as we know so far. Some differences, naturally. America's done better than we have, for instance, but they had more room to play with in their planning. The Dutch have had a rough time because they're so vulnerable to flooding. Spain's survived better than we have, France worse and so on. But what matters is that all the government machines seem to have come through and will be able, like us, to function, isolate themselves and take control when the time comes.'

'What about Surface – here in Britain?' Brenda presumed to ask.

'Today's reports add up to pretty well total destruction of buildings on the lower ground, under about two hundred metres – which means most of the urban concentrations – and more moderately above that. East Anglia seems an exception; earthquake damage was lighter there but as you might expect, it's been badly hit by floods. The Great Glen, in Scotland, is apparently a total disaster – the water hasn't settled down yet but the Highlands north-west of it are now virtually a separate island. . . . We'll know a lot more over the next week or two, because there are going to be tidal waves to beat anything on record, Arklow predicts. (By the way, to reassure you – Beehive's ventilation inlets can be sealed off against flood for as long as ninety-six hours at a time; we have stored oxygen for that.) We're making practically no public radio broadcasts for a few days, as you know – better to let Surface look after itself to begin with, till they're ready to listen to us. But we *are* warning people to evacuate the coasts . . . I think it's safe to say that the world's shipping and navies will have ceased to exist within a week.'

He paused, and then went on: 'As for casualties – there will be no way of telling for some time, if only because

Arklow was wrong about one thing. He thought the Dust, on this occasion, would be very localized or non-existent. In fact it was very widespread indeed. . . . That damnfool broadcast about the vinegar masks was either too early or too late. If we were going to make it at all – and the experts' advice was that it was unnecessary – we should have made it days before so that people had time to prepare. Yesterday was the worst of both worlds. Only a minority will have been able to benefit from it – but Beehive showed its hand and people will guess that we *could* have told them earlier. Jennings and the Prime Minister made a terrible mistake there. One the Prime Minister will live to regret.'

Brenda did not notice the subtle distinction at the time. She was too torn between horror at the overall picture and shamefaced relief at her own safety to be aware of subtleties.

'But, Reggie – if the Dust was widespread and only a few had vinegar masks – what's Surface going to be like in three or four days' time?'

'If I were you, my dear, I shouldn't give yourself night-mares trying to imagine it. After all, we shall be spared the unpleasantness of witnessing it.'

Over the next few nights Brenda found difficulty in sleeping. But horror, however factual, was distant and un-real; security and status were present and real, and one could only take in so much. Little by little Brenda redis-covered sleep at the side of her sultan.

15

Hiding was less easy than Philip, Betty and Tonia had hoped. Their best prospect, Philip had thought, would be East Anglia; Suffolk and Norfolk were the most thinly populated areas within reach of London and in any case offered the closest open country to their starting-point. So they had headed in that direction taking the smaller roads through Great Dunmow and Haverhill and in spite of diversions and detours had begun to bypass Bury St Edmunds by the evening of the first day.

But the looked-for rural emptiness had proved a mirage. Refugees from devastated London were everywhere on the move, merging with others from Chelmsford, Colchester and Ipswich – and, as the day wore on, with still more from the coastal and river-valley villages as well on the run from the rising floods.

About sunset BBC radio had come on the air again. Philip had been trying the car radio every half-hour or so and to his surprise suddenly heard music. To judge by its volume, it came from an emergency transmitter. The music – Vaughan Williams' *Fantasia on 'Greensleeves'* – continued to its end, after which the announcer said:

'This is the BBC. Here is a Government announcement. As a result of the world-wide earthquakes, serious tidal waves are building up in the Atlantic and will be affecting coastal areas of the British Isles during the next few days subsiding gradually thereafter. People living in these coastal areas, at less than 100 metres above sea-level, are warned to move inland immediately and to take refuge on land higher than the 100-metre contour. Craft now at sea should be beached at the nearest suitable point and abandoned. Coastguard personnel are officially relieved of their duties and should also move inland. That is the end of the Government announcement. I will now repeat it at dictation speed.'

After the repeat, Elgar's *King Arthur Suite*.

Philip stopped the car and they pored over the map.

'East Anglia's going to be a death-trap,' Betty said. 'Look – even if 100 metres is grossly exaggerated, to give a safety margin, places like Bury and Cambridge are way below it. . . . And right now we've got the Ely fens between us and the high ground. If we don't get the hell out of it, it'll be a toss-up whether the water or the stampede from the coast hits us first.'

'Double back south of Cambridge?' Philip suggested.

'I'd say it's the only way. Drive all night – we can take it in turns to sleep. And not stop till we're well into Bedfordshire or Northants.'

Tonia took her turn at driving but they only slept one at a time; with hazards every kilometre in the shape of wrecked cars, refugee bottlenecks (especially in the villages) and the occasional fissure, they needed at least two pairs of eyes. It took them some time to find a way across the Cam upstream of Cambridge because the first two bridges they tried were down. In the end they had to cross by the A 14, where the refugee stream was thicker but at least moving. As soon as they were over, they left it again, taking the side-roads towards Abbotsley and St Neots.

Another advantage of the side-roads was petrol. It could no longer be bought but there were wrecked cars everywhere from whose tanks petrol could be siphoned. On the main roads most of them had already been drained dry but full or half-full tanks were still to be found in the quieter places and Philip topped up at every opportunity. One family saloon from which he took the last three or four litres had hit a tree head-on (the road surface had tilted sideways by five degrees or more) and there were still two bodies in it, a man and a woman crushed by the impact and covered in dried blood. The sight of them, and the fumes of petrol in his mouth as he sucked at the siphoning-tube to start the flow, combined to make him vomit. But he managed to complete his task, and on a quixotic impulse used about half the salvaged petrol to turn the wreck into a funeral pyre. Betty and Tonia, who had stayed in the car, did not ask him why.

By the afternoon of the second day they had found a surprisingly quiet little wood west of Kettering where they decided they must stop and sleep because their exhaustion was beginning to make driving unsafe. Two other refugee families were camped in the wood but they were obviously unaggressive and just as exhausted. And most important of all, none of them had the bronchitic coughing and wheezing they had heard so much since yesterday – the symptoms of a Dust-breather. So there was no danger, from them, of the sudden violent madness which was the terrible secret that Philip's little group nursed.

Since yesterday morning they had seen many thousands of refugees as well as those who clung stubbornly to ruined homes and had had personal contact with dozens of them.

One thing they had found heart-rending and one disturbing.

The heart-rending fact was that, in the face of universal disaster, people had been astonishingly cooperative with each other, astonishingly willing to give and receive help. Frayed tempers there had been, naturally, and the occasional selfish bully; but in general people had seemed eager to prove and to be reassured that even if Nature had turned on them, human nature at least had reserves of unity and ingenuity that might save something from the wreck. What tipped the balance in favour of non-aggression was that at least three-quarters of the refugees were already more or less ill with Dust 'bronchitis'. The healthy ones were anxiously making allowances for them and trying to nurse them through what they had no reason to believe would be more than a bad period of illness – for the Premier's broadcast had not hinted at anything worse. Philip, Betty, and Tonia, only too aware of the truth that all would soon know, found this unwittingly forlorn hope, this doomed tenderness, almost unbearable to watch.

The disturbing fact was that the anti-witch hysteria, which Betty had hoped would be less evident away from the hothouse environment of the Beehive mess, had not been swept aside by the disaster. It was not universal, certainly, but here and there it was virulent. In more than one village, they had passed fanatical street orators (Crusaders, probably, they thought) haranguing listeners on the responsibility of the witches for the visitation of God's wrath – and gathering surprisingly large and sympathetic audiences. Outside Sharnbrook, they had passed the most dreadful sight of all: the bodies of an elderly woman and a teenage girl hanging from a makeshift gallows, with 'WITCH' placards round their necks. Philip wanted to stop and cut them down but Tonia, who was driving at the time, accelerated suddenly past them.

'Hell, we can't just leave them there!' Philip pleaded.

'We can, you know,' Tonia said grimly. 'You didn't see what I did – the two guys along the hedge with shotguns. Reception committee for guys like us. . . . It's rough, Phil, but it looks like the human race is sorting itself out into the living, the mad and the dead. Let's concentrate on Category One, huh? Otherwise we might join Category Three.'

'She's right, you know, darling,' Betty said. 'If there'd been a chance to save them, we might have had a bash. While they were still alive, I mean. But we'll get no thanks for saving corpses.'

Philip had to agree but the vision of the two dangling bodies still haunted him as they settled down to sleep in the quiet wood, huddled under blankets in the car seats. Some time during the hours that followed they invaded his dreams, vividly, and their twisted features were those of Betty and Tonia. He woke gasping, to find himself held tightly in Betty's arms as she tried to soothe him.

'Sorry,' he muttered. 'Nightmare.'

'I know, love,' Betty whispered. 'I've been listening to it. Try not to wake Tonia. . . . I'm glad she's with us, aren't you? Makes us stronger.'

He drifted back into sleep, wondering confusedly what she meant by that.

They all three woke at first light, having slept the clock round through sheer weariness, but stiff with discomfort. They lit a small fire in a clearing, gathering sticks from the woodland and crouched and stamped round it till they got warm. Betty managed to get a saucepan of water hot enough to make instant coffee; they had sugar but no milk but the black sweet liquid refreshed them. Breakfast was a strange mixture – a tin of herrings in tomato sauce followed by one of sliced peaches. Tins and jars had been the only usable stores in Betty's ruined kitchen; bread, milk, butter, cheese and vegetables had been a long-decayed mess.

'We're going to have to do better than this,' she said. '. . . Phil – you're the only one who's read the official reports. When does the Madness start?'

'After about three days, in brief fits. By the fifth or sixth day it's continuous.' He felt a new vigour this morning, a new sense of realism; yesterday he could not even have discussed it without tension but today he could answer calmly. 'The violence, that is – there may be bouts of harmless delirium before that. The pattern's pretty uniform, apparently. As I remember, eighty-seven per cent of the cases in the Emergency Units followed that three-day, five-day timetable. The rest took a little longer – up to a week for the whole development.'

'So we've got till tomorrow morning to take cover somewhere.'

'Looks like it.'

'And for looting,' Tonia said.

'Looting?'

'What else? You don't imagine anyone's interested in money any more, do you? And we can't take cover without food.'

Philip sighed. 'True enough. It's just the word . . . Still, we might as well call a spade a bloody spade. . . . Not from the living, though. The way the towns collapsed, there must be enough ownerless shops in them.'

'And fields in the country,' Betty pointed out. 'We've passed God knows how many hectares of vegetables. And it's been a good year for blackberries. . . . Another thing – there'll be cows to milk with too few people to milk them, especially as it'll have to be by hand. I wish *I* could.'

'I can,' Tonia said unexpectedly. 'Learned when I was a kid, on vacation on my uncle's farm. Might come in useful at last.'

Other people in the wood had apparently been talking along the same lines. They were still sipping their second cup of black coffee when a delegation of three men and a woman came to their camp-fire from the other two refugee families. They talked cautiously for a few minutes, exchanging experiences, and then the eldest of the men – a tall man in his forties with a middle-class accent – came to the point.

'Look – we need food and I expect you do too. We were thinking of making a sortie into Kettering or Market Harborough to see what we can find; we had a quick look at both yesterday, from the fringes – there's hardly a house left standing, and a lot of the survivors were getting out. There should be pickings without actually having to fight for them.'

'We were talking about it, too,' Philip said.

'Right. Point is, we've got kids with us, and one old woman and two younger ones. And there *might* be fighting, whether we go looking for it or not. If we add your lot, there's six men, five women, and kids. . . . How about five of the men going on the sortie, in one car – and leaving one man to watch over the women and kids, here? We've got a shotgun we can leave with him. The bigger the sortie, the better our chances. Want to join us?'

Kettering was as devastated as the tall man – whose name was Harry – had reported but not quite as empty. They were able to drive the car in as far as the railway bridge over the A 6, half a kilometre from the centre, and park it there facing back the way they had come; then they had to go ahead on foot, keeping close together and watching their flanks. People were busy in the ruins, mostly trying to make parts of them livable and did little more than glance warily at the five strangers.

'What we want's a supermarket,' Harry said. 'Let's go on a bit.'

'There's a noise ahead,' Philip told him. 'Sounds like a crowd arguing.'

'Hell. The last thing we want.'

They rounded the right bend in Lower Street and saw it.

'My God! Troops! First we've run into.'

'Troops' was perhaps an exaggeration. A young lieutenant, a lance-corporal, and four privates were strung out in front of the smashed windows of a big supermarket. The officer had a revolver in his holster and the five soldiers carried their rifles at the port. The crowd of men and women who faced them looked angry and resentful. One of the men was arguing with the officer. As Harry and his group came up behind the crowd, the young officer raised his voice.

'Look, everybody – go home. Until I get new orders, my job's to prevent looting. And that's what I'm going to do. So clear this crowd.'

'Orders from where, sonny?' somebody called, mockingly. 'There's no one to give 'em.'

The officer flushed. 'Don't you count on that. Anyhow, that's my business. Go home.'

'Stupid puppy,' Harry muttered to Philip.

There was a chorus of 'What homes?' and another cry from the mocking voice. 'Stop looting, eh? Six of you? There's dozens of shops, sonny.'

'This is the biggest and it's where the food is. So we'll go on protecting it.'

A woman pushed forward out of the crowd towards him, shouting furiously: 'Too right it's where the food is! And we've got hungry kids! What the hell d'you think you're trying to do? You and your "orders"! Get out of our way!'

She was almost on him and he drew his revolver, taking a hasty step backwards. The crowd sensed his nervousness and at the same time were angered by his threat to the woman. They moved closer.

Harry said, 'Jesus, he's asking for it.'

A moment of poised silence was broken by noises from inside the supermarket. The lance-corporal said, 'They've got in the back way, sir.'

'Hendry – Powers – through the shop! Stop 'em!'

The soldiers never had a chance to obey. As the officer shouted his order, the crowd rushed forward. Two shots rang out and that was all; the crowd was instantly an enraged mob, overwhelming the khaki figures, milling around them for a few seconds and then pouring into the shop.

It was all over before Harry and his group had caught their breath.

They stared down at the six soldiers; the officer was certainly dead, the rest either dead or stunned. The woman who had challenged the officer lay at his side with a bullet through her chest, and another civilian was staggering into the shop after the crowd clutching a bleeding arm.

'Come on!' Harry cried. 'It's done. Might as well get our share.'

They began to run. Philip shouted to Harry: 'The guns! Get the guns!'

'Christ, yes!'

It took them half a minute, at most, to strip the soldiers of their arms and ammunition. Harry ordered one of his men back to the car with them and the remaining four hurried into the supermarket.

Inside was chaos; displays tumbling as people grabbed at tins and boxes, bottles smashing as they stumbled into each other. Strangely, few had thought of taking a trolley – perhaps fearing it would hamper them. There were still four left and Harry's group seized them, trying to keep calm and work methodically, choosing the most compact goods, remembering small unnoticed valuables such as yeast and sticking plasters and salt and a card of throwaway lighters, trying an unopened door which might, and did, hide more meat (the meat counter had been stripped in seconds), and paying a flying visit to the hardware shelves, where Philip found a treasure they lacked – a camping-gas ring with spare cylinders.

Harry was a natural commander. He managed to keep an eye on all his group, coordinate their efforts without fuss, avoid clashes and order withdrawal at just the right moment.

They must have been a bizarre sight, four grown men careering through Kettering with loaded supermarket trolleys like women in a perambulator race. But nobody stopped them and they reached the car with all their loot. The man who had carried the guns ahead was very relieved to see them. He was standing guard over the car with the revolver, while a group of young men across the road eyed him speculatively.

They drove back to the wood without incident and were welcomed as returning heroes. But the women had not been idle. Tonia proudly produced a plastic pail of still-warm, frothy milk.

'Found a cow,' she announced. 'Poor old girl was in the hell of a state. Well, we've all got to help each other with our problems, these days – haven't we?'

They never did solve the puzzle of the abandoned farm. It was about a kilometre from the wood and they were led to it by another cow's distressed mooing – Tonia's friend's companion was obviously confined there and equally obviously unattended. Harry and Philip, with Tonia as the nearest they had to an agricultural expert, went to investigate. Tonia's opinion, after administering emergency relief to the cow and examining such telltale evidence as the hencoops and the kitchen, was that the farm had been empty of humans for at least two days. Beds and clothing suggested that a couple and a young man, perhaps their son, had lived there. Maybe they had been in one of the market towns when the earthquake struck and been killed. Maybe they had taken fright at their isolation and fled to relatives. Whatever the explanation, they had plainly gone, and all the signs were that they would not be back.

The three of them returned to the wood and called a conference, at which Philip told the others the truth about the effect of the Dust, and the coming need for the utmost in self-defence. The debate was not long. Within an hour, they had packed their cars and moved to the farm – six men, five women, two girls aged fourteen and eleven, and a seven-year-old boy.

It was plain from its equipment and the bills and receipts that littered an old roll-top desk that the farm had not commanded many hectares. But the building itself was old and rambling, probably a relic of more prosperous days, and it had bedrooms enough for all of them if the three single men used the loft as a dormitory. It was also virtually undamaged; four broken windows and a fractured pantry wall.

They had two milch cows, a somewhat elderly horse, three young pigs, some poultry, a questionably adequate stock of hay and other feed, plenty of potatoes and vegetables and a water-pump that worked. They also had enough adults for round-the-clock sentries, five rifles, a shotgun, a revolver and some, if not much, ammunition.

Given luck, they reckoned that they could manage.

Fewer of the Vyrnwy river valley people had survived than their neighbours in New Dyfnant had hoped, and most of the scattered handfuls that did fell to the madmen.

In the first minutes after the earthquake, the majority had managed to reach the vinegar masks they had prepared. But house damage had been greater than in New Dyfnant. Many had been trapped or crushed; vinegar and gauze carefully kept ready had often been buried in wreckage; the untrapped desperately trying to free the trapped had often forgotten about their masks till it was too late. And almost at once, into the middle of this chaos, had swept the great wall of water from the burst dam.

How the few refugees from the flood who had been able to reach higher ground on the other side of the valley had fared, New Dyfnant did not know as yet. But thirty or forty of them from the near side had reached the village and been taken in by families with relatively undamaged homes or housed temporarily in the village hall. All but three of them had arrived holding vinegar masks to their faces and claimed to have been using them from the start. The three without masks had been locked up with Tom Jenkins – two of them were too numb with shock to protest. The third resisted so violently that Dai Police had had to handcuff him till he cooled down, which had taken half an hour while Dai talked to him, using up time the constable could ill spare.

Over the next few days, the four prisoners loomed large in the village's conscience and its fears. Everybody knew what would happen to them but nobody knew what would have to be done with them. Dai Police had no cell, so they had to be kept in the safest place available – one of Jack

Llewellyn's lock-up garages, which they made as comfortable and warm as they could for them.

Once Eileen had made sure that everyone in the forest camp was well and safe, she had come down to the village to offer her help to Dr Owen. The doctor, rushed off his none-too-young feet, was very grateful, not only because of the number of injured he had to attend to, but because Eileen was the only person with direct experience of handling Dust victims. Her advice was grim but inescapable: strait-jackets would have to be improvised as quickly as possible and they would have to be worn continuously from the third day. She insisted (which Dr Owen considered very brave of her) on explaining this to the four men herself. She softened the facts as much as she could; they knew that the Dust would drive them mad because they had been told so when Eileen's warning had first been passed to them – this had been essential, both to drive home the warning's importance and to prevent the unafflicted from being caught unawares. But in talking to the four, she deliberately gave the impression that this madness came in fits, intermittently, with periods of sanity in between and that the strait-jackets were needed because the fits were unpredictable and they might injure themselves and each other when they were seized by them. It would be more cruel than they could bear to tell them the whole truth, that very soon the madness would be continuous and without hope. They were sick enough and frightened enough, already.

She managed, she hoped, to persuade them and to keep her poise while she did so. But as soon as she was out of their hearing, and the lock-up door clanged down behind her, she burst into tears in Dr Owen's fatherly arms.

'I'm sorry, Doctor . . . I . . .'

'Don't you say that, Eileen fach. You were a bloody

marvel and that's a fact. Have a good bawl now and be done with it.'

'But what's to become of them?'

'God alone knows, my dear. I daren't think of it or I'd weep myself. Come along now. Let's see how they're getting on with those damn jackets.'

Dai Police's wife Joan had organized a sewing party who were hard at work making the jackets from sail-cloth commandeered from a dinghy in somebody's back garden – a dinghy that would never sail on Lake Vyrnwy again, because Lake Vyrnwy was now a sea of mud with a stream in the middle. 'Feel as though we were plaiting hangmen's nooses, we do,' Joan said glumly but got on with it.

The strait-jackets were never used.

They were ready on the third day with Eileen growing increasingly nervous and impatient, but there had been delay in finding adequate thread. Dai Police, the doctor and Eileen set off for the lock-up with two strong men as escort in case of trouble. The escort carried shotguns; there had been a noticeable tendency, since the earthquake, for those who possessed them (as most families did, with so many rabbits and other game to hand) to keep them within easy reach. Carrying arms went against the grain with Dai Police; he had in his safe a .32 automatic and a hundred rounds of ammunition which had been handed in by the executors of a retired colonel, recently dead, but so far he had not overcome his reluctance to wear it.

When they reached the lock-up it was empty. The door had been smashed open from the inside.

For a moment nobody spoke; they all stood staring, perplexed and paralysed, at the ruined door. Then a faint call from the garage forecourt set them running to where Jack Llewellyn lay, bloodstained and half-stunned. Jack waved a feeble arm along the street and croaked, 'After them, for God's sake!' before he collapsed again.

The doctor cried, 'See to him, Eileen!' and the four men sprinted away up the road. It was just as well Eileen was occupied with attending to Jack's injuries, because it saved her from witnessing what followed.

They caught up with Tom Jenkins and the others outside the school. That Tom himself, and one of the valley men, were completely in the grip of the violent madness was obvious at once. The other two seemed disorientated and hesitant, as though they had been infected by the first two's madness and swept along by it, but were uncertain what was happening. All four turned to face their pursuers, glaring at them wild-eyed, and Tom gave a terrible wordless roar like a bull.

'Easy, now, Tom,' Dai said, with little hope of getting through to him, but feeling the attempt had to be made. 'Easy now. You know us. We want to help you, man.'

For a fraction of a second the eight of them were a frozen tableau – whether the madmen would attack or take flight seemed to hang in the balance. It was broken by the sound of children laughing and running.

Geraint Lloyd's contribution to the crisis, after the first day, had been to keep the school working and parents had been only too glad to have the children off their hands. Now, at just the wrong moment, a dozen of the younger ones poured out of the school door into the street.

The high-pitched clamour seemed to infuriate the madmen. Snarling, they turned on the children.

Dai and the others raced forward but Tom reached the children first, snatching up seven-year-old Becky Reece in his great hands, holding her at arms' length, roaring, crushing . . .

By chance, Becky's father was one of the escort. Without a word, he put his twelve-bore to Tom's head and fired.

The whole scene was over in seconds, but it stuck in Dr Owen's memory for the rest of his life. Geraint yelling to the children to come back in. Three more shots. The children's stampede back to the schoolhouse. The sudden silence. The four dead madmen in the village street. Becky's father, his gun dropped, clutching his bruised and weeping daughter, babbling reassurance to her.

They held a village meeting that evening. It did not last long; even the pale and shocked Rev. Phillips acquiesced in the decision, though by common consent he was excused from voting.

From that night, until the madness danger was known to be over, a rota of armed men would guard the approaches to the village from the valley. Dr Owen had described the symptoms of the madness in detail, though in fact they could not be mistaken. Healthy refugees would be admitted. Refugees with bronchial symptoms would be locked up in Jack Llewellyn's garage, which would be repaired next morning and made impregnable; they would not be released until the doctor had pronounced them clear.

Madmen – and madwomen, even mad children – would be shot on the spot, as both safety and mercy demanded.

Reality, even grimmer than the reality of the earthquake, had come to New Dyfnant.

In the forest, Peter O'Malley was facing a reality of his own and dealing with it single-handed. His employers, the Forestry Commission, had presumably ceased to exist and the statistical side of Peter's work had become too academic to continue. But the animals remained and one thing Peter had to know, even if only because human life and health might be involved – their reaction to the Dust.

Peter and Father Byrne had become part of Dan and

Moira's camp, moving Peter's trailer into the laager the day after the earthquake. But the others had been quick to understand the importance of what Peter had to do and he was excused all camp duties to get on with it.

Day by day, he roamed the forest, watching carefully. Birds and insects seemed completely unaffected by the Dust; so far, so good. Fish too; the camp had eaten several trout before it occurred to them that the fish might have taken in Dust from the water surface, and the eating of fish was immediately banned. But no one developed any symptoms and after a few days it was considered safe to lift the ban. This was a relief because although they had built up quite a stock of tinned and other preservable food in the cave, winter was coming and all fresh food was precious. The longer the cave stocks could be made to last, the better.

Mammals were another matter; they were affected in varying degrees. The camp goats, Ginger Lad the cat and Peter's own two whippets – merely seemed listless and reluctant to eat for a few days; then they picked up and within a week were back to normal. (Meanwhile the goats' milk, too, had had to be banned.) Peter also kept as much of an eye as he could on New Dyfnant's livestock, asking the few village smallholders to keep him informed of any symptoms developed by cattle, sheep, pigs or horses. The villagers were glad to help him, because the nearest veterinary surgeon had been in Llanwddyn and nobody knew his fate. Mainly they had reacted like the goats, though two cows and a sheep had failed to recover and had died.

Of the wild animals, stoats, weasels and the few pine martens Peter knew of came through fairly well. They simply went into hiding while they felt ill and about eighty per cent of them re-emerged a few days later, apparently recovered. Badgers, for some reason, seemed totally immune and only one or two deer showed the temporary listlessness.

Two species, however, were badly hit. Squirrels, both grey and red, developed symptoms unlike any other species; about three-quarters of them were affected and they died slowly and painfully, becoming increasingly helpless, rather like rabbits with myxomatosis. (Rabbits themselves reacted like their enemies the stoats and weasels.)

The other victims – the foxes – were the only ones who were affected in the same way as humans, even to the time factor. Three days after the earthquake, Peter was attacked by an enraged vixen, who flew at him snarling in a forest fire-break. He had managed to dodge her first snapping onslaught and to shoot her before she could renew it. Within a week there were no sane foxes to be seen and Peter had issued an urgent warning to camp and village.

For many days, Peter was occupied hour after hour with a tragic but necessary slaughter of doomed squirrels and crazed foxes. He had been stockpiling ammunition ever since the Midsummer tremors had given him a fore-boding of crisis, and was probably better supplied than any-one in New Dyfnant or the camp. But he knew his reserves were not limitless and he guarded them carefully, using traps and snares when he could, and even gassing fox-earths (a thing he hated doing). He hoped with all his animal-loving heart that a few immune foxes would survive somewhere to revive the species, but he dared not be any-thing less than ruthless with the affected ones and so far he had come across none unaffected.

He piled the corpses, both squirrel and fox, in a clearing not far from the camp, being reluctant to let them lie where he killed them because he had no way of knowing if their bodies might be infectious to living animals. Once a day he lit his crematorium bonfire. On the fourth day of the slaughter, Eileen came out of the trees just as he was lighting it.

He straightened up to speak to her but the expression on her face silenced him. After a second or two she turned and ran and he could hear her retching and sobbing as her footsteps died away.

Distressed, he waited for a chance to speak to her alone that evening by the camp-fire. She gave him a nervous half-smile, quickly extinguished, as though she wanted to make amends but he knew the barrier was there.

'It has to be done, you know,' he said, 'and there's no one but me to do it. Those foxes could be killers – and the poor bloody squirrels . . .'

'I know.'

'Keep away from that clearing, eh? I won't burn 'em anywhere else.'

'It's not just that. I can hear every shot you fire. Oh, Peter . . .'

He laid a hand on her arm but she jerked it away. 'You see?' she went on 'I can't bear . . . Please, Peter – I *know* it's me and it's stupid and wrong and unfair to you – but I can't *help* it! Killing makes me physically sick. I *try*, but . . .'

She broke off and for a long time they both stared into the fire without speaking. He was still trying to find what he could possibly say when the others joined them, and the moment was gone.

That was the evening when the forest camp 'changed gear'. The phrase was Dan's and he introduced it in the usual camp-fire discussion of the next day's work.

'It's all very well sitting here and fixing duty shifts for washing-up and what have you,' he said, 'but I think it's

286

time we changed gear. Time we started thinking about the future.'

'Haven't we?' Angie asked. 'I'd say we'd been pretty far-sighted, the way we've been laying in stores and thinking out what'll come in useful and so on.'

'Yes, Angie – but those days are over. We can't go on shopping sorties any more; if there is any trade, it'll be by barter and that won't be till things have settled down. We don't even know *how* they'll settle down. Let's face it, we don't know how many people'll be left alive. We don't know how widespread the Dust was or how many were caught by it or what'll happen to them. *Can* they survive, Eileen?'

'I don't see how,' Eileen answered. 'They can't look after themselves, they'll be fighting and killing each other, and the rest'll be killing *them*. Like they did in the village.' She said it in an expressionless, brittle voice.

'They had no choice, love. They were already attacking the kids.'

'*One* was.'

'I know how you feel but it's done – and what's going to happen in places where they aren't just three or four but hundreds – the majority, perhaps? The sane ones'll have to kill or be killed – the mad ones'll give 'em no option.' He could feel Eileen withdrawing into her shell, so he slid away from the subject. 'Anyway, let's just say we don't know what the size of the population will be, what with the earthquake itself, the Dust and the tidal waves. The Government broadcasts tell us damn all – discounting the hourly repeats, they add up to a couple of hundred words a day. They're obviously battening down the hatches and letting us stew in our own juice till the worst is over. Then I suppose they'll come out and take charge.'

'If they still really exist,' Greg said. 'All right, they've

287

still got a transmitter – though they've scrapped TV and that's a pointer in itself . . .'

'No, it isn't. There aren't enough battery sets to make it worth while with power gone. And *they* run off car batteries which most people can't recharge. But radios will go on for a long time yet. So Beehive sticks to radio.'

'All right, granted that. My point is that the earthquakes might have virtually wiped the Beehives out as an effective force. These broadcasts may just be a bluff.'

'We don't *know*,' Moira said, 'and we shan't, unless and until they do come out – so there's not much point in discussing it, is there?'

Greg grinned, unabashed. 'Okay, okay. What *were* you on about, Dan?'

'Just this,' Dan said. 'Before the quake we were camping here, hoping that with Peter's help the Forestry Commission wouldn't notice us. But now, no Forestry Commission. We *live* here and bloody lucky we are with it. And the winter's coming. I think it's time we started cutting down trees to build cabins and ploughing the meadow for autumn vegetable-sowing, getting Greg's alternator rigged at the waterfall for charging batteries and so on. In other words, start turning this into a *permanent* camp.'

Once stated, it was obvious, and nobody disagreed. They all fell to discussing priorities and the only surprise came when Rosemary said, 'As it's going to be our home, it ought to have a name', and Father Byrne (who spoke little but helpfully) suggested: 'How about Camp Cerridwen?'

They all looked at him in astonishment.

'Father!' Moira said, laughing. 'You're very tolerant of our pagan ways even though you thoroughly disapprove of them. But I never thought you'd suggest we call our camp after a pagan goddess.'

The old priest looked apologetic. 'It must be the Celt

in me but I have a great affection for the old legends. I don't base my theology on them, that's all. . . . But here we are in the Welsh mountains, making our home in a hidden valley that's like a fertile cauldron. The Cauldron of Cerridwen. So why not Camp Cerridwen?'

'I think it's a marvellous name,' Moira said. 'I propose we vote on it.'

'Point of information,' Angie asked. 'Who *was* Cerridwen?'

'A Welsh Mother-Goddess, who had a cauldron representing several ideas – abundance, inspiration, rebirth . . .'

'Enough said. I'll vote for that.'

So did everybody; and Camp Cerridwen it was.

They worked hard, isolated from the outer world from which no news came. The few refugees who straggled into New Dyfnant came from no further afield than the devastated Vyrnwy valley and knew nothing outside their personal stories – except for terrible rumours of the Madness in Llanfyllin a dozen kilometres away and Welshpool twice as far, which were always second- or third-hand and might or might not be wildly exaggerated.

The hourly BBC official broadcasts, cryptic and repetitious, told them little except by inference. The only specific information they gave and that only in the first week or so, came in tidal wave warnings; particular areas were warned of imminent disaster. Angie, the camp's best geographer, noted the warnings and checked them on the map. The danger-line had been lowered to the fifty-metre contour, she noticed – presumably on more exact data – but the overall picture was still calamitous. No coastal area escaped but it was obvious that funnels like the Scottish firths and the Severn and Thames estuaries, urban plains like Lancashire and Cheshire and low-lying marine counties in

East Anglia must be suffering terribly from the mountains of sea that surged round the British Isles. With that coming on top of the earthquake and the Dust, it was not possible to begin to imagine what the death-toll might be. Angie did not communicate the scant news she had to the others except when they asked – and they rarely did. None of them was callous but the disaster was almost too vast for compassion to be meaningful. They were alive, and safer than most, so all they could do was work to stay that way until the outer world thrust itself upon them.

Their first decision was that, barring extreme emergencies, the motor vehicles were not to be used. Every litre of petrol would be saved for the chain-saw and the rotovator which were now in action round the clock. Dan and Peter went down to the village to see what could be done about bartering for a horse and cart. The result was almost embarrassing. They returned with one sturdy draught horse, two saddle horses (with saddles and bridles), and a farm cart with a plough and a harrow in it; and any suggestion of payment was brushed aside.

'Look now, man,' Dai Forest Inn told Dan when he tried to argue. 'We are alive and sane in New Dyfnant, if sane we ever were, that is, thanks to you people up there. Only one man gone mad through the Dust, of our own people, and his own fault, wasn't it? And but for you, it might have been the whole bloody lot of us. Witches you may be but that's between you and God and your own business. But you looked after us and what's a horse or two compared with that?'

'All the same . . .'

'All the same nothing, Dan bach. Their owners died in the earthquake, so they're communal property, like, see? And who better to look after them than our friends in the forest? Come now, and have a whisky while I've still got a bottle or two left.'

Another strange gift was wished on them by official decision of New Dyfnant council: two ruined farmhouses on the edge of the forest, from which only they had the right to salvage usable items and materials, the original owners also having died in the earthquake. The villagers were warned off and meticulously observed the ban. Camp Cerridwen appreciated this privilege greatly, because there were many things there, from doors and window-frames to a kitchen stove which would burn logs, all invaluable for the cabins they were building – not to mention hen-houses, garden tools and so on.

One of the farms had nearly half a hectare of vegetable garden, and that too was allocated to the camp. Most of it was potatoes, now ready for lifting, but there were also brussels sprouts and cabbage, carrots, and a few rows of beans. Everybody was delighted, especially old Sally, who had been appointed storekeeper and rationing-calculator.

The cabin-building went ahead surprisingly fast, considering that none of them were experts. All they had was Peter's knowledge of timber, Greg's flair as a handyman and two photographs of Finnish log cabins in a travel book of Angie's. At least there was suitable timber a few metres away. Greg and Dan felled it, helped increasingly by Peter as the afflicted foxes and squirrels became fewer through his culling and through natural deaths. Angie, who was remarkably strong, gave a hand with the trimming in spite of their protests, and the draught horse was used to drag the timber to the site. They also had regular volunteer help from a muscular but inarticulate village lad who fancied Eileen but was getting nowhere with her. He accepted his failure philosophically and went on helping.

There were technical problems to be solved, mostly by

trial and error – such as the shallowness of the topsoil over the rock plateau (how deep should holes be pickaxed for the uprights?) and the choice of suitable material for packing the crevices between the trunks (would mud bound with straw stand up to the weather?) – but they got round these one by one, and their first cabin took shape. It was to be a central, communal, living-and-eating room with a stove, in which the tent-dwellers could also sleep as a temporary measure if the cold weather came before sleeping-cabins were ready; the caravan-dwellers would be all right, though attention was paid to lagging and screening Angie's caravan and Peter's trailer for greater warmth.

With so much building to be done, there seemed little hope of tilling much of the six-hectare meadow yet. So they selected the easiest stretch – about a hectare of clean grass with no more than a dozen small bushes to be dug out – and began to rotovate it. But here Eileen's mute admirer took over and harnessed the draught horse to the plough they had been given. He was a very bad ploughman and the result was not pretty but the soil *was* turned and deeper than the rotovator could reach. Learning from him, after a few hours Dan found he could do almost as well as far as straightness of furrow went, though the horse paid little attention to his commands and the whole process was very time-consuming.

'It'll look better when we've harrowed it,' Greg said hopefully.

Moira, Rosemary and Eileen felt a little guilty and frustrated about the building and ploughing, because being young and healthy they wanted to help more but simply had not the muscles for this stage of the work. Even Dan and Greg, town-bred as they were, were exhausted at the end of each day.

The camp-fire was very welcome in the evenings, for the

first chill of autumn was in the air. They dug a second hearth farther away, for use on the odd evening when the wind (which mostly was funnelled either up or down the valley) blew at all strongly towards the trees. It was round this more exposed fire that Geraint Lloyd found them huddled one evening when he rode up to visit them on his bicycle, as he did fairly regularly to give them what news he had been able to pick up on his ham radio and to bring up batteries for recharging. Greg had jury-rigged a water-wheel to drive his alternator, pending a more durable structure and was only too glad to help Geraint keep his radio going. (Geraint, as ingenious as Greg in his own way, had converted an old baby-carriage into a trailer for his bicycle to carry the batteries.)

Geraint found them more depressed than usual this evening; it had been a tiresome day, full of problems and false starts, and everyone seemed to feel that not much progress had been made. Nor had a gusty wind and a couple of rain-showers improved tempers.

'We've *got* to get the first cabin roofed and weathertight pretty bloody soon,' Greg was grumbling, 'so we can get cracking on the cook-house. We can't have the girls cooking in the open once the winter sets in.'

'We can always cook in the caravans,' Angie said.

'And use up all our gas bottles when we've got a wood-burning range? Not bloody likely. Anyhow, the caravans are bedrooms. Ought to keep 'em for that, if we're going to have any kind of comfort.'

'I know today's been a bad day. But you'll get it done.'

'If we have a month of rain?' Greg asked gloomily.

Geraint listened for another minute of semi-bickering and then interrupted: 'At least you *can* get on with it. D'you realize what it's like outside? Damn lucky you are –

and we in the village, too – tucked away in a defensible cul-de-sac. You should listen to my ham friends.'

Everybody fell silent. They were well aware that the Madness had become, by unspoken agreement, almost a taboo subject at Camp Cerridwen. It was now a fortnight since the first madmen had been shot in New Dyfnant, and at the Camp only Dan, Greg and Peter knew, from the villagers, how many had since been shot at the barracades on the two approach roads – forty-three men, women and children so far. More than one villager who had hitherto been regarded as tough had had to be taken off the sentry roster, because he had come home from a necessary execution sick and trembling. And those forty-three could only have been a random handful of the insane, because they wandered aimlessly with no evidence of the purposeful seeking of shelter. Any who came up the approach roads did so by chance and against the odds, for the main road was steep and the other one winding and long. Only Geraint Lloyd, crouched for hours on end over his radio exchanging piecemeal local news with his fellow-hams, had any kind of perspective of the overall picture.

Dan and Greg had good reason to keep the news to themselves and they had no difficulty in persuading Peter to do the same. As in most witch covens, so in theirs, it was the women on the whole who were the more psychically sensitive; Moira unusually so even for an experienced High Priestess, Sally to a lesser degree but consistently, while Rosemary's came and went unpredictably but could at times find her painfully vulnerable. Greg seemed resigned to the fact that, after years of trying, he still 'couldn't pick up a bloody thing' – but he nevertheless had great psychic power which the others could tap, and with which he could surround Rosemary, in her vulnerable moments, like a wall. Dan himself was more mentally than psychically sensitive, so although he did not 'pick up' a great deal, he was remarkably astute at interpreting what he did pick up (a process in which many otherwise gifted clairvoyants mar their own gift).

From the first days of the Madness, the sheer magnitude of the violence raging in the psychic atmosphere, as it did over the physical Earth, had hung over the women's awareness like a thundercloud. On the fifth day after the earthquake, the astral shock-wave had hit them. Moira, shaking, had ordered a Circle; Dan had taken one look at her and assumed command (a thing he very rarely did), casting it himself. He had included everyone but Father Byrne; to the priest he had explained quickly what they were doing and why, and had suggested that he might be happier – and more effective – in the caravan confronting the powers of darkness in his own way. Father Byrne, who was anything but insensitive himself, had nodded, said 'God bless you all', and gone not to his caravan but to the little open-air sanctuary he had made for himself in a clearing in the forest. Dan had then taken charge of the building up of their psychic defences; Angie, Eileen and Peter had cooperated willingly and very soon the whole group had felt stronger and calmer. Moira, rejuvenated, had taught the non-witches the basics of psychic self-defence – concentrating particularly on Eileen, who although quite untrained in psychic matters was all too factually aware of the nature of the Madness and therefore specially vulnerable.

Since then, everybody had borne up well during the day and a nightly Circle had been cast around the camp to protect their sleep. (Dan, half-teasingly, asked Father Byrne if he minded sleeping inside it. Father Byrne had replied that if God had forgiven Naaman for the political necessity of bowing down in the House of Rimmon, He would doubtless forgive a somewhat aged priest for the domestic necessity of sleeping in it. He had then hastily added that he was only joking and that as far as he was concerned, the camp was protected by a circle of love and goodwill which was more important than the formula used.) And when Peter brought back the first news of the grim operation at the barricades, he had readily agreed with Dan and Greg that it should be kept from the women unless and until it was necessary to give it to them. 'They're our psychic antennae,' Dan had said. 'Let's keep the air as clear as we can for them.'

Nevertheless it was Moira who asked tonight: 'It's really bad, Geraint, isn't it?'

The schoolmaster nodded. 'I'm afraid so, Moira. . . . In the first week after the earthquake, I was in touch with eighteen hams still operating in Britain and two in Ireland. Now I'm in touch with five British and one Irish. That's fourteen gone. Four of the British and the Irishman lived in coastal areas so they'd announced they were getting out; whether they got clear, God knows.' He looked apologetically at Eileen. 'I hope you don't mind – but they *are* all my friends, even if I've never met most of 'em, so I tipped 'em off about the vinegar masks in time. So no one got caught *that* way. And the Irish knew in any case. But that's still nine out of the twenty who survived the earthquake but have since disappeared – and none of the others picked up a signing-off message from any of them, though we'd all promised to broadcast one if we could. . . . And all those nine were in bad areas, big towns and so on. . . . Some of them had pretty dreadful stories to tell, locally – and the ones who are left are still telling them. We're damn lucky here. We hate what we're having to do at the barricades – but that's nothing to what's happening in the towns and the open country. The sane minority are having to kill the insane majority, whenever they meet face to face. Either that or get killed themselves. And since not one in a thousand of the sane ones has a gun or anything, a hell of a lot of 'em *are* getting killed. . . . Ireland's been better off, as far as my friend there can tell me, because they got the Dust warning and only a small minority were caught by it. But about half their population, North and South, live in seaports, and the casualties there must have been ghastly. It looks as though Ireland got the tidal waves first, and worst, on top of earthquakes just as bad as ours. . . . Can't tell you much about the rest of the world yet, I'm afraid. I've been too busy trying to build up the British Isles picture and cooperating with the other hams to do it. Anyway, long-range radio conditions were lousy after the quake and they're only improving slowly. But from the odd contacts I *have* had, I'd say our state of affairs is pretty typical. . . . It's like the end of the world.'

They were all silent for quite a while. Moira looked around them; Father Byrne with his eyes shut, his lips moving, the rosary slipping rapidly through his gnarled fingers. Eileen rigid, unmoving, the tears trickling down her cheeks from her unblinking eyes. Peter watching her, longing to put his arms round her in protection and love, and not daring to. Ginger Lad, sensing the tension, snaking himself round Angie's ankles and staring up at her anxiously. Rosemary clinging to Greg, her shoulders quivering . . .

'You said "the sane minority", Geraint,' Dan asked at last. 'How many?'

Geraint hesitated. 'Christ knows, Dan. I've been trying to make a wild guess, piecing together everything I've been getting. For one thing, it depends on how long the mad ones last. Everyone says they don't eat unless food's right in front of their noses, they hardly sleep and then it may be a field or a pavement, they injure themselves and do nothing about it – they *must* die off before long, from malnutrition or exposure or disease or injury; they can't just go on rampaging about indefinitely. . . .' He drew a long breath. 'And when *that's* all over – my guess, for what it's worth, is that if one person in fifty in Britain is still alive, sane and healthy enough to go on living, then Britain will have been damn lucky.'

16

There were times, during the two or three weeks of the Madness, when Philip thought the killing would never stop.

The little Garth Farm community had been better prepared than most, because Philip had been able to warn them of the violence and incurability of the Madness. After the first incident when a madman blundered suddenly into the farmyard and half-strangled Harry's wife before Harry shot him, there was no argument about what had to be done.

From then on, a duty roster of armed sentries was drawn up and nobody was to be out of sight of them at any time. There was plenty of work to be done in the fields if the farm was to be kept running but they always went out in parties of at least three, with an armed look-out who kept round his neck the binoculars they had found in the house. The madmen were easily identifiable even at a distance; after you had seen one or two, you could no longer mistake them for sane people who were merely distressed or ill. So since the defenders of Garth Farm had good Army rifles, the binoculars, by giving more warning, helped to make the necessary act a little less gut-wrenching by depersonalizing it slightly. The attacker could be picked off at a greater distance, according to how good a shot you were, instead of waiting until you were face-to-face as would have been necessary with a shotgun. At first the defenders had hoped that a warning shot might scare the madmen off, because none of them had any desire to kill them unless they actually attacked. But the first few tries proved that this was an illusory hope. The madmen ignored bullets. They even ignored wounds if the first shot merely winged them. They seemed motivated by one consuming obsession – to close with and destroy any sane person they saw. (For some reason no one could explain they rarely attacked each other.) So the rule became simple; shoot on sight and shoot to kill.

Garth Farm seemed to attract them – perhaps because it stood alone on a slight rise, visible from several kilometres away in the Kettering direction. Once the Madness took hold there were shootings every day. The toll ranged from two on the most peaceful day to seven on the worst. Light seemed to increase the attacks – bright sunlight meant maximum danger, an overcast night apparently none at all but there were several attacks around the full moon when the sky was clear.

Disposing of the bodies was an unpleasant and time-absorbing business; an old quarry in the woods about a kilometre away provided a cliff over which they could be tipped into mercifully concealing trees, for burial was out of the question. But they had to be carted there under armed guard as always and this made the farmwork intermittent.

None of the defenders managed to become indifferent to the slaughter, with the possible exception of Harry's younger brother who had a vicious streak and seemed almost to enjoy it. Strangely, Harry himself betrayed the most distress; he had been a regular soldier and had seen action in both of the small localized wars which had disfigured the 1990s. But that had been the killing of armed enemies as sane as himself, and *this*, by its very contrast, went against all his soldier's instincts. So in some ways it was even harder for him than for the others who had never been trained in 'honourable' warfare. For Harry was both briskly practical and unsubtly honourable, so while he did not hesitate over the necessity he could not hide the anguish. He never put it into words except in the simple phrase 'poor sods', but somehow that muttered epitaph was more poignant than most graveside orations.

After two weeks of shooting came the first signs of a change. They began finding the bodies of madmen who had died of their own accord.

They had expected it, logically, having reached the same conclusions as Geraint Lloyd; the exposed, underfed, self-injuring lunatics could not survive for long. All the same, the first bodies took them by surprise. They all seemed, by some bizarre mercy of Providence, to have died in their sleep; they were curled up under the lee side of hedges or against haystacks (one had even crept into an outlying barn), as though in the hour of death they had rediscovered their lost instinct to seek shelter. That they had been madmen and not mere refugees was beyond question – they had the torn and festering fingernails, the encrusted eyes, the strangely emaciated necks and the yellowish pallor which the defenders had come to recognize as symptomatic.

There was in fact one other phenomenon of these 'natural' deaths to which only Betty was a chance witness and of which she could not bring herself to tell even Philip: a last-minute return of sanity. It was she who discovered the shelterer in the barn. Philip was a hundred metres away, on armed guard, and Tonia was near him. Betty, needing a bucket, had gone to the barn alone – breaking the rules a little but all was quiet (the madmen were usually heard before they were seen) and she had an automatic in her belt. She came across the man without warning, when she was almost on him, lying foetally curled in the hay. He was unmistakably a madman and her hand flew to her gun, but he did not move, merely stared at her, and Betty (breaking the rules again) hesitated. After a few seconds, the man smiled, said 'Hullo there!' in a calm friendly voice, closed his eyes and died.

Betty somehow knew, beyond a shadow of doubt, that he was dead. She was so certain that she put away her gun and knelt beside him, bursting into tears for the first time since the earthquake. Philip heard her sobs and came running. When he found her with the body, he helped her up, soothing her, saying 'I know, love, it's bloody . . . I know . . . I know . . .' again and again.

No, darling, you don't, she thought as she clung to him; not this new heart-breaking thing. And I'm not going to tell you. I hope you never find out. One of us is enough.

Over the next few days, the number of discovered bodies increased and the number of attacks grew fewer. At last the attacks ceased altogether. The Madness was over. They carted the last bodies off their land and began, warily and a little increduously, to relax.

Even the BBC, in the first of its brief bulletins that had meant anything at all since the flood warnings, announced that 'reports from Government agents throughout the country' showed that the last of the madmen (whom the bulletins called 'afflicted categories') was dead. It ended with a vaguely worded exhortation to 'those of us who have survived' to form small self-supporting communities and live off the land.

'Thanks very much,' Harry said scornfully as he switched off. 'We're doing that already and so's everyone else with any sense, I imagine. Bloody so-called Government!

Whose fault was the Madness anyway? Who didn't tell us about the vinegar masks till it was too bloody late?'

'Did you notice the "Government agents" bit?' Philip asked. 'That was deliberate, I'd say, knowing how Beehive thinks. Plant the idea that Big Brother is watching you, wherever you are.'

'You bet I noticed. . . . Why didn't they tell us something useful, like how many people are still alive, and where? Let their bloody spies earn their living. . . . I wonder how many *are* alive? We've seen nobody for days, except the Robertsons at the farm down the hill and that small bunch we saw on the move yesterday.'

'Yes . . . I wonder why they didn't stop? They saw us, too.'

'Just being cautious, I expect. People will be, for quite a while. You can't blame them.'

In the sudden empty peace of the land, the Garth Farm group were not, as it turned out, cautious enough.

Half a kilometre from the farm stood an isolated, practically undamaged cottage to which Betty and Tonia had taken a fancy. Sleeping accommodation at the farm *was* a little cramped and if Philip, Betty and Tonia moved into the cottage, the three single men could move out of the dormitory into warmer bedrooms. The could still cook and feed communally but everyone would have more elbow-room. It seemed a good idea to all concerned and the move was made.

Now that they were able to concentrate on the work, they made fair progress. Harry and his wife, Harry's brother, and Tonia all had some agricultural knowledge and were able to direct the efforts of the others; and the farm, though it was not large and seemed to have been under-capitalized, had been well cared for and the land was in good condition. It would be hard work without fuel to drive a tractor or other machinery, but unlike the vanished owners they would be concerned not with cash crops but with feeding themselves, so they could horse-plough enough for vegetables and increase their livestock – their neighbours the Robertsons, grateful for the gift of one of the Army rifles during the Madness, had already promised help with that. The Robertsons also owned more than thirty hives and had offered them half a dozen. Honey would be vital in the absence of sugar and none of them had any idea if beet-sugar production was possible on a domestic scale or how to set about it if it was. Garth Farm had half a hectare of orchard and a sizeable soft-fruit garden, while the Robertsons had virtually no fruit at all, so the beginnings of a mutually beneficial barter relationship already existed.

All in all, for eleven adults and three children, Garth Farm looked a viable proposition; rather a lot of mouths to feed, perhaps, until their production plan had been working for a season or two – but even that was taken care of; the Robertsons' place was about the same size but only had three adults and two children, so they were only too willing to offer food in exchange for help.

'When you look at it, this place is a bloody godsend,' Harry decided. 'It could have been designed for people like us, in a survival situation.'

There were others who thought so, too, and for years afterwards Philip found it hard to forgive himself for their naïveté in believing that they could forget defence once the Madness was over. If they had been a little more realistic, a little more quick-witted, Harry and the others might still be alive.

They had even, in a sense, had warning. A man and a girl on horseback had ridden up to the farm one morning, saying they were looking for relatives who had been somewhere in the area just before the Madness set in. Harry and the others had received them politely and given them a cup of their fast-vanishing tea but had agreed afterwards that they didn't like them much. They had been, as Tonia put it, 'too goddamn nosey', asking questions and peering around with a persistence that seemed somehow out of tune with their assumed friendliness. Everyone was relieved to see the back of them and promptly forgot them, instead of realizing the possible implication that the 'friendly visit' was in fact a reconnaissance for a raid.

Luckily, Philip, Betty and Tonia had not yet moved to the cottage when the visitors came, so that piece was missing from the reconnaissance jigsaw puzzle. It was the missing piece which saved not only them but Harry's children, eleven-year-old Finola and seven-year-old Mark.

They moved into the cottage, as it happened, two days later; and three days after that, just before breakfast-time, the raiders took Garth Farm.

In the cottage, Betty and Tonia were tidying up and Philip was still shaving – ten minutes later, they would have been on their way past the orchard to the farm for the communal breakfast. Philip thought he heard hooves but told himself it was probably Harry and his wife out for an early ride on the two hunters Robertson had quartered with them because his stable was overcrowded and there was plenty of room in Garth Farm's. Or it could be old Bunty (as they had christened the farm's own veteran mare) frisking in the pasture behind the cottage, where she had spent the night after working yesterday pulling the cart which was kept in the cottage's lean-to. Bunty did have bouts of skittishness on fine mornings like this.

Philip rinsed his face and was still drying it when he heard the shots. Ten, fifteen of them, maybe more; in the sudden fusillade he lost count but the firing was over by the time he had run to the upper window from which he could see the farm. Betty and Tonia were hard on his heels.

'Oh, Christ – what the hell was that?'

'Look – six, seven horses, tethered to the rail fence . . .'

There was somebody with the horses, shotgun in hand; it looked like a girl, though it was hard to tell from this distance, as she or he was half hidden by a tree. Almost at once, two men walked out of the farmyard towards her; they too carried guns and moved with the confident ease of victors who need not fear a shot in the back. The girl – it was a girl, they saw now – stepped away from the tree to meet them.

'It's that bitch who came the other day,' Tonia said, grimly. 'God, we were *blind*!'

Philip took a deep breath. 'Look, girls – I'm afraid it's bloody obvious what's happened. They've raided the farm and they've *won*. A hell of a lot of shooting, over quickly, and then those three walking about as though they *know* it's over. The rest – there must be at least four more from the number of horses – they'll be inside, with Harry and the others either dead or prisoners. Question is – what do *we* do? Try a counter-attack, to rescue them if they're still alive?'

'What with?' Betty asked. 'One pistol and a four-ten? We've got some rifle ammo but all the rifles are at the farm.'

'Hell!'

'Our only chance'd be to hide in the woods and wait till dark. We *might* get away with something in the small hours.'

'*If* there's anyone left to rescue,' Tonia said. 'That shooting sounded – well, kind of purposeful, to me.'

'We'll have to get out of *here*, that's for sure,' Philip told them. 'That lot know what they're doing – and from their recce they know we three are missing. They'll take a look at the cottage any moment now.'

Suddenly Betty gripped his arm and pointed.

Running through the orchard, obviously keeping out of sight of the farm, were Harry's two children. Finola, awkwardly but determinedly, clutched a rifle. Little Mark, close behind her, hugged a carrier bag.

'Get 'em in – quick!' Philip rapped. 'Tonia, you keep watch here – right? Anyone comes this way – downstairs like the clappers!'

'Right.'

The two children cannoned into their arms in the garden – Finola white-faced but calm, Mark sobbing quietly, spilling his bag of cartridge-clips on to the lawn.

'They're all dead,' Finola said woodenly. 'Everyone but us.'

Betty put her arms round the two children, tightly, and they clung to her. 'Catch Bunty, Phil,' she said over their heads. 'We'll chuck what we can into the cart. We'll at least *try* to get away on wheels. But if Tonia gives the alarm, we'll have to drop everything and run.'

They did get away, the five of them, with a haphazard cartload of possessions and loaded weapons, making as little noise as they could as Bunty hauled the cart down the lane away from (and fortunately out of sight of) the farm. Tonia drove, Betty kept the children under cover behind piled bedding and Philip sat by the tailboard, rifle in hand. They had gone about three kilometres before the pursuers appeared behind them – two mounted men, one of them the man who had come to the farm before. Philip hid his rifle till they were within range and then brought down one of the horses with his first shot; the rider hit the road, either stunned or dead. The other man spurred forward, not pausing to unsling his rifle but firing with a revolver. Philip heard two bullets smack the tailboard before he got the second man in the chest.

'Pull up, Tonia!'

Tonia reined in and Philip jumped to the ground. The first man *had* been stunned and Philip had no compunction at all about shooting him through the head; the man was a murderer anyway, and no report of them must get back to the farm. He collected the dead men's weapons and ammunition, caught and mounted the surviving horse and rejoined the others.

They set off again, moving as fast as Bunty could manage and concentrating on finding unlikely routes to lose any other pursuers.

Mark was still in shock, but Finola, a fiercely intelligent child who had been aware of the possibility of disaster throughout the slaughter of the past few weeks, managed to tell them the story. She and Mark had been upstairs with 'Uncle John', Harry's aggressive younger brother, when the raiders swooped on the farm. Everyone else had been caught unprepared and unarmed in the kitchen or the yard and had been herded into the yard. John had loaded the rifle he always kept beside him, and motioned the children to keep quiet. Then, from the bedroom window, he had tried to shoot the raiders' leader. Somehow he had missed ('the man must have moved just as he fired – Uncle John was a good shot') and as he re-aimed he was shot dead himself. Whether the family tried to seize the opportunity to rush the raiders, or were shot down at once in cold blood, Finola did not know. She was busy dragging Mark into the loft and through the trap-door to the water-tank space under the roof. But as they ran, they heard the fusillade. There was a skylight by the tank and peering cautiously through it Finola had counted the bodies in the yard and realized that she and Mark were on their own – unless they could reach the cottage unobserved. She had kept her nerve astonishingly well, quietening Mark as the raiders searched the upstairs rooms and miraculously missed the little trap-door, creeping out when they had gone downstairs to search the outbuildings, finding her father's rifle and ammunition in the bedroom, leading Mark down the back stairs and hiding with him in the fruit bushes till the raiders were indoors again. ('I'd have used the rifle if they'd found us,' she declared and Philip for one believed her.) Then they had slipped away through the orchard.

'You did marvellously, darling,' Betty told her. 'It was horrible, but you're safe now.'

Finola shook her head, gravely. 'Oh, no, we're not. None of us. Anything could happen any moment, couldn't it? Things are like that always, now. But I'm glad we're with you. Where are we going?'

17

Brenda liked Gareth Underwood. Not merely because he was clearly in love with her but because he really was a very nice young man. Both these facts were, she felt, out of character. Intelligence agents weren't supposed to be either emotionally vulnerable or nice. Sexual buccaneers maybe, in accordance with popular tradition – sweeping women off their feet with casual unconcern, but not politely, undemandingly adoring. Charming bastards maybe but not genuinely and transparently *nice*. She told herself, amused, that he must be a very incapable spy. Yet she knew he was not. He ranked high for his age in Beehive's Intelligence Section.

Gareth was responsible every Monday (when he was not on some nameless mission on Surface) for bringing Brenda the weekly Intelligence Digest for filing in her library's Top Secret Archive Room. The drill was laid down. He would bring the sealed envelope to her personally; they would go, together and alone, into the TSA Room and lock themselves in; they would then sit on opposite sides of the table and Brenda would open the envelope and sign for the contents before filing them. Today, as she locked the door from the inside, she couldn't resist the quip 'We can't go on meeting like this' – and felt slightly ashamed of herself, for Gareth, while laughing politely at her conventional little joke, actually blushed.

Brenda's security classification, of course, entitled her to read the Digest, and she always skimmed through it in front of Gareth before she filed it. She could have waited till he'd gone, but hell, the boy enjoyed the few minutes' privilege of looking at her, so why not let him? Besides, she could always ask him questions on it and *she* rather wickedly enjoyed seeing how far he was prepared to bend the rules in answering her.

Today, however, the first page of the Digest jolted her into seriousness.

'I knew it was awful, Gareth, but I hadn't realized it was quite as awful as this.' She read out: ' "It is now possible, therefore, to estimate that the total surviving population of England, Wales and Scotland, on Surface, is about 620,000, with a maximum error of ten per cent either way. To this must be added the known total of 11,374 Beehive personnel." . . . Gareth, that's less than one per cent!'

'I know . . . At least the Madness is over. The survivors will *survive*. And multiply.'

'And if there'd been no Madness or practically none? If people had known about the vinegar masks weeks earlier – even days earlier?'

She should not have said that she knew, but Gareth did not freeze up as he might have done. 'I know, Brenda. That was . . . a terrible misjudgement, if you ask me this side of that locked door. But to be fair, you can't blame the Government altogether; they went on what the experts told them and the experts said a major Dust outbreak was unlikely.'

'Was "unlikely" a firm enough prediction to gamble on? . . . Oh, I'm not trying to trap you into dangerous thoughts. I'm just a bit stunned, that's all.'

'Aren't we all? And being safe down here, we've all got Guilt with a capital G nagging at us, so it's not enough to blame natural disaster.'

'I haven't noticed all that much sense of guilt,' Brenda said. 'Mostly it's "I'm all right, Jack".'

'Sometimes both – and that makes it worse. . . . God, this isn't a dictatorship yet. We're still entitled to our own views on policy.'

Not a dictatorship? Brenda asked herself – can he really believe that? But she said no more than: 'Even Intelligence agents.'

He smiled. 'Even us.'

She read for a while in silence and then asked: 'There are things that don't even go into the Digest, aren't there? That don't go down on paper at all?'

'Well . . .' he said, cautiously. 'It's only Top Secret, after all. Which means it goes to quite a lot of people. . . . What did you mean, anyway?'

She tapped the page in front of her. 'For instance – it mentions the witch-hunt thing. More than mentions, in fact – it names the areas where it's strongest and weakest – lists the kind of incident that's taking place, everything from a form of trial claiming to enforce the Order in Council, to straight lynchings – says where witches are reported to have consolidated themselves in static communities or defensive bands – even analyses how well the Crusader network has survived and how much influence it has. The only thing it *doesn't* give is Beehive's attitude.'

'To the Order in Council?' he asked, drily.

'Oh, come off it, Gareth. To the witch-hunt. To these impromptu "trials". To the lynchings. It doesn't say if

Beehive agents – putting it baldly – are trying to calm things down or stir them up.'

'You know I can't comment on that.'

'I know you can't. I was just pointing to the omission which would strike any careful reader as deliberate.'

He paused and then said: 'Let's just put it this way. I hope *I'm* never sent on that kind of job. Only for God's sake don't tell anyone I said so.' He smiled diffidently and all her instincts told her his smile was genuine.

She had pushed him far enough. He must know that, as the Chief's mistress, she was perfectly well aware that the witch-hunt was a deliberate creation from the start to deflect anger from the Government, and as such was still being fomented and encouraged by Gareth's own colleagues in the field. Did he think she was testing his loyalty? Perhaps . . . She sighed inwardly. They were both trapped by love; she by her love for Reggie into the smothering of conscience, Gareth by his love for her into the abandonment of caution.

'You know I'd never hurt you, Gareth,' she said gently. 'I may be . . . well, what everyone knows I am. But I am *not* a listening-post.'

Gareth blushed for the second time, whether from the intimacy of her remark, or from jealousy of Reggie, or both, she did not know. She smiled at him anyway and got up to file the Digest away.

When he had gone she took the file down again and re-read the Digest from start to finish, thoughtfully.

Moira and Dan thought very carefully before they even suggested the 'lighthouse' to the rest of the coven. The temptation to leave things as they were was strong; Camp Cerridwen was consolidating itself gratifyingly well, the central cabin was now roofed and warm, the cook-house was almost ready for use and thanks to an exceptionally mild autumn the ploughing and sowing had progressed faster than they had expected. Relations with the villagers of New Dyfnant, already excellent, were being cemented by growing personal friendships. From the point of view of geography, defence and natural and stored resources, Camp Cerridwen was probably as secure as any survival-group in Britain – and far more secure than most, if the reports Geraint Lloyd was exchanging with his handful of ham radio friends were at all typical. The handful had now increased to six in Britain and two in Ireland, apart from intermittent foreign contacts. Two of those who had fled from the floods had managed to return after the waters subsided, and having been prudent enough to seal their equipment in polythene sacks before they left, were able to get them working again. Another, whom Geraint had not heard from since before the earthquake because his set was mains-powered, had succeeded in converting it to battery power, and had rejoined the network. Recharging or scavenging for batteries remained a problem, of course; one ham had succeeded in building a water-wheel charging plant similar to Greg's, while another pedalled a bicycle-dynamo contraption the whole time he was on the air; their ingenuity, fortunately, seemed to match their compulsion to communicate.

Four of the six reported active witch-hunting in their areas, of varying degrees of intensity. One of them, in Warwickshire, guessed shrewdly that it was being deliberately and centrally fostered. But it was the news from a ham near Marlborough that Moira and Dan found particularly disturbing when Geraint passed it on to them.

'There seems to be a whole stretch of Savernake Forest where the situation's the other way round,' Geraint reported. 'It's a bunch of witches who are doing the persecuting and everyone's shit-scared of them, Joe says. A right black lot they must be, by the sound of it. They threaten disaster to anyone who offends them and if he goes on doing it, the disaster *happens*. . . . Joe can't make up his mind if it's suggestion, real black magic or sabotage organized to *look* like magic; point is, people have found it does happen, so they toe the line. Most of 'em believe it *is* magic.'

'Are they camped in the Forest?' Dan asked. 'This black lot, I mean.'

'They were, till a couple of weeks ago. Then they commandeered a village – a more or less undamaged one but there were only about a dozen survivors in it after the Madness. The witches simply ordered them out and they went. By then they were too scared not to. And since then, more people have been drifting in – almost as if once they were dug in in the village, they sent out a call to their mates to come and join them.'

'Does anyone know who they are? Any names?'

'Joe says not – but their queen bee's got a local nickname: the Black Mamba. Joe's talked to people who've seen her. Young, good-looking, long black hair and a holy terror. She and some man are the leaders but when they deal with anyone she does most of the talking and she's the one they remember.'

'I'm afraid,' Dan said, 'that sounds very much like Karen and John.'

'You *know* them?'

Dan nodded. 'Karen Morley and John Hassell. It was John's wife who got killed on Bell Beacon – the Sabbat Queen. . . .'

'Oh, God, yes. I remember.'

'John was terribly bitter afterwards and you can't blame him. But he'd have come through, on his own. Karen was the coven Maiden; she took Joy's place as High Priestess and got working on him. Persuaded him to fight back by going black. They wanted us to join them and when we said no, they set off – about twenty of them altogether – for Savernake Forest. We never saw them again but by God we heard about them. They're the Angels of Lucifer.'

'The ones who killed Ben Stoddart? – or at least said they would and then staged that terrible thing at Eileen's old Unit?'

'The same. And Ben Stoddart died.'

'Jesus! . . . Could they really *do* that?'

'They could and they did, Geraint. We're certain of it. If I were you I'd tell your friend Joe to stay clear of them. . . . Oh and don't tell him you know their names or who they are. It wouldn't do any good and if word got to them that he knew . . .'

'I get the message . . .' Geraint looked a little embarrassed. 'Look, if I said this at the parent-teacher meeting (we're still holding 'em, did you know that?) I'd be in trouble. But *I* know damn well that witchcraft works. And if the Angels of Lucifer have power, then so have you lot. Can't *you* do some thing about them?'

Dan looked at Moira who said: 'Not yet, Geraint. We may have to one day but the time's not ripe. Consolidation's our job right now. Because when we *do* clash with them . . .'

'Pistols for two and coffee for one?'

'Something like that, yes.'

When Geraint had gone, Dan said: 'I'd hoped we could put off the lighthouse till *we* were dug in. But if the Angels are mobilizing already . . .'

Moira nodded and they called the coven. It still consisted only of themselves, Rosemary, Greg, and Sally. Eileen and Peter had both, separately, asked to be initiated, but Moira, although she welcomed them to most of their Circles, would not bring either of them fully into the coven as long as the tension between them and Eileen's tormented ambivalence were unresolved. And Angie, while benevolently disposed, said she felt 'more at home on the sidelines'.

It was five years since Moira and Dan had last created an 'astral lighthouse'. The house next door to them had been put up for sale and with thoughts of forming their own coven already in their minds, they had very much wanted it to be bought by the right kind of neighbours. They had set up a Circle in their bedroom, and enacted the Great Rite together with dedicated solemnity and in a white heat of love; at the moment of orgasm they had forged the thought-form of a shining light over the empty house, and fervently envisaged its purpose. Within a week, Greg and Rosemary had appeared, liked the house at once, and paid their deposit on it. (Nine months later little Diana had been born; 'And that,' Dan said contentedly when he first held his daughter in his arms, 'must have been some lighthouse.')

Tonight, three days before the full moon, the coven talked together for an hour, and then Moira and Dan, Rosemary and Greg, withdrew to their own tents, while Sally took Diana for a walk by the river in the moonlight as a special late treat. As they watched the water, a fish jumped, and a minute later, a few metres downstream, another. The old woman and the child looked on, fascinated, while first one silver ring and then the other spread, shimmered, and disappeared into the eddies of the current.

'Magic Circles!' Diana whispered.

'Yes, darling. Magic Circles.'

On the day of the full moon, Camp Cerridwen heard a long unfamiliar sound; a motor vehicle coming up the logging road. When it rounded the bend they saw it was a big Dormobile motor caravan with four people in it. Dan was the first to recognize them and called out 'Fred! Jean!' excitedly as he ran towards them. Big and grinning, Fred

317

Thomas braked and jumped out, with Jean behind him; then a shy-looking younger couple, Bruce and Sandie Peters, vaguely remembered as members of the Thomases' coven in Chertsey – the coven which had hived off from the Hassells' and had been invited, but refused, to go with John and Karen to Savernake Forest.

By now the rest of the Camp had come running, and after a babble of welcomes and introductions, Fred told Dan: 'They said in the village we'd find you up here.'

'But *driving*, for God's sake! Where did you get the petrol?'

'Oh, that . . . We've been saving it. We've been holed up near Chipping Norton till the Madness was over, and ever since then we've been trying to pick you up. Tarot, I Ching, map-dowsing, the *lot* and getting nowhere. Then suddenly, three nights ago, Jean said she *knew*. Somewhere in these mountains, a forest near a lake. We thought it was Bala at first but she was positive it was somewhere around here. So we reckoned it was worth the last of our petrol and headed this way – then in Llanfyllin we picked up your trail from a family who said you'd saved their lives by telling their cousin in New Dyfnant about the vinegar masks. So here we are – and if there's a litre left in the tank, I'll be surprised. . . . May we stay? Have you room for us? We'll work hard.' He grinned again. 'I know I'm only a bloody clerk but Bruce here is a builder. And both the girls are gardeners.'

'Room for you?' Moira smiled back. 'Look around – you bet there is. And I've a feeling you're only the first.'

18

'If Mac sounds off once more about the evils of witchcraft,' Beaver grumbled, poking the fire viciously, 'I'll . . .'

'Yes, Beaver? *What* will you do?' Wally's question was crisp and sardonic and when he was crisp and sardonic he was dangerous.

Beaver moderated his voice. 'Just that his preaching's a bloody bore. We're clobbering witches, aren't we? – and doing all right out of it. Can't we just get on with it and manage without Mac's lectures?'

Wally poured himself a whisky. 'Let him talk. You don't have to listen.'

'Easier said than done. He's got a voice like a dentist's drill.'

'All the same, you'll do it. Mac's our lifeline to Beehive. Where'd we be without that? No petrol dump, no ammo – we'd just be one more brigand group putting the fear of God into the locals. The couple of dozen we can reach in an hour's walk. No future in *that* because they've got nothing worth looting.'

'They've got some cattle and things.'

Wally laughed. 'I can just see you settling down to a quiet

life milking Buttercup every morning.' He switched off the laugh and went on incisively: 'We are mobile and we have fire-power. They're the things that matter and it's Mac who supplies them. All *we* have to do is wave a Crusader banner for him. Personally, I don't give a damn if we're clobbering witches or flat-earthers or guys with red hair. But it's witches we're paid for – in petrol, ammunition and other things. And that's worth a few boring speeches from Mac. He really *believes* in it. And he's ready enough to do his bit if a raid turns into a fight. So let him talk, if he wants to.'

Beaver sighed. 'I suppose you're right . . . Tell you one thing, though. Petrol and ammo are fine but here's the six of us in a nice cosy manor house and it's like a bloody monastery. If Beehive really wants to keep us happy why don't they send us some women?'

'Poor deprived Beaver.' Wally regarded him thoughtfully. 'You have a point, though – some resident crumpet would be good for morale. It might even be able to cook.'

'There's Little Big Tits, at the mill. I could sort that man of hers with one hand.'

'For Christ's sake, Beaver – I've told you before. Foxes don't rob the farms they live on. So hands off the locals. We want 'em scared of us, sure – but not hell-bent on revenge. No aggro within five kilometres of base and that's an order. *Again.*'

'It was just a thought.'

'I'll do the thinking around here.'

'Think me up a redhead, then.'

Wally was silent for a minute, then narrowed his eyes into the chilly smile that announced an idea. 'Would you mind if she was a witch?'

'I'm not Mac. She can be a Confucian Methodist Jewess if she's built right. And preferably under eighteen.'

'Business and pleasure,' Wally mused. 'Two birds with one stone. Yes, why not?'

'There's six of us,' Beaver pointed out. 'That means six birds not just two.'

'Fair enough. . . . Have you ever heard of Woodbury Croft? Well, I have. I keep my ears open, which is more than you do. And I've been saving that one up.'

Molly Andrews had looked at the sky, sniffed the air, tapped the barometer and decided it was not going to rain. 'Right, Jane. If you get Team A on to lifting onions, I'll take Team B for sowing summer cauliflowers – that'll be a quicker job, so when we've finished we'll come over and help your lot. Barbara, Team C on the cows.'

'Where are we storing the onions?' Jane Hooley asked, with her usual slightly anxious frown. The youngest of the three teachers, she was earnest and meticulous; the girls had teased her a good deal when she had first come to Woodbury Croft a year ago and Molly had wondered if she was going to prove suitable. But she had won the girls over by some indefinable alchemy of her own and the teasing had petered out.

'In the end garage, dear. Spread them on that long bench by the window, where the sun can dry them. If there are too many for the bench, we'll make some wire frames to extend it. . . . And, Barbara, see what you think about Snodgrass, will you? I'm not happy about him, and he's the only bull we've got till Peppy grows up. Hell, I wish we had a vet.'

They discussed Snodgrass's symptoms while the girls assembled in the gym for the morning briefing. Molly had been a teacher for twenty-three years, and Principal of Woodbury Croft for the past nine, and she was still both bewildered and exhilarated by finding herself, all of a sudden, more farmer than teacher, in charge of what she called 'this agricultural nunnery'. In the summer term there had been seven staff and ninety-three pupils; now there were only three staff and eighteen pupils. The crisis and the witch-hunt had hit the school badly, for Woodbury Croft was, in its modest way, as well known for its pagan orientation as Saffron Walden and Sidcot were for their Quakerism. Four out of five of the girls had come from witch families and Molly and her deputy Barbara Simms were both open witches. The non-witch girls had been withdrawn by their parents and two of the staff had resigned at the time of the first Order in Council. Molly, though naturally worried, could not blame them. The rest had simply not come back for the autumn term, except for Jane and Barbara and the eighteen girls who were still with them, and with the witch-hunt in full swing, Molly was surprised that any had returned at all. Then, with the earthquake, she had found herself responsible for them all. No word had come from any of the parents or from Jane's brother in Huddersfield or from Barbara's fiancé in London. They must all be presumed dead till proved otherwise. Meanwhile they themselves were alive, thanks to a good stock of vinegar for pickling, and Molly's prompt reaction to the Prime Minister's broadcast.

The period of the Madness had been a nightmare. They had no defence but a twenty-year-old revolver that had belonged to Molly's soldier father and exactly six rounds of equally ancient ammunition. Molly had managed to stockpile some food but it had had to be rationed to near-starvation level because they had no idea how long the siege would last. For siege it was. Woodbury Croft was in isolated Midland country but they saw roving madmen almost every day. Molly had had no choice – with eighteen girls aged eleven to seventeen on her hands – but to barricade the school's main building and stay inside it. On three occasions, when all seemed quiet, she had made a quick sortie with two of the senior girls (she picked the best sprinters) to gather what they could carry from the vegetable garden, Molly armed with the revolver and the girls with axes. The third time, they had been taken by surprise by a barefooted madman who had rushed at them out of a shrubbery. The bigger of the two girls had tried to hold him at bay with her axe and then Molly had shot him, astonished that the gun worked.

They had not visited the vegetable garden again until the Government radio confirmed that the Madness was over.

Since then, they had seen no one but two nomad families who had passed by with little to add to what they had guessed already – that there were no neighbours in evidence for several kilometres. Woodbury Croft was on its own.

Molly, her two assistants, and one or two of the older girls had started planning. The vegetable garden was fortunately large, for home-grown vegetables had been part of the school's policy and it could be extended. They had some seeds and looted more from the shop in the tiny abandoned village four kilometres away. (Why it had been abandoned remained a mystery; there were only four corpses – all obviously madmen – and all of the few vehicles which they were used to seeing there were gone.) They had rounded up three cows, two calves, and a bull, and about a dozen hens with a cockerel. Until their own vegetable area's extension began to produce, there was plenty to see them through the winter in the deserted fields and gardens.

Molly had begun to feel more confident; the girls (with the one or two inevitable exceptions) had rallied remarkably well; the work was getting done, and they were even managing to put in a few hours a week of classroom education, for Molly was determined that as far as possible the school should continue to be a school. Farther ahead she could not see.

She hoped they would not remain in all-female isolation for too long; it was not healthy or natural for growing girls, and Molly herself, though unmarried, frankly liked male company. She particularly missed Jock Innes, her own High Priest, and his brother Alec, who had visited the school without fail for all the festivals, and oftener if they could, to hold Circles for the staff witches and for those of the girls whose parents wished it. ('Like a convent's confessor,' he used to joke.) Perhaps Jock and Alec were dead too, now. One night, in a crisis of loneliness, Molly had sat quietly in her bedroom and opened up her astral awareness, trying to pick them up. She had been so swamped by the horror that pervaded the astral plane, at the height of the Madness, that she had withdrawn from it at once, gasping and weeping, and had not tried again.

Doreen and Kathy worked their way along the line of onions, Kathy doing most of the talking as usual. They did not look like sisters; Doreen, almost seventeen, abundant red hair caught in a waist-length ponytail, already full-breasted and wide-hipped, of whom everyone had always said 'she's the quiet one'; Kathy, just fifteen, with her short black mop and boyish figure, who was never still and never silent. Yet they had always been close and although each was in her own way essentially feminine, they seemed aware of a creative polarity of difference which they enjoyed as a man and woman might. They were the only children of witch parents who would have been reluctant to send them to boarding school, if their father's job as a foreign correspondent for *The Times* had not kept him (and their mother, once the girls were old enough) constantly on the

324

move. Their mother had always arranged to be at home for the school holidays, or to take them with her, if it could be managed, to where their father was. A very gifted witch herself, she had spent much of their time together training the girls in the Craft, and they had taken to it like ducks to water, working very well as a partnership because of that very polarity of difference. It was just as well that they were close, now, because they knew it was almost certain they were orphans.

'I hope we'll be growing some *spring* onions, too,' Kathy was chattering. 'These big fat ones are nice, specially for cooking, I like 'em with mashed spuds, but fried is best – only fat's hard to come by now, isn't it? But spring onions, come salad time, salad's so *boring* if it's just lettuce and things . . .'

'Hey, Kath – shut up – listen . . .'

Then Kathy heard it too and straightened, incredulous. All along the line the girls were stopping their work, staring towards the drive. It couldn't be . . . but it was, *engines* – a big van and four motor-cycles, winding up from the road. Then they were all running, excited, Miss Hooley with them and across the field they could see Big Molly and her lot running too, and Miss Simms and the others from the cow-shed.

Doreen, as she ran, felt a flash of unease. Something about the way the van drew up, two men jumping down from it to left and right, and the motor-bikes halting spread out in a neat arc, two on each side of the van – all happening together, like a military operation. . . . Don't be silly, she told herself, these days people do behave like soldiers if they've any sense, keep together, ready for anything, eyes open. . . . She kept running, Kathy beside her and soon everybody was gathered in the drive, staring at the visitors.

'My name's Walter Crane,' the man who was obviously the leader was telling Molly. Doreen didn't like him; his eyes never seemed to blink and he stood with his feet apart like a poised boxer.

'And mine is Marie Andrews,' Molly said. So Big Molly isn't happy about him either, Doreen thought; I've only heard her use her proper name about twice, when she was upstaging people. 'We are what is left of Woodbury Croft School. Where are you from?'

'North of here . . . Is this all of you?' He made an economical gesture to include the assembled women and girls.

Taking him very literally (another upstaging sign, Doreen knew) Molly did a roll-call with her eyes. 'Yes, all of us. . . . You're very lucky to have petrol, aren't you?'

'It's Government issue. From a special concealed dump.'

'Oh? Then you have some official function?'

'You could call it that, Miss Andrews.' He snapped his fingers. In a moment, all his five followers had guns in their hands. Automatics appeared from inside anoraks and two light machine-guns from motor-cycle pannier bags. Several of the girls screamed but Walter Crane snapped 'Shut up!' with such frightening authority that the screams became mere whimpers. Doreen, who had not screamed, remembered her mother's training: *If anything frightening happens, breathe slowly and keep your nerve.* Doreen breathed slowly, taking Kathy's hand in her own. She realized that her instinct about the arc of motor-cycles had been right; the raiders had them neatly penned.

'And what is that function, Mr Crane?' Big Molly asked. 'Terrorizing schoolgirls?'

He still did not blink. 'Our function, Miss Andrews, is rooting out witches.'

Big Molly must be breathing deeply too, Doreen thought,

because she kept her cool splendidly. 'Indeed. May I see your authority for that? I presume you have one.'

'Certainly.' He had not yet produced a gun himself but now he did, and fired a single shot into the air. More screams, even more quickly smothered. When the echo had died away, he said: 'That is our authority.'

'A typical one.'

'Oh, don't misjudge us, Miss Andrews. There is always a proper trial.'

'I'm sure there is. With you, Mr Crane, as judge and jury.'

'You're misjudging us again. I am the judge. Four of my friends are the jury; allow me to introduce them – Beaver, Mac, Jake and Fatso. And Garry over there is the executioner.'

Breathe very slowly. Very, very slowly. And don't scream, whatever you do. Kathy's convulsive grip almost cracked Doreen's fingers but she was managing to keep silent, too.

'You're the headmistress, I take it, Miss Andrews?'

'I am.'

'Then since everybody knows this is a witch school, you're the one to stand trial . . .' He looked around, unhurried. 'The netball field, I think. Garry, bring what we need from the van. The rest of you, take everybody over there.'

Most of the girls were by now numb with shock and it was a stumbling procession that made its way to the netball field, flanked by the four gunmen. When they reached it, all but Big Molly were herded together in a group facing one of the tall posts.

'Which of you is Miss Andrews' second-in-command?'

Barbara, who had been trying to soothe one of the youngest of the girls, stepped forward without speaking.

'Your name?'

'Barbara Simms.'

'Right, Miss Simms. Come here to me . . . Now turn round.' He pressed his gun into the back of Barbara's neck and raised his voice. 'Understand this, all you girls. If anyone misbehaves, or tries to interfere, or doesn't do exactly what she's told, I shall blow Miss Simms' head off. . . . Garry – tie Miss Andrews to the post.'

This can't be happening, but it is – she looks like Joan of Arc, roped to the netball post – and that ring over her head, it even looks like a halo – oh, Big Molly, how can we help – Aradia, Cernunnos, let her feel no pain. . . .

'Marie Andrews, you are charged with the crime of witchcraft. You are further charged with the crime of corrupting these girls by teaching them the evil and illegal beliefs and practices of witchcraft. Do you plead guilty or not guilty?'

Molly's voice trembled a little but was still clear. 'I do not recognize this so-called court and I therefore refuse to answer.'

'The court takes note that the prisoner is obstinate and uncooperative but interprets her statement as amounting to a plea of not guilty. . . . Marie Andrews – are you a witch?'

'I refuse to answer.'

'The court is merciful so it gives you a second chance to reply. Are you a witch?'

'I refuse to answer.'

'The court's patience is exhausted. There are no further questions, so I will sum up for the jury. If the prisoner were not a witch, she would say so honestly. Her refusal to answer is tantamount to a confession. That being so, the second charge, of corrupting young people by teaching them witchcraft, follows naturally, for a witch in charge of a school cannot do otherwise. Gentlemen of the jury – do you find the prisoner guilty or not guilty?'

The four gunmen chorused 'Guilty!'

'Then only one sentence is possible. Executioner, do your duty.'

When the man called Garry flung the canful of petrol all over Molly's clothes, the screaming really started; and when he set light to it, most of the girls hid their faces, clutching each other. Even Kathy buried her head in Doreen's shoulder; only Doreen, summoning strength she didn't believe she possessed, stood upright and wide-eyed, trying to pour her soul's help into Big Molly at the moment of flaming death, trying to remember in one impossible instant all that her parents had taught her about fighting against evil. She believed, then and afterwards, that her help reached Big Molly, for Big Molly never screamed, only opened her mouth in a single gasp which became without pause the rictus of physical death.

Big Molly herself was gone.

A few minutes later, the twenty survivors lined the wall of the gym, five gunmen facing them like watchful NCOs while Walter Crane inspected them.

'Right,' he said when he had finished walking along the line. 'You're witches, every one of you – we know that. And you're damn lucky not to be going the same way as *she* did. Remember that – and remember we can always come back another day. Right now, we're letting you off lightly, but it'd be wrong to let you off altogether. So I'll tell you what is going to happen. Six of you are coming with us, for penal servitude on behalf of the others.'

Doreen called out, loudly and deliberately: 'And just what do you mean by that, you sadistic, murdering bastard?'

Miss Simms, beside her, tried to shush her but it was too late, it had been said, and Doreen felt better for her defiance. Walter Crane merely smiled and walked unhurriedly across to her. He looked her up and down, slowly, unblinking as ever.

'Beaver, come here.'

One of the gunmen, who looked more muscle than brain, joined him. 'Yes, Wally?'

'You wanted a redhead. How about this one?'

Beaver repeated Wally's up-and-down inspection but less coolly. 'Not bad.'

'Then as she's apparently too stupid to realize what six men mean by penal servitude for six girls – strip the bitch and show her.' He pulled Barbara Simms out of the line and once more held his gun to the back of her neck. 'The other boys can hold her down. And, girls – remember what I said about blowing Miss Simms' head off. Because if the rest of you so much as move, I'll do it.'

The van bumped and wove along the country lanes with the six of them locked in the back. Every few minutes Wally slid open the inspection window from the driver's cab to glance at them before sliding it shut again; otherwise they were on their own.

Doreen barely felt the pain of her ruptured hymen or the bruises on her wrists and ankles; she was transfigured by a magnificent hatred, a beautiful and treasured hatred, ice-cold, calculating and patient. She was armed with a new, strange deadliness and she was glad of it. Everything, for the first time in her sixteen and three-quarter years, was black and white without a hint of grey; fierce love for her friends, alive or dead, fierce and merciless hatred for her enemies – the six men with the guns. It was all so simple.

She looked around the other five girls and knew, with a confidence that transcended pride, that she was their leader. Wally himself had picked Kathy, of which Doreen and Kathy were both glad, because grim as their outlook was they needed each other. Mac – the humourless fanatical one – had chosen Gina, slow and cow-like and looking more bewildered than frightened. Jake, whose apparently colourless personality Doreen could not make out yet, had picked Helen, a doll-like fifteen-year-old; he would find she had a fiery temper. Helen seemed to be bearing up well. The one Doreen was most concerned about (she had one protective arm round her as they travelled) was little Muriel, who was only thirteen and had been selected by the obese and sweaty Fatso. She was trying not to cry but was trembling uncontrollably, and no wonder. The sixth, Miriam, an eighteen-year-old Jewess, had been picked by the executioner Garry. Miriam, Doreen felt, would be a tower of strength for she was conscious of her inheritance, and two millennia of ghetto wisdom burned in the brown eyes which gazed into Doreen's across the van and seemed to be saying 'This is nothing new, my friend'. Doreen was grateful that Miriam *was* her closest friend apart from Kathy. The three of them should be able to hold the others together.

Muriel turned in Doreen's arm and moaned: 'What are we going to *do*?'

'Do?' Doreen glanced at the the inspection window to make sure it was closed. 'We're going to do exactly as we're told and be good, obedient, submissive little prisoners, until the chance we'll be looking for comes. And when it does, God help those bastards.'

Philip's little group had been on the move for a week, living off the land and not quite knowing what they were looking for. They knew they should settle somewhere, with the winter coming on, and preferably in a community of some kind, particularly as they had the two children, Finola and Mark, to look after. They wondered what conditions would be like in the smaller towns, now that the Madness was over, and had taken a wary look at Kettering and Market Harborough. Kettering was silent and virtually empty, with occasional survivors always scuttling out of sight as soon as they saw them; much of what had not already been destroyed by the earthquake had since been gutted by fire, which seemed to have been widespread in several parts of the town – though how the fires had started, they could only guess. They had managed to scavenge one or two things which they needed from ruined shops and houses, though earlier looters had left little worth scavenging. Their most useful finds were enough heavy-duty polythene to turn the cart into a covered wagon, and – for Tonia – a cassette recorder, several cassettes and a whole box of batteries. Tonia, though now readerless, had all the frustrated instincts of a communicator and it cheered her up a lot to be able to keep a recorded journal, and it cheered the others to be able to tease her about it.

Kettering they found insupportably depressing. Market Harborough was not merely depressing, it was hostile. There seemed to be a few more people there than in Kettering, but they, too, flitted on the edge of vision. In one street, three or four arrows were shot at them – not very efficiently, because only one hit the wagon, burying its head in the woodwork. They put on the best speed Bunty could manage and headed out of town. A couple of hundred metres farther on, they were fired at by a rifle from somewhere behind them. The intention was apparently merely to hasten them on their way, because the bullets ricocheted off the pavement exactly the same distance to each side of them, suggesting that the marksman could have hit them if he had wanted to. They took the hint and kept going.

But the chief reason that would have decided them against taking refuge in a town in any case was the profusion of corpses, in various stages of decomposition. Most of them, if they were recent enough for the mad and the sane to be distinguishable, seemed to have been madmen – but by no means all of them. The stench of death was everywhere and doubtless the disease-germs of corruption as well.

'Anyone who stays in those fever-traps must be crazy,' Betty said, 'or else too stupid to be able to survive where they can't find cans to open. For God's sake, let's stay in the country.'

Nobody argued. Finola said, 'The horses don't like towns, anyway.'

Some of the villages were corpse-strewn like the towns and had been abandoned once the looters had done their work. But one or two had been cleared of bodies and colonized by refugees. These varied in their reaction to new people who came their way. One, a few kilometres from Market Harborough, had just had two typhus deaths and would admit no newcomers unless they quarantined themselves for three weeks in a designated cottage. Another was occupied by eleven men and three women, two of whom were over fifty; Philip's party were urged to stay a little too warmly, and Betty and Tonia had no difficulty in persuading Philip to move on. Another would have welcomed them and they were tempted, but although friendly the villagers seemed shiftless and impractical, and their ability to forge a working community seemed doubtful. At another, they were simply turned back at a street barricade without explanation.

They were beginning to wonder if, after all, they would have to find a small farm they could run by themselves, when they met the Ramsays.

They had bypassed Leicester and Burton and were working their way across country south of Uttoxeter, heading for the more open lands of the Welsh border. The going had been rough this particular day with many diversions and back-trackings because of fissures, and when in the evening they saw a likely looking field with a stream and a copse that promised firewood, they were glad to stop. A horse-caravan was there already and as usual Philip rode up to it a little ahead of the wagon to make sure that the people were friendly.

A man was building a camp-fire near the caravan, and as Philip approached a woman and a small boy disappeared into the caravan with the signs of caution which Philip had learned to recognize. The man, who was about his own age, watched him warily but after the habitual tentative exchange of greetings apparently decided he was not dangerous. Very soon the wagon was parked beside the caravan, the women and children were making friends and Philip was helping the man to get the fire going.

They introduced themselves as Jack and Sue Ramsay and their eight-year-old son Clive. They had lived in Uttoxeter, which was completely destroyed, they said. After the earthquake, they had fled by car, but had only gone a few kilometres when it broke a half-shaft. They had been determined to remain mobile, and all petrol would have vanished within a few days; so they had, like Philip's group, salvaged a horse and cart. Only more ambitiously and ingeniously they had then hunted for an abandoned caravan trailer which they had managed to roll on to the flat top of the cart, jack up to remove its wheels, lower on to the cart and lash in place to make a very serviceable horse-caravan.

'Only snag is, it's a bit longer than the cart-top,' Jack said. 'So the driver has to ride the horse. Ever tried that, between shafts? But we manage.'

'It's a marvellous job,' Betty said. 'Much better than our covered wagon thing.'

They cooked a communal meal of rabbit-and-vegetable casserole. Philip had shot the rabbits that morning and although they were a brace of big ones they did not supply much meat for eight people. But to the Ramsays any meat was a luxury; they had no gun, and admitted they had not yet mastered the art of snaring. They had caught the occasional chicken but by now almost all stray poultry had either been killed by hungry refugees or rounded up and jealously guarded by static families or communities.

'How did you live through the Madness?' Philip asked.

'Oh, God, don't ask. We found a good solid barn and turned it into a ruddy fortress. Every time I went out for vegetables, I wondered if I'd make it back.' He shuddered. 'I had to kill two of them. I carried a bottle of ammonia in my pocket, to chuck in their eyes and an axe to finish 'em off. Thank Christ *that's* over – poor bastards. They were just the same as the rest of us. Only unlucky.'

They were all silent for a moment, remembering. Then Sue said, unexpectedly: 'I wish we *could* say it's over.'

'Oh, it's not too bad now,' Philip said. 'Since the raid that drove us out, we've covered a good hundred kilometres and we've met no more actual violence. We were shot at in Market Harborough but only to warn us off, I think. Compared with the Madness, that's nothing.'

'Then if you don't want to see more violence, you'd better do what we're doing in the morning – get out of here. As far as you can from this area.'

'Why? What's happening?'

Sue's next remark was even more unexpected. 'Are you witches?'

'No, we're not,' Philip told her. 'But we're not against them either. And we think the witch-hunt's barbaric.'

'Good. Because we *are* witches. . . . Ever heard of the Crane Mob?'

'Don't think so. Who are they?'

'A gang of organized witch-hunters. Witch-killers. Their base is about fifteen kilometres east of here, a big old manor house. Somebody's keeping them in petrol. There are six of them, all with motor-bikes and guns. Sometimes they bring a van with them, to take away any useful loot when they've finished. . . . They had been working east and south, pouncing on witch families and wiping them out. But in the last day or two we've heard they're raiding this way. So we're moving.'

'Point is, we're known around here,' Jack said. 'We ran a coven in Uttoxeter before the trouble, and everyone knows our faces. On top of which, that caravan's pretty well unique – recognizable from kilometres away. And yesterday a friend tipped us off we're on the Crane Mob's list. We haven't a gun, so we'd be sitting ducks. We're leaving at first light, travelling west. Out of the Mob's territory. And if I were you, I'd do the same. Our site may be known and the Mob isn't fussy. They might knock you off just in case you were friends of ours.'

Betty murmured in Philip's ear: 'Let's join forces.'

'Good idea,' Philip said. 'Look, Jack – we're heading west, too. And we *have* got guns – three rifles, a four-ten shotgun and two pistols. *And* a spare horse, as outrider. Why don't we stick together? We'd be stronger . . .' He grinned. 'The kids'd be company for each other, too.'

Sue's face lit up. 'Not to mention the grown-ups and the horses. How about it, Jack?'

'I feel better already,' Jack said.

They had worked very carefully on the listening-holes. Wally's bedroom (which was also, like it or not, Kathy's) and Beaver's (Doreen's) were immediately above the big sitting-room where the men always gathered in the evening. Loosening a floorboard in each, which could be hidden by rugs, was not difficult and since the sitting-room ceiling was richly moulded, the little holes they cut in the plaster under the loosened boards were practically invisible even if you knew where to look.

Doreen and Kathy had made the listening-holes while the men were out on raids. They went raiding two or three times a week and to begin with they had always taken one of the 'wives', as they called them, locked in the van as a hostage for the good behaviour of the five left behind – and had also taken all the spare firearms and ammunition (of which they seemed to have plenty) stored in the cab of the van. But after the first week, though the weapons still remained in the van, Wally decided that the hostage was an unnecessary encumbrance. The girls had no transport and nowhere to run, and the locals, well enough aware of the conditional nature of their immunity, would have been quick to inform on the direction the girls had taken if they did try to run.

Besides, Doreen's policy of apparent submission was working. Though it was horribly difficult, the other girls had seen the sense of it and had pinned their hopes on Doreen's leadership. Doll-like Helen, as Doreen had foreseen, was unable to control her sporadic outbursts of temper but ironically they had merely resulted in the other men teasing Jake about being hen-pecked. Thirteen-year-old Muriel had an unexpected reprieve – for Fatso proved to be impotent. Advised by Doreen, she was careful to give no hint of this to the other men while the other girls were equally careful to give no sign that she had told them. Fatso, terrified of ridicule, was grateful for her silence and anxious not to provoke her into breaking it; so she did not manage too badly. Gina and Miriam had not been virgins, which made their ordeal a little less traumatic; Gina, too, was helped by her bovine resilience, and Miriam by the dedicated hatred which she shared with Doreen and Kathy.

They lulled the men further by efficient housekeeping, to which the Mob were not accustomed; and Gina and Helen were excellent cooks.

Eavesdropping on the Mob's plans, once the listening-holes were made, was simplicity itself. When Wally wanted to brief his men on the next day's operation, he dismissed the girls from the sitting-room. It was then natural and unsuspicious for Doreen or Kathy or both to go to their bedrooms. They preferred to have two listeners; it made for more accurate and comprehensive reporting.

The night that Wally planned the raid on the Ramsays, Doreen and Kathy were both at their listening-posts.

'Jake, you've recced the ground,' they heard Wally say. 'Let's have your report.'

'The site's fourteen and a half kilometres from here,' Jake replied. 'No occupied houses within a kilometre of it. You can't mistake their caravan – it's a car-trailer one lashed on to a flat-topped farm cart. The field's triangular, with a river along two sides and a small wood along the third. The road runs behind the wood. If we come at them through the trees, we've got 'em trapped. The stream looks too deep to wade and anyway we could pick 'em off while they were trying.'

'Any firearms?'

'I couldn't see – but they might have 'em hidden. Our contact didn't think so.'

Wally considered for a moment, and then asked: 'Any gradient on the road?'

'Enough to coast the bikes for the last kilometre to the

338

wood. But not for the van, I'd say. She doesn't coast easy, that thing.'

'She's noisy, too. . . . Right, then, we'll do it the simple way. Beaver, you'll take the van, leaving here five minutes after us. We'll go ahead with the bikes, quietly for the last couple of kilometres to the top of the hill, then coast. We'll take up our positions in the wood. When we hear the van coming down the hill, we attack. If the noise brings them out to look, so much the better; we pick them off at a distance. . . . How far's the caravan from the edge of the wood?'

'Eighty metres. Hundred, maybe.'

'Just right. And how wide's the wood, between the road and the field?'

'Fifty metres, say. Easy to move through but plenty of cover.'

'Good. . . . Now remember, everybody – this is a quick kill. No hanging about, no "trials", no lectures. There's no point, because there's no audience. Only the two of them and the kid, so we kill 'em on sight. Lay out the bodies where they can be seen. As soon as we've got 'em, I'll blow my whistle and Beaver will bring the van round. Loot what we need, fire the caravan and leave. The shooting will bring snoopers when it's all quiet and the message will get around. The Ramsays are known as witches. Their bodies will *be* our lecture. Any questions?'

Garry asked: 'What if others have joined them, since Jake did his recce?'

'The plan's the same. Get them too. Guilt by association.'

'What about the horse?'

'Shoot it. . . . Anything else?' Nobody spoke, so Wally went on: 'Give the girls a yell. I want a drink.'

Quickly, Doreen and Kathy replaced their floorboards and rugs.

Later, when they and Miriam were alone together washing-up, Doreen said: 'This is it, I think. It'll be the first time the van's left after the others. Now here's what we'll do . . .'

It was hardly surprising, when the girls served breakfast an hour before dawn, that Beaver was still a little besotted with his 'wife'. She had given him astonishing cause to when they went to bed, playing on everything she had learned about him till he fell asleep in an erotic daze. She was still giving him meaningful glances as he ate his breakfast and Beaver glowed. That was women for you. Show 'em who's boss and before you know where you are they're begging for it.

As the bikes left, all the 'wives' were out there to see them off. Doreen chatted with Beaver while he timed his five minutes, and when he said it was time to go, she put her arms round his neck, said 'Good luck, Beaver' and kissed him powerfully.

His grunt of pleasure changed to a brief scream as the well-honed kitchen-knives were driven into his back by Kathy and Miriam. Then he was dead.

It took less than a minute to distribute the arms and ammunition from the cab. Doreen, Kathy and Miriam were the only ones with knowledge of firearms, so Doreen drove with Kathy beside her, while Miriam rode in the back with the other three, teaching them all she could about loading and firing in the quarter-hour they had available. Kathy navigated from the marked map Beaver had prepared.

'I just hope nothing holds them up,' Kathy said. 'We don't want to overtake them on the road.'

'When Wally plans an operation,' Doreen told her, 'that's the way the operation goes. Only this time, he doesn't know about *us*.'

Jack and Philip were backing the horses into the shafts as the sun cleared the eastern horizon; apart from that, everything was ready to move. Philip had allocated rifles to Jack, himself, and Tonia who was the best shot of them all, and pistols to Betty and Sue. Until they were well clear of the Mob's area, each of them was to keep his or her weapon ready to hand. The three children had been given clear instructions; at the first sign of danger, they were to shelter among the piled bedding in the covered wagon and keep low. They had accepted the drill, though Finola was furious at not being given the shotgun.

Jack's harnessing was finished first and he crossed over to help Philip.

'Healthy-looking old mare, your Bunty,' Jack said. 'She's in as good shape as our Viscount, even though he's younger.'

'Not bad,' Philip agreed. 'I think she . . .' He broke off, cocking his head. 'Did you hear something?'

'What?'

'Car, or van . . . Over there, beyond the wood.'

'Oh Christ – yes!' Jack snatched up his rifle. 'It can only be them. Tell the women – I'll see to the kids. Then firing positions, quick. They'll be coming from the wood, there's no other way.'

They only just made it before the firing started. Prone behind a bush, Philip was firing every time he saw muzzle-smoke; the raiders could not have expected them to be armed, because two or three of them had emerged from the trees, firing as they came, and had only run back when they met the answering fire. Philip thought Tonia had got one, but could not be sure; the man had fallen out of sight into a dip in the ground.

After the first exchange, both sides seemed to have found cover, because the firing settled down to sporadic sniping

341

with no observable hits. Stalemate, Philip thought; someone's going to have to make a rush and it'll have to be them because we can't leave the kids.

When the rush came, Philip's heart sank for an instant; four men, and the two wingers had light machine-guns. We shan't have a hope, unless we get them *now*. . . . He fired at the man on his right, and missed, dropping his head flat as a burst zipped over him.

This is it. Oh, Betty, my darling . . .

There was a sudden crescendo in the firing, which puzzled Philip though he had no time to analyse why. He aimed again at the wing machine-gunner but somebody else got him first; he flung up his hands and crumpled half a second before Philip pulled the trigger. Without pause, he changed targets, and got a man himself. Then he realized what had puzzled him: too *many* rifles . . .

The firing stopped.

In the silence, he could hear one of the women whimpering in smothered pain. Tonia? Sue? He would have known if it were Betty. . . . *Why* had the firing stopped?

A girl's voice called from the wood: 'Are you all right down there?'

For a moment the defenders were all too astonished to answer. The girl's voice came again: 'You're safe. They're all dead. We're coming out and so can you.'

Philip could hardly believe his eyes. From the edge of the wood, holding rifles above their heads to show they came in peace, six girls walked out in line abreast. All of them looked like teenagers and one couldn't have been older than twelve or thirteen.

Jack came to his senses first. 'Come on down,' he called. 'My wife's got a flesh wound, otherwise we're all right. And thanks for your help, whoever you are!'

Round the relit camp-fire – for it was a chilly morning –
the schoolgirl Amazons told their story. 'Once we'd dealt
with Beaver and got the van and the guns, it was easy,
really,' Doreen said. 'We knew what the plan was, so we
just came up behind them through the wood, and as they
started advancing we got them. At least, we got the three you
hadn't got. One of you hit Fatso before we opened fire, then
I think it was you who got Jake while we were all firing. . . .
I'm sorry we didn't start a minute earlier. Then maybe
you' – to Sue – 'wouldn't have got hit.'

Sue patted her bandaged arm. 'Not to worry, it was only
a nick. It hurt like hell for the first minute but it's fine now.
. . . Thank God you came at all. We'd all be dead, otherwise.'

'Oh, I don't know. You were doing fine. They only
thought there'd be the three of you and they didn't expect
you to be armed. . . . Will you stay here now?'

Jack said: 'Not Sue and me and Clive, anyway. We've
got a sort of hunch about the Welsh mountains. . . Phil?
Betty? Tonia?'

'If the girls agree, I think we'll stick with you,' Philip
said, and Betty and Tonia nodded. 'But what about Doreen
and her lot? I don't know how much petrol they've got left,
but we could pack them in our wagons somehow when it
runs out.'

'Thanks, but we've got to get back to school,' Doreen
told him.

Jack began to laugh, helplessly, and soon even the girls
were laughing, too. 'I suppose that did sound rather sur-
realist,' Doreen admitted, 'but we do have to. There's only
two staff and twelve girls left to keep the vegetable garden
going, and that. Besides, they'll be worried sick about us.'

'Doreen,' Miriam said, 'would you mind if I opted out
and went with them? I'm the oldest, and I only came back

343

this term for more "A" Levels, so what's the point now? You can manage without me and I'm getting wanderlust.'

Doreen looked doubtful. 'Woodbury Croft's your only home, now. The Welsh mountains seem a long way away, somehow.'

Miriam smiled slightly and shrugged. 'A long way from where?'

Doreen was silent, obviously still uncertain. Sue looked at Miriam and said: 'There are four bunks in our caravan. You'll be welcome if you want to come. Eh, Jack?'

'Of course she will. . . . The old question, isn't it?' he said to Miriam. '*Voahin zoll ish gehn?*'

Miriam looked surprised but pleased. 'You don't look Jewish.'

'Only a quarter, but my grandmother's English was never very good.'

'Well, Miriam?' Sue asked encouragingly.

'Thank you very much. I'd love to come with you.'

'That's settled then. . . . Are you *sure* the rest of you want to go back to your school?'

'Oh, yes, we must,' Doreen said. 'We've got to get all these guns to them, haven't we? Then it can't happen again.'

19

Beehive claustrophobia had become a familiar affliction. According to the Health Department Digests reaching Brenda's desk, it was serious to the point of incapacity for work in 0.19 per cent of the London Beehive personnel, sufficiently marked to require drug treatment in a further 2.803 per cent, and estimated to affect about one in five of the remainder 'mildly' – though the Digest admitted this last category was practically impossible to define.

Brenda was beginning to wonder just where on the scale she herself fitted.

She knew she was becoming increasingly restless. She had always been a quick and voracious reader, somehow managing to read the whole of four of five books, selected parts of a dozen others and a good many newspapers and periodicals, every week, however busy she was; and she had realized that recently a disproportionate amount of her reading was on natural history, gardening, travel and all the open-air subjects. Although national television had stopped, Beehive personnel were served with several hours a day of closed-circuit programmes from the film and videotape library, on two channels; and here, too, she found herself switching to the same kind of material – even developing a quite uncharacteristic taste for horizon-galloping Westerns.

I must be getting concrete-cramp, she told herself in the current colloquialism. But she was too self-aware to be able to pretend that that was the whole of it. She knew that her attitude to Reggie was undergoing a change and one which did no good to her self-esteem.

She had accepted, earlier on, that strong and capable command was necessary to the survival of Beehive as an effective organization and therefore (surely?) to the ultimate revival of Britain. And Reggie was, without any doubt, strong and capable. But she had been asking herself more and more lately the question which no dictatorship can ever answer: *quis custodiet ipsos custodes* – who guards the guardians? And if the 'guardian', the unchallenged dictator, was not quite sane . . . ? She had been able, so far, to thrust that terrible doubt away, to persuade herself that he knew what he was doing, at least better than anyone else would have done. To persuade herself, too, that even a benevolent dictator was dependent, in scientific matters, upon his expert advisers – and that the experts had been wrong about the Dust. And yet sometimes, in her occasional dark sleepless hours, oppressed almost beyond bearing by the knowledge that the majority of her fellow-countrymen were dead and that many of the survivors would succumb to the coming winter, she found the experts fading to rather insubstantial scapegoats and she was haunted by the guilt of the man asleep beside her. At best, he had made an unforgivable mistake by gambling on the experts' advice; and at worst . . . *No!* – from the other possibility she still shied away, but part of her knew it was there.

Did she love him? She no longer knew. She had believed so, in the first exciting weeks of the consolidation of Beehive, watching with admiration and a semi-maternal pride the success with which he made himself the most powerful man in Britain. And she still used the word 'love' to herself in considering their relationship. Certainly her sexual need for him was stronger now than it had ever been, not only because power seemed to have sharpened his virility, but because in this complex of artefacts which was Beehive – without trees or grass or even pets, where Nature was represented by the occasional potted house-plants which individuals had remembered to bring, where earth and sky were concrete surface 2.35 metres apart – in this suffocatingly unnatural world, copulation seemed the only breakthrough of Nature, the one field where banished Pan could run goat-footed and free. Without it, Brenda felt she would have joined the Health Department's claustrophobia statistics.

For her erotic need she did not have to apologize to herself; it was genuine and, she knew, reciprocal. But what did humiliate her was the knowledge that she enjoyed the privileged status which (both practically and subtly) being Reggie's mistress gave her. That, too, was a weapon against claustrophobia because it gave her psychological and social elbow-room and she was not sure she could do without it. At the first sign of a fall from favour, the wolves – the would-be successors – would be at her throat.

There was no hint of any such fall at the moment; Reggie seemed to regard their liaison as permanent and exclusive and to trust her absolutely. She probably knew more of what was going on than anyone except Reggie himself, for it was his habit to hold some of his most confidential discussions – with General Mullard, for example, or with Intelligence agents he was briefing personally – in the privacy of his own quarters; and he never asked her to leave the room. He seemed almost to need her there, because on the one or two occasions when she had tried to slip out during such an interview, he had asked her to pour drinks, or drawn her unnecessarily into the conversation, as an obvious device to make her stay. She could sit quietly in her armchair and read, or play patience, or work out a chess problem, so long as she was *there*.

That was how she came to witness his briefing of Gareth Underwood for the mission to Savernake Forest.

Reggie had not, recently, discussed the witch-hunt with her. He would mention this or that incident in it, but give no indication of his own attitude. She knew well enough that he had played a key-role in the launching of it and that Intelligence were actively involved in keeping it going – which he obviously could have stopped but had not. She had the impression that he was allowing it, and Beehive's involvement in it, to continue of its own impetus while he watched and brooded over it. That he was brooding over it, and in a new way, she knew from the books he was reading, for it was naturally she who brought him the books he wanted from the library. In the early stages of the witch-hunt, he had read *Malleus Maleficarum*, Robbins' *Encyclopedia of Witchcraft and Demonology* and other works on the methods and psychology of the great persecution of the sixteenth and seventeenth centuries. But more recently he had been ordering books on magic itself by modern writers from Gardner, Crowley, Regardie and Valiente onwards, and reading them with a deep absorption quite unlike his usual rapid, note-taking scan. Brenda observed and wondered.

She also made a point of at least skimming through the books before she returned them and they made her uneasy, or to be more honest with herself, it was Reggie's interest in them which made her uneasy. She had no doubt in her own mind that, in one sense or another, magic 'worked';

as a very widely read librarian, she knew that the basic facts (if not the explanation) of telepathy, clairvoyance, telekinesis, psychometry and other paranormal functions had been established beyond doubt. Parapsychology, over the past quarter-century, had become a respectable science – even if the attitude of other scientists to its findings had remained nervously ambivalent. Brenda recognized that paranormal abilities existed and could be trained and developed and used for good or ill, like any other natural gift, and Reggie's preoccupation with the subject disturbed her. What was he up to?

His briefing of Gareth Underwood did nothing to reassure her.

When she had poured drinks for the three of them (Gareth carefully addressing her as 'Miss Pavitt') Reggie came straight to the subject.

'You know about the witch colony in Savernake Forest?'

'The so-called "black" group, sir? Yes, we know of them.'

'I want you, very discreetly, to go and speak with their leaders. Could you manage that?'

'I'm sure we could.'

'Not "we", Underwood – you personally. I'm borrowing you from the Section, and your chief knows this is a confidential mission, not to be divulged to any of your colleauges, even to him. You will be briefed by me and you will report to me. You may ask your chief and he will confirm it.'

'Very well, sir.'

'Right. Tell me what you know about the group – or will you have to refer to records first?'

'Only for details, sir. I know the outline. We're almost certain they are the Angels of Lucifer, who . . .'

'I know of the Angels of Lucifer. Go on.'

'Well, sir, since they commandeered their village base, they're believed to have grown to about thirty or forty strong, possibly more, since a lot of their new recruits come in at night, and in country like that our agents can't watch the whole perimeter. Our men say there's something purposeful about the way the new people come in, as though they're being *called* in on a mobilization plan. Only an impression, of course, but a strong one.'

'Interesting.'

'The leaders are a man and a woman. We don't know their names, but all the local people call her "the Black Mamba". A very attractive woman in her middle twenties with long dark hair and a rather oriental face. Type-cast, one might say. She's known as a holy terror. The man is perhaps a year or two older, tall and quiet. The locals are very careful not to offend them, because various unpleasant things happen to those who *do* offend them and some of those things aren't easy to explain.'

'What kind of thing?'

'Two or three apparently causeless deaths. A few fires which have broken out in places that were well guarded. Illnesses which disappeared again as soon the victim toed the line. . . . The general feeling in the Section, sir, is that these incidents *are* natural but so ingeniously organized that they *look* like black magic – which most of the locals believe they are.'

'And what's your own feeling, Underwood?'

'Frankly, sir, I'm not sure. I'm keeping an open mind. But anyway, however they're working it, it's very effective. They have everyone within five or ten kilometres doing what they're told. Those who do are left in peace, so now everybody does.'

'H'mm . . . Is the group armed?'

'Not heavily, sir. Nobody's seen more than a couple of

shotguns. They're brought along by escorts when the leaders deliver a warning in person. They've never been used, so far as we know, except for hunting rabbits and game.'

'How do the group survive? Feed themselves and so on?'

'The village is a vegetable-growing area, sir, with some cattle and pigs and poultry. More or less self-supporting. If they need anything extra, they demand tribute – but never exorbitantly. It looks as though they want the locals disciplined but not antagonized to the point where they move out.'

'They sound very intelligently organized.'

'They are, sir. All our agents agree on that.'

'And ruthlessly "black" in magical terms.'

'They certainly seem out to create that image of themselves,' Gareth said cautiously.

'You don't believe they are, in effective practice?'

'As I told you, sir – I keep an open mind.'

'Very professional of you. But whatever the truth of it, Underwood – in practical politics a very interesting polarization is taking place. We know of at least a dozen witch communities that have managed to establish themselves; three are openly "black" in their attitudes and behaviour, the rest "white". The two stances seem quite distinguished and deliberate, but the viability and success of the various groups differ considerably. Two "white" and one "black" have not survived; they were destroyed by local action, with or without undercover Beehive encouragement. The most important "white" centre is in North Wales, in an excellent defensive position and with local public support . . .'

'New Dyfnant. We know about it, sir.'

'Of course you do. The Section is perfectly well aware of all this – but has not, I think, realized the importance of the black/white polarization. . . . We could not, for example, destroy the New Dyfnant group – which, as you doubtless also know, is growing in the same way as the Savernake Forest one – short of mounting an overt Army offensive, and the time is not yet ripe for such activity. All anti-witch action must appear to be spontaneous popular anger, for the time being at least. . . . But understand this, Underwood. Savernake and New Dyfnant are natural enemies. And it is to exploit that fact that I want *you* to go to consult with our friend the Black Mamba and her – er – consort.'

' "Friend", sir?' Gareth ventured a faint smile.

'She may well prove to be – as long as it suits them and us. Are you beginning to understand me?'

'I think so, sir. You want a secret alliance between Beehive and the Savernake Forest group, against New Dyfnant and the other "white" groups.'

'Exactly. Though if I substitute "myself" for "Beehive" in your definition, I hope you won't think it for megalomania. It's merely to underline the extremely confidential nature of any such arrangement.'

'I get the message, sir.'

'Good. Now, you may offer the Black Mamba's group whatever material help they find attractive – food, equipment, weapons, medical supplies – use your discretion; I'll back you up. We'll find ways of getting it to them. As for non-material benefits, you'll have to play it by ear. For example, you can offer them immunity for themselves when Beehive emerges in due course to take charge but I doubt if they'd believe you for a moment. You and I wouldn't, in their place, because there's no way of guaranteeing that the promise would be kept, and they know it as well as we do. But immunity as long as the pact lasts – obviously yes. And there may be *something* they want. Information on the white groups' activities, for example. You'll soon find out, I'm sure.'

'If they're willing to talk at all,' Gareth said, 'they'll tell me what they want. But what help do *you* want out of *them*, Sir Reginald? Guerilla-military? Informational? Or . . . well, magical?'

'Your mind is still open, I see,' Reggie said drily.

'I just want to know what I'm expected to ask for.'

'Quite so. You will ask for their *help* against the white groups in general and the New Dyfnant group in particular. Throw "informational" into the ring as a starter. Try to learn, diplomatically, what *they* believe they can do and encourage it. The objective at this stage is to establish the alliance, not to demand specific commitments from their side.'

'But I may make specific commitments from *our* side.'

'You may indeed. There are times when apparent generosity is a good investment and I think this will be one of them.'

'When do you want me to go, sir? Immediately?'

'As soon as possible. But how well versed are you in their particular field of activity – and its language?'

'Black magic, you mean, sir?'

'Black *and* white – though they have a common terminology.'

'No more than the next man, I suppose.'

'Then before you go, spend a couple of days in Miss Pavitt's library – in one of the private rooms, I don't want anyone to see what subject you're studying – and read up on magic and witchcraft. You can advise him about suitable books, can't you, my dear?'

Brenda said: 'Of course. And he can use the TSA room – his rating allows it.'

'Excellent, excellent. I shall expect you to be leaving in

four days at the most, Underwood. And if you think of any more questions you want to ask me before you go, arrange an appointment through Miss Pavitt, not through the usual channels. But let her know when you're ready to leave, in case *I* want to see *you* again.'

For the next three days, Gareth was closeted in the TSA room for as many hours as either Brenda or her deputy (the only other librarian entitled to use the TSA room key) were on duty – which amounted to about sixteen hours a day with a couple of breaks for meals. He was a glutton for work, almost as rapid a reader as Brenda herself and apparently gifted with a remarkable memory. By the second day she found herself wondering if his concentration was purely professional, or if he, too, was becoming infected by the same kind of fascinated absorption with the subject that she had noticed in Reggie. His few comments as she brought him more and more books (he soon outstripped her own recommendations and was asking for material she'd never even heard of) suggested that he was thinking about it deeply, though at no time did he imply any judgement on the brief Reggie had given him. He avoided this so studiously, even when she lunched with him and they had time to talk, that her intuition began to tell her that he was not happy about it. She remembered his one revealing remark of a week or two back, 'I hope *I'm* never sent on that kind of job. Only for God's sake don't tell anyone I said so.' He seemed almost by his very silence on the matter to be begging her to forget his brief indiscretion.

My God, Brenda thought – am *I* becoming psychic? All I know is that I'm not happy about this 'alliance' either. Not happy at all.

When Gareth finally left on his mission, and thanked her for her help in the privacy of the TSA room, she wished him luck and a safe return – and on impulse, kissed him. It was a very sisterly kiss. At least, she hoped it was.

Forty-eight hours later, Gareth found himself face to face with the Black Mamba, and he admitted to himself that the reports had been right – she *did* look almost too type-cast for the role of Black Priestess. Her large eyes, slightly tilted at the outer corners, were warm yet unnerving, and her long black mane, which she wore falling free, might have been designed by a wigmaker for a pantomime witch, though Gareth's sharp eyes could see it was all hers. That she was aware of her own powerful sexuality was evident from the way she moved and from the way she dressed, with a hint of the barbaric chieftainess that could only be deliberately calculated. Gareth appreciated it from a safe distance; for himself, he thought, he would as soon go to bed with a real black mamba.

Her man was very different, withdrawn and watchful, speaking one word to her ten. Gareth, though he kept the fact to himself, recognized him; for John Hassell's photograph was in the Section's file of prominent witches, having been added to it after the Bell Beacon disaster. He was the husband, Gareth remembered, of the Sabbat Queen who had been impaled with a ritual spear. Enough to turn any-one black, he thought with a twinge of compassion – espe-cially with a bitch like this one working on him. Gareth did not miss much.

He had had to do a lot of talking on the edge of the village to get himself brought in to see Karen (as he learned her name was) and John; and even then he had been strip-searched, not too gently, before he actually did see them. That did not worry him at all; all that concerned him, as a professional, was that he was now where he had aimed to be. Karen and John received him in what had been

355

the lounge of the village pub, with a shotgun sentry outside the door, and spent the first ten minutes grilling him with questions to satisfy themselves of his bona fides.

He had an uncanny feeling that not all of the grilling was by way of the spoken questions, though he treated this feeling with suspicion. He had learned a good deal, during his studies in the TSA room, about the theory of telepathy, of clairvoyance, of the 'reading' of auras; and he guessed from the steadiness of John and Karen's eyes on him and from a sensation almost of static electricity in the room that these methods were being tried. Suggestibility, he insisted to himself. Obviously their tactic would be to create that impression. But the feeling remained and Gareth did not like it.

His awareness of it at least mitigated his surprise when the atmosphere suddenly changed, as though Karen (it was she who determined it all the time) had flicked a switch to earth the static. She smiled for the first time and walked relaxedly behind the bar to produce a bottle (Glenfiddich, for God's sake) and three glasses from under the counter.

'Right, then, Mr Underwood – what's your first name?'

'Gareth.'

'So you're a genuine messenger, from Big Chief Harley himself. And you heartily disapprove of the message you bring but you're a professional so you'll deliver it faithfully. . . . Water, soda or straight? No ice, I'm afraid.'

'Very little water, please.' He was genuinely astonished; shrewdness was one thing but this was outside his experience. He smiled back at her, deliberately. 'Messengers have no opinions – if, as you say, they are professionals.'

'Haven't they, Gareth? But leave that for the moment. What does Harley want from us?'

'Help from the Angels of Lucifer against the white witches.'

John said: 'Angels of Lucifer! That was a try-on, wasn't it?'

'The Angels have proved their effectiveness in a very dramatic way, over Ben Stoddart. If you weren't the Angels, Harley wouldn't be so interested in your cooperation. . . . Intelligence Section may not be clairvoyant but they're reasonably efficient in their own way.'

Karen laughed. 'All right, give you that one. We're the Angels of Lucifer, and *if* we made a deal with Harley, he'd get his money's worth. But what *is* his "money"? Actual cash would be so much waste paper on Surface. What's he offering?'

'It's part of my mission to find out what you need. Food, equipment, medical supplies, horses, weapons – *you* know what would be useful to you and he's prepared to be generous.'

'I see. And in exchange, he wants us to fight the white witches. Does he mean magically? Surely he doesn't believe in magic?'

'You killed Ben Stoddart,' Gareth pointed out. 'You took over this village without any need for violence, in the ordinary sense. You have fifty to a hundred square kilometres completely under your thumbs. So whether your methods are magical, or "normal" screened by clever propaganda, is almost academic. The point is that you *succeed*. And Harley appreciates successful allies.'

'Oh, I like this man, John, don't you? He'd make a lovely diplomat. . . . Has Harley got any specific targets in mind?'

'Yes. The New Dyfnant group.'

There was a moment's unexpected silence. Karen did not move but her eyes seemed to brighten. John paced across the room, expressionless, and stood looking out of the window with his back to Karen and Gareth.

'I will *not* harm Dan and Moira Mackenzie themselves, Karen,' he said. 'And that's flat.'

Gareth caught Karen's warning glance; while John's back was still turned she laid a finger briefly on her lips. So, Gareth thought; the Mackenzies are John Hassell's old friends and he still has a soft spot for them; but the Black Mamba would have their guts for garters without turning a hair. I have to play along with her but not alienate him. He felt inwardly sick but his brain worked fast.

'I know I'm talking in ignorance,' he said, carefully diffident. 'But isn't there a magical technique called "binding"? To neutralize your opponent's efforts, without doing him any personal harm?'

'There is indeed.' The approval in her voice was unmistakable. 'And John knows it as well as I do. There'd be no need to hurt your pals, darling. But they *do* have to be neutralized, you've said so yourself. . . . You know more about magic than you pretended, Gareth.'

Engaging frankness called for. 'A good agent does his homework."

Karen laughed and even John seemed to relax a little.

'Have another scotch,' she offered Gareth.

'Please. I haven't tasted Glenfiddich for months.'

'We found a dozen in the cellar. We keep it for special guests. . . . Do you think Big Chief Harley would like a bottle?'

'I'm sure he'd be delighted. But I doubt if I'd be strong-minded enough to take it to him unopened. There are limits even to *my* professionalism.'

This time, even John laughed.

'That wasn't what I had in mind,' Karen said. 'I think it would be a good idea if I took it to him myself.'

John's laugh evaporated. 'For God's sake, Karen . . .'

'No, but seriously, darling. This proposal of Harley's is

important. And although Gareth's a conscientious messenger – for all his private disapproval, and *he* knows I'm right about that – it's something that ought to be discussed face to face, with the Big Chief himself. . . . Are you offended, Gareth?'

'Not in the least.' Gareth was torn between an acute wariness and the tempting prospect of being relieved of his abhorrent role as go-between. 'I could get you to him safely.'

'But why *you*?' John cried. 'It's a bloody dangerous trip for a woman. Why not me?'

'Because, my darling male chauvinist, you're needed here, to keep control of things. I wouldn't trust anyone else in charge. As soon as you were gone, there'd be quite a few men hoping you'd never come back.' (Crafty bitch, Gareth thought; watch her undulate her body to drive the point home.) 'But I would came back. All Beehive couldn't stop me.'

'Immunity's one of the things I'm empowered to promise you,' Gareth said. 'You certainly would come back. Because this is where Harley wants you.'

'But the journey itself,' John protested.

'How did you get here, Gareth?' Karen asked.

'Bicycle.'

'Horses would be better. We could spare a couple. . . . Or three, if you like, John; one of the boys could come with a shotgun if it'd make you happier.'

'And I left a gun hidden outside the village,' Gareth said. 'We'd make it all right. . . . Only one thing,' he smiled, 'legend has it you ride about your domain side-saddle, Karen. I'm sure that helps the tribal chieftainess image, and I'd love to see it – but I think it would be a little over-dramatic for travelling incognito. Would you object to a normal saddle, just this once?'

'For you, Gareth – even that.'

Gradually, between them, they lightened the atmosphere and watched John become less tense. Within half an hour, it was all agreed. Next morning, Gareth, Karen and a shot-gun escort rode away to London.

The escort, a taciturn man called Joe, took his duties seriously. Where he thought there was possibility of an ambush, he always rode ahead to satisfy himself there was no danger. This gave Karen her first opportunity to speak to Gareth alone and she took it immediately it arose.

'You backed me up very well, Gareth,' she said without preamble. 'I'm sure you get the picture; John could *not* be in on the real talking. Harley needn't worry – he'll get what he wants. I can handle John.'

'I'm sure you can handle most men.'

'Yes, Gareth, I can. But *you* needn't worry, either. Bitch I may be but I never bite the postman.'

And Harley? he was tempted to ask. But he held his tongue.

Gareth had been away for five days and Brenda was missing him. She had no one else with whom she could share her unease; the sharing with Gareth had been almost entirely unspoken but there had been a mutual awareness of it (she was sure she did not deceive herself about that) which had somehow made the unease more bearable. And in Gareth's absence, Reggie made it worse. There was an air of expectancy about him, an excited impatience which was also unspoken and which made Brenda feel more excluded than ever from his private thoughts, more than ever the sultan's odalisque whose sphere of usefulness was precisely defined and never to be exceeded. Reggie's habit of using her as a sounding-board, of thinking aloud to her in virtual monologue for the ordering of his own thoughts was now confined to routine trivialities. The matter that really absorbed his attention was never referred to and loomed all the larger in Brenda's anxiety because of its deliberate avoidance.

It's crazy, she thought. When Gareth avoids a subject, I nevertheless feel comforted. When Reggie avoids it, I feel disturbed.

Gareth's call came to her library desk on the morning of the sixth day, and the unexpected sound of his voice gave a lift to her spirits.

'Brenda? This is Gareth.'

'Yes, Gareth. Good morning to you.' There was the unmistakable quality of a radio link on the line and Brenda knew better than to ask where he was. Secret communication-points existed around the country from which agents could contact Beehive and he might be anywhere. 'What can I do for you?'

'Would you please tell our friend that I'm bringing the lady in to see him, at her own request?'

'I'll tell him. . . . Any idea how soon?'

'By this evening, if the going's easy. Tomorrow afternoon at the latest.'

'Right.'

'Be seeing you, then. 'Bye, Brenda.'

'Good luck, Gareth.'

She went straight to Reggie, who was in conference with the Head of Personnel, but admitted her at once on his secretary's announcement – as she knew he would, for she never interrupted him trivially. She greeted the Head of Personnel with a polite apology and handed Reggie the message which she had already typed out. He read it and said, 'Ah . . . Would you be good enough to arrange accommodation, my dear? And please let me know as soon as they arrive?'

'Of course.'

They arrived in fact just before seven that evening, Gareth phoning her as soon as they were inside Beehive by the secret entrance. She directed him straight to the guest cubicle she had booked for 'the lady' and was at its door to meet them.

She had been prepared, of course, to dislike the Black Mamba. But she was astonished at the depth and intensity of her antipathy from the moment Gareth introduced Karen to her, and she had no doubt whatever that the antipathy was mutual. They purred at each other suitably, of course, and Brenda saw to the guest's needs with meticulous hospitality before they left her to 'freshen up'; she had ascertained Karen's size, and promised to be back in half an hour with an appropriately unobtrusive uniform.

Alone with Gareth in the corridor, Brenda let out an explosive 'My God!'

Gareth said, 'Yes.'

Forgetting discretion, Brenda went on: 'Gareth, that woman's poison. Highly efficient poison, in full control of herself. If I had any say in it, I wouldn't let her within a hundred kilometres of Beehive – let alone Reggie.'

Somebody else passed them and Gareth waited till he was out of earshot before he replied. Then it was to say, obliquely: 'I'm never quite sure of the boundary between woman's instinct and clairvoyance.'

'You don't have to be a woman to pick up *her* vibes.'

He smiled wrily. 'I can confirm that. . . . Oddly enough, I kind of liked the man, though. He's *become* evil but the thing that started him off would have made *me* bitter, too. But she was evil to start with, I'd say – and with her beside him, knowing exactly what she's doing, he'd never have a chance to draw back. . . . I'd like to tell you all about it, next time we're in the TSA room.'

'Should you, Gareth?' Having released her feelings, she found discretion was seeping back.

'No, but I will.' Then with a change of tone: 'When's the Chief receiving us?'

'Eight-thirty. Dinner for four in his quarters. I'm to escort her there, and you're to arrive independently. He's being very rumour-conscious on this. Doesn't even want her identified with Intelligence Section. And *I'm* to cook and serve dinner.'

'Go easy on the hemlock,' Gareth said.

There was no doubt about it, Brenda told herself with growing alarm as the dinner progressed: the rapport between Karen and Reggie was as immediate as the antipathy between Karen and herself. Reggie was at his most charming and he and Karen monopolized the conversation. Almost all of it was about the practical problems of survival on Surface which they discussed as cheerfully as though Karen had just returned from a camping holiday. The rest was about horses for which they shared an enthusiasm. Reggie was delighted to find that she had learned side-saddle from Janet Macdonald herself, which apparently put her among the élite.

How their talk finally turned to serious business, Brenda could never quite remember. It must have been over coffee, because she clearly recalled the *zabaglione* and Karen's fulsome praise of it. After that, everything became frighteningly vague. One sentence stood out in her mind; Karen asking Reggie: 'Do you *really* want to know if it works?' – and then Karen's big eyes moving from her face to Gareth's and back again. . . .

It could not be said that she and Gareth *woke up* in her own quarters, sitting opposite each other with drinks in their hands. They simply became aware, abruptly and simultaneously, that they had been there for some time. Even that this was their second drink.

Brenda nearly screamed. Gareth must have realized it, for he quickly grasped her free hand in his own, holding it tightly till she was in command of herself.

'Hypnotism,' he said at last. 'The bloody woman hypnotized us, right there in front of the Chief's eyes. Christ, that *must* have impressed him!'

After a pause, Brenda said: 'It was more than just hypnotism, Gareth. She brought us out of it, together, when *she* was ready, by remote control. An ordinary hypnotist couldn't do that. It calls for telepathy.'

'Not necessarily. She could have ordered a trigger. For example – "You will go back to Brenda's room, sit down and pour yourselves drinks and when you take the first sip of your second drink you will wake up, remembering nothing of what has happened in between." This *is* our second drink, isn't it? And we've both just tasted it.'

'Yes, it is. But that's all I know. I don't remember getting here or what we've been talking about, except that we *have* been talking.'

'Me too. But you see? It could be a normal hypnotic technique, without telepathy or anything.'

'*Normal!* . . . Gareth, I'm hypnosis-resistant. A doctor tried once and I wanted to cooperate but no way could he put me under. But *she* did it across a dinner-table, just like that. And I'm pretty sure I *felt* her command to wake up – not any trigger situation that she'd ordered but her *command*, coming through as she gave it.'

'I must say, so did I. But that could be post-hypnotic

suggestion. She could have told us we'd believe that when we woke up.'

'All of it *could* be. But do you know what, Gareth? I'm frightened. Scared out of my bloody wits – for myself, for you, for Reggie, for Beehive . . . Hell, I'm scared for *Britain*. Does that sound melodramatic?'

Gareth did not answer for a moment; then he shook his head, slowly.

'Dare we have another drink?' she wondered. 'Or will there be some post-hypnotic suggestion attached to that, too?'

He smiled, for the first time. 'I guess we'll risk it.'

'After all,' Brenda said as she poured, 'she's achieved her purpose. Put us in our places, shown Reggie what she can do and got him to herself. . . . I wish her joy of him,' she added venomously.

'That remarks sounds a little . . . uncharacteristic.'

'Yes, it does, doesn't it? . . . Cheers.'

'Cheers.'

They sat for a while, wrapped in their separate thoughts. Then Brenda asked: 'Gareth – you love me, don't you?'

He lowered his eyes. 'Yes, Brenda, I do. You know I do. I have . . . well, since about the second time I met you.'

'Then this'll sound incredibly selfish of me. I don't love anyone, right now. But by God, I *need* your love. I need to trust you and I need you to trust me or I'll go bloody mad. . . . You're an Intelligence officer. For what we've already said and will say to each other, you could destroy me – and I could destroy you. But we won't. We need *each other*. Don't we?'

Gareth looked up again, into her eyes. 'Yes, we do. And I think we're going to have to do more than talk. We're going to have to *do* something about it.' He blushed, suddenly young and vulnerable. 'Oh, I didn't mean . . .'

'I know you didn't,' she told him gently.

He recovered himself and went on: 'We're going to have to do something about *her*. About what's going on and what's planned. . . . You said you were scared for Britain. You know what, Brenda? So am I.'

20

'Ye Lords of the Watchtowers of the North; Boreas, thou guardian of the Northern portals; mighty Cernunnos, Lord of the forest; great Cerridwen, Queen of earth and sky; we do thank you for attending our rites and ere ye depart to your pleasant and lovely realms, we bid you hail and farewell!'

Behind her, everyone echoed 'Hail and farewell!' as Moira drew the Banishing Pentagram in the air above the altar with her athame. She laid the knife on the altar and turned, smiling at them and they all broke into talk and laughter. Some put their clothes back on by the row of hooks along the end wall, others, in no hurry to cover their comfortable nakedness, gathering around the big wood-burning stove. Dan began clearing the ritual tools from the table which had been placed against the north wall to serve as an altar; Greg switched on the twelve-volt lighting of which he was justifiably proud, and little Diana exercised her privilege of blowing out the candles one by one.

Eileen, perennially anxious to learn, came over to Moira and asked: 'Why do you only mention Boreas? Why not the winds at the other quarters?'

'Do you know who they are?' Moira asked back.

'Eurus in the East, Notus in the South and Zephyrus in the West,' Eileen answered promptly. 'And Aeolius who's the master of them all . . . That's my trouble. I collect facts but I can't always work out reasons.'

'Well, East, South and West are Air, Fire and Water, and to mention winds for all of them might make it harder for people to hold the elements in their minds. But North isn't only Earth, it's the altar as well so it's rather special; you thank the God and Goddess there, so you make it more ceremonious. Besides, Boreas is the doorkeeper of Caer Arianrhod . . .'

Two or three others had joined them and began asking their own questions. It was the same after every Circle now, for the coven had become something very different from the tight little group in half-forgotten Staines. To-night, for instance, there were eighteen adults and four children crowding the Central Cabin for the regular Friday Circle: Moira's group of five plus Diana, eight witches who had joined Camp Cerridwen over the past two or three weeks with three of their children, and five interested non-initiates including Eileen and Peter. What with getting the incoming witches attuned to Moira and Dan's particular methods and customs and explaining things to the non-initiates, 'I feel more like a schoolteacher than a High Priestess, sometimes,' Moira had said to old Sally.

'Since when were the two different?' Sally wanted to know. 'Maybe we'd got too cosy, love.'

Even the attunement process required care, for although all the witches realized the importance of harmony in their embattled situation, it was of the nature of Wicca that every coven had its own character and was a law to itself; so unless differences were examined and adjusted, misunderstandings could arise. Most bewildered, sometimes, were

Sam and Elizabeth Warner, who were Traditionals trained in a very different set of rituals from Moira and Dan's Gardnerian/Alexandrian ones, but their determination to work with the majority was fortunately aided by a healthy sense of humour.

'Cheer up,' Dan told them. 'We'll put out an astral call for more Traditionals, then you'll be able to do your own thing in parallel with us.'

'What?' Sam exclaimed in mock horror. 'All this re-education for nothing? Besides, I rather like holding two passports.'

Altogether, Camp Cerridwen now numbered twenty-four adults and six children. Father Byrne even had a congregation, for one couple with a year-old baby were Catholics; they had come in with the husband's brother and sister-in-law, who were witches. 'I'm past being astonished,' Father Byrne had said, smiling, when Dan informed him that a little chapel now had high priority on the building programme, immediately after the minimum sleeping accommodation.

Building was, in fact, going ahead well, for more hands meant more efficient working, and Bruce Peters, the quiet young builder who had arrived with Fred and Jean Thomas, had proved to be knowledgeable and ingenious. The Central Cabin, kitchen and three family cabins were all finished and three more were at framework stage.

Camp Cerridwen was becoming a village.

Liz Warner had proved an asset in another way: she was a schoolteacher and as soon as she arrived she started daily classes for the children – who, leaving out the Catholic couple's baby, ranged from five to thirteen years old. But within a week, she and Geraint Lloyd, the New Dyfnant schoolmaster, had arrived at a better arrangement. A pony-cart was found for Liz and her five pupils and every morning she drove them down to Geraint's little school. Geraint, who had been coping single-handed with seventeen children of various ages, was delighted. He took charge of the older ones and Liz of the younger. 'Now we might actually get some teaching done instead of just keeping the little devils quiet,' he told her happily. The New Dyfnant parents obviously appreciated Liz too, for she rarely returned to camp without gifts of vegetables, eggs or cow's milk, sometimes put anonymously in the pony-cart while she was busy teaching.

Camp Cerridwen's own little farm was making fair progress, all things considered. Much winter sowing had been done, goats and poultry were thriving, some soft fruits had been planted and the bees in their six hives seemed to be hibernating healthily (since they were newly installed, some of the camp's precious and dwindling sugar had been allocated to their autumn settling-in feed). But with winter closing in, first priority had to go to seeing that everyone was housed and warm, so there was a limit to the amount of time that could be devoted to farming. And it would be many months before the planting produced food or the hives honey. The half-hectare of vegetable garden in New Dyfnant which had been earmarked for their use was a considerable help and the cave in the woods still held useful stocks of food; but with the camp's population growing and perhaps more recruits to come, old Sally as ration-organizer kept an anxiously watchful eye on the reserves.

An extra hazard had arisen once the Madness was over. With movement much safer, occasional nomad pilferers appeared. Organized bands, strangely enough, were not the danger. A couple of raids had been tried on New Dyfnant but the villagers, themselves well organized and favourably sited, had dealt with them firmly and word must have got around for no more attempts were made, although more exposed communities in the neighbourhood (and according to Geraint's ham-radio contacts, in other parts of the country) suffered sporadically. But lone infiltrators were another matter. One had been shot while trying to steal a goose on the outskirts of New Dyfnant, and two hens had disappeared during the night from Camp Cerridwen itself. Peter O'Malley, who still ranged as much of his beloved forest as his share of the camp work allowed, occasionally came across signs of what he called 'fly-by-night bivouacs', never of more than one to three people, and always abandoned by the time he got there. Though once he had shouted after a man running away through the trees a couple of hundred metres from him. The man had gone on running and vanished.

'If the bloody fools are hungry, why don't they come and ask if they can join us?' he grumbled to Dan.

'Natural cowards or natural thieves. Or both. Or maybe they've heard we're witches and they're scared we'll turn 'em into frogs.'

'Only thing that really worries me is the cave,' Peter said. 'If one of them finds that, we could be in trouble.'

Dan agreed and the evening meeting discussed the matter. Reluctantly, they earmarked a newly finished cabin as a store, and next day transferred the contents of the cave to it; even more reluctantly, with so much work to be done, they kept one man at a time, night and day, patrolling the camp as an armed sentry.

One of Peter's duties fitted in well with his forest-ranging. They were almost out of tinned meat and there was no fresh to be had from livestock, for both camp and village had banned all slaughtering – even of poultry – till the spring brought renewed breeding. So Sally had asked Peter to supplement the rations by regular hunting, helped when possible by such good shots as Angie; only good shots could be allowed to hunt, for their stocks of ammunition, though not yet dangerously low, were still not limitless. Peter had agreed and had supplemented his gun by snares (which he hated). The result had been a fairly steady flow of rabbit, wood-pigeon and the occasional pheasant; and also a renewed withdrawal from Peter by Eileen, who had been beginning to relax in his company.

Angie, exasperatedly observing her young cousin's behaviour had for once thoroughly lost her temper. 'My God, Eileen, I wish we had a damn shrink in the camp – because that's what you need, my girl. You've got the nicest man in the place following you around like a puppy-dog and you bite his head off because he's keeping us fed. What the hell do you think you're up to? A bloody psychiatrist's couch is the place for you – if the word "bloody" doesn't trigger off this stupid obsession of yours.' She could see the tears in Eileen's eyes but she couldn't stop. 'For Christ's sake, none of us enjoy killing. I don't. *Peter* doesn't. And that's another damn stupid thing. When I kill a rabbit, you just look the other way. When *he* kills anything, you crucify the poor bugger.'

'I *don't*,' Eileen burst out. 'I only . . .'

'You only kick him where it hurts, that's all. Because, God help him, he's as much in love with you as you are with him. Which you *are*.'

Eileen, white-faced and miserable, looked at her in silence for a moment and then walked away, leaving Angie – once she had cooled down – thoroughly ashamed of herself.

Moira and Dan watched the approaching convoy with some surprise. It was usual for one or two of the New Dyfnant villagers to escort newcomers to Camp Cerridwen, to satisfy themselves that they were both harmless and acceptable.

But this group – a farm cart tented with sheet polythene, an odd-looking contraption of a wheelless motor caravan lashed on to a flat-topped cart, and two horsemen – was headed by Dai Police himself riding with Liz and the children in the returning pony-trap, and two more villagers, mounted and carrying shotguns, brought up the rear.

''Afternoon, Dai,' Dan called when the convoy was a few metres away. 'What's all this, then? Wells Fargo?'

Dai signalled the convoy to halt and jumped to the ground. 'Just being careful, Dan bach. They seem all right and there's three young kids with 'em – but it's enough guns they have to be a raiding party.'

'Guns?'

'Three Army rifles, a four-ten, three pistols and a good bit of ammo. We took it all off 'em and stashed it in the pony-trap here. They didn't complain – and that's a good sign. Only reasonable, they agreed it was, seeing that they want to join you.'

'Hey – Moira, Dan – remember me?'

They turned at the call and saw the man who had jumped down from the caravan and was walking towards them.

Dan replied: 'I know your face, but . . .'

'Jack Ramsay – and my wife Sue's still in the van. We met last year at that healing seminar in St Pancras Town Hall. Gardnerians, from Uttoxeter.'

'*That's* right – I remember – don't you, Moira?'

'I do indeed. We lunched together and you and Dan blinded us with science about Kirlian photography . . . Blessed be!'

'All right, then, are they?' Dai Police asked, relieved.

'If Jack here will vouch for the others . . .'

'Absolutely,' Jack said. 'We owe 'em our lives, for a start. Them and half a dozen battling schoolgirls – but tell you about that later. . . . Oh, just one of us is a stranger –

the fair-haired one on the chestnut. We fell in with him this morning, on the way in. Name of Underwood. Say's he's got a message for you. One of the pistols is his, by the way. He *doesn't* want to join you but the rest of us do. May we?'

The Central Cabin was packed to meet the newcomers because everyone was intrigued to learn that three of them – Philip and Betty Summers and the American journalist Tonia Lynd – were escapers from Beehive. They were bombarded with questions, and Tonia had some of her own when somebody mentioned that there was a radio ham in the village who had recently, with improving conditions, picked up at least some fragmentary news from America. It was all they could do to dissuade her from rushing straight back to New Dyfnant to meet him; Liz Warner promised to take her down to the school in the morning and introduce her. The young Jewish girl, Miriam, too, asked as many questions as she answered; Moira had a feeling she would be an intelligent and useful recruit to the camp.

But Moira was puzzled by the fair-haired man who had introduced himself as Gareth Underwood, but had said he would deliver his message to her and Dan in private when things were quieter. She noticed that he spoke little and that he listened to what the Summers and Tonia had to say about life in Beehive with what seemed to her to be an inner amusement.

Moira whispered to Tricia Hayes: 'What do you make of the Underwood man?'

Tricia, who had found her way to Camp Cerridwen all by herself, was perhaps their most gifted clairvoyant with an almost unnerving talent for reading people. Fiftyish, with an unmemorable face and thin mousy hair, she looked too frail to be the determined survivor she in fact was, and at first sight no one would suspect her of being gifted at anything.

'I've been watching him,' Tricia whispered back. 'He's strange. Knows a lot but very self-controlled – and he's swimming against the tide.'

'What tide?'

'The tide of whatever he's supposed to be doing. I think he's official. None of this talk about Beehive is new to him. But he's not *supposed* to be here and he's on edge.'

'Can we trust him?'

'Yes, I think you can. *Because* he's not supposed to be here, you know? Though he'll tell you something you don't like. He doesn't like it, either.'

Moira had confidence in Tricia but she was still wary when she and Dan were able to talk with Underwood alone, walking together along the river-bank out of earshot of everyone else.

'What's your message, then, Mr Underwood?' Dan asked. 'And who's it from?'

'It's not really a message because it's only from me. It's a warning – a tip-off. . . . Look, I'm an Intelligence agent from Beehive but I'm here off my own bat. If my boss knew, I'd end up in the cells or worse. I'm supposed to be on my way back to Beehive from Savernake Forest – does that ring a bell with you?'

'It does. Go on.'

'I'll be reporting back four or five days late but I've got a good story to explain the delay. All the same, I'm pushing my luck a bit. . . . The tip-off is that Harley, who's pretty well the absolute dictator in London Beehive now, has made a secret alliance with the Angels of Lucifer.'

'Jesus! . . . An alliance for what?' Dan asked.

'To fight against the white witches in general and this group above all.'

'I don't believe it!'

'Why don't you believe it, Mr Mackenzie?'

'Because John . . .' Dan broke off, as though he had second thoughts about giving a reason.

The agent smiled. 'Because John, whatever he's done or become, is still too fond of you two to harm you personally? You're right. But Karen – the locals call her the Black Mamba – has no such scruples. She'd *enjoy* harming you. She knows how to handle John and when Harley sent me down to contact them and offer the alliance, she fixed it that I took her back to negotiate with Harley alone. She was in Beehive for three days, incognito except to Harley and me and one other person, and then I had to escort her back. I came straight on here, because I wanted you to know.'

'*Why* did you want us to know? What's in it for you?' Dan asked.

'There's nothing in it for me except sticking my neck out. I just think the Black Mamba's pure poison and I don't like the way things are going. I know Beehive's got a lot to answer for – but it could, conceivably, serve a function in due course to get what's left of Britain back on its feet, *if* it keeps its nose clean. But if this alliance is symptomatic of the way Harley's thinking, I haven't much hope of that. . . . And look – if I'm an *agent provocateur*, what's the object of the exercise? To stir up conflict between the white witches and the black? That exists already and nothing *I* say is going to turn it into a pitched battle. Or am I here to spy on you? If so, why have I said all this and why am I rushing straight off again? I'd do better to claim to be a refugee, stay a few days, and then disappear. Sabotaging your radio-ham friend's equipment on the way out – because that's the only significant thing I've learned. If I'm not speaking the truth, why am I here?'

'I think you *are* speaking the truth,' Moira said. 'Dan?'

'Yes, it all figures. . . . What did Karen and Harley agree on?'

'That I don't know. They spent hours by themselves and all I was told at the end was to organize the secret material help he'd promised her. I was able to do some of the simpler things at once – like filling a rucksack with pistols and ammunition – and the more complicated ones, like more horses and saddles, I'll organize when I get back.'

'But what practical action does Harley want from *them*?' Dan asked. 'A physical attack on us? Not very practicable. Surely not magical action? He wouldn't believe in it.'

'On the contrary,' Underwood said, 'I think he's hooked on it. And possibly on Karen as well.'

'Now I'm taking you really seriously,' Moira told him. 'Karen's terribly ambitious. If she's been offered *that* kind of a pact with Beehive, she's going to do something about it, and if John gets in the way she'll get rid of him. . . . Your warning is worth having.'

'Can you look after yourselves, when she starts anything?'

'We can. Our psychic defences are as good as hers. But without you, we might have been caught napping. . . . Do *you* believe in this kind of thing?'

'A month ago I'd have said "I don't know". But I've seen and learned a lot in the last couple of weeks and now I wouldn't take any chances. I hope you won't, either.'

Moira thought for a moment, then asked : 'Why go back to Beehive at all? Why not stay with us here? They'd write you off as dead, wouldn't they? It could happen to anyone, riding about the country solo.'

He shook his head. 'Call it professional habit but I've a hunch I can be more useful as a double agent. Might even be able to give you more tip-offs. Tell you what –

I'll go down with your Yankee friend on my way out and have a word with the radio ham. Is he trustworthy?'

'Yes.'

'Then I'll give him a frequency and a daily listening time, and a simple code for "Expect physical attack", "Expect psychic attack" and so on – half a dozen basic messages I might want to send. I'm always giving the radio operators timed code messages for Beehive agents and I don't have to explain them, so I could slip an extra one in if it was urgent to tell you something.'

'Watch that neck of yours.'

'I will.' He smiled. 'Frankly, I'd like to stay with you. But apart from anything else, "where a man's treasure is, there will his heart be also". So I'll be on my way in the morning.'

'What's the treasure's name?' Moira asked.

'Brenda. Throw in a spell for her, when you've a moment. She could do with it,' Gareth Underwood said.

'Have you got a typewriter?' Tonia asked eagerly.

'Typewriter, yes,' Geraint Lloyd said, 'but I'm having to watch the paper. This is a school, remember.'

'You could spare a dozen sheets a week, say, I'm sure. We could do one copy for the village and one for the camp, on notice-boards – and each place would keep the back numbers as archives. Goddam it, man, you're a community asset. You're in touch with the world, even if only in bits and pieces. Passing it on by word of mouth isn't enough. We can have a *newspaper*.'

Geraint had to admit he found the crop-haired American's enthusiasm infectious. She had arrived with Liz and the camp children and the mysterious Underwood, at nine o'clock, and had been barely able to contain her impatience while Underwood insisted on fifteen minutes in private with

Geraint before he went on his way. Geraint had come out to find she had already arranged for Liz to take charge of both classes for the first hour so that she could have him to herself. Within forty minutes she had sucked his brain dry of everything he had learned and could remember of his radio-collected information from Britain and abroad. She had particularly wanted to know, naturally, about America. He had to tell her that radio reception had been very bad after the earthquake and had only just begun to improve to the point where he could manage occasional exchanges with American hams; a tall aerial which Greg had built for him had helped a lot. The States, from what his scattered contacts could tell him, were in much the same situation as Britain. Population loss seemed to have been slightly less disastrous because although the vinegar-mask announcement had been simultaneous with Britain's, the clock-difference had meant the Washington announcement had been made while the shops were still open and also the quake had hit America a couple of hours later than Europe, so more people were prepared. But this advantage had been partly offset by the fact that unlike Europe, where the Dust had cleared within hours of the earthquake, the Western Hemisphere had suffered from it with irregular renewed outbreaks for nearly a week, by which time the less fortunate had no vinegar left, while others, believing the first outbreak would be the only one, had become careless.

When Tonia had gleaned all she could, she insisted on being shown his equipment and asking if he would teach her to operate it, so that between them they could increase its hours on the air. Once she had his promise, she plunged into her plan for a village-and-camp newspaper.

'For God's sake,' he laughed when she paused to draw breath, 'not so fast! You'll choke yourself.'

She grinned back at him, engagingly. 'Never get in the

way of a frustrated journalist who smells an outlet. You're apt to get run down.'

Liz Warner put her head round the door and asked: 'Could I have him back now, do you think? It's been *two* hours.'

Eileen stood in the cabin door, tasting the air of sunrise and finding it good. Nobody was yet up except for Greg on sentry patrol and very probably Peter out doing the round of his snares – but she turned aside from that thought; it was too lovely a morning to examine distress. She closed the cabin door behind her and walked.

There had been some reshuffling of sleeping arrangements now that three family cabins were ready. Old Sally had moved in with Angie to share her motor caravan, which by now was cosily lagged and just right for the two older women, who had become close friends. Eileen and two unmarried girl newcomers, now joined by Miriam, had been allocated one of the family cabins which had promply been dubbed the Spinster Shack. Since the oldest of them was twenty-four, they had taken no more than pretended offence at the name.

Although it was late October – only a few days to go to Samhain – the weather, apart from a couple of damp and chilly weeks at the end of September and beginning of October, had been exceptionally kind with temperatures over 15° almost every day and mild nights. Dan, who had found a maximum-minimum thermometer in the greenhouse of one of the ruined houses in New Dyfnant which had been allocated to them for 'looting', and an old barometer in the kitchen (he wished it had been a barograph), kept daily records. He wondered out loud whether the world cataclysm had produced permanent climatic changes. Peter, for one, hoped not; he had no desire to see Wales or anywhere else for that matter lose its character, its evolved natural balance. Others, still only half-adjusted to rugged pioneering, were not so sure. 'If Wales goes sub-tropical,' Sam Warner said, 'that'll suit me fine. Nature will find a new balance. When interfering man is as thin on the ground as he is now, ecology has a chance to be self-adjusting.' The discussion was academic in any case; it would be years before any permanent changes became discernible from chance fluctuations.

This morning Eileen cared nothing for long-range climatology. It was enough that today's sky was soft and clear, that only the gentlest of breezes made sea-sounds in the treetops, that the ground was dry under her rubber sneakers and that she felt no need for a jacket over her sweater and jeans.

She strolled over to Greg who had stopped to talk to the goats tethered among the tree-stumps where daily felling was pushing the edge of the forest back. The goats looked at them with their strange primordial eyes and went on munching. They laughed and left them, Eileen walking beside Greg as he continued his patrol towards the logging lane, round the bend of the tree-line.

'Still an hour to breakfast,' Eileen said. 'I think I'll climb up to the Giant's Bed.'

'Wish I could come with you. It'll be marvellous up there, on a morning like this.'

She waved to him from the edge of the plantation and started walking up one of the dark, straight, two-metre-wide paths that quartered the forest like a chessboard. It was more a tunnel than a path, for the tall conifers brushed each other's branches above her head. Every now and then she came to a little clearing, some of them dictated by outcrops of mountain rock. She was heading for the bigger outcrop, known locally as the Giant's Bed, half a kilometre above the camp and when she reached it, it was worth the climb. She picked her way through the brambles that guarded the foot of the grey bastion, scrambled among the bilberries and mosses that hugged its crevices and found herself at last on its table-top, jutting into the sky clear of the downhill trees. The whole of the camp's private valley spread below her and the ring of mountains faced and flanked her, under a vast kindly sky. She could see one or two of the camp roofs and the woodsmoke of the kitchen stove being lit for breakfast, through the ranks of Christmas-tree fingers that pointed up singly from each tree, seeming to admonish her: *Be still, watch, listen . . .*

Eileen sat cross-legged on the rock, absorbing the morning's contentment, till she realized it must be time for breakfast.

She skipped happily through the brambles and down another tunnel leading more directly to the camp.

It was at the first intersection that she glimpsed, briefly, the strange man leading away the stolen goat. She jumped back quickly into cover, trying to collect her thoughts. The thief must have sneaked the goat away while Greg was at the other end of the camp and while the people who were up were still either in their cabins and caravans or busy in the kitchen. It was all too easy; the goats were a few metres from the forest edge but a good hundred and fifty metres from the buildings. A quick dash from cover, a knife through the rope . . .

Which way was he heading? She had only seen him for a second and although she could find her way around, it was hard to build up a map of the forest paths in her mind. Anyhow, what could she do about him? He must be armed, at least with a knife. She would have to try to get another glimpse of him, fix his direction and then run for help. He could not move very fast pulling a goat, and even if they failed to catch him, they might frightened him into abandoning it.

She hurried through the trees in what seemed to her the most likely direction, doing her best to move quietly. Her guess had been all too accurate; she emerged into a clearing at the same moment as the thief – and in that moment they both saw Peter.

Eileen shouted a warning. Peter, sprawled on the ground loosening a rabbit's body from an awkwardly placed snare, jerked his head round, saw the stranger coming for him knife in hand and leaped to his feet. His twelve-bore was propped against a tree a few paces away. He lunged towards it but the man headed him off.

For a few seconds they faced each other, half-crouching, while Eileen held her breath. The man's eyes flicked to the shotgun and back again. He seemed to realize he could not reach it without risking the advantage of his knife, for Peter would be on him as he grabbed at it.

The goat, released and indifferent, moved away in search of tastier grass.

Point forward, the man's knife-blade wove menacingly in the air – one quick feint, which Peter side-stepped – then a determined rush. Eileen screamed and Peter tried to side-step again, but his foot struck a root and he stumbled. The man leaped on him and the two of them were wrestling on the ground, Peter disadvantaged by his fall, the man's knife within a finger-length of his throat.

Eileen's paralysis broke, swept away by a berserker tide of love and fury. She leaped for the gun, cocked both hammers with hands that barely knew how, jammed the muzzle into the man's ribs and pulled both triggers.

The explosion seemed to stun her, physically and mentally. The recoil jerked the gun out of her inexperienced hands and it fell across the bleeding corpse as Peter pulled himself from underneath. He jumped to his feet, still panting from the struggle and put an arm round her shoulders as she stood staring wide-eyed at what she had done.

Gently he turned her and led her away from the body, sitting her down against a tree, facing where she could not see it.

'I killed him,' she said at last, in a voice of halting amazement.

'I know, love. And you saved my life.'

'I killed him. I took a gun and shot him to bits because I love you. *And I'd do it again.* Peter, what's happened? What *am* I?'

'You? You're the most wonderful woman in the world. The only woman I want, now or ever.'

She turned and looked into his eyes, still bewildered, as though she had not heard him. 'But don't you see? If anyone tried to hurt you, I'd do it again! *Me!*'

They went on looking at each other and gradually the bewilderment in her eyes faded away and she began to smile, a smile of love and longing. Quite how it all happened they could never remember afterwards, but all their clothes were away, and they were clasping and entwining and searching and discovering and adoring, naked and lovely to each other on the forest floor, a stone's throw from the forgotten dead enemy, and then, merged and triumphant, they were swept into that nodal point of joy where the meaning of the universe is clear and never quite forgotten.

She lay afterwards cradled in his arms, gazing up through the branches at the shifting glimpses of sky, still too transfigured to ask herself if she was cold.

'This is a new and different Earth,' she told him, wonderingly.

Peter shook his head, holding her close, caressing her. 'No, it's not. It's the same Earth as ever. But we've been blind to her and to ourselves for too long. Now she's bringing us back to our senses – the ones that are left.'

She mocked him tenderly: 'How like a man, to put it into words and draw a moral.'

'Sorry – did I sound pompous?'

'No, my love, my darling. Besides, you're right. But for me . . . We're alive and we're part of *Her*. That's enough.'

PART TWO

Phoenix

21

'Only four this week, is it?' Dr Owen said, leaning back in his chair and swinging his stethoscope. 'You are all too damn healthy up here and that's a fact. I don't know why I come.'

Eileen grinned at him. 'You know very well why you come. For a morning out from the village and a lunch of grilled trout.' She patted her five-month belly. 'And to see how Junior's doing. Anyone'd think you were its grandfather, you fuss so much.'

'Junior is doing fine without any help from me. I will concede your point about the trout, though. . . . And to be honest, Eileen fach,' he continued more seriously, 'I worry about young Brian. A crying shame it is, a promising lad like that, only two years at Guy's and no way of ending his training. I feel *I* should be teaching him more.'

'Don't be silly, Doctor. He's learning a hell of a lot from you, working in the village with you two days a week, borrowing all your books, helping me in the clinic here – and I'm teaching him all I can, too. He'll end up as real a doctor as if he'd finished his time at Guy's. . . .'

They strolled out together into the May sunshine, still

discussing Brian Sennett, the medical student who had reached Camp Cerridwen with his sister Olive in January. His arrival had been very welcome to Eileen, who in spite of Dr Owen's weekly visit to the little clinic that had been built on the end of Peter and Eileen's cabin, and his availability in a crisis, had begun to feel a little worried about her responsibility as the rapidly growing camp's resident 'medical officer'. She had, after all, only qualified as a nurse herself a couple of years before the quake. Peter, too, had been relieved. They had only just become reasonably certain that Eileen was pregnant and he was more anxious than she was about her overworking, so even a partially trained colleague for her eased his mind a good deal.

Camp Cerridwen was barely recognizable after a winter of work which had only been halted by one week's snow and (according to the village experts) slightly less than average rain. The camp now numbered 173 people, about three-quarters of them witches or children of witches and although some cabins were still overcrowded, everybody slept indoors, either in a cabin or in a lagged caravan. Building was now in full swing and within a month or six weeks was expected to catch up at least with the existing population, to an acceptable standard. They had stuck to the original C-shaped plan, with the buildings spread in an arc along the edge of the forest and facing towards the centre of the little plateau whose heart was the camp-fire. Cabins had their own rock-built fireplaces but it had become a social habit to light the central fire each evening, small or large according to the weather, and to gather around it.

The forest had, in fact, already receded from behind the first arc of buildings as felling progressed, and a second row was springing up behind the first on the cleared ground. The biggest building of all was no longer the Central

Cabin, which was now used for a variety of small-group purposes such as practice sessions of the Music Club (the village had donated a battered piano and various people owned instruments from guitars to violins, an accordion and a cornet), Geraint Lloyd's surprisingly well-attended Welsh classes and talks by experts (such as the camp's solitary professional farmer) on their specialities which had now become necessary knowledge for everyone. Considerably larger than this, and a building achievement of which they were rather proud, was the Mess Hall. Central catering still had to be the rule, for the most economical use of their slim food resources.

The farm had been growing fast but still not as fast as the population. The six-hectare meadow had been fully ploughed before the winter and in much of it new sowings had replaced the winter vegetables. Every seed was precious, though fortunately several of the newcomers who had had both the time to prepare their flight and the foresight to think of it had brought more; but even those who were experienced gardeners were having to learn the unfamiliar skill of growing for seed as well as for consumption, with the next crop to think of and nowhere to buy new seed.

But the six-hectare field no longer sufficed, with the absolute necessity of keeping as much livestock as could be acquired and managed. So every patch of river meadow between camp and village had been pressed into service and the camp farm had become a necklace of meadows stretching the whole four kilometres to New Dyfnant.

With the onset of winter, the area around the Vyrnwy valley below New Dyfnant had become relatively peaceful. The scattered survivors had almost all drawn together into little communities, clearing and patching up villages, and there were large stretches of country without a soul in sight. Many cattle, sheep, and pigs and a few horses and goats,

391

roamed wild; there had been much hunting and slaughtering of them for food and the wiser communities had been rounding them up for stock as well but with population less than a hundredth of its former size there were still many wandering free. On two or three occasions, New Dyfnant and Camp Cerridwen had organized joint round-up expeditions, with every rideable horse for which there was a rider, and had brought in a gratifying number which were shared out between village and camp in proportion to their populations. These expeditions had been careful to avoid clashes with other communities, conceding any disputed territory without argument, for there were still unclaimed animals to be found and the last thing most people wanted was any local feud springing up.

Also still to be found, fortunately, were a few hayricks and hay-filled barns far enough from communities to be unclaimed and winter feed was badly needed, so slower cart-expeditions were sent out for these. The cart-expeditions took with them one of the bee-keepers (of which there were six in New Dyfnant and two in the camp) on the look-out for hives, which in their winter somnolence could be sealed for the journey and brought home.

As a result, by the spring Camp Cerridwen possessed one bull and eight cows, a boar and two sows, six ewes (but as yet no ram, though they could borrow one from the village) two billy-goats and seven nannies, four geldings and three mares (again, no stallion but the village had several). Two of the mares were in foal, both sows were in farrow, only one cow as yet in calf and two of the nannies had been February twins of one of the adult nannies, while another was in kid. The ewes had not been found till April, so no increase was expected there for a while. They also had eighteen hives, sixteen of them flourishing, the other two colonies having failed to survive the winter, but their bee-keeper was confident he could re-stock the two empty ones during the summer.

Four cockerels and sixty-three hens in the hen-runs were mostly of their own rearing from the original handful, for wandering poultry, being easily caught and cooked, had quickly become very scarce. No geese as yet but a drake and two ducks had been recently acquired and were being carefully guarded (especially from the camp's twelve dogs and five cats) for breeding. (Of the cats, incidentally, Ginger Lad was the undisputed king and two were heavily pregnant by him.)

One other thing had come from growing contact with the local small communities; the beginnings of barter and of the planning of output with barter in mind. One village, for instance, had once had a reputation for hand-weaving and two of the surviving older villagers remembered their skill; three looms and five spinning-wheels had been salvageable and the experts had set to at once training other spinners and weavers. In New Dyfnant, Jack Llewellyn had restored his grandfather's forge and remembering what he could (he knew metal in any case, being a proficient welder) was also training two youngsters; and already woven cloth was coming into New Dyfnant in exchange for ironwork and repair jobs. Two tiny villages down the valley, a couple of kilometres apart and manned by no more than half a dozen adults in each, had agreed to specialize, the one on livestock and the other on crops, to keep each other supplied. Other communities were beginning to wonder how they, too, could improve their position in the makeshift economy that was developing.

Inevitably, the internal economy of each 'tribe' became more or less communal, because at such a level of day-to-day survival nothing else would work. Camp Cerridwen, having started from scratch in survival conditions, was completely communal, both in the organization of work and in the use of products; the facts of life, not political or economic theory, dictated this. New Dyfnant stood at the other extreme, for thanks to Eileen's vinegar-mask warning, its population had survived almost completely, though the quake had done a good deal of physical damage; so the social and economic structure remained with all the impetus of habit, family pride, mutual knowledge and Welsh independence. But even that could not survive entirely; damage was uneven, community effort was needed for re-building and the closing of road-fissures and outside services and supplies had vanished. No stocks came into Bronwen's shop, no petrol to Jack's garage, and no liquor to Dai Forest Inn's cellars. No county salary to Dai Police, no church stipend to the Rev. Phillips and no National Health pay to Dr Owen or Ministry of Education pay to Geraint Lloyd. No money existed anyway. Yet all these people's services were still needed (even Bronwen's as barter organizer, Dai Forest Inn's as by now full-time Council chairman and Dai Police's as arbitrator of disputes and occasional enforcer of community decisions) and the village did not resent having to feed them. So gradually an *ad hoc* mixed economy had evolved with the boundaries between its public and private sectors constantly being ad-justed by trial and error.

At the camp, Dan's chairmanship had become as full-time as Dai Forest Inn's in the village. He was still the undisputed leader, though by now he had an active camp committee to help him and was able to delegate a lot of the organizing work. The committee's most important function was the deciding of priorities and the division of labour, for between building and farming there was more than enough to be done. There was always, too, a balance to be drawn between the effective use of available experts and the need to give individuals a variety of work – for their own encouragement and morale, for the development as far as possible of a community of all-rounders and for the fair sharing of popular and unpopular tasks.

Moira, also, retained her unchallenged spiritual and Craft leadership – though the situation had changed somewhat. There were over a hundred adult witches at Camp Cerridwen now, so the time had passed, early in the winter, when they could still be a single coven. In fact, there were now fourteen of them, none of which exceeded the traditional maximum of thirteen members. Three of the fourteen had hived off from Moira and Dan's original one, so she now wore four proud buckles on the Witch Queen garter Dan had made for her as soon as three covens had entitled her to that status. Five of the other covens had arrived independently, four had hived off from them and the remaining one had been built around a High Priestess and High Priest who had turned up covenless. It had been a wrench when Rosemary and Greg had hived off from Moira and Dan but they all knew it had to be done. Eileen and Peter, initiated at Samhain and intensively trained, had set up their own coven in March and another first-degree couple, arriving in November, had been similarly accelerated and were doing well, though Moira still nursed their young group from the sidelines. The coven maintained the Wiccan tradition of independence and autonomy, but the leaders met regularly as a Council of Elders to discuss progress and any differences that arose or to agree on transfers in the few cases of personal friction.

'I still can't get used to it,' Dan told Moira. 'Remember the old law that covensteads must be at least a league apart? And the years people used to wait sometimes for second and third degree?'

'The league law belonged to the Burning Time,' Moira

said. 'It couldn't work once the Craft went public. And as for waiting years – well, it's like an army – in peacetime it takes years to train an officer but in wartime you do it in months. You've got to or no army . . . And this is war, darling. We've felt the Angels of Lucifer probing often enough this winter, haven't we? Half our work's been psychic defence, just blank-walling them. But there *will* be a showdown, so our army's got to be ready.'

'I know . . . Anyway, with a hundred and twelve witches in one camp, and two or three dozen more asking to be initiated – what else can we do?'

'One thing about having fourteen covens,' Moira smiled, 'it fits very neatly into the calendar. Though the way things are growing, *that* won't last long.'

The calendar-fitting concerned the Temple which had been completed in time for the Spring Equinox and stood at one end of the arc of buildings. It had not had to be large, as it was never used by more than one coven at a time, on a fortnightly rota of formal Circles. Larger-scale rituals, such as Festival get-togethers, were held in the Mess Hall. Covens also met informally in between as they felt the need or for training purposes mostly in family cabins.

The promise to Father Byrne had been kept, though it had surprised some of the newcomers and even provoked some grumbling; his little Catholic chapel was built at the same time as the Temple, facing it from the other tip of the arc. His congregation was now four adults and one baby, for two other newcomers – unknown to each other before they arrived – were Catholics, a forty-year-old carpenter and a nineteen-year-old girl art student. Shy but not hostile with the witches (both of them had arrived with witch neighbours who had picked them up as lone survivors of their families), these two had gravitated together and two months later had taken everyone by surprise by asking

Father Byrne to marry them. The wedding had been an extraordinary affair; Greg and Geraint between them had rigged a public address system for the Chapel, and the Catholics and half a dozen Protestant non-witches had gone inside, while the rest of the camp had listened to the service from outside. A nearly completed cabin had been rushed ahead in time for the bride and groom to move in and they had been escorted to it in procession after a memorable wedding-breakfast – to which Dai Forest Inn, one of the village guests, had contributed one of his three remaining bottles of champagne for the 'top table' and a cask of home-brewed cider for everyone else. The newly-weds had remained shy but were clearly happy.

Spiritual leader Moira might be, but she – and in due course even those who had grumbled at the priority given to the Chapel – had come to appreciate the elderly Father's contribution deeply. From his doctrinal stance he never wavered; his own faith was total and he would always say, if asked, that the witches' religion was mistaken. But his humanity was total, also, as was his respect – practical as well as theoretical – for other people's sincerity. More than once he helped Moira to counsel people in distress, on a basis of simple human wisdom and innate spiritual strength without trespassing in Moira's beliefs or betraying his own.

'How do you manage it, father?' Moira asked wonder-ingly after they had, quite fortuitously, dealt together with a woman who did not know whether her son in Bradford was alive or dead and had been suffering bouts of acute depression as a result. Moira and the old priest, strolling together and discussing the cultivation of lettuces, had come across her moping on the river's edge. Twenty minutes later, after a kind of spiritual pincer-movement of consola-tion, she had gone away almost smiling.

'Manage what, my dear?'

'To work so well with us when you don't agree with us.'

'But *you* manage it with *me*. I could ask you the same question.'

'Yes, but . . .'

'Moira, we have many differences but we have certain things in common. A concern for human beings and a belief in the reality of psychic power. And neither of us believes that the duty of converting the other is more important than the harmony of this camp. So we work together on the things we believe in and keep our own counsel on the things we disagree about.'

'Is it really as simple as that?'

'Did that poor woman go away a little happier – after you and I had talked to her together?'

'Yes, she did. I'm sure of it.'

'Then it *is* as simple as that.'

They walked along the river-bank for a while in silence and then he said: 'You and Dan and many of the others – you are good people.'

Moira flung an arm impetuously round his shoulders and gave him a quick squeeze. 'And you, my friend, are the nearest thing I've met to a saint. . . . I suppose it's disrespectful to hug saints, though.'

'An interesting point of protocol,' he said with mock gravity, 'but since I am most certainly nothing of the kind, God help me, the point is academic. . . . Let me see, what were we talking about? Lettuces, wasn't it?'

Camp Cerridwen's quota of schoolchildren had risen to twenty-three, so the daily 'school bus' down to Geraint Lloyd's school was now a convoy of pony-trap and farm cart. One of the passengers, for the past month, had been Geraint himself.

The first indication of his intention of moving into the camp had been his request, in February, to the camp committee for permission to build a radio cabin in his own time at weekends.

'With this news network of ours building up,' he had explained, 'it'll be much easier if Tonia and I are in the same place. So I'd like to shift my equipment up here, if that's all right by you and sleep beside it. I can come and go to school with Liz and the children every day. And Tonia could do her camp duties more easily if she wasn't always commuting to take radio watches in the village. Besides, I have to charge my batteries up here already.'

The committee had agreed gladly and of course there had been a lot of volunteer help for him when he started building. The helpers had noticed at once that the plans for the cabin were larger than would have been needed for a bachelor and a radio bench but had said nothing, taking their cue from Tonia's smiling inscrutability, since she was not usually one to keep silent about anything that occupied her thoughts. When the cabin was finished, Geraint carted up his belongings from the village, culminating in a bed which was blatantly double. Tonia then abandoned the Spinter Shack and moved in with him. When somebody had commented on this with heavy-footed obliqueness, Tonia had said: 'Hell, we've been sleeping together for weeks, so why not do it in comfort? I love the guy and I guess he loves me. Any questions?'

There had been no questions. Mating was in the air at Camp Cerridwen; the tribal atmosphere, the survivalist way of thinking, the immediacy of manifested nature, all seemed to stimulate it. One or two of the partnerships, Moira feared, had been a little too hastily formed and sexual rivalry and jealousy were the predominant cause of such conflict as the camp suffered; but this she knew was natural and inevitable and she and Dan were reluctant to exert their influence unless things were getting out of hand or to give their advice unless it was asked for. When the people concerned were witches their own covens could keep an eye on any potentially explosive situations, and when they were not, the witch leaders were particularly anxious to avoid any suggestion that they were trying to dictate to the minority on personal matters.

'I hope the camp never becomes *too* large,' Dan said at one of the Elders' meetings. 'We've pretty well reached our optimum size. Everybody still knows everybody else, even if sometimes it's only slightly. So we still work like an extended family. A lot of things get sorted out by tribal opinion which'd have to be legislated for formally if we were any bigger. And legislation has to be impersonal. Once *that* creeps in, the whole nature of things changes.'

'It can't last, though,' Sam Warner said. 'On a national scale, I mean, once Britain's re-populated – which'll happen a hell of a lot faster than it did in medieval times because we've got the memory *and* the technical knowledge of modern civilization. We'll be instinctively moving towards it again, even if most of us don't really want to. Three or four generations and we'll be back in the old groove – or at least the beginnings of it.'

'Hardly our immediate problem,' his wife put in.

'I'm not so sure, love. Look – right now Britain's a land of small tribal communities and so's the whole bloody world if Geraint and Tonia's news sheets are anything to go by. And whatever's evolving *inside* those communities will have a big influence on what evolves *out of* them. The tribes and their ways of thinking and living will be the bricks with which any new State will be built. And the mortar will be the memory of urban civilization plus salvaged technical knowledge. So what tribes like ours are doing right now *is* important for the future. It could determine the whole shape of the building.'

'Don't forget,' Greg said, 'that the bricks might get hit by a shower of mortar without warning any time. And it could be very uncomfortable.'

Moira laughed, 'When you lot have finished with the metaphors – what do you mean, Greg? Beehive coming out and taking charge?'

'Of course I mean bloody Beehive. *Their* way of thinking will be completely old-establishment. Probably nineteenth-century establishment, at that, because they'll have tightened up into a military and administrative clique convinced they've got a divine right to rule.'

'With a nasty extra dimension, though,' Moira pointed out. 'If Gareth Underwood was right about Harley – that he's not just made a strategic alliance with the Angels of Lucifer but got involved in black magic himself – Gareth's actual words were "hooked on it" . . . . Well.'

Sam asked: 'What do you think that will mean in practice, Moira?'

'Dan and I have been thinking about it a lot,' Moira told him. 'All winter we've been picking up the Angels of Lucifer every now and then, but they've never been more than probing attacks, have they? It hasn't taken too much effort to fend them off. They've never tried a real psychic offensive, the sort of thing they did at the Banwell Unit against Ben Stoddart. We'd have known if they had. And frankly, after Underwood's warning we *expected* them to. So what are they waiting for? *We* think they're waiting till Beehive's ready to come out. That they'll synchronize their all-out attack with that.'

'Will we be able to hold it?'

'We will, Sam. We've *got to* believe we will or we're weakened from the start. But more than that – we've got to be ready to hit back. You know the rule: if you're under psychic attack, put up your defences and if the defences are strong enough the attack will bounce back on the attacker.'

'The Boomerang Effect.'

'Precisely. And in ordinary circumstances, white magic must confine itself to that and leave what happens to the aggressor to the Lords of Karma. Anything more than that is black. But there *are* times, particularly when thousands of innocent people are threatened, when the Boomerang Effect – or even binding – isn't enough, and deliberate counter-attack is called for. Only your conscience can tell you that. . . . You may even have to hit first, once you know the attack is being prepared. And *our* conscience tells us that one of those times is on its way. Does anyone disagree?'

Several of them said 'No' emphatically and the rest shook their heads. Liz asked: 'Are we strong enough to mount an attack? . . . No, I don't quite mean that – we've got the strength all right but are we *organized* to do it? Psychic attack isn't exactly a thing we've trained ourselves for.'

'Haven't we? We attack disease often enough by launching concerted power at it from the coven working together. We've been taught not to launch it against people but if we have to, the technique's the same.'

'All right – but you say "from the coven". How about *fourteen* covens? What do we do – work under you and Dan as one giant coven? Or in separate covens but at the same time? Either way we ought to know about it and be ready. Even practise it somehow, if we can find a way of doing that without alerting the Angels of Lucifer.'

Moira looked at Dan. 'Time to tell them our suggestion, don't you think?'

'Yes, love, I do.'

'Right, then. We think we need a psychic assault group – and here's how it would work . . .'

22

Without Karen's help, Harley knew, the situation might have been far worse. Not that the *putsch* would actually have succeeded, of course; that was unthinkable. The gods had not put supreme power into Sir Reginald Harley's hands to mock him. His mission was inexorable because only to him had the vision of Destiny been fully revealed, the vision of a Britain purged and cleansed of its degenerate multitudes, a purified stock on to which he, Harley, was to graft the future, a wiped slate on which only he could write. Yet the gods still had their secrets, which they unveiled to him, their chosen instrument, layer by layer as the time was ripe. And he had no doubt that Colonel Davidson's attempted mutiny and Karen's part in rooting it out, had been such a lesson. There is poison within as well as without, the gods had been telling him; the human battalions which were his instruments of Destiny must be immaculate, worthy of their task, before the next step on the ordained path could be taken. The lesson had confirmed, as well, what he had already partly understood – that to fulfil his mission he needed his complement, the Dark Angel the gods had sent to him, Kali to his Siva, the magical consort of the bright male destroyer-creator.

He wondered sometimes (though he seldom thought of her now) how he had ever been content with Brenda. He had believed she had satisfied his masculinity. But that had been in the old half-blind days when he had relegated maleness to a mere biological function, instead of the godlike creative essence which Karen had taught him it was. Their first coupling, a transformatory experience for him, had been on her second visit to Beehive. Since then she had come every month. John, she assured him, had been easily persuaded of the need for these visits, for there was much to plan between Harley and the Angels of Lucifer and the material benefits to the Angels had been immediate and continuing. But her real purpose had been the magical training of Harley and to this he had surrendered himself wholeheartedly, discovering in it a new dimension of power and awareness. Analytical habit had made him ask himself, at first, whether this was an illusion engendered by sexual euphoria. He had even put the question to her for she was always urging frankness in him.

Karen had smiled. 'Illusion? All right, let's try an experiment. Has anyone annoyed you today?'

'Annoyed? . . . My God, yes. Our so-called Prime Minister. He does as he's told, of course – but it's when he's trying to help that he's most disastrous. He created quite unnecessary problems at this morning's conference by sheer stupidity.'

'Right. Let's teach him a lesson . . . Make love to me, Reggie. But *slowly*.'

He was briefly taken aback by the apparent irrelevance but soon forgot about it. She conducted their mutual arousal with her usual (though never repetitive) skill and once he had entered her, commanded him to keep still. He obeyed, astonished at his own control, and she kept talking to him softly, unmoving herself. How long they stayed thus, he could not tell; locked in a motionless intimacy, tension mounting to an unbelievable pitch and then still higher, a mystical rapture in which body and mind and spirit were indistinguishable, a trance of almost intolerable brilliance which could not continue yet must not be broken . . .

Karen whispered: 'Picture him. Picture the Prime Minister. Hold his image in your mind . . . Now, command him to be silent. For a night and a day he cannot speak. *We* command him. Hold the image and the command, right through the orgasm. Are you ready?'

'Yes.'

'*Now!*' – and in that instant her pelvis began thrusting. They cried out together in a tornado of release, but somehow, he managed to hold on to the image and the command. He felt exhausted of every atom of his strength and it was minutes before he could even summon up enough strength to dismount her.

'How long did that take?' he wondered at last. '*I* haven't the remotest idea.'

She glanced at her watch, relaxedly matter-of-fact. 'Just under an hour.'

'It was incredible . . . Will it work?'

'Of course it will.'

She spoke with complete confidence but Harley still found himself nervous, next morning, about calling on the Prime Minister. He found the doctor with him, puzzled by a complete loss of voice which nevertheless had none of the other symptoms of acute laryngitis. The patient's voice came back suddenly, and equally completely, at half past ten that evening. The doctor bluffed an explanation, not daring to mention the word 'hysteria'.

Harley never doubted Karen again.

It was during her May visit that he asked her help in questioning Colonel Davidson. The colonel had been caught red-handed, in treasonable conference with one of his captains, a lieutenant and a signal corps sergeant. The lieutenant had been the weak link in the plot, some unguarded words of his arousing the suspicions of a lance-corporal who was in fact one of Intelligence Section's 'ears' in the Army. The Section had planted a bug in the colonel's quarters and had pounced on the conspirators next time they met, as soon as they had said enough to condemn themselves. In their enthusiasm the section had incurred Harley's wrath, for as he pointed out, they had pounced too soon. 'For God's sake – if you'd given them a bit more rope they'd have hanged others as well as themselves. They're only the ringleaders and I want *everybody*. You'd better get names out of them and fast.'

The Section had got to work. After twenty-four hours Davidson had still said nothing except to rail at Harley as 'a witch-ridden megalomaniac'. The implications of a leak about his relations with Savernake Forest had alarmed Harley and he had ordered the interrogators to be less squeamish in their methods. This proved unfortunate, for the lieutenant died under questioning, and the captain and the sergeant, who had been brought in to watch what to expect when their turn came, somehow managed to commit suicide in their cells.

Left only with Davidson, who seemed impossible to crack, Harley did some rapid thinking.

Colonel Davidson, bruised and aching though he was, knew better than to be surprised when he was cleaned up, brought a fresh uniform, given a good meal, and taken under escort to Harley's private quarters where the escort handcuffed him to a chair and left. Here comes the softening-up bit, the sweet reasonableness, the proffered deal, he told himself. God damn Harley, that won't get him anywhere, either.

Harley came into the room, a young woman with long black hair at his side. So that's the Black Mamba, Davidson thought, deliberately ignoring her. The colonel's own spies had been efficient.

'I'm sorry about the handcuffs,' Harley said pleasantly. 'I'd have done without them but my watchdogs won't let me. They insist on you being physically harmless before they'll leave you alone with me.'

'How right they are,' the colonel told him.

'Come now, Colonel, the time's past for dramatic gestures. So pointless. Your conspiracy has lost its leaders and hasn't a chance of succeeding. You may disapprove of me but I'm sure you'll agree that with *your* chance gone, even my regime is preferable to anarchy. So why not be sensible and cooperate?'

'With you – and *that*?' He jerked his head towards the woman.

The woman laughed.

Apparently unruffled, Harley went on and on, calm, reasonable, placatory. The colonel was puzzled. He sensed that it was all meaningless, that Harley knew perfectly well it would not succeed but that he was continuing the interview for some hidden purpose.

The woman just sat there, unspeaking, a faint smile on her face. In spite of himself, the colonel found himself glancing again and again in her direction, drawn by that face, drawn by those eyes. They were an unusual shape; the colonel, who knew his Far East, was certain there was no oriental blood in her but could understand why people thought there might be. And the *size* of them . . . the depth . . .

He was back in his cell, sitting bolt upright with a start.

When they had dressed him for the interview, they had given him back his watch. It was still on his wrist and he looked at it incredulously. He had lost at least an hour and a half, between succumbing to those great eyes and receiving the mental order to wake up. He *knew* it had been a mental order; he could still feel the impact of it, the quality of mocking triumph, even the femaleness of its sender.

What had he said before he was led back to the cell? In that hour and a half, what names had he given, what plans explained, what good men and women betrayed? Had black sorcery achieved what torture could not?

Colonel Davidson could only feel, with an awful certainty, that the pockets of his mind had been picked, emptied, rifled. For the first time in years he lowered his face on to his hands and wept.

General Mullard, anxious about morale, wanted the executions to be carried out secretly. But Harley decided otherwise. Seven officers, twenty-three other ranks and nine civilians were marched, handcuffed, for half a kilometre along frequented corridors to a large empty store-room, where they were led in and dealt with four at a time. The firing squad had been picked by Harley personally from the Hub Defence Battalion which was known colloquially as 'the Big Chief's Own'. Thirty-nine prisoners, four at a time, meant ten volleys, which echoed down the Beehive corridors for quite a distance. Six of the thirty-nine had been women.

At the same hour, five were executed in the Cardiff Beehive and two at the Norwich one, the only places outside London where Davidson had managed to plant supporters.

There were no more conspiracies and informing on even flippant critics of Harley's regime became a normal self-defensive reaction. General Mullard, a little grudgingly, admitted to Harley that he had been right.

Brenda, no longer in Harley's confidence, had known nothing of the would-be *putsch* until the mass arrests had included one of her own library assistants. Within an hour, news of the swoop had been all round Beehive and it had been a nerve-racking hour for Brenda, quite apart from her distress over the assistant whom she had liked and known for years. She was frightened both for herself and for Gareth. She expected to be picked up and questioned because of her closeness to the arrested assistant and she had feared that Gareth might be involved in the conspiracy. She did not think he was but knowing his secret views she had to face the possibility of it and of his having hidden the fact from her for her own safety. But no questioning occurred, then or afterwards, and Gareth rang up her up with a routine library query the obvious purpose of which was to let her know that he was not in trouble.

He came to her room that evening and, signalling to her to be careful, began a meticulous search for any newly installed microphone. Brenda understood and kept up a harmless conversation till he had finished.

'All clear,' he announced at last. 'I was pretty certain you hadn't been bugged since the last time I looked, when the Chief chucked you out – but with all this going on, I'd rather be quite sure. . . . I heard about your chap Farmer. I really am sorry about him. Been with you a long time, hadn't he?'

'Yes, he had . . . Were you . . . ?' She did not know quite how to put it.

'In on the round-up? No, love, I wasn't. I knew Davidson and the other three had been arrested, the other day, but the whole business suddenly became very hush-hush.

No one in the Section was told what was going on except the people actually working on it. Next thing the rest of us knew was this morning when the other thirty-eight were pulled in simultaneously.'

'What'll happen to them, Gareth?'

'The charge is treason, Brenda. Every single one of them, including your pal – I'm sorry, love.'

'So Reggie'll have them shot. Oh, my God . . . Who else will they find?'

'My guess is no one. With a thing this size, I know how the Section works. If they *did* expect ramifications, every last one of us would be on overtime, questioning the prisoners' contacts. But we're not. It was neat, quick and complete. I know the signs and I'd bet a year's pay they're satisfied they've rounded up everybody. One of the leaders must have talked and convinced them he'd left nothing out. Don't ask me how. It's all very untypical.'

'I did wonder myself,' Brenda admitted. 'When they arrested Jerry Farmer, they didn't question me or any of the staff. They didn't even search his desk. Just took him away . . .' She smiled bitterly. 'A grilling was the least I expected, now that I'm out of favour. . . . Though it's a couple of months now since Reggie dropped me. I suppose I'm not even "out of favour" any more. Just unimportant.'

'Not to me,' Gareth said quietly.

'I know . . . Why do you put up with me, Gareth? I use you as an emotional punching-bag and you never complain.'

He shook his head diffidently and after a while he asked: 'Do you still miss him?'

'I wish I could answer that one,' she said, frowning. 'I just don't *know*. Sometimes I think I miss the man he *used* to be – but how much of that is really nostalgia for the old days, before the earthquakes and the witch-hunt and the

Dust? . . . I thought I'd miss the status of being Madame Pompadour, with everyone afraid of offending me. But I don't. There's no real satisfaction in having everyone scared of you. I thought the wolves'd be on me as soon as I fell from grace – but do you know what, Gareth? Most of them just steered clear of me, as though I were going round with a bell crying "unclean, unclean". . . . And the *real* people were much more relaxed with me, as though I'd rejoined the human race. . . . The worst time was in between, when I knew that bitch had taken him over already but he kept me on out of habit – when *she* wasn't in Beehive, at least. I was humiliated but I was as stubborn as hell. I was *not* going to give in to her. . . . You said he "chucked me out". He never actually did, Gareth. Just treated me as part of the furniture till the humiliation outweighed the stubbornness. Do you know how it happened in the end? We'd come back to his quarters together and I let us in with my key. I always kept it separate from my key-ring – don't know why, caution I suppose. Anyway, he was being emptily charming, talking about nothing and not thinking of me at all and all of a sudden I hated him for excluding me. I put down the key on the table – sort of instinctive gesture of rejection. I went to pour a drink and when I came back the key had gone. I had a feeling he wanted me to . . . to abase myself by asking for it back. I couldn't. He went on being emptily charming, as though nothing had happened – he still is, if we meet by accident. I never went back and we never mention the fact.' She smiled unpleasantly. 'My God, Gareth, if *I* were a black witch I'd have his wax image right here, stuck full of rusty nails. Hers, too. Does *that* mean I miss him? Go on, psychoanalyse me.'

He shook his head again. 'I almost wish you *were* a black witch. You'd be doing the country a service.'

'Don't tempt me . . .' Her smiled faded. 'With your dangerous thoughts, I'm surprised *you* weren't in there with Colonel Davidson. Thank God you weren't. I'd as sure as hell miss *you*.'

'No, Brenda. When the time comes, that won't be *my* way of fighting him.'

Brenda took a deep breath.

'*Our* way, Gareth,' she said.

23

'I sometimes wonder,' Norman Godwin told his wife, 'why the hell we ever took on this bloody Castle.'

'You've been wondering that every week for months – and you know very well why,' Fay said.

The early sunshine bathed the perfect mandala of the sunken garden, below the East Terrace on which they stood, and softened the massiveness of the thousand-year-old fortress of Windsor at their backs. The lawns of the quartered circle were not as immaculate as they had once been, certainly; but they were still not bad, for the Castle group kept them mown on a rota system, as a labour of love. Only one feature was new – the two-metre-wide altar, neatly built of stone blocks, where the north-pointing path of the equal-armed cross met the outer circular path. The ornamental pond at the centre, too, was kept meticulously clear of floating leaves.

'It might really have been designed as an outdoor witches' temple,' Norman mused.

'You've said that before, too.'

Norman smiled. 'Stop taking the mickey, girl. You were the one who spotted it in the first place.'

They stood brooding, remembering the day they had come; the three covens from Slough, banding together for defence through the worst of the Madness, with friends and families making up nearly sixty people. They had been lucky to survive, for this part of the Thames Valley had been hit hard; and they had owed that survival to the nostalgia of a middle-aged woman from County Limerick. Maeve Kiernan was a quiet hard-working member of the Godwins' own coven, who had lived in Slough for thirty years or more, but who still tuned in to the Radio Eireann news almost every day. So she had picked up the Taoiseach's announcement on vinegar-masks days before the earth-quake – and those who listened to her had escaped the Dust. Apart from the covens and their immediate friends, there had been few enough to listen; for the anti-witch mania was intense locally and on one occasion Maeve had narrowly escaped lynching as a panic-mongering witch when she had bravely stood up and tried to pass her news to a cinema audience.

The defensive band, practically unarmed, had fled from Slough in convoy during the demented hand-to-hand fighting, and dodging fissures, had found themselves at the gate of the Castle. Strangely, there had been few people about and those that there were had been busy fighting each other. The band had managed to lock themselves in the Round Tower, where they had been unassailable, till the peace of death had settled on the turmoil outside.

They had emerged and decided to make Windsor Castle their home.

That it was defensible was a strong argument in favour; the heating problem was a strong argument against and had troubled them throughout the winter and spring – hence Norman's remark after an unseasonably cold May night. They had managed, somehow, to find enough small rooms as living accommodation which could be kept reasonably warm and yet were close enough together to be defensible. By some freak of geology, the Castle hill had been barely touched by the earthquake, which had inflicted no more than a few cracks in the Castle's inner walls and caused the partial collapse of the Salisbury Tower – though nearby Eton was a desert of rubble and fire had destroyed most of Windsor. The Castle, although cold, was a fortified oasis.

But that, they knew, had not been the real reason why they had stayed. They were surrounded, almost too profusely, by a millenium of the history of their now-decimated people and its hold on them grew as the days passed. If they abandoned it, rats and vandals, broken windows and damp, perhaps fire from careless nomads, would make short work of much of it. Almost without debate, they were overtaken by a compulsion to become its *de facto* guardians.

So the situation had arisen, bewildering to the odd stranger who came and went, of a survival group as short of food, facilities and warmth as any other, solemnly taking on the extra burden of lighting great wood-fires in the hearths of the State Apartments in rotation to fight off the worst of the damp, and searching methodically for tremor cracks to make good, new rat-holes to plug up, loose roof-tiles to fix, burst pipes to mend and broken panes to reglaze.

Most of them being witches or sympathizers, they had been regular in their esbats and sabbats. In fine weather the sunken garden was, as Norman said, an ideal outdoor temple, with its great Circle and four cardinal points already laid out. Indoors, the King's Dressing Room served admirably, being only five and a half metres square, comparatively easy to warm and free from any obtrusive symbolism, even the pictures being confined to Royal portraits which looked on undisconcerted by the skyclad rituals. (So far no one had been hardy enough to be skyclad in the sunken garden; that could wait for a week or two yet.)

Fay and Norman, knowing the strong tradition that the Order of the Garter had witchcraft roots, had been tempted to suggest using St George's Chapel for one of the Great Sabbats but had decided against it; there were Christians in their community who might well be offended, thus endangering the friendly relations which had been achieved. They had compromised by suggesting the Garter Throne Room, where the three covens had held a very successful joint Imbolg festival on 2 February.

Today, with the climbing sun already banishing the chill, Norman soon regretted even the appearance of doubt. The whole thing, he decided, had been worth it.

He put an arm round Fay's shoulder, turning to go back indoors. To his surprise, she halted and stiffened. He looked down at her questioningly.

'Norman – hush, listen . . .'

He listened but could hear nothing.

'I thought I heard an aeroplane,' she said.

'Oh, darling – don't be daft. It's months since we heard even a motorbike . . .' But then he broke off, amazed, as a slight change of wind brought the sound to his ears too.

They listened incredulously as it grew louder.

'It's a chopper,' Norman said at last. 'And it's getting closer.' Defensive instinct made him pull Fay down to crouch behind the wall of the terrace; strangers were treated with caution till proved friendly and a *helicopter* . . . His hand touched the butt of his automatic which he always carried when he was out of doors.

'There it is. Look.'

The helicopter had materialized on the eastern horizon

and was coming straight and fast for the Castle. Norman and Fay kept out of the sunlight, watching.

Minutes later, the helicopter settled on the lawn below them, swinging slightly to reveal RAF roundels and cut its engines. A middle-aged man jumped out (his flying jacket did not seem to cover a uniform) and turned to hand down the passengers; a handsome woman about his own age, a younger man and woman with a baby and two teenage girls. The group stood together for a moment, looking up at the Castle. Then the pilot said something to the younger man and they both took out pistols and began to move forward warily towards the terrace's central flight of steps, the women and girls behind them.

Norman waited till they were about twenty metres away, then called out from behind the wall.

'Drop those guns, please.'

The two men turned towards him, saw his pistol and obviously realized they were infinitely more vulnerable than he was. The older man dropped his weapon and the younger followed suit after a second's hesitation.

'Move away from them. . . . I'm sorry but we have to be careful. We've been attacked before. We wish no one any harm but we have to be sure. . . . Right. I'm coming down to join you.'

The older man smiled as Norman walked down the steps, gun in hand. 'I do understand. We're fugitives, too. But definitely peaceful.'

Norman asked: 'Who are you?'

The smile became a laugh. 'One might say – your landlords. I know a lot has changed but technically I own this place.'

Norman heard Fay gasp beside him and then awareness hit him as he recognized the face . . . *all* the faces. For a moment, the conflicting impulses of caution and respect paralysed him. He suddenly felt the absurdity of the situation and he pushed his gun back into his belt.

'Forgive me, sir,' he stammered. 'We weren't exactly expecting you.'

Once the first astonishment and embarrassment were over, the day went remarkably well. Norman had the feeling that the King and his family, while courteous, were uncertain at first how to treat the squatters at whose mercy they obviously were, even though Norman had given them back their guns at once. Norman, in turn, hardly knew how to treat his refugee Sovereign in such a bizarre situation, so fell into the same kind of watchful politeness.

But fortunately, from the moment they went inside, the evidence of the group's attempts at preservation (however makeshift) was all around them; and as the King came to realize their attitude and the work they had put in – a quixotic effort, in the circumstances of winter survival – he thawed rapidly. By the time they were all seated in the communal dining-room, he and his family were treating the squatters as friends. There were nearly a hundred people at the meal, for the group had grown since its beginnings, and rumour, running round the Castle in minutes, had made sure there were no absentees.

Norman had never been either royalist or anti-royalist, tending to take the institution for granted, and to regard any debate on its principle as being of purely academic interest with so many more immediate problems to think of. But today he had to admire, if only on a personal basis, the way his unexpected guest (or should it be host?) managed to combine an interested and interesting friendliness with an *ex-officio* dignity. This was an unreal situation, yet its unreality was here to stay, so must be accepted as real. He hoped he was coping as well as the King seemed to be. . . . He glanced across at Fay in animated conversation with the Queen and the younger Princess; no awkwardness there, apparently.

The meal was finished but nobody left. The King turned to Norman and asked: 'Would you mind if I made a kind of after-lunch speech?'

'I wish you would, sir. I'm sure everyone's – er . . .'

'Full of questions?'

'Well, yes.'

The King nodded. 'I'll see if I can forestall some of them.'

Norman stood up and banged his mug on the table. In the instant silence which followed, he announced, hoping that his words sounded neither pompous nor abrupt: 'Ladies and gentlemen, His Majesty would like to speak to us all. But before he does, *I'd* like to say something – I don't know anything about protocol, so I hope it's in order. Just that, of all the strange things that have happened to us in the last few months, this must be about the strangest. I don't know what His Majesty's plans are, except that they don't tally with Beehive's. Perhaps he'll tell us. But I do know that in a sense he and his family are in the same boat as we are and for that reason alone, quite apart from any others, we're very glad to welcome them – if one can welcome a family into its own home . . .' There was a murmur of laughter, in which the King joined. 'Anyway, sir – this may not be exactly a royal welcome but it's a genuine one and we're delighted you're here . . .' He did not know how to finish, so he gestured awkwardly at the King and sat down.

Fay smiled across at him, reassuringly, during the applause.

The King stood up with a little bow of acknowledgement to Norman and the applause cut off quickly.

'Thank you very much, Mr Godwin – ladies and gentlemen . . . Mr Godwin needn't worry; *I* haven't the faintest
idea of the protocol for such a situation, either. I don't
think it's arisen before. But believe me, for anyone as
hungry – and I will admit it, frightened – as I and my
family were this morning, this has been a *very* royal welcome. . . . I won't speak for long, for a very practical reason;
I'm probably the only helicopter pilot present (it has become an hereditary skill of our family, fortunately) and it
occurs to me that the sooner we get that machine under
cover and out of sight, the safer we all are from any
reconnaissance sorties that may be out searching for me and
my family, as they probably will be soon enough. Beehive
has several concealed helicopter bases which is how we
managed to escape – and that should tell you a good deal
about the situation in which we found ourselves. . . . In
brief, as Sovereign, I can no longer regard the Beehive
administration as being the legitimate authority of this
country and therefore – if the Crown has any function left
at all – I have a duty *not* to appear to be its formal head.
For that reason, I got out. Fortunately I was able to bring
my immediate family with me. Any man would want to do
that, of course, but I had an additional reason; if Beehive
should claim that I have abdicated or died and should try
to impose as my successor some relative of mine who is
still in its power, it would have to compel some unfortunate
cousin. And since my son and my elder daughter are both
of age – and, as you can see, in good physical and mental
health – such a manoeuvre would be rather unconvincing.
. . . Mr Godwin has asked what my plans are. Frankly,
ladies and gentlemen, I do not know yet. I hope the time will
come when I shall know. Meanwhile, if you will have us –
and if you feel our presence does not add to your own
dangers – we would very much like to stay with you . . .'

The rest of his sentence was drowned in an outbreak of applause. When it had died down, he went on: 'Thank you for that; we appreciate it very much. This is, after all, our home, or one of them – I don't mean that in the sense of economic or constitutional ownership which has become pretty irrelevant these days, but in the sense that we love it. And our more intimate knowledge of the place might even be useful in your admirable work to conserve it. . . . I think it will be best if we neither regard ourselves as your guests nor think of you as ours, but instead regard all of us as one working community. . . . One day, perhaps, what is left of our country will find once more a useful function for a Sovereign or perhaps not. I can't foresee the answer to that question. If it does, I will hold myself ready to fulfil that function. If not – and in the meantime in any case – my family and I will do our best to make our own contribution, as individuals, to the survival and rebirth of our tragically tiny nation. One thing I will *not* do, ladies and gentlemen – I will not be paraded as the figurehead of a corrupt and dictatorial clique, cowering underground in comparative safety until it feels ready to emerge and take control, by force, of those who have done the real work of surviving.' He paused and then suddenly turned and smiled. 'And now perhaps, Mr Godwin – will you and some of your friends help me to hide that chopper?'

Two or three hours later, the King and Norman were walking round the Castle precincts, the King answering the shy greetings of the people they passed. They found themselves at the entrance to St George's Chapel and the King went in, Norman following him. They stood for a moment looking along the nave and up at the delicate tracery of the fan-vaulted roof.

'You're witches,' the King said at last. 'You know what they say about the Order of the Garter?'

'Yes, sir.'

'I've often wondered if it's true – that Edward III was really a supporter of the Old Religion?'

'There seems to be quite a case for thinking so . . .'

'I know, I've read Margaret Murray too.' He chuckled. 'I was totting up, a week or two back, sitting angry and frustrated in Beehive – apart from my own family, there are just two Garter Knights still alive so far as we know and one of *them* is senile. . . . Perhaps if I do ever get my job back, I'll recruit some rather more interesting new blood into it. After all, since Disestablishment stopped me being Head of the Church, I can be far more elastic in matters of religion. If anything, I have an obligation to be ecumenical. . . . Wasn't there a controversy in your Craft, oh, about forty years ago, over whether there was such a thing as a King of the Witches?'

'Quite a heated one.'

'Wouldn't it be ironical if people started calling *me* that?'

24

'What are we going to do with Bill Lazenby?' John asked, after he and Karen had been riding for some minutes in silence.

'He tried to desert, John. That can't be forgiven.'

'Of course not. He's got to be punished, as an example. But he can't be re-absorbed afterwards. He'd be unwilling and resentful and a weak link. . . . Oh, I know resentment *can* be harnessed and channelled, as a source of power – but not continuously in an operation like ours. We'd have to waste too much attention on him.'

'Of course.'

'And we can't just banish him because then he *would* escape. Join a white group somewhere – and we can't have that because he knows too much.'

'A great deal too much.'

'So we have to punish him and afterwards . . . Karen, there can't *be* an afterwards for him.'

'In other words, he's got to be executed.'

John sighed. 'Yes.'

'I'm glad you recognize it, darling. . . . Come on, race you!'

She spurred her horse and was away but John was soon beside her, for riding was one acomplishment in which he equalled and even excelled her, and in his more analytical moods he sometimes wondered if she gave him opportunities to prove it as a calculated sop to his self-respect. She was his superior in magical power, in ruthlessness and in charisma – he had long accepted that – but she still needed him so she took care to nourish his pride.

He was still captivated by her, more so than ever (Joy was a ghost from the golden past, too painful to dwell on), but he could look at her reasonably objectively. Could admire, at this moment, as she galloped with streaming hair towards Stonehenge, the brazen effectiveness of her barbarian-chieftainess image which indeed he had helped her to create, for he had a good eye for theatrical effect. Always side-saddle and black-booted, from the waist down she was fashion-plate Edwardian, but she had topped it with a startlingly flamboyant, close-fitting blouse of scarlet brocade, covered in bad weather by a scarlet cloak. A sheath-knife hung from a silver belt. For ten or fifteen kilometres around, this extraordinary figure, with its long black hair unbound in fair weather or foul, had become the symbol of the awe in which the Angels of Lucifer were held. Once she had become known, she had only to make an appearance and people hurried to do as they were told.

At Beltane, the Angels of Lucifer had lit a huge bonfire, on high ground near their village, which was visible through the night from border to border of their territory; their subjects within those borders had looked towards it uneasily, and drawn their curtains. May Day itself had dawned fine and warm and Karen had astonished them with an action which, in some way that none of them could explain, increased their superstitious fear of her still further. She had ridden the bounds of her realm, erect and regal, with John beside her and an escort behind. Skirt, boots, belted knife, and side-saddle were as always, but from the waist upwards she was naked except for a large silver inverted pentagram that flashed between her breasts. Her nipples were painted as scarlet as her lips. The total effect, which other women might have made absurd, she made terrifying.

Since Beltane, rain or shine (she seemed impervious to either) she had always ridden abroad like that. She was an intensified symbol of the Angel's power and men quailed before it. But she insisted on being its unique focus. When Jenny, the ex-Banwell nurse, riding with her one morning, had presumed to strip off her own shirt in imitation of her leader, Karen had merely looked at her in commanding silence. Jenny had flushed and replaced her shirt. Since then, no one had dared.

Today, jumping from the saddle as she arrived at the Henge a length behind John, she was the laughing warrior queen. The escort stayed respectfully beyond the encircling earthwork while John and Karen walked together among the huge sarsen trilithons, recovering their breath after the hard ride.

'I like your idea, John,' she said after a while. 'What did you call it? – "testing our heavy artillery" . . . Yes.'

'It almost frightens me,' John admitted. 'There's so much power here. Have *we* the strength to handle it?'

'Strength? After all we've achieved?'

'Even after that.'

The sun had disappeared behind a heavy bank of cloud and the lowering greyness reinforced John's doubts. His question had been almost rhetorical, for until then Stonehenge had merely challenged him, not troubled him. But suddenly, in retrospect, it was no longer rhetorical. John shuddered.

Karen walked over to the Altar Stone at the focus of

426

the bluestone horseshoe. She fingered it for a moment and then lay face upwards upon it throwing back her hair. She smiled serenely up at the sky. 'I dare anything that the Henge can do.'

'Don't try to frighten me with melodramatics,' John said, covering his unease with casualness. 'In spite of popular belief, that was *not* a sacrificial altar. The evidence is that it once stood upright.'

'A fallen phallus. All the more appropriate as an *execution* altar.'

'You mean Bill Lazenby?' John was no longer casual. 'God, Karen – we've never done *that* before.'

'We have *killed* before.'

'But ritual human sacrifice . . .'

'Bill has to die – you've said so yourself. Why not make his death serve a purpose? That would be a *real* test of our "heavy artillery".'

He looked down at her, fascinated and half-repelled, knowing that in their own terms she was right and almost despising himself for his reluctance. There were no half-measures possible, along the course to which they were committed. Yet still . . .

As he gazed, the sun broke through, bathing Karen and the Altar Stone in unexpected light. It was surely a sign, an endorsement of her intent. But could she draw the others along with her? . . . Most of them, yes, without hesitation, but one or two might baulk. His own support, he knew, would swing the balance; together they could command the Angels of Lucifer, as they had done from the start. If he failed her now, what breaches would he open?

'Very well, Karen. Tomorrow at dawn? New moon's the day after tomorrow, so it'll still be in the waning phase.'

'Tomorrow at dawn,' Karen said.

The eastern horizon was clear, with only the thinnest gauze of morning mist hugging it, so there would be no difficulty about timing the sacrifice. The Angels of Lucifer, their bodies glistening with the belladonna 'flying ointment', insulatory and hallucinatory, which Stanley Friell had prepared for them, danced in a wild ring widdershins between the outer ring and the horseshoe, keening and yelping; they had been at it for half an hour, enraptured and tireless, a dynamo of power that built and built, a charge awaiting detonation by the sacrifice, and ready to detonate in turn the vastly greater power locked in the ancient stones.

Inside the great horseshoes of trilithons were only Karen, John and Sonia the Maiden, grouped around the victim spreadeagled on the Altar Stone. There had been no need to bind him, for Stanley had prescribed for him too, with a dose that paralysed his limbs but left him conscious and wide-eyed. The Maiden stood behind him, stroking his head and shoulders, crooning to him, whispering flattery to him, telling him what a fine man he was, what a worthy sacrifice, filling his field of view with a last inverted vision of the living. John faced East across the Altar Stone, awaiting the first glimpse of the sun, ready to give the command to Karen as she stood opposite him, ceremonially astride with the knife held high.

A sliver of golden fire flickered on the horizon, and John cried: 'Now!'

As the blood pulsed on to the Altar Stone, Karen led them to join the ring of dancers, the red knife still in her hand, laughing in exultation as the earth shook beneath them and the towering megaliths groaned.

'The epicentre was in the area of Salisbury Plain,' Professor Arklow told Harley. 'A strange phenomenon. It could be felt as a slight physical sensation in the Cardiff and

Manchester Beehives – and, as you know, here in London – but not apparently in the more distant Beehives. And yet I've had no reports of actual damage. Have you, Sir Reginald?'

'Not so far, Professor. All the Beehives reported at once, of course – that's an established drill whenever the seismographic duty officers report a sizeable tremor. All negative, except that as you say Cardiff and Manchester felt it. But agents on Surface within reach of radio points in the area have been reporting all morning, as well. They all say the same; considerable public alarm, naturally, but only trivial damage . . . What's your prognosis? Are we in for more?'

'That's what I mean by a strange phenomenon,' the professor said. 'After the past few months, we pride ourselves on having become more skilled than ever on reading the signs. A tremor of that magnitude *should* have given us warning. It did not. I've even been back over the last few days' recordings to see if we'd missed anything but there was nothing. The tremor did not fit into any normal pattern nor has it been followed by any normal aftermath. It just *happened*, Sir Reginald. And to be frank with you, as a scientist I find that most disturbing. I keep asking myself: "Why?" – and finding no answers. . . . What's so unusual about Salisbury Plain?'

I have a very good idea, Harley smiled to himself. But if I told you, my dear professor, you would not believe me.

Moira sat bolt upright in bed, jerked awake by a vertiginous awareness of evil. Her movement woke Dan, who sat up beside her, looked puzzled and grasped her hand.

'Did you feel it?' she asked as the wave subsided.

'I felt *something*. Something very nasty. From over there.' He pointed south-east and Moira nodded. Although Dan was less psychically sensitive than herself, she knew from long experience that he had a better sense of direction.

'Savernake Forest?'

'Could be.' He was already out of bed and pulling on clothes. 'Hadn't we better call Tricia? If it's Karen and John, we need all the facts we can get.'

'If it's them and strong enough to wake us up,' Moira said grimly, 'we need the Elders.'

Within a quarter of an hour they were all gathered in the kitchen, the warmest place in that early dawn; the High Priestesses and High Priests of all fourteen covens, Tricia Hayes their best clairvoyant and old Sally who had heard them moving about and had got up to stoke the fire and make them a hot drink. Dan and Moira had not had to rouse them all; Tricia herself and several of the others had also been wakened by the psychic shock-wave and were already getting dressed.

'Well, Tricia?' Moira asked. 'What can *you* tell us?'

'Blood,' Tricia said. 'That's what I got first. And tall stones – megaliths. Then I pulled myself together and tried to be calm – it wasn't easy, I'd been overwhelmed at first . . . It's the Angels of Lucifer.'

No one asked 'Are you sure?' because they knew Tricia. If she was not sure, she said so.

'Megaliths,' Dan said. 'Stonehenge and Avebury are both on their doorstep.'

'It's not Avebury,' Jean Thomas insisted, a little unexpectedly because she was seldom emphatic about her own clairvoyance. 'We know Avebury inside out and we love it. If it *had* been Avebury, we'd have picked it up. Wouldn't we, Fred?'

'Yes, I think we would . . . Could it be Stonehenge, Tricia?'

'I've never been there, oddly enough,' Tricia told him. 'Let me try . . .' She closed her eyes and everybody kept quiet, waiting. 'I suppose it must be. Nothing else could be that *big*. . . . A road with a tunnel under it . . .'

'That's Stonehenge,' several people said.

'I'm going to stop now, if you don't mind,' Tricia said. 'I'm not getting anything new and that awfulness *hurts*.'

'Leave it, then, love,' Dan told her. 'Sally, anything hot for Tricia yet? She's shivering.'

'Coming up right now.'

'Do you realize what this means?' Greg asked. 'They're using the Henge as an amplifier. Animal sacrifice, if Tricia's right about the blood . . .'

'Not animal,' Tricia interrupted. 'Human. At least, I think so. If it had been animal, the blood wouldn't have . . . *swamped* me like that.'

They stared at each other, appalled; for a moment no one felt like speaking.

'I think Greg's right,' Sam Warner said finally, in a determinedly level voice. 'I reckon Liz and I have put in more study on stone circles than anyone here, although I'm sure most of you know at least something about them. They *are* focal points of power, even most detached psychical researchers accept that by now. We're certainly convinced of it. . . . We all know the Angels of Lucifer are powerful. They're completely ruthless and they know what they're at. Well, if they're using human sacrifice to raise power *and* using Stonehenge as an amplifier – no wonder they woke us up!'

'Any suggestions, Sam?' Dan asked.

'Yes. We all know that sooner or later we're going to have to fight the Angels of Lucifer head on. That's what we set up the Psychic Assault Group for and it's been shaping up well. So why shouldn't the PAG use an amplifier, too? The *power's* the same – it's there for the godly to use, as well as the ungodly. . . . So is there a stone circle anywhere near here?'

'Geraint will know,' Moira said. 'And if he doesn't, he'll find out. He's got plenty of archaeological books in his school library.'

Geraint did know, because he had helped to excavate it; a small but well-preserved megalithic circle a few kilometres away in the rising mountains west of Dyfnant Forest. It had lain for centuries buried under an ancient landslide, till gradual weathering of the topsoil had, in 1998, revealed a tell-tale pattern on an Ordnance Survey aerial photograph. The local archaeologists had moved in, Geraint among them, and in two years of volunteer labour had dug out the site. Now the circle stood clear and stark, looking a thousand years younger than its counterparts elsewhere because of its long burial.

Geraint wanted to take the Psychic Assault Group – the PAG as it had come to be called – to the circle himself but Tonia would not hear of it. He was still recovering from a bullet-wound in the right leg and was firmly confined to camp.

The wound was the result of the only shooting battle that had so far taken place in Camp Cerridwen itself. It had been quick and decisive and Geraint had been the only casualty apart from the two dead attackers. That the attack had failed was thanks to Gareth Underwood. Since his brief visit, Geraint or Tonia had been listening meticulously at 0745 hours every day on the designated frequency but none of the arranged code phrases had come through for several weeks. Then one morning Tonia had heard 'Jerusalem artichoke gammon' repeated twice. That had puzzled them. 'Globe artichoke' meant 'expect psychic attack' and 'Jerusalem artichoke' meant 'expect physical attack' – but there was no 'gammon' on their list. Obviously Gareth was trying to tell them something extra.

It was Greg who had hit on the answer. 'Gammon – ham – he's saying they're going to have a crack at your ham radio!'

They had posted concealed marksmen all round the radio cabin, day and night. Just before dawn on the third night they had seen two armed strangers moving silently towards the cabin. They had let them come far enough to have them surrounded, and Peter O'Malley, in charge of the night's guard, had called on them to halt. They must have been very determined raiders, for they had tried to rush the cabin, one of them firing as he ran, the other pulling the pin from a hand-grenade. In the dim light, Peter had managed to wing the grenade-thrower so that it dropped at the man's feet. The other man had tried to kick it clear, but too late, and the explosion had killed them both. Geraint, jumping from bed, had been hit by a shot through the wood of the door.

'Quite a compliment,' he had joked shakily as Eileen bandaged him up. 'Our little news network must be bothering them.'

The raiders were in civilian clothes, carrying Army issue weapons but wearing no identity discs. Father Byrne and the Rev. Phillips from the village had conducted an ecumenical funeral service at their burial. Earlier raids on New Dyfnant and the Madness had produced many unidentified but probably Christian bodies, so the priest and the minister had worked out an agreed procedure. The minister, reared in an atmosphere where Popery was anathema, had been suspicious at first but growing respect and liking for the gentle old priest had dissolved his doubts.

The attack on the radio cabin had not been repeated but the armed watch had been maintained.

The PAG had been the product of Dan's tidy mind but it was psychically sound and had been quickly agreed upon. Each coven had nominated its most psychically powerful member, which was not necessarily the same thing as the most psychically experienced. These formed the PAG, under Moira and Dan's leadership (Moira and Dan's coven being handed over to their senior couple while the PAG was in action). The idea was that when a psychic attack was to be mounted, the PAG would be its spearhead, raising the power as a group and directing it at its target. At the same time, each coven would be meeting and concentrating on feeding power to its own representative on the PAG. A simple two-tier pyramid of dynamism, with Moira and Dan at its tip.

Putting the theory into practice had involved some trial-and-error. First, each coven had chosen its own 'delegate', and practised feeding power into him or her within the coven's own Circle, while the delegate tried to direct the total to a single objective such as the telekinetic moving of a compass-needle, or a specific work of healing, according to the delegate's known talents. As a result, two of the delegates had proved unable to carry such a charge and had shown signs of distress, so had had to be replaced by others perhaps less talented but more robust. Again, by the original plan the PAG should have totalled fifteen – Moira, Dan and one delegate from each of the other thirteen covens. But three of the covens had found that their most effective delegate was in fact a duo (two married couples and a pair of identical twin sisters) who were used to working powerfully together but were no more than average apart. So the final total had become eighteen.

The next stage had been to weld the eighteen into a working group. Moira and Dan had begun 'limbering them up' by practising simple and familiar rituals with them, to get them used to each other. This had resulted in the replacement of one of the delegates, from the Warners' Traditional coven, who admitted he found the strangeness of the Gardnerian-type rituals too distracting for him to be able to concentrate on the task for which he had been chosen. His replacement proved much more adaptable and fitted in well.

At last the team seemed ready and they tried some directed work – at first without calling on the support of the covens. They had begun with telepathic projection of selected images, Tarot trumps, to three volunteers outside the group: Tricia Hayes the expert, one moderately experienced witch and one helpful non-witch who claimed to be completely insensitive. Their correct guesses, which on pure chance should have been around one in twenty-two, were one in four and three-quarters by Tricia, one in twelve by the witch, and a fraction under one in eight by the non-witch (who was so gratified that she began taking an active interest in witchcraft and was accepted as a postulant in Rosemary and Greg's coven). Moira and Dan were delighted; any group which could project with that degree of success, in an experiment which was uncharged with emotion, should, they knew, be a formidable force in the urgent determination of battle.

They had then repeated the experiment with the full pyramid, the covens being unaware of the cards being projected, but concentrating on feeding power to their respective delegates. The runs had only been short, because the camp was too busy to immobilize two-thirds of its population too often for too long – but the results had been startling. Tricia's success rate became almost complete, while that of the other two approximately doubled.

This was the stage the PAG had reached when Sam made his suggestion about the stone circle.

The sun was lifting clear of the forest behind them as the PAG reached the high ring of megaliths. They had left while it was still dark but they knew that by now all the covens would be up and assembled. The experiment was to take place between 8.00 and 8.30, with its climax timed for 8.30 exactly. Moira and Dan had reconnoitred the place two days before and decided what they intended to do, but had left the briefing of the PAG till they were in position in the stone circle. The covens' minds were to be uncluttered by any concepts other than power-feeding.

All the group were fully clothed. Moira and Dan much preferred to work skyclad or for special purposes cere-monially robed; but they had decided that the PAG must be as mobile – and, if necessary, inconspicuous – as a military unit, so they had trained in ordinary clothes, of a cross-country serviceability, from their first meeting.

They arrived just after 7.30 and rested within the ring, getting the feeling of the great stones.

Just before 8.00, Moira told them: 'You see that wooden hut over there, about a hundred metres away? It's where the excavators used to keep their tools. Geraint said it'd still be here. . . . We're going to set it alight, by psychic effort from inside the henge, at half-past eight exactly. Right – take your places, everybody and we'll cast the Circle.'

For the next half hour, they welded themselves together mentally, flexing the psychic muscles they had trained, building up the power to a higher pitch than they had ever reached before. After a while they began to feel the henge responding, the ageless currents which its builders had understood so well, stirring and resonating with their own group mind. The thought came to Moira as the perspiration beaded on her brow: *We've been learning to walk, then run – now we're riding a stallion.* She could feel, too, that other confluence of currents, the tide of supporting power from Camp Cerridwen in the heart of the forest. . . .

It was going to succeed. She knew it.

At half past eight, she cried: 'Go! Go! Go!', pointing the ritual sword straight at the wooden hut.

Her whole body shook and it was as though a white-hot flame surged through the veins of her arm. In the distance – it seemed leagues away, yet impaled on her sword-point – the wooden hut began to smoulder; she knew the surge of extra confidence in the group behind her and gasped again as it swept through her.

The hut burst into flames.

Moira did not move till it was burning fiercely and the immense tide flowing through her spirit and body had begun to ebb. Then she turned. Several of them lay panting and exhausted, their eyes closed. Others sat gazing at the flame-wrapped hut, still hardly believing it.

Dan put his arm round her, lowering her gently to the ground as she slipped into grateful unconsciousness.

25

'Don't misunderstand me, Harley,' General Mullard said. 'I am *not* saying that Operation Skylight will be a failure. It has to succeed, because it will be the end product of Beehive's very existence. We came underground to preserve a governmental and military machine which could survive while Surface was in chaos and emerge to take charge when the time was ripe.'

'I am aware of that,' Harley said, with the complacency the general found increasingly hard to put up with these days. 'Also that the time *is* ripe and that Operation Skylight will therefore take place on 21 June. Three weeks gives us plenty of time to prepare. What is your point?'

'My point,' the general said patiently, 'is that we shall be mounting Operation Skylight with about one half of the forces we originally envisaged. The virtual destruction of the hives at Birmingham and Bristol by the earthquake and the losses at other hives depleted the Army badly. And I know Davidson's lot were only a handful but they were in key positions, so that didn't help. . . . Operation Skylight will take control of the country for you, as ordered. But we shall be thinner on the ground than I should like. There will be local reverses, guerilla activity from uncooperative elements and so on. Some of these Surface communities have had plenty of practice, dealing with the Madmen and with bandit groups.'

'A disciplined Army is rather a different proposition from stray lunatics and bandits.'

'Of course it is. But there are thousands of these communities, scattered over nearly a quarter of a million square kilometres of Britain. The population is estimated at just over 500,000. To control them, I have fewer than 6000 men. One infantry brigade plus supporting arms. I'd have been happier with a division. So don't expect instant miracles.'

'You have been training Beehive civilians as military reserves. I'll authorize you to call up two thousand of them.'

'But good God, man . . .' General Mullard took a deep breath to control himself and then went on with deliberate calm: 'In the first place, there is a limit to the amount of effective military training one can give to civilians in a concrete rabbit-warren. They will have their uses but not as reliable assault troops in a guerilla situation. And in the second place, what is Beehive *for*? To provide an effective administration which can start getting what's left of the country back on its feet as an organized State. To establish the King's peace . . .'

'Don't mention that man!' Harley snapped – his first show of real feeling since the interview began.

'All right, the State's peace. To provide services, a uniform system of law, meaningful currency – all of it very makeshift at first, of course, but beginning to work, and showing that it *can* work right from the start. The first days and weeks will be vital for establishing confidence in the Government. *Vital*. And if you give me two thousand of your five thousand skilled administrators, how are you going to manage *that*?'

'I suggest, General Mullard, that you deal with your side of the problem and leave me to deal with mine. The administration has some aces up its sleeve of which you may be unaware.'

Exasperation made the General indiscreet. 'Such as the Black Mamba and her little brood?'

Now it was Harley's turn to control himself. After a moment he said icily: 'Do not underestimate them. They have demonstrated their effectiveness in ways of which you certainly *are* unaware.'

'Oh, I'm sure they have. But I'm just a soldier. I stick to the old motto – "Trust God and keep your powder dry, in reverse order of priority". God being on the side of the big battalions. How many battalions the Devil is worth, remains to be seen.'

Harley stood up from his chair, 'Since you have mentioned priorities, General, let us get ours clear. Beehive's first task is to *control* Britain – swiftly, completely and ruthlessly. Civilian resistance will not be tolerated and your orders to the Army will make that quite plain. Where necessary, for example, hostages will be taken to ensure obedience and shot if it is not forthcoming. You have stated the problem yourself: our forces are small and our territory large. To establish control, therefore, they must be feared. What you so vaguely describe as "confidence" can wait. Instil fear, General, and you will have played your part in Britain's rebirth. And my two thousand administrators will be better employed helping you to instil it. They can return to their desks once our hold on the country is secure. And now, if you will excuse me, I have work to do.'

The general left, not trusting himself to speak. Is Harley quite sane any longer? he wondered as he strode along the corridor. Does he see himself as a rehabilitator of the country or as Genghis Khan? . . . And yet there's a horrible logic in what he says. Too few men to impose discipline on seventy or eighty times their own number – what other means is left but terror? It might have been different if over the past months Beehive had shown a few signs of being helpful to Surface, even if the daily BBC bulletins had given useful advice to communities struggling to survive, instead of conveying nothing but a sense of detached, quarantined omnipotence, biding its time. . . . It is too late now. I must play the hand I have been dealt.

Deeply depressed, General Mullard went to draft his Army's orders.

Harley had already forgotten him and was working his way through the morning's pile of documents that required his personal attention. Near the top was a note from Head of Intelligence, reporting that operative Gareth L. Underwood was missing, presumed killed, having failed to return from a mission in the Croydon area where gang warfare was rampant. Damned nuisance, that – Underwood had been a very useful courier between Beehive and Savernake Forest – he shouldn't have let the Section borrow him back for the Croydon mission. Now he'd have all the trouble of briefing a replacement.

Further down in the pile was a sealed envelope marked 'Personal'. Harley frowned, recognizing Brenda's handwriting. What now? . . . He slit open the envelope and took out the single sheet of private notepaper.

My dear Reggie, – I never thought I'd be writing you, or anyone, a suicide note. But here I am doing just that. I've got hold of a gun and I'm going up to Surface for a last look at the sky and the sun – and to save Beehive the embarrassment of disposing of my corpse. It's not just the ending of our long relationship that has brought me to this point, though it has, I will admit, contributed to my decision, because being involved with you helped to distract my attention from a problem that has since become intolerable. (Don't blame yourself for that – we were so careful from the start not to become dependent on each other.)

The real reason – which I hope I always managed to hide from you – is that almost from the beginning I suffered from Beehive claustrophobia. I used to dream about open skies and fields and rivers and wake up desolate. Waking up beside you, my dear, helped me to push these dreams aside. But in the past few weeks, they have become nightmares. I cannot suffer this troglodyte existence any longer. And since I am not equipped, by either temperament or toughness, to survive on Surface – nor in my present empty state particularly tempted to try – the quickest solution seems also the most desirable.

It's ironic, I suppose, that my access to the TSA room also gives me access to the list of secret Beehive exits! But don't hunt for my body. I shall walk it well away from my escape hatch before I dispense with its services.

Good-bye, Reggie. Remember, if you think of me at all, the good times.

Brenda

Harley sat back, examining his reactions with some curiosity. Relief, yes; she was finished with, for him, and he preferred her out of his sight. Nostalgia? No; it was not an emotion he suffered from. Guilt? . . . *No!* He would not be blackmailed by those little barbed phrases – 'my present empty state', 'if you think of me at all' – revealing inserted among the sentences of pretended detachment. And she was no more claustrophobic than he was; of that he was certain. The whole letter stank of self-pity, of a determination to use her only remaining weapon – her own death – to punish him for rejecting her. Well, it wouldn't work. Let her rot, wherever she now lay.

He turned his attention to the next document on the pile.

Brenda's body ached in every muscle; she had not ridden a bicycle since she was a schoolgirl and even the fifty kilometres to which Gareth had considerately limited their daily target she had found heavy going at first. She had been driven, for the first two days, by an obsessive compulsion to get as far away from London as she could, as quickly as she could. Gareth, too had wanted to be away from the risk of any chance encounter with other agents who might know he was supposed to be going south not north-west. After that, she had pedalled doggedly, knowing that Gareth could have moved twice as fast and determined not to let him down. By the fifth day she was getting into the swing of it but her body, so long deskbound, still protested.

Nevertheless she was happy. She realized that the Beehive claustrophobia which she had pretended in her 'suicide note' had been more real than she had thought. Aching and tired, she could still not keep a smile (no, a grin, a great big adolescent grin) off her face when she heard a bird sing, or resist calling to Gareth to stop for a moment when they crossed a river, or feel anything but pleasure at the smarting of her sunburnt forearms. The outside world – even fraught with danger and pockmarked with catastrophe – was a beautiful place.

Danger there was, though less than Brenda had expected. They both carried revolvers at their belts, and on their second day, during their mid-afternoon rest near Aylesbury, they had very nearly been surprised by four young men who tried to jump them and steal their weapons. Brenda had been overpowered, but had rolled on top of her gun long enough to keep her attacker from getting hold of it while Gareth knocked down one, evaded another and managed to draw his own gun and seize control of the situation. The attackers had withdrawn, shouting insults – Gareth had not needed to fire – and they mounted their bicycles and ridden away. Gareth had been furious with himself for such unprofessional carelessness, and Brenda only slightly less remorseful at the knowledge that she had been absorbing his attention at the time. After that, they had rested in places where they could not be approached unseen.

But all in all, Brenda was surprised and heartened to find how peaceable the decimated population was, how ready to be friendly once the first cautious mutual appraisals were over. Of their four nights on the road so far, one had been spent in a ruined and deserted house but three as guests of communities, the smallest being a family of six and the largest a village commune of more than fifty. One was already known to Gareth – he had a cousin in it, discovered by chance on an earlier mission – so there was no problem there. The other two they had approached with their hands clasped on top of their heads (this seemed to have become the recognized gesture for armed strangers seeking peaceful contact) and, after questioning, had been accepted. One had required them to hand over their guns till they left; the other had not even asked for them. At each place, they had paid for their keep with gifts from their rucksacks and pannier bags. Gareth knew from experience what was both easily portable and generally acceptable: tea, instant coffee, dried milk, chocolate, ballpoint pens, antibiotics, packeted seeds, concise medical and veterinary handbooks (which had quickly disappeared from library and bookshop shelves), clinical thermometers, batteries for digital watches, safety pins and other small treasures. He had smiled when Brenda, during their secret planning of escape in the TSA room, had announced her intention of bringing some lipsticks, compact refills, eyeshadow, and tights, but had been surprised to find how eagerly some at least of their hostesses accepted them.

It had been the evening talk that had been balm to Brenda's soul, and which made her memories of Beehive's daily preoccupations increasingly unreal. Talk of the practical problems of keeping alive, well, fed and warm; of big or little triumphs of ingenuity or determination; of the success or frustration of experiments in division of labour and inter-community barter; even in one place (Brenda could hardly believe her ears) of that perennial problem of Christendom, the repair of the church roof. Talk of human relationships, as absorbing, tender, foolish, astonishing, obtuse, splendid, farcical or transfiguring as anywhere, and yet, to Brenda, a world away from the hot-house pettiness and bitchiness of the equivalent talk in Beehive. Some talk of possible futures, mostly diffident, as though the speakers were afraid of being thought too hopeful too soon. And yet Brenda sensed this undercurrent of hope, this tentative dawn of confidence that what had been achieved so far could be built on – even if the achievement had been no more than survival and a wary friendship with scattered neighbours.

'I don't know whether it's magnificent or pathetic,' she told Gareth as they rested by the roadside under Wenlock Edge. 'I love their sheer guts and their . . . well, sort of shy optimism – you know? But then I think of Reggie and

General Mullard – and the Angels of Lucifer – and 21 June, and I wonder just how much chance these people really have, once the bayonets and the bureaucrats move in on them. . . . You know what? I've a feeling they'd do better without any imposed government *at all*. Does that make me an anarchist?'

'You said "imposed" government. There could be other kinds, in due course. Would you object to that?'

'Not if it emerged *from* these people. Beehive's kind will be alien to them – to everything they've been through. It is already, in their minds . . . Look, except for the Bicester place where they didn't ask, we've been telling them frankly we're Beehive deserters. And it's always made them even more friendly, hasn't it? That shows what they think of "the government". . . . What's it done for them, since the quake? Nothing at all, except to stir up this damn witch-hunt thing – which seems to have died out, by the way.'

'Not everywhere, Brenda. I've seen places where it's very much alive, I'm afraid.'

'So I've been lucky with the three communities I've met. But I'd like to think they're fairly typical – or if they're not already, they soon will be.' She laughed. 'I must be a naïve optimist *as well* as an anarchist. Only five days out of Beehive and I'm starting to believe in people again.'

'It's the fresh air that does it.'

'And you, St George-on-a-bicycle.'

'St David, do you mind? I was born in Carmarthen.'

They fell to teasing each other; it was impossible to remain solemn for long. Besides, they both had an additional reason for a sense of well-being. On their second night out, lying in her sleeping-bag next to Gareth in his, still awake after he had gone to sleep, she had been oppressed by a feeling of self-reproach. Gareth was her only friend and had been for weeks; he was her comrade in a dangerous venture, which would have been far less dangerous for him on his own – though of course he had not said so. She was a liability gladly accepted because he loved her and she repaid his devotion with mere friendship. She remembered a phrase which had caught her imagination while she was studying ancient Irish tribal mores for her history degree: *cairdes sliasait*, 'the friendship of her loins.' Did he not at least deserve that, in a partnership where death might be round any corner – or would it be an insult to his love, when she was not in love with him? And yet she *loved* him, as she had loved her dead brother or her longer-dead father. . . . Her debate with herself had become more tortuous and amorphous as the sleep of physical weariness overtook her. Next morning she had tried to recapitulate it with a clearer mind and had realized with some surprise that consideration of her affair with Reggie had not even entered into it. The following night, unpacking their things in the room which the village commune had offered them, while Gareth put their bicycles away, she had with sudden decision zipped up their two single sleeping-bags as one double one and laid it out on the bare mattress of the big bed. He had not seen it till later, for she had gone down to join him and they had been immediately drawn into their hosts' company. When they had finally said good night and gone upstairs and he had seen what she had done, he had stopped short, unable to find words. She had smiled at him, hiding her own doubts, and had prepared for bed with deliberate unconcern. Once they were lying together, his respectful tenderness had brought a lump into her throat, and she had forgotten her trepidation in her determination to make him relax, even laugh. She had succeeded; and now, after three nights of increasingly natural lovemaking, she no longer tried to analyse the difference between loving and being in love. She only knew that in spite of her uncertain future and the muscular weariness of their journey, she had never been so content in all her life. Certainly not with Reggie.

They arrived at Camp Cerridwen on the evening of the sixth day. Gareth received almost a hero's welcome, because the camp knew they owed the survival of the radio cabin (and probably of Geraint and Tonia) to his warning message; Brenda was swept up in it too but not merely by way of reflected glory. She felt an immediate rapport with Moira in particular, and since she was a librarian, schoolteacher Geraint and journalist Tonia adopted her at once as their personal property and virtually shanghaied her into the news network team before she could draw breath. They were eager to pump Gareth for information, too; he had to curb their enthusiasm a little, or they would have rushed on to the air to their British and foreign ham contacts with facts that could only have come from within Beehive – which, so soon after Gareth and Brenda's 'deaths', might have caused someone in Beehive to put two and two together. The two-man raid on the radio cabin, Gareth told them, had been made on the Army's initiative in consultation with Intelligence Section. It had not been repeated because, with the advantage of surprise lost, it would have required a larger force, which the Army could not spare during the preparations for Operation Skylight. But if they drew attention to themselves by being not merely a nuisance exchanging what news the hams could gather, but a real danger by transmitting Beehive secrets, Harley might order the Army to attack at once, regardless.

An Army attack was coming anyway; that was the central grim fact in the news which Gareth brought. But at least he could tell them the date and the time.

As soon as the welcoming was over, Gareth, with Brenda

beside him, spoke to Dan, Moira and the camp committee.

'Operation Skylight – the surfacing of Beehive to take control – is fixed for 21 June. Zero hour is 0600 hours but some units will be setting out before that and others after. It'll all be carried out in waves, by shuttle-service from the secret helicopter bases around the various Beehives – the main forces coming from London. On the first day, they'll establish headquarters in about thirty places spread out over the whole mainland but thicker where the population's thickest. The places have been carefully chosen – mostly relatively undamaged small towns or large villages. The nearest one to here is Corwen, about thirty kilometres away. They won't be doing it with kid gloves. They'll requisition whatever they need and anyone who resists eviction or disobeys the Army's orders will be shot. On the second day they'll start imposing control over the surrounding communities, starting with the largest – and at the same time they'll begin announcing regulations and provisional tithe laws and so on.'

'*Tithe* laws?' Dan asked, incredulously.

'That's what they're calling them. How d'you think the administration and the Army are going to be maintained? The Beehive stores won't last for ever. . . . And get this straight. It's going to be a military dictatorship, with no holds barred and Harley's administrative machine as the ruling caste. Big Chief Harley himself is the absolute dictator of Beehive and he has every intention of being absolute dictator of Britain. The Prime Minister's a puppet. My own guess is that after Operation Skylight, Harley won't even bother to use him as a figurehead. The Premier will either be framed as a traitor or simply meet with an accident.'

'Where does the King fit in?' Sam Warner wanted to know. 'The BBC broadcasts are still in the name of "His

Majesty's Government", even though we never hear his voice.'

Gareth smiled wrily. 'Apart from Brenda and myself, the most distinguished defectors from Beehive have been the Royal Family. A few weeks ago the King, the Queen, the Prince of Wales and his wife and baby, and the two Princesses took a helicopter from one of the secret bases and disappeared. Being the King *and* a helicopter pilot, he was able to get away with it – though Harley still had the officer of the base guard reduced to the ranks. Intelligence Section did their nut trying to get wind of them. It wasn't till just before we left that an agent located them. Windsor Castle, of all places – the sheer cheek of it fooled Beehive, the Section never dreamed they'd go there. Holed up in it with a witch community, too . . . It's one of the priority targets for D-Day. Special task force to seize the Castle and take the Royal Family alive. Just like Camp Cerridwen. Dan and Moira are to be taken alive, too. I've a feeling that's a special request from the Black Mamba. I don't think Harley would have bothered with the "taking alive" bit as far as Dan and Moira were concerned.'

'Yes, that would be Karen,' Dan said.

'Never mind, they needn't catch any of you. Listen: the task force aimed at Camp Cerridwen is two platoons in four helicopters, taking off at Z minus one, which means they'll be here about 0630. They have orders to kill everybody except Moira and Dan, but *not* to fire the camp – it'd start a forest fire and even Harley knows that every hectare of Forestry Commission plantation is going to be precious. The radio equipment is to be wrecked. So all you have to do is to move out on the twentieth – every man, woman and child of you – and hide in the forest, somewhere kilometres away, there's plenty of it. If you can do that, without leaving clues or even hinting at it in the village, you can save yourselves *and* the camp. . . . If you ever have a chance to come back to it, that is,' he added sombrely.

'We'll worry about that afterwards,' Moira told him. 'We can hide ourselves *and* take Geraint's radio stuff with us. But there's something else you'd better know about. Eighteen of us, including Dan and me, will almost certainly be busy somewhere else on D-Day . . .' and she told about the Psychic Assault Group and the stone circle.

'Do you find that . . . shall we say, a little bizarre?' Dan asked when she had finished.

'Setting fire to a hut by psychic effort? Three or four months ago I'd have thought you were either lying or suffering from group hallucination. But since then . . . Not only have Brenda and I personally experienced what the Black Mamba can do – which *might* be put down to hypnotism, just – but there's something else you *don't* know. You heard about the recent earth tremor, down south?'

'Yes. Two of Geraint's ham pals reported it.' There was a sudden gleam of extra interest in all the witches' faces and Gareth wondered why.

'The epicentre was Salisbury Plain. And just at that time, the Angels of Lucifer conducted a human sacrifice at Stonehenge. If that was coincidence . . .'

'It wasn't,' Moira and Dan said together, and Moira went on: 'We picked up the ritual – in fact, it woke several of us up. And our best clairvoyant insisted it was a human sacrifice. She saw the big megaliths, too. That's what gave us the idea of experimenting with a stone circle. . . . Then when we heard about the tremors we thought it must have had something to do with it.'

They launched into a discussion of earth currents, ley lines and foci of power which left Brenda bewildered, though Gareth seemed to be taking an unsurprised interest in it. She was not disbelieving because the evidence was plain enough but she was soon out of her depth in the technicalities. But when they started talking about positive action against the Angels of Lucifer, she ventured to intervene.

'Did the Angels *intend* the earth tremors, do you think?'

'We don't know,' Dan told her, 'but we think it's unlikely. They were probably testing their own strength, seeing what power they could raise by human sacrifice at the Henge and not worrying too much about what the power actually did once they'd raised it. And they *are* powerful, even without ritual human sacrifice or a stone circle as an amplifier. So I'm not surprised at what did happen.'

'If I know Karen,' Jean Thomas said, 'she'll have been delighted at what happened.'

'But if you try to do the same thing – without the sacrifice, of course – couldn't it be dangerous?' Brenda asked. 'Couldn't *you* trigger off an earthquake or something equally disastrous?'

Moira shook her head. 'We'll be defending Mother Earth, not outraging her like the Angels of Lucifer. She looks after her own.'

'Do you really see her that way? As a conscious entity, able to decide who's on her side and who isn't?'

'Experience points that way,' Moira smiled. 'But yes – the short answer is, we do. We see the whole universe as conscious, at various levels of complexity and on various time-scales – various wavelengths, if you like. Witchcraft is largely a method of learning how to tune in to the right frequencies. All religion is, really . . . The Earth-Mother is one aspect of the Goddess, of what we conceive as the female polarity of the Ultimate – the side that gives birth and nourishes and re-absorbs and re-shapes, while the other side – the male polarity, the God – impregnates and energizes. We see all creation and activity as the outcome of polarity, even at Divine level. . . . Again, all religions do, however they obscure it . . . The Earth-Mother is how the Goddess expresses herself on and in our planet, our particular corner of the universe. For the past two or three thousand years, mankind has over-emphasized the God-aspect and tried to push the Goddess into the background or deny her altogether. In the end, that's as much an offence against the God as against the Goddess; deny him his complement, and you deny *him* . . . Do you know what Camp Cerridwen is? Not just a survival community trying to feed and house and organize ourselves. We're trying to get ourselves back on the Earth-Mother's frequency, to talk to her and listen to her. Not only the witches, either – all of us, in our own way. Father Byrne, for instance; if ever a man talked to her face-to-face, he does, whatever he calls her . . . Am I answering your question – about our running into danger, I mean?'

Brenda hesitated. 'Yes, I *think* you are – though it's a bit much to take in all at once. Can we discuss it some more, when you've time?'

'Of course we can. But right now the point is – we've *got* to fight the Angels of Lucifer on the Earth-Mother's behalf, if you see what I mean. And when we do, it's by putting ourselves on *her* frequency and calling on *her* power, so it can't be destructive except to her enemies. Does that sound naïve?'

Brenda laughed, suddenly. 'I like you people. You make the most extraordinary statements without batting an eyelid and then ask solicitously if we think you're being "bizarre" or "naïve". Tell you the truth, I don't know. But you're on the right side and you're *doing* something. So just tell me how I can help and we'll philosophize about it afterwards, win or lose.'

'Fair enough,' Dan grinned at her. 'Now, Gareth – down to business. Do you know how the Angels of Lucifer fit into Operation Skylight? From what you say, Harley and Karen must have planned something for them to do.'

'I'm only piecing hints together,' Gareth said, 'but I'm damn certain they've planned something. I was still courier between them and escort for her when she commuted with Beehive, up to a fortnight ago, and I kept my eyes and ears open. Karen has some kind of operation arranged for D-Day. And it's silly the way you pick things up – but their kitchen at her headquarters has a big calendar on the wall, where the cook notes things. I got a look at it last time I took her back and the cook had scribbled "Breakfast 3 am" opposite 21 June. That's two hours before sunrise and three before zero hour. My guess is that at sunrise, they'll be at Stonehenge, raising all the power they can to back up Operation Skylight. What else was their last experiment at the Henge *for*? It must have been a rehearsal for the time when Harley will need their support. And that means D-Day.'

'It makes sense,' Dan agreed. 'And that means our PAG must be in action at the same time.'

Jean Thomas turned to Gareth and asked: 'When you were at Karen's place did you hear anything about Avebury?' Everybody smiled; Jean and Fred Thomas's devotion to Avebury, the megalithic site nearly thirty kilometres north of Stonehenge, was known to everyone in the camp. Avebury was less spectacular and world-famous than Stonehenge, and its stones were smaller, but it covered a far greater area with Avebury village at its centre; many witches and occultists, and even archaeologists, found it more interesting and rewarding than its famous neighbour.

'Not much,' Gareth answered. 'I know it's outside the territory they control. I heard a bit of conversation about it once – someone suggested taking it over but Karen said no, it wasn't worth it, Stonehenge was enough. I sort of gathered there were only a handful of villagers living there.'

'That's good,' Jean said, and Fred nodded with her.

'What's your point, Jean?' Greg asked. 'Want a second honeymoon there?'

'All right, all right, have your joke. But Fred and I have been thinking. We knew the battle with Karen's lot was coming; now we know it's on 21 June, and it's pretty certain they'll be at Stonehenge. If we want a power-house for the PAG, why not Avebury? There's more power locked up there than anywhere in Britain – even than Stonehenge, though I know you think we're a bit biassed about that, so let's just say it's in the same league as Stonehenge. And they've been linked together in people's mind for so long, the psychic channels will be there between the two. We could make it the weak point in Stonehenge's armour.'

Greg was already peering at the map. 'But it's about 150 kilometres from here, love.'

'So what?' Fred supported his wife. 'We could rustle up enough bicycles and horses to reach there in four days at the most. Or even take one of these useless vans we've got parked here – we've got enough petrol stored and you do still see the odd vehicle on the move, using its last tankful to look for new *lebensraum*. People don't pay much attention to them – just look up at the unfamiliar noise and then get on with what they're doing. Especially if they see guns . . . We could take the PAG, which is eighteen, plus half a dozen strong-arm boys to protect them. Two vanloads altogether, say.'

'But what for?' Sam Warner interjected. 'Tire ourselves out travelling, just to get a little extra power out of Avebury? We could end up even.'

'Not with Avebury,' Dan said. 'You know what? – I like

455

the idea. Oh, we all pull Jean and Fred's leg about the place, but some of us do know just how powerful it really is. *And* it's a psychic "in" to Stonehenge, as Fred says. What's more, the Angels wouldn't be expecting an attack from there. It *could be organized*. . . . What do you think, Moira?'

'I think Jean and Fred may have something,' Moira said.

26

On a hill by the Swindon road, a kilometre or two outside Avebury, twenty-six men and women watched the sun go down on 20 June from an abandoned house on the edge of a wood. They had been there for two days; Dan had allowed eight days for the trek from Dyfnant Forest, to be on the safe side, thinking that Fred's estimate of four days was probably an underestimate. He had been right. With diversions to avoid communities and having to cross the Severn above Cheltenham (the motorway bridge at Chepstow was reported to be held by a brigand group), the journey had taken six days.

They had decided, after some discussion, that motor transport was worth the expenditure of stored petrol. The camp's petrol reserves were higher than they had foreseen, chiefly because Greg's water-driven power system was increasingly efficient and an electrical circular saw meant that the petrol-driven chain-saw was rarely needed, and ploughing and harrowing were entirely by horse. So with much back-tracking to avoid fissures, they had travelled with two mini-buses, a car and one motor-cycle for scouting ahead. The total party had grown to twenty-eight – eighteen in the

PAG, eight armed guards and two radio operators trained by Geraint and Tonia. The pack radios, ingeniously built by Geraint and Greg from cannibalized ordinary radios and useless TV sets begged from the village, had a maximum range of about fifty kilometres; one operator, with a guard to defend him and keep him company, was already in position, well concealed, with a good view of Stonehenge and further armed with a pair of binoculars. Every hour, on the hour, he sent the code word 'Cabbage', which meant 'No activity at the Henge', and Miriam, who manned the set with the PAG, acknowledged. She kept continuous watch in case of developments but otherwise they kept radio silence except for the brief hourly report. The crucial code word would be 'Aconite', meaning that the Angels of Lucifer were occupying Stonehenge – for the watching operator was Bruce Peters, who knew Karen and John and several of their group by sight.

The time would come, obviously, when the dozen or so prepared code words would no longer be adequate and Bruce would have to describe what he saw in clear for the benefit of the PAG. But by then the ether would be alive with the Army messages of D-Day and one short-range voice on a non-Army frequency (Gareth had been able to inform them on that) would with any luck pass unnoticed.

Two of the guards had spied out Avebury village as soon as the PAG were installed in the empty house. The little cavalcade had apparently managed to arrive without alerting the village; the approach had been very circumspect, by moonlight and without lights, and with slow and careful reconnaissance ahead of the main party. The vehicles were well hidden in the wood and camouflaged.

The Avebury community, the spies reported, consisted of seven adults and four children; they slept, without posting sentries, in the Red Lion, the village pub which had (the

Thomases remembered) several bedrooms. This was good news, for it made the PAG's plan of operation simple. The last thing they wanted was a battle.

The White City stadium, on the western fringe of central London, was a fortress. The Army had commandeered it ten days before Beehive Red and since then no one had seen inside it. There had been much coming and going of helicopters in those ten days and nobody living around had bothered to keep count, so it was anyone's guess how many remained there after the earthquake. The wise deduced that it was a Beehive helicopter base, and the wise (even, very soon, the foolish) kept away, because anyone who approached within a hundred metres was sniped at – one shot as warning and the next to kill. Nobody, of course, could get high enough to see inside. It was something of an anomaly, as the only known Beehive presence on Surface – though gradually rumours circulated of other stadiums and football grounds (all of them completely surrounded by stands or high walls) scattered around the capital which it was inadvisable to approach. As the months went by, the few local civilians who had survived the Madness and the winter had come to take them for granted and ignore them, from a safe distance.

But tonight those who lay awake noticed there were unprecedented noises of activity inside White City. Peering out of their windows they saw the glow of many lights reflected from the thin night mist above the stadium and they wondered. Then, in what should have been the deadest hour of the night, no one slept any longer, for the first of the helicopters clattered up into the sky.

Harley, sitting at General Mullard's side in the Operations Room five hundred metres below Primrose Hill, glowed with a euphoria which for once did not exasperate the general. Mullard was a soldier to his marrow; intelligent and sensitive, he could be plagued with doubts beneath his impassive exterior as long he was confined to sedentary planning but once the die was cast (he had a habit of muttering '*Jacta est alea*' with a puffed-out breath of relief) the doubts faded away. Action, for good or ill, was an elixir; his expression did not change but his eyes had a new sparkle and his staff could depend on hair-trigger decisions from him even in the face of reverses – *particularly* in the face of reverses. Operation Skylight was going smoothly into action; the intricate timetable of troop movements out to the helicopter bases was running without a hitch; the Z-minus-four helicopters, first of the day's flow of shuttles, were all reported away. The first entries had appeared on the virgin wall-charts, and the WRAC girls, like uniformed croupiers, were sliding the first coloured symbols on to the huge map of Britain painted on the Ops Room table. For the first time in months, General Mullard felt one hundred per cent alive.

If Harley effervesced with excitement and confidence, who was he to criticize? At least the man recognized that this, for the moment, was the Army's show and did not interfere.

At Windsor Castle the entire community was barricaded in the Round Tower, with every firearm they could muster and the approaches barbed-wired. The courier from Camp Cerridwen had warned that the attack was to be expected at 0900 hours – the assumption being, apparently, that by then most of the community would be up and about in the grounds, unsuspecting, and even if the attackers met with difficulties, hostages could be taken to be shot at regular intervals unless and until the Royal Family surrendered.

But now it would be the attackers, not the defenders, who would be surprised.

As the Prince of Wales put it to Norman Godwin: 'If they want to take us alive they're going to have to blow us up first.'

At the village in Savernake Forest six prisoners huddled in the schoolhouse under armed guard, their hands tied behind them. Their bonds were hardly necessary, because they were all in a dream-world, thanks to the drugs which Stanley Friell had prepared for them. The drugging was purely to make them easy to handle and transport to Stonehenge; once they were there, an antidote would restore them to full awareness for Karen insisted that all sacrifices' terror would add to the power raised. Four of them – three men and a woman – were locals who had offended the Angels of Lucifer; the other two were an itinerant man and woman who had tried to pass through the village in their wandering, unaware of its reputation.

The seventh chosen sacrifice was sitting, unfettered and undrugged, with Karen and John, and she had chosen herself. Ever since Bill Lazenby had been offered up on the Altar Stone, Sonia Forde, the Maiden, had been trans- figured. For her, the blood sacrifice had been a transcendental experience, sweeping through her in a blinding vision of power – literally blinding, for she had had to be led home and had not seemed to recognize her surroundings for three or four hours. Since then she had been in a state of mysic rapture. Two days ago she had not *asked* Karen but had *told* her, that she, the Maiden of the Angels of Lucifer, had been touched by their Master and granted the privilege of being the first Midsummer Sacrifice. Karen (who believed in neither God nor Devil, only in an impersonal cosmic power which she had the knowledge to tap and direct) had seen the light of ecstatic madness in Sonia's eyes and had agreed at once. It was an unexpected bonus to her plans; Sonia was twenty, auburn-haired, slim and nubile but (for neurotic reasons, Karen knew) *virgo intacta*. By all traditional standards, she was ideal. And her willing sacrifice would have a valuable psychic effect on the others.

Sonia sat now between herself and John, erect and proud. She had dressed her hair with great care and made up her face, heavily but skilfully and dramatically – as well as her nipples, for she wore nothing but a spotlessly white skirt and a necklace of pearls. To this infringement of her own regal monopoly, Karen had raised no objection; nothing must challenge the martyr's vision of herself.

Karen glanced past the entranced girl at John, wondering, with a rare flash of unease, at his expressionless face. Usually she could read his thoughts like a neon sign but as D-Day drew nearer, a screen had dropped between them. He had not argued with her and he had played his part in the planning efficiently and with apparent determination, but he had said little and none of that at all revealing.

She banished the unease deliberately. *I* am the channel of power, *I* am the leader. Nothing shall stand in my way today. Certainly not John. He will do what is required of him. As will Harley, afterwards.

At three in the morning, silently and keeping to the shadows as far as possible on this bright moonlit night, the PAG and their seven guards and Miriam approached the Red Lion. The PAG were to take no part in the capture, for they must remain as calm and rested as possible for the later psychic battle. Four of the guards surrounded the building to prevent anyone escaping through windows or back doors. The other three broke into the front door with a jemmy.

The sound woke the house and for two minutes there was uproar and shouting, but – thank heaven – no shooting. Five minutes later, all eleven of the villagers had been herded into the dining-room, the curtains drawn, and candles lit. They looked indignant and bewildered as Dan began to address them.

'I'm sorry about this, but please believe me, we don't want to hurt you or your property or to steal anything. You'll have to forgive us for the damage to the front door – that was necessary. All we need to do is to stay here for the next few hours. We can't say yet exactly how long it'll be. But it's absolutely vital that nobody realizes we're here. So we have to keep you all under guard till it's over and see that none of you leave or try to signal anyone outside. You can come and go as you please inside the house as long as one of us is with you.' He smiled, he hoped reassuringly. 'We've been as considerate as we can – you'll notice that two of our guards are women, and *they'll* conduct the ladies to the loo and so on. The only place you must keep out of is the lounge bar, because we'll be using that. And please make as little noise as possible when you're anywhere near it. If we eat or drink anything while we're here, we'll pay for it – we've brought a couple of sacks of assorted goodies for the purpose and I'm sure there will be things in them that you'll find useful.'

'But what's it all *about*?' the obvious leader of the group asked. He was a solid-looking man in his fifties whom they had heard addressed as Lenny. 'Bandits I could understand and serve us right for not posting sentries – we've had no trouble for months, so we got careless. But all this politeness with a gun at our heads. . . . It don't make much sense, tell you the truth. What are you up to?'

'A fair question, Lenny – that's your name, isn't it? . . . Have you heard of the Black Mamba and her lot?'

The frightened reaction, of the women in particular, was immediate, and Lenny swallowed. 'Everyone round here has. But they've never troubled us. Are *you* from there?'

'Not on your life. They're everybody's enemies. . . . Do you remember the earth tremors last month?'

'You bet we do.'

'And did you hear what the Black Mamba's gang did at Stonehenge that day?'

Even Lenny could not hide his fear at the question. 'Word got around.'

'Yes, I'm sure it did. Well, this morning two things are going to happen. We've had word that they'll be doing it again today, probably at sunrise, and probably worse than the last time. And we've also had word that the Army's coming out of Beehive to try and take control of the country. Now I don't know what you people believe or how you feel about witches. But we're witches – *white* witches – all of us. And while the other lot are making use of Stonehenge for evil, we're going to do everything we can to use Avebury for good, to fight against the evil they're doing. The Red Lion's right in the middle of Avebury Circle. And that's why we're here.'

Dan paused, waiting for reactions. Lenny and the others looked at each other and then Lenny spoke.

'I'm Church of England, myself, and so's the missus here and the kids, and some of the others. Young Jane over there, she reckons she's a witch but she's a good girl and my wife's cousin, so we've been keeping quiet about it and looking after her. . . . The way I look at it – if you're telling the truth, and I'd say you are, we're not going to stand in your way. I've lived with these stones all my life and *I* know there's power in them, whatever the Vicar used to say. Stonehenge too but that's dark to my way of thinking, never felt easy there even before all this. But *our* stones, they're light, they're different. And I'd leave it to them. If what you're trying to do is good, they'll help you. If it ain't, they won't – and they might even punish you for it, some ways. An' may God forgive me for saying it. . . . You carry on, lad. We won't cause you any trouble. But keep your guards on us – you'll be too busy to have to worry about whether I'm lying to you. I ain't but I might be, mightn't I? So tell 'em to keep their guns loaded and then you'll be easy in your mind. . . . Those others without guns, in the lounge – they'll be doing the magicking?'

'That's right, Lenny. Me too.'

'Well, good luck to you. Is there time for the missus to brew up some hot soup for everybody before you start?'

It had been a greater wrench than Rosemary had expected, the exodus from Camp Cerridwen into the forest. Most of the campers (there were nearly 160 of them, after the PAG had left) believed, against all apparent logic, that they would be able to return. The witches believed it by conscious decision with the object of bringing it about by envisaging their return with concerted willpower and imagination, and the non-witches had been generally infected by their confidence. Anxiety over Moira and Dan and the PAG, so far away and with the two leaders on the Army's wanted list, was inevitable and hardly unexpected. But the actual leaving of the camp, on the morning of the twentieth, had been a sadness whose intensity took them by surprise. They had built and ploughed and planted it with their own hands and leaving it empty was like abandoning an only child.

Everything of particular value that could be moved had been hidden in the storage cave and the entrance effectively camouflaged. It would be extremely bad luck if it were discovered and the witches did not believe in bad luck. Rosemary and Greg, with their coven, had spent an intensive half-hour on a spell to turn inquisitive eyes away from it.

Gareth had originally suggested that no hint be given to the New Dyfnant villagers of the evacuation plan but a few days' acquaintance with the relationship between camp and village had made him admit that this could be modified. Three old people, two sick, and three couples with young babies had been adopted by village families 'for the duration of the emergency', and the village, to a man, would have cut their own tongues out rather than betray them. Eileen, at six months the most advanced pregnancy in the camp, had been offered an almost embarrassing number of homes (New Dyfnant had not forgotten that she, above all, had saved them from the Dust) but had insisted on joining the exodus, clinching her refusal with the argument that her face, too, might be on the wanted list – and Gareth could not be sure it was not. To minimize dangerous knowledge, all arrangements, by common consent, had been through one person, Bronwen Jones the Shop, and only she had any idea of what was actually planned, though neither she nor anyone else in the village knew or needed to know just where the exodus was heading. Only she, indeed, knew the hour of departure – and two hours after it she passed the word to Dai Police and Dai Forest Inn to send up a herding party to bring the camp's livestock down to the village for lodging around the farms.

By that time all the men, women, and children of Camp Cerridwen had melted into the forest.

It would take a large-scale operation with hundreds of men to find them, for in the past quarter-century the Forestry Commission had extended the Dyfnant plantation till it covered more than fifty square kilometres south and south-west of Lake Vyrnwy. Peter O'Malley had chosen their destination and planned the route, for he knew the forest better than anyone in Camp Cerridwen – and knew, too, which species of tree would give them maximum cover from the air. He had ordered dark clothes and drilled everyone in what to do at the first sound of a helicopter engine. He had chosen an area towards Llechwedd Du, four or five kilometres to the west, where he knew of a small group of caves that could accommodate the whole party – and, most important for D-Day, could give the fourteen covens working space separated from the children and the non-witches who would look after them, so that they could concentrate without distraction.

It had been a heavily laden procession that had set out from the camp along the plantation 'corridors', for nobody knew how long they would have to hide, and they were carrying as much food as they could. Bedding was less of a problem; it was a warm June and the weather seemed set fair. Geraint and Tonia had been tempted to lug their radio equipment with them but it would have been impossible to carry the batteries as well, and since transmitting was out of the question and the PAG pack radios were much too far away to receive, it would have been of little use. So they had buried it, well wrapped in polythene sacks, half a kilometre from the camp the day before they left.

On the journey, Rosemary had kept an anxious eye on Greg, for although he had said little and maintained the cheerful exterior required of one of the founder members and acknowledged leaders of the camp, she knew that he had been worse hit than almost anyone by having to leave it. No one had put more ingenuity, craftsmanship and sheer hard work into it, from the start, than he. She could have wept as she watched him carry his precious alternators from the little river power-station to the cave with his own hands and then the heavy-duty batteries in a wheelbarrow – nothing, she knew, would he leave undone to make a new start possible if the chance came. She had had, finally on the last night, to order him to bed so that he would be fit for the march, otherwise he would have been up till dawn removing and hiding more and more pieces of treasured equipment.

But once the trek was over, the people under cover, and a meal organized, she was relieved to sense that his cheerfulness became more convincing. A new phase had begun and he was responding to the challenge. When everybody had begun to relax a little, he had started urging her, as convener of the Elders in Moira's absence, to call them together to plan tomorrow's support effort for the PAG, and shepherded Tricia into a quiet corner with instructions to see what she could pick up from Avebury. Then, at last, Rosemary could smile; for Greg, she saw, the worst was over. What tomorrow's worst might be, remained to be seen – but with the trauma of the exodus firmly behind him, he was prepared to face it.

An hour before sunrise, the covens were assembled and ready, in three caves so close together on a broken hillside that they were virtually interconnecting. Rosemary and Greg's group was in the centre cave, where Rosemary's voice could be heard by everyone if necessary. Tricia sat beside Rosemary, made as comfortable as possible with rolled bedding, for though her clairvoyance was usually in full consciousness, she could sometimes go into trance without warning. One Circle could have embraced them all but Rosemary would not tamper with the arrangements they had practised already when the covens were less closely packed; so each High Priestess cast her own, even though the smallest was barely two metres across. That done, Rosemary cast a Great Circle mentally, whispering to Greg that she was doing so. He nodded and suddenly she remembered – and knew he was remembering – the last time they had sat in their own Circle, one among many inside a Great Circle. A year ago today; the Midsummer Grand Sabbat on Bell Beacon. . . . The wheel had come fully round. Some – perhaps twenty or thirty – of today's gathering had been there too; were they remembering?

Was John Hassell, on his way to Stonehenge, remembering his golden Joy? And if so, was it adding rage to his corrupted intent – or opening for him a chasm of doubt? Such wondering was wasted effort; they would need all they could summon up to feed power to Moira and Dan and the others.

Rosemary closed her eyes and slid her hand into Greg's. Curling her fingers, she could feel the fine hairs on the back of his hand and she was overcome with love for him. He gave a faint rumble in his throat, his habitual acknowledgement of any love-signal when other people were around and squeezed her palm against his own.

'Moira and the others are ready,' Tricia said suddenly. 'I can see the dark woodwork and the open fireplace . . . They're in their Circle, holding hands.'

With slow deliberation, Rosemary strengthened her union with Greg, and expanded it in her mind to include their whole coven. She could feel the ring of individualities closing and integrating, the group mind awakening, and when she knew it was ready she said quietly, '*Deosil* now, *deosil*'. She urged the power to her left clockwise, into Greg and the girl beyond him, and felt the surge from the man on her right. Soon the current was flowing as they had practised, a flywheel of psychic power through their unmoving bodies, *deosil*, *deosil*, amplifying itself with its own momentum. She knew, on the fringe of consciousness, that the other covens were picking up her cue and doing the same and she could sense the growing battery of sunwise whirlpools around them; but she diverted no attention to them, that was not her function. Her coven's power must all go to their link at Avebury, young Olive Sennett of the quicksilver mind, while the others concentrated on their own links. The flywheel of power was building, growing into a cone with its tip a shimmering vortex above the centre of their Circle, vividly clear to Rosemary's astral vision.

Rosemary said: 'Olive.'

She visualized Olive, sitting as they had arranged on Dan's left; the rather bony young body, the pony-tailed brown hair, the wide mouth and surprised-looking eyes, the habitual crouch with one leg curled under her and the other thrust straight out. . . . She felt an echo, an interlocking, and knew they had her. She said: 'Feed her.'

She was barely aware of the cave around them or of their physical bodies any longer; only of the ring of astral bodies, of linked minds, of the bright vortex of power they had created. On her command, the vortex reached out, not leaning, not losing its momentum, not changing its shape, but reaching out in another dimension to mesh with Olive and invigorate her.

Olive felt it, and exulted, and Rosemary knew. The current was flowing, steadily and strongly.

Then, astonishingly, with the current still unwavering, the cave and the hills and the forest recaptured Rosemary's awareness. The earth was real and alive around her; and not only *here* but Avebury as well, the mandala village with its sidestepped crossroads, its tree-crowned earthworks, its immemorial ring and avenue of stones. And all the land between, the rock and soil and water of Wales and England; a living organism, living and breathing and feeling, and they all a part of it.

The vision sank again into the background, leaving the astral power-line to fill Rosemary's world. But she knew.

The Earth had spoken to her and She was on their side.

Miriam, sitting in a corner outside the ring of the Group with her earphones clamped to her head, broke the silence with one word: 'Aconite'.

Moira said 'Thank you', and the Group, unmoving, braced themselves.

The Army helicopter settled outside the ditch, west of the Henge and facing it. As the pilot cut his switches and the noise died, John could see the main group pacifying their frightened horses, three hundred metres away to the north of the perimeter, their reins tied to the road fence.

The main group of the Angels of Lucifer had come ahead on horseback, leaving Karen, John, Stanley Friell, Sonia and the six prisoners with their guard to arrive just before sunrise in the helicopter Harley had provided. John had not seen the necessity for the helicopter but had acquiesced. Only Karen knew its real purpose. It was to stay with her till Harley signalled that the success of Operation Skylight was beyond doubt and then fly her to Harley's side with the dozen or so Angels who really mattered and whom she had already secretly briefed. John and the others would be left to fend for themselves. If they caused any trouble – which Karen, despising them, did not envisage – a word from Harley to the Army would settle the matter.

But that was for later and Karen barely thought of it. Her whole mind was on the coming sunrise and the magical offensive whose impact would be felt across the length and breadth of Britain. Of that, Karen had not even a sub-liminal flicker of doubt. And when the smoke of battle cleared, she, Karen Morley, would be High Priestess – not merely of a handful of black witches, however effective, but of Britain itself. Power was her destiny. And on the path to power, John was an outworn tool and Harley a new and keen-edged one.

Karen stepped to the ground, the others following.

When his passengers were all clear, Captain Brodie leaned back in his seat and blew out his cheeks. 'What an incredible bunch,' he said to his co-pilot.

'That boss-woman gives me the creeps,' Lieutenant Denning replied. 'And who are those poor sods with their hands tied? They look bloody hypnotized.'

'Drugged,' Brodie said. 'The other chap's a doctor, the one with the bush-jacket on. And you know what, Den? If my guess is right, I hope those "poor sods" stay drugged.'

Denning grunted. Neither of them had any real doubt what was afoot. Harley's relationship with the Black Mamba was no longer a secret in Beehive and stories of her magical powers (most, but not all, apocryphal) had been circulating for weeks. The name 'Angels of Lucifer' had been whispered, though cautiously. Once Beehive had got used to the idea, the general reaction had been 'At least they're on our side'. From that, among people already attuned by the witch-hunt to the idea of magic being powerful and dangerous, it was an easy step to accepting as reassuring the knowledge that a group of black witches had been enlisted as Beehive's allies in Operation Skylight.

But like meat-eaters with abattoirs, acceptance was one thing, and having to watch the physical reality was quite another. The two officers gazed after their departing passengers with an uneasy fascination. The two young women naked to the hips, made up and jewelled, the black-skirted and black-haired one vibrant with a terrifying authority, the white-skirted and auburn-haired one surrounded by an aura of spiritual madness almost as terrifying. The unsmiling man in the black robe with the knife at his belt. The

bush-shirted doctor, the very ordinariness of his garb unnerving beside the others. The six drugged prisoners, barefoot and clad in plain shifts like the Burghers of Calais.
Their watchful guard in jeans and boots, carrying a shotgun. All moving towards the heart of the Henge, around
which the twenty or thirty men and women who had been
with the horses were now arranging themselves, all stark
naked and even at this distance grimly but eagerly purposeful.

'I don't think I want to watch this,' Brodie said.

'We're not going to be able to help watching it,'
Denning told him, and, sickly, the captain knew he was
right.

Sonia shed her skirt, laid herself gracefully supine on the
Altar Stone and began to sing. The song was wordless, a
quiet atavistic keening, an enraptured salute to the Master
she longed to embrace, a resonant consecration of the blood
still imprisoned in her veins and demanding the freedom of
sacrifice.

The sound cut through John like a knife, sharper than
the blade in his right hand. It was scarcely to be borne and
Karen's evident gratification at it enhanced the torment.
Still John did not doubt; he was here for a purpose and the
purpose had been grasped to his soul since he had first set
out for Savernake Forest. But would the sun never rise so
that the unbearable song could be ended?

The Angels were circling wildly, widdershins between
the megaliths as before, their cries in eerie counterpoint to
Sonia's keening. Karen, arms high and wide, was intoning
an invocation, its charged sentences weaving in the air like
smoke. John, entranced by his pain, stared alternately at
the horizon and at Sonia's pulsing throat on which the pearl

necklace rolled gently back and forth like the creamy edge of a wave on a smooth beach.

Time stood still but sound and movement and rhythm did not.

Then, at the end of timelessness, the edge of the sun blistered the horizon.

John struck at the white throat. The song ended in a bubbling hiss, and the blood rippled down from pearl to pearl and spread over the Altar Stone. Sonia's head rocked sideways and the eyes, sightless and blissful, gazed into his own.

Moira felt the shock-wave of evil sweep over them and gasped, tightening her grip on the hands to right and left. Fighting back, she rallied. One of the Group had fainted but his neighbours had joined hands across him; the rule had to be 'no stopping for casualties'.

She knew, with a flash of certainty, what she had to do next.

She ordered: 'Joy Hassell! Project Joy to John!'

The Group heard and understood. Some had known Joy and the others had been given a photograph to study, for she was one of the prepared weapons. Bracing themselves against the black tide still flowing from Stonehenge, they worked together, building up Joy's image.

Sonia's body had been removed and the first of the prisoner-victims, bound and gibbering with terror from Stanley's reviving injection, had been flung down on the Altar Stone. He had slipped on Sonia's copious blood, and the two men responsible for bringing forward the victims were having a struggle to place him for John's knife. Karen's incantation had become specific, launching the tide of power in support of the 6,000 soldiers already fanning out in the skies of Britain, strengthening their resolve, binding any urge to compassion, numbing and paralysing all who would resist them. John, in a rage of destruction now that blood had flowed, roared at his assistants to hold the sacrifice still. He raised the knife.

In that instant the earth moved. The great uprights of the trilithons groaned at the tremor and one of the capstan lintels screeched.

Briefly, the screech merged with John's scream, and Karen failed to distinguish the two. Then she realized that John had dropped the knife and was staring transfixed past her shoulder. Karen spun round and saw what he saw: misty but unmistakable, Joy, his dead golden wife, as she had been at the Grand Sabbat before the lance impaled her but with a face of infinite love and infinite sadness.

John screamed again, then turned and ran.

Joy flickered, was gone – and reappeared, running ahead of him.

Half blind with fury, Karen snatched up the knife and dispatched the sacrifice, ordering the next to be prepared. She knew the source, now; Moira and Dan, her mortal enemies, were nearby and striking back. She flung venom at them and then directed all her power at John, who had reached a horse and leaped into the saddle.

He tried to ride away but could feel her power drawing the horse back, in a tightening spiral round the Henge, inwards and inwards though he tugged at the reins till the horse's mouth bled. Joy was away, beyond the earthworks, still calling to him, but he was helpless. He screamed again in misery and despair. The horse brought him almost to the Altar Stone and then reared in panic at another victim's dying cry. John was thrown from the saddle, hitting one of the uprights. He fell to the ground inside a trilithon archway and the horse bolted away, trampling him as it turned.

John lay there, three-quarters stunned, but conscious enough to know that his back was broken. He would never move again and he did not care. He watched, almost with detachment, Karen at her murderous work. Dimly he heard the exultant cries of the circling Angels of Lucifer and the shrieks of the victims. He did not care. He had willed all this and he was past redemption.

The earth was trembling again, quaking and shuddering under his ruined back. He saw, against the sky, the uprights of the trilithon move, scraping a hand's-breadth outwards along the underside of the lintel. A shower of splintered sarsen fell around him. What did it matter?

But through the haze of pain, golden Joy would not let him rest. She stood by the upright, urging him, pleading with him; it does matter, there is still something you can do, you can help to stem the tide you unleashed. . . . There were others with her. He lay in a circle of people – Moira, Dan, other familiar faces . . . No, they must leave him, it was not to be borne . . . His eyes were drawn back, despite his shame, to the figure who pleaded with him, his golden Joy, his accuser, his dead beloved . . .

Then she was blotted out by Karen, towering over him with the knife, the two helpers behind her. Her face was a mask of hatred and she pointed at him with an arm that was red to the elbow.

'*Now him!*'

John was not afraid; death did not matter. But he was furious at her for obscuring Joy and he could feel the shadowy ring of Moira, Dan and the others, urging him.

The earth trembled again.

Something broke loose in the dying John and he cried: 'Mother Earth! Great Mother! Destroy her!'

The last thing he saw was the uprights falling outwards

and the huge lintel crashing down to obliterate Karen and himself.

At Avebury the battle had seemed endless; two more had fainted and even Moira, locked in a nightmare of clashing darkness and light, was beginning to wonder if she could survive much longer. But near the worst of it, she had felt John, or a part of him, reaching out to them; tormented and confused, he was a breach in evil's armour and she had hung on, gasping.

Then, without warning, the dark wave had shattered.

Knowledge of victory swept over them. Moira could feel the tears of relief running down her cheeks, hear the others laughing in triumph, some of them near to hysteria; feel Dan's arms around her; hear Miriam excitedly relaying Bruce's reports.

She bathed in the tide of success for a few moments longer, then pulled herself up. Quietening the Group, assuring herself that the three unconscious ones were all right and re-establishing control, she made them listen.

'We've broken the Angels of Lucifer, with the Goddess's help. They challenged her once too often. But she's still challenged. Right now the soldiers of Beehive are setting out to steal or destroy what the survivors have built. They'll be on their way to Camp Cerridwen at this moment – and to all the other places, some good and some not so good – but even the worst aren't as evil as what Harley wants to impose. He's damned himself by the allies he sought and the methods he used. He mustn't be allowed to succeed – I don't have to tell you that. . . . Our people at home in Wales are still working to feed us power. So let's *use* it. Make victory complete . . . And remember, the Earth Mother's with us. You heard what Bruce reported – an earth tremor hit Stonehenge and brought down the stones on Karen and John. *But it didn't reach here* – or anywhere else, is my guess. And what does that mean?'

She held out her hands and the ring re-formed. When she knew it had re-formed mentally and astrally as well, she gave the word.

'Speak to the soldiers. Speak of peace.'

'It's as though the Earth had punished them,' Captain Brodie said, wonderingly.

The two pilots had watched the whole murderous ritual, held almost hypnotically in their seats, feeling its evil like a corrosive vapour in the air. When the huge sarsen trilithon had splayed outwards and collapsed on the Black Mamba and her High Priest (who seemed to have lost his nerve but been dragged back, in that crazy horseback spiral), Brodie had instinctively reached for his switches to take off, visualizing a shock wave that might damage the helicopter. But he had realized at once that no shock was coming, only the faintest tremble. It did not make sense because the trilithons were barely 200 metres away, and a narrow fissure had appeared in the ground across the heart of the Henge and reached almost halfway to where they sat. The chopper should have been shaken like a child's rattle. . . . The horses, away on their right, had plunged and pulled at their reins and three of them had managed to tear free from the fence and had bolted. But then animals, Brodie told himself, sensed many things that men and helicopters did not.

'They're finished now,' Denning said. 'Look – without *her*, they don't know what to do.'

It was true. Most of the Angels of Lucifer were wandering or crouching among the megaliths, bewildered and aimless. Three or four were arguing between themselves, as though they had the will to assume leadership but not the agreement. The seven sacrificed bodies lay in a row out-side the sarsen horseshoe, bloodstained and forgotten.

'What do *we* do, Skip?' Denning asked.

'I don't know, Den. I just don't know.'

Denning glanced at his commander and friend, con-cerned. It wasn't like the Skipper to be indecisive. He must be as numbed by everything as he felt himself. . . . Denning turned his eyes to the Henge again and suddenly froze.

'Skipper – the Dust!'

Out of the fissure the dreadful miasma of the Madness was seeping, unnoticed by the Angels till it was already enveloping them. Brodie and Denning, well conditioned by drill, grabbed their respirators and snapped them over their mouths while the drifting cloud was still 100 metres away.

Then the Angels realized and panicked.

For a few seconds they ran hither and thither, hopelessly trying to dodge the Dust. Then two or three of them began to race towards the helicopter and, like a cattle stampede, the rest followed. Brodie took one look at the wild-eyed naked mob, coming closer every second, and hit his switches. The rotors whirled into life and the chopper rose, sliding briefly over the vision of crazed upturned faces and plead-ing outstretched arms, then banking as though to shake free of the horror. . . . Up and up into the dawn sky till Brodie felt free and content to hover.

'They were doomed already – they'd breathed it,' Den-ning said.

'More than that, Den. They didn't *deserve* rescuing.'

'Do any of us? If Operation Skylight's allied to *that* sort of thing?' It was almost a seditious question and he won-dered how Brodie would take it; for the captain, much as he liked and respected him, was a conventional soldier with a very simple sense of duty.

'That depends,' Brodie said, to Denning's astonishment, 'on what we do now.'

'Our orders say "In the event of complete loss of contact with Karen Morley and her group, you will report the fact, and your position, to Base, and await instructions",' Denning pointed out.

Brodie did not answer for a while but rotated the chopper slowly so that the horizon passed before their eyes in a stately panorama. Then he smiled and said, 'Damn the orders. We will spend a little time sweeping the area with our detector scoop open, to see if what I suspect is true – that the only Dust outbreak was at Stonehenge. Then we'll put her down in a nice field somewhere and think. Not awaiting instructions, Den – awaiting enlightenment. . . . Are you with me?'

The lieutenant leaned back in his seat, feeling a contentment he had not yet even begun to analyse. 'I'm with you, Skip. I'm with you all the way.'

'B' Company was being transported by the RAF and the major resented the fact. Once, his company had had its own choppers, flown by pilots under his personal command; but all such privileged units had been stripped of their aircraft on Beehive Amber, every machine being transferred to a flexible common pool. The major knew it had been necessary; Operation Skylight, for example, could only have been mounted on a shuttle basis. But at least he might have had the luck to be shuttled by Army machines. The RAF had an infuriatingly irreverent attitude to 'Pongos'.

He felt unreasonably relieved when the RAF had deposited 'B' Company on the outskirts of the little Suffolk town of Needham Market, his alloted HQ, and departed. Not even a decent salute from that puppy of a flight-lieutenant. Oh well – forget them. 'B' Company had work to do.

The major wished he could pin down the vague feeling of unease that possessed him. He didn't dislike the RAF *that* much. And, anyway, they had gone.

He watched his three platoons deploy for the advance into the town – left front, right front and one in reserve in case of trouble. Of course there would be none.

Even as he formulated the reassuring thought, the firing started. Shotguns by the sound of it, from that house ahead of No 5 Platoon. But why weren't No 5 replying? The target was clear – he had seen the muzzle-smoke himself. . . .

He rapped a fire order to the mortar section corporal beside him. A couple of mortar bombs through that slate roof and the rats would come running.

No 5 Platoon still hadn't replied to the single opening volley. What the hell were they up to? They were out of shotgun range anyway – they had the bastards on toast!

He realized the mortar hadn't fired yet, either, and he rapped over his shoulder: 'You heard me, Corporal! Get cracking?'

'Why?' the corporal asked, calmly.

The major could not believe his ears. He spun round to face the corporal, who stood by the mortar with his thumbs stuck in his belt.

'Why, man? Because I gave you an order! By Christ, I'll have your stripes!'

'There are people in that house, sir.'

'Of *course* there are bloody people! That's why I want it demolished. They're firing at us!' And what the hell was *he* doing, arguing with an NCO?

'Only warning shots, I think, sir. Our lads are still out of range. And the firing's stopped.'

'It'll bloody soon start again when they're *in* range!'

'I don't think so, sir. Look.' The corporal pointed past him towards No 5 Platoon.

The bewildering unreality of the scene left the major, for once in his life, without even an expletive. The men of No 5 Platoon were walking relaxedly towards the house. Some had their hands shoulder-high; one or two waved white handkerchiefs; some even had their hands in their pockets. And not one of them carried a weapon. The major saw, incredulously, the rifles and LMGs lying abandoned on the grass where the platoon had first deployed. . . . And coming to meet No 5 Platoon, three civilians were emerging from the house, their shotguns broken open and cradled casually in the crooks of their arms.

'If I were you, sir,' the corporal said kindly, 'I'd take a walk into the town – more of a village really, isn't it? – and start making friends. There's bound to be a committee or something. See how we can fit in with them, like. After all, it's not many weeks to harvest. They could probably do with our help.'

He watched as the major stumbled away towards the houses without so much as opening his mouth. Not a bad old stick, as company commanders go, the corporal thought. Bark worse than his bite. Just a bit slow on the uptake, sometimes.

At Camp Cerridwen some of the Army assault group lay on the grass enjoying the sky – after all, they hadn't seen much of it recently – while others strolled around the cabins inquisitively. Those with an eye for craftsmanship admired the way obvious amateurs had solved the problems of building. The Signals sergeant, who had been an electrician before he enlisted, muttered in frustration because the water-powered generating system had had its vital parts removed; it was obviously a neat job and he'd have liked to see it in action.

The assault group commander, a young captain with a face like a Mafioso, sat on the river bank arguing with his two platoon commanders and the CSM.

'I'd like it, too, for Christ's sake. But there's nearly 100 of us – and if we can get the wives out of Beehive (and take that grin off your face, Sar'-Major, you randy sod) we'd be more like 150. This place just couldn't absorb us. By the look of it, it's about the optimum size already – they wouldn't thank us for turning it into a ruddy town.'

'Couldn't we build another, downstream a bit?' one of the lieutenants suggested. He was, after all, a Welshman.

'Not enough hectares to support us,' the CSM said. 'You could see as we came up – they've got every meadow and clearing in use, right down to the village. No, it's a pity, but I reckon the OC's right.'

'What do we do, then?'

'Look around for somewhere with elbow-room, is my idea,' the captain said. 'Settle in and as soon as things are quiet, send the choppers for the wives.'

'I hope they'll be able to refuel.'

'Well, if they can't, the girls'll have to walk, won't they? Good for their figures. We're not leaving them in that stinking warren, that's for sure. Besides, if we didn't get 'em to the lads quick, we'd have a mutiny on our hands. And you know how seriously I view mutiny.'

Everyone smiled politely at the OC's little joke.

'I wish we could hang around for a day or two and meet the dreaded witches,' he went on. 'They've done a grand job here and it'd have been interesting to talk to them. But they'll probably stay under cover till we're well away. You can't blame them. After all, they may not know what's been happening.'

'Bet they do, sir,' the CSM said. 'They're bloody telepathic. My aunt was one. Unnerving – we couldn't keep a thing from her.'

'I think I'll stick to radio,' the captain said. 'You can always switch that off. . . . Right, Sar'-Major, get 'em fell in. Take-off in twenty minutes. We'll put down at the village and ask if there's a site around here where a mob of old sweats can plant spuds and things. . . . And tell this undisciplined shower that if they leave so much as a fag-end littering this nice clean camp, I'll have 'em on jankers for fourteeen days.'

The Royal Navy had, naturally, suffered worst from the great earthquake of the year before, with its attendant tidal waves. Of its total tonnage, 64.3 per cent had been lost at sea, either sunk or flung against various coasts; 27.1 per cent had been damaged beyond repair in port; and the remainder, with the proud exception of HMS *Ringo*, had also been in port but less damaged so that repair might be possible when and if the facilities became available. No estimate of how many men of the lost ships' companies had survived was possible, because those fortunate enough to be ashore or to reach land had been cut off from all channels of command, and had had no choice if they wanted to survive but to regard themselves as discharged and try to join local communities.

So all that had been left of the Senior Service, as a functioning organization, was the Admiralty command structure in Beehive, unhappily lent piecemeal to the Army and RAF to keep them employed – and HMS *Ringo*, alive and well and living at Stornoway on the Isle of Lewis in the Outer Hebrides.

HMS *Ringo* (Commander J. B. MacLeod, RN) owed her escape from the universal disaster to her function. A nuclear submarine designed for maximum-depth work, she had been on a survey mission 6000-plus metres down in the Cape Verde Basin at the time. Her mother ship on surface, *Ringo*'s only contact with the outside world, had received the Admiralty's urgent warnings, and realizing that *Ringo* had not a hope in hell of surfacing *and* reaching port in the hours available, had wisely ordered MacLeod to stay where he was for as long as he could. The mother ship had then raced her guts out to reach Dakar, the nearest port, where she had in due course been smashed to scrap-iron by the tidal wave – though most of her ship's company got away and were absorbed, with seamanlike adaptability, into the life-style of various villages in the Senegalese hinterland, where the earthquake had wreaked much havoc and extra hands were welcome. *Ringo* had stayed below, riding out currents and buffetings unprecedented at such a depth, for another twenty-three days, till MacLeod calculated that surface conditions should be manageable.

The Admiralty had been incredulously joyful to learn, by atmospheric-laden radio, that they actually had a sea-going ship under their command, in full working order. They had ordered MacLeod to Stornoway, which was known to be usable and relatively clear of wreckage and MacLeod, a Hebridean himself, had been glad to comply. There, he was to await further orders, which were unlikely to be forthcoming until Operation Skylight.

There had been much to keep MacLeod and his men busy, for the Isle of Lewis had been hit by earthquake, tidal wave, and one – fortunately localized – Dust outbreak. *Ringo*'s greatest gift to the island's survivors was her nuclear engines which could run virtually for ever. Within three weeks they had rigged a power supply to Stornoway itself and in the following months had steadily extended it to neighbouring homesteads. There had been nine marriages, during the winter and spring, between members of the ship's company and island girls, for the tidal wave, catching all too many Lewis men at sea or vainly trying to secure their precious boats at the last moment, had left many widows. MacLeod himself had every reason to believe that he was a widower, and only the impossibility of confirming the fact had kept him back from regularizing his very satisfactory relationship with the Provost's eldest daughter.

The warning order for Operation Skylight had seemed to come from an unreal world, but it was an order, and MacLeod and his officers had made the necessary preparations.

When the operational order came, MacLeod and half a dozen ratings were a kilometre outside Stornoway, puzzling over the problems of a blown-down power line that had to cross some awkward terrain, and for which new poles, which were in short supply, would somehow have to be improvised. The Yeoman of Signals came hurrying up the hill on a bicycle and handed the signal from to MacLeod.

'From C-in-C Home Fleet, sir.'

Commander MacLeod found himself strangely reluctant to look at the signal. He was aware, too, of the sudden anxious silence among the men at his side. With an effort, he read the signal – for some reason, aloud, which was not his habit.

'C-IN-C HOME FLEET TO HMS RINGO. PROCEED FORTHWITH TO STRANRAER WIGTOWNSHIRE AND PLACE YOURSELF UNDER COMMAND OF ARMY OFFICER I/C STRANRAER AREA TO ASSIST IN CONTROL OF CIVILIAN POPULATION.'

MacLeod looked around the faces of his men. He looked at the fallen line. He looked down the hill at the little harbour town. Then he turned back to the Yeoman of Signals who stood with signal pad and ballpoint ready.

Commander MacLeod said, loudly and firmly: 'Make: "HMS RINGO TO C-IN-C HOME FLEET. NO THANK YOU. WE LIKE IT HERE." '

At Windsor Castle it took a little while longer than elsewhere for the position to become clear. For an hour or two, the wary defenders could hardly believe that the soldiers who strolled in the garden at the foot of the Round Tower were not setting some devious trap to tempt them out. When this misunderstanding was finally cleared up, the lingering military instincts of the assault group were a little disappointed that the King would not allow them to mount a ceremonial Royal Guard until *after* lunch. In the event, the mounting of the Guard was put off until the following morning, for the King decreed major inroads into the hitherto carefully rationed Castle wine cellar and the lunch – with soldiers, witches and the Royal Family amicably intermingled – became celebratory and somewhat prolonged.

General Mullard's professional nose told him that something was going wrong long before the truth penetrated Harley's megalomaniac euphoria. At first it was only a vague feeling; the sense of gathering momentum which always marked a well-conceived operation was taking longer to reach him than it should have done. The big Ops Room map was full of symbols, indicating units already airborne and reporting their positions en route. The progress chart on the opposite wall to Mullard's high desk had also begun to fill up on schedule; it listed the designated HQs and special objectives by name, and had blank columns for 'Take-Off', 'Landing', 'Occupation Achieved', with a wider one for 'Remarks'. Similar but smaller charts flanked it, for reports from regional Hives of the progress of their own operations. On all of these, actual departure times for the first waves had been entered in the 'Take-Off' column with commendable punctuality. The 'Landing' column had also begun to fill but too many of the times were anything from five to twenty minutes later than the ETAs laid down. If the weather had been bad, Mullard could have understood this, because the ETAs had been calculated on the basis of normal June flying conditions. But the day was fine, clear and almost windless everywhere. Some unknown factor was slowing down the flights by a roughly uniform percentage and the puzzle nagged at Mullard's mind.

As the shuttle proceeded, the delay was becoming cumulative. Second-wave entries were beginning to appear in the 'Take-Off' column and they were all behind schedule – some of them even more so than could be accounted for by the mysteriously longer flying times. Delays were taking place on the ground too, at the helicopter bases where all should have been going like clockwork. The general detailed a GSO 1 to chase up the bases and the other Hives for explanations. The replies were all blandly reassuring; the shuttle was going smoothly, any delays were due to the late return of the first shuttles, there were occasional technical or refuelling problems but nothing more than had been allowed for in planning. General Mullard did not like it. Even the tone of the reports lacked the note of slightly nervous self-justification normally to be expected when the top brass asked questions. They were *too* bland and it was the general who felt nervous.

Beside him, Harley clucked with delight every time a new entry was made in the 'Take-Off' or 'Landing' columns. After a while Mullard felt in duty bound to remark 'The reported times are lagging behind schedule, you know'.

Harley brushed it aside. 'What's a few minutes here or there? This is a military operation, General, not Trooping the Colour. Your boys are doing splendidly.'

Maybe, Mullard thought, with a sudden angry flash of dislike for the man beside him. But all he said was: 'There should be more in the "Occupation Achieved" column by now.'

'There are three – no, four. The others are probably too busy to report.'

'A force commander,' Mullard snapped, 'whether he's a lance-corporal or a bloody general, is never too busy to report.'

Harley smiled loftily. 'You're an old Blimp, Mullard.'

Mullard bit back a retort and instead snatched a phone. 'Get me Needham Market,' he barked, having picked one of the four 'Occupation Achieved' names at random. It took about seven minutes for him to be put through, announce himself and demand to speak to the force commander, and another two for a mere lieutenant to be brought to the radio.

'Sorry, sir, the OC's busy. The committee chairman's showing him around the place.' The boy's voice was amiably casual.

'Are you in charge in his absence, Lieutenant?'

'I suppose so, yes.'

'You *suppose* so.' The general's voice was pure ice. 'Then give me your own progress report.'

'Oh, we're settling in nicely, General. Nice place, nice people.'

Some instinct warned General Mullard not to react as he would normally have done to this incredible conversation, but to handle it like a nurse with a slightly delirious patient. 'Any casualties?' he asked calmly. 'On either side?'

'Oh, no. Of course not.'

489

'So I take it you have established control without trouble.'

'The question doesn't arise. I don't think you quite realize how things are, General. The war is over.'

This boy is mad, the general told himself. He's *got* to be. 'Is there any other officer with you at HQ at the moment, lieutenant?'

'Yes, sir. Lieutenant Spillman.'

'Put him on.'

After a pause, another voice. 'Spillman here.'

'Lieutenant, this is General Mullard. Did you hear the other end of this conversation?'

'Ye-es.'

'Then you will realize that your brother officer's mind has become unhinged, for whatever reason. You will place him under arrest and have your commanding officer report to me personally by radio the moment he returns.'

Spillman's laugh was relaxed, genuinely amused. 'Oh, really, General Mullard. Get stuffed.'

The radio went dead.

Mullard stared at the telephone in his hand. In that moment, with awful certainty, he knew that he was not dealing with one mad officer or even two or even with a mutinous unit. He knew, and he could not tell how he knew, that Operation Skylight faced total, irretrievable, inexplicable collapse.

Like an automaton, he had himself connected by radio with Ashford in Kent, Ripley in Surrey and Lechlade in Gloucestershire, the three other names that had so far appeared in the 'Occupation Achieved' column. He deliberately watched his words because Harley was within hearing and he did not want to be involved with him for the moment. At Ashford he got a sergeant. At Ripley, he actually got the commanding officer. At Lechlade, a platoon commander's batman. To each, he listened carefully.

When he had finished, he put down the telephone and turned to Harley.

'Sir Reginald,' he said, 'your dream is over. Operation Skylight no longer exists.'

Harley stared at him. 'What *are* you talking about? Have you gone mad?'

'That's a question I'll have to go into with myself, later. But I am telling you. All four of those units have torn up their orders and laid down their arms. They have not merely fraternized with the local civilians – they are busy merging with them. They are not *rebelling* against Beehive. They have merely brushed Beehive aside as irrelevant. And you can be absolutely certain that all the other units and assault groups will be doing exactly the same. You're finished, Harley.'

Harley had jumped to his feet. 'Finished?' he hissed. 'You don't know what you're saying! . . . Get me the man at Stonehenge!'

Mullard shrugged and picked up the telephone. 'Get Captain Brodie, in the helicopter standing by at Stonehenge.'

While he was waiting, a stunned-looking Admiralty officer appeared at his elbow with a message in his hand. Mullard took it from him, read it, and laughed, passing it to Harley. *'Far-called, our navies melt away; On dune and headland sinks the fire: Lo, all our pomp of yesterday Is one with Nineveh and Tyre . . .'* he quoted softly, and then into the phone, 'Yes? . . . Thank you.' He laid down the receiver. 'There is no reply from Stonehenge.'

Harley screamed 'Colonel! Take over command! General Mullard has been taken ill!'

The GSO 1 came running and looked at Mullard in bewilderment. The general stood aside, gesturing towards

491

the command chair. 'You heard the man, colonel. Take over. For what it's worth.'

General Mullard walked out of the Operations Room without looking back. He went to his quarters and changed into civilian clothes. While he was doing it his wife came in. She looked at him, at first with astonishment but then with dawning understanding, though he had said nothing, only smiled at her.

'Where are we going?' she asked.

'Wherever the sun shines, Debbie.'

Deborah Mullard nodded and started packing two ruck-sacks. They hadn't used them since their last rambling holiday, three years ago. Her husband had often teased her for the nostalgia which had made her bring them to Beehive.

'You're taking it very calmly,' he said.

'Service wives are always ready to move, darling. . . . There's only one thing worries me, a little. Your face is well known. Might someone up there feel like taking it out on you?'

'If they do, my love, I've asked for it. But do you know what? Up there, I don't think anyone will be bothered.'

The WRAC corporal let the long rake with which she had been pushing symbols about fall disregarded on to the huge map. The map had become meaningless, anyway, and it was much more interesting to watch the Big Chief going mad, bellowing that single word over and over and over again.

'How about getting out of this mess?' the young flight-lieutenant beside her asked. 'We might as well, now. Coming with me?'

Dear Ned, of course she was going with him. If he didn't know that yet, he never would. . . . They elbowed their way out of the disorganized crowd into the corridor, Harley's monotonous cry fading graudally behind them as they went.

'What does *Götterdämmerung* mean, anyway?' Ned asked her, curiously. 'I never was a Wagner buff.'

In the lounge of the Red Lion at Avebury, Lenny's wife was serving her standard panacea, hot soup. The three who had fainted were still a little pale but fit. Young Jane, who 'reckoned she was a witch', was skipping around on Cloud Nine. She had begged to be allowed to join Camp Cerridwen and after a talk with Moira and Dan, Lenny and his wife had agreed.

Four of the guards had gone to fetch the vehicles; the car would pick up Bruce and his guard from near Stonehenge, keeping an eye open for drifting Dust according to Bruce's radioed warning, though on this windless day the outbreak seemed barely to have moved beyond the Henge itself. The leaderless Angels of Lucifer had disappeared at once, Bruce had reported, heading towards Savernake Forest with every symptom of panic.

The PAG and Lenny's group sat around the lounge, drinking their soup and talking animatedly until the vehicles arrived.

Dan stood up. 'Well, Lenny – all of you – thanks a lot for your hospitality. I'm sorry we had to descend on you like that and I'm sorry about the front door. We'll look after Jane, don't worry.'

'Don't you apologize for nothing,' Lenny told him. 'I ain't figured it all out yet, and maybe I never will, properly. But I know a battle when I smell one – and I reckon something happened under our roof we can be proud of.'

'Can you smell victory, too, Lenny?'

Lenny smiled. 'Like a garden full of flowers.'

'Me too,' Dan said. 'Come along, boys and girls. Time to go home.'

EPILOGUE

There had been many handfastings and several Christian weddings at Camp Cerridwen in the year and three-quarters of its existence; but the handfasting of Mary Andrews and Nigel Pickering was a very special one. For one thing, until a week before it, they had not seen each other for two years – nor, since the great earthquake, had either of them known if the other was alive or dead. Very soon after the catastrophic Grand Sabbat on Bell Beacon, at which Mary had been Sabbat Maiden and Nigel her Priest, Nigel had been called to Yorkshire by the death of his father and the need to take over the family's small printing business. He and Mary had corresponded almost daily, for although not lovers or even engaged, they had been a close working partnership in their coven and they had missed each other very much. But with Nigel tied down by work and Mary by an invalid mother, they had not been able to visit each other. Nigel had at last been able to arrange a weekend journey to see her, at which (he had decided and she had sensed) he was going to propose to her.

The earthquake had struck a week too early.

Both had survived by the skin of their teeth. Mary and

her mother had been adopted by a neighbouring family, after the earthquake had destroyed their house; but three days later the family had succumbed to the Madness and Mary had been lucky to get her mother away in a stolen car, her sick mother driving while Mary nursed a broken arm. They had found a doctor in a Berkshire village who had set the arm and had settled down with the village's tiny group of survivors, defending themselves in a barricaded farmhouse on meagre rations till the Madness was over. Mary's mother, whose illness required special food, had died in spite of all the doctor could do for her.

Nigel, his home town of Elland a burning shambles, had taken to the moors with his brother, and they too had teamed up with a small community struggling to keep alive on poor land.

Mary and Nigel had both tried, especially after the collapse of Operation Skylight had brought a strange peace to the country, to get news of each other, however forlorn the hope. But after a travelling group had told Mary that Elland had been wiped out and Dan (whose brother's marriage to the only unattached woman in the community had made him even more aware of his loneliness) had actually trekked to Cookham in search of her and had found no clue, in both of them hope had faded to a dream.

Nigel had not returned to his moorland group. Camp Cerridwen was known by repute to virtually every witch in the country within two or three months of Skylight – as Midsummer 2004 was now called by everybody, transferring the name of the failed Operation to the dawn of the peace which had followed it. So Nigel had decided to see Moira and Dan again, and had made his way to Dyfnant Forest at the end of August. He had been welcomed with delight and persuaded, without difficulty, to stay. Camp Cerridwen had unanimously decided to limit their population to a maximum of 200, to keep it agriculturally viable and to preserve its character. But immediately after Skylight, when dozens of civilianized Army radio operators became aware of Geraint and Tonia's ham network and had enthusiastically joined it, news of survivors in search of friends and relatives had become a major part of its traffic. So about thirty people, including one complete coven from Camp Cerridwen, had departed with everyone's blessing to reunite families believed dead or to pick up old threads believed broken. And that left room for desirable recruits like Nigel.

Nigel had settled in well, his printer's instincts drawing him to Geraint and Tonia. He and they dreamed of a printed newspaper but that was out of the question for the present. He had, however, scoured nearby ruined towns with a horse and cart and in Llanfyllin had unearthed treasure in the shape of a stencil duplicator and a good stock of paper, ink and stencils. Foraging parties, which were now a regular activity of most communities, had been briefed on what to look for and the stock had grown substantially. So with the Samhain 2005 issue as No 1, Camp Cerridwen's news sheet had become a weekly 'newspaper'. They called it *The Cauldron* after the Welsh Goddess's legendary vessel, and in memory of a respected Wiccan newsletter of the 1970s and '80s. It circulated in the camp and New Dyfnant and travelled with the trading carts over an area of twenty or thirty kilometres around. Soon its example was being followed in other places, based on the radio network which was becoming a well-organized news agency with Camp Cerridwen as its acknowledged nerve-centre.

Radio reception had improved steadily and news from abroad was beginning to take on a coherent shape. The world picture ranged from outright military dictatorship in one or two countries (Belgium, for example) to a situation very like Britain's, where a complex pattern of spontaneous cooperation between varied kinds of community was evolving in the absence of any State coercive apparatus. France and Denmark were outstanding examples. In the Arab countries, bedouin habits had been naturally readopted and in Israel, her rapidly expanding industry almost completely destroyed by the earthquake, a renaissance of kibbutzim had been equally natural. In some countries, such as Holland, the struggle to control the environment demanded large-scale cooperation as rapidly as it could be forged; the Dutch already had a functioning democratic government, an empirical but energetic structure, organizing the repair of the dykes and the reclaiming of polders by methods they would have regarded as crude two years before but which were getting the job done. Though completely unaggressive, they were having a marked moral effect on their Belgian neighbours, who resented the military clique in power and were likely to sweep it away before long, with 'Benelux' as their slogan of revolt.

In the Soviet Union, as Dan remarked to Geraint when after several months the picture became reasonably clear, 'the Earth Mother seems to have intervened in person'. Moscow Beehive had been completely wiped out by the earthquake, and with typical Russian centralism it had housed virtually everyone who mattered. Regional hives had attempted some kind of a Skylight-type takeover but, shorn of its real leaders, the *Apparat* had had little impact. The conscript armies, unequal in any case to the vastness of the territory, had been dissolved by the urge to go home. Here, too, a useful pattern for survival existed: the collective farms. Heavily depopulated as they were, they formed natural rallying-points for disbanded soldiers and fugitive townsfolk, and many of them seemed to have revived admirably.

What was happening in China, it was still too early to say; news was too thin and at too many removes. But such hints as there were seemed to point to a development similar to Russia's.

In India, the Dust had taken a terrible toll; New Delhi had given a vinegar-mask warning in good time, but the organization of supplies had been difficult and millions had been affected. Of those who were left at the end of the Madness, hundreds of thousands had contracted plague as they looted the uninhabitable cities for food. The remnants of the once-vast population had reverted to their immemorial village life and after disaster probably unparalleled anywhere else in the world, were achieving some kind of stability. Strangely enough, radio news from India was fairly plentiful; skilled refugees from a vanished technological civilization seemed to have an urge to communicate and enough of them had found or improvised the means.

America, being a continent and not a country in the ordinary sense, reflected most of these patterns. Urban life had virtually ceased to exist; New York, Los Angeles and other great cities were unapproachable rubble-heaps. There had been a general tendency to revert to State identity and in one or two places – Vermont, Illinois, Idaho – embryo State organizations were already struggling into being. Elsewhere – Oklahoma, Maine, Montana – the pattern seemed to be purely tribal and family, paralleling the British. There were pockets of brigandism, particularly on the fringes of the agricultural areas, and other pockets of fervently religious cohesion; Mormon Utah had a positively Messianic sense of identity. In California, as might be expected, a confusing patchwork of differently motivated communities vied with each other for attention. The American Beehives, with local patriotism as a morale factor in mind, had been organized in general on a State-by-State basis (with much cross-posting of personnel to give units a local character – a political decision which had greatly annoyed the top brass). But this had largely backfired. For the ordinary GI, and for many of his officers, home was too close, and in the face of universal destruction, too tempting. In many States, after Skylight, the Army had dwindled to a hard core of ex-townsmen whose homes, and even the remnants of whose communities, had vanished – and they were surrounded by independently minded farming groups, many of them armed deserters from their own ranks. Some wise commanders, in these circumstances, had abandoned all ideas of control and tried instead to provide useful services and protection against bandits.

One factor, in Europe and America, interested Dan in particular; in how many places had the witchcraft movement and a psychic battle been significant? He was collecting a dossier on the subject, but he was only at the beginning of his research, for in many places witches were cautious about talking on the air about such things. But he had some evidence already; for example, he was pretty certain that in West Germany, northern Italy and the Basque areas of France and Spain the witches had been well organized and had played an effective part. Interesting, he told himself, that those were the places where the emerging pattern of life seemed closest to that of the British Isles, and where armies had most quickly melted into the working population.

The Cauldron carried at the bottom of its last page the imprint: 'Editor, Geraint Lloyd. News Editor, Tonia Lynd. Published by Nigel Pickering at Camp Cerridwen, Dyfnant Forest, Montgomeryshire, North Wales.'

Mary Andrews first saw a copy early in June, a gift from an intinerant barter-pedlar. She had read it all through, eagerly, for Moira, Dan, Rosemary, Greg and one or two other old friends were mentioned in the camp news. Then she came to the imprint.

Within twenty-four hours – as long as she needed to bargain for a bicycle and to say goodbye to her community – she was on her way to Camp Cerridwen. It took her three days, all of them tormented by doubt. Was he married or involved with someone? Had he changed? Had she herself, too much for him?

She need not have worried. She rode into the camp on the third evening, too impatient to seek out Moira and Dan and announce herself, but simply asking the first stranger she met where she could find Nigel Pickering. The stranger directed her to a cabin from which came the churning sound of a hand-operated duplicator.

He answered the door and stood for a second gazing at her incredulously. Then he flung his arms round her, almost knocking her over; and when they both got their breath back, his first words to her after two years were 'Will you marry me?'

'I am attending the – er – handfasting,' the Reverend Phillips explained, 'I will not say "under protest", because that would be unneighbourly; let us say "with a certain sense of impropriety". But I will *not* stay till the evening and be a party to their pagan festival.'

'Oh, come now, my friend,' Father Byrne smiled. ' "Be a party to"! – it sounds like being an accessory to a crime. *I* never actually *attend* their rituals, of course, but neither do I scurry away out of sight of them if they are held in the open air. And I often gladly accept an invitation to enter one of their Circles once the ritual is over and the sociable part begins. . . . And where's the "impropriety" about a wedding?'

'You call it a wedding?'

'Of course it's a wedding. Two rather likable young people are being joined together, as man and wife, in front of their community and by a procedure recognized by that community. That defines a wedding – all the more so in the absence of any civil machinery for the purpose. If they choose to call it a "handfasting", I find it a charming word. Etymologically, "wedding" means "a surety" – sounds like a mortgage, doesn't it? "Handfasting" is much prettier.'

'It is still a *pagan* ritual, father. And you and I, as ministers of God – how can *we* be involved?'

'We are involved by our love for the people concerned.' The old priest sighed. 'And increasingly – God forgive me if I err – I have come to regard "pagan" as a rather meaningless label, in the two years since these young Samaritans picked up a sick old priest by Lake Vyrnwy and brought him to this camp. The Good Samaritan was a heretic, too, remember – which was the point of our Lord's parable. . . . If you did watch tonight's Midsummer Sabbat, you would see 150 witches, as naked as the day they were born . . .' He smiled at his friend's shudder and went on: 'Shame at nakedness was the first symptom of the Fall, was it not? . . . As naked as the day they were born, joyfully saluting their Maker and honouring the Earth which is the Maker's gift. It matters less than I used to think, that they visualize that Maker as a duality of God and Goddess. You and I visualize Him as a Trinity – and the vast majority of *my* co-religionists at least worship a Goddess in the shape of the Blessed Virgin, whatever we theologians may try to tell them about the distinction between *latria* and *hyperdulia*. . . . Are *any* of us wholly wrong, John? Have any of us a monopoly of the Mystery? . . . Do not mistake me; I am a Catholic and I believe as you do that Christ is the way and the truth and the life. I believe that these good people –

and they *are* good, you know that as well as I do – are missing much by not following that way. But nor will anyone convince me, any longer, that their way leads in the *opposite* direction. Or that I should be too proud to learn something from them. Etymologically, again, "pagan" means "of the countryside" – and we are certainly that here, all of us. And when tonight, the thirteen covens gather in their little Circles within the Great Circle, I shall be outside that Circle, but in a sense not alien to it. When they dance around the fire in honour of the Earth and the God-given currents that flow in her, I shall be with them in spirit, and I believe – if I may put it this way – that God will be, too.'

The minister was silent for a while and then said: 'I will agree with you on one point, anyway. These *are* good people, however misguided their ways. And rightly or wrongly, I am happy to wish Divine blessing on the – er – handfasting.'

Tactfully, Father Byrne managed not to smile at the younger man. 'The Prince of Peace,' he said, 'moves in mysterious ways.'

The Circle of cut blossom on the grass contained the members of Nigel's coven, and Nigel and Mary themselves facing Moira and Dan, who had been invited to perform the handfasting. They were all robed, out of deference to the many village guests among the remainder of the community squatting on the ground outside the ring of flowers. There was little human sound apart from the crooning of Eileen and Peter's nine-month-old daughter Deirdre, who thought the flowers were very pretty and wanted to reach and eat them.

Moira asked: 'Who comes to be joined together in the presence of the Goddess? What is thy name, O Man?'

'My name is Nigel.'

Dan asked: 'Who comes to be joined together in the presence of the God? What is thy name, O Woman?'

'My name is Mary.'

'Mary and Nigel, we greet you with joy. . . . Unity is balance and balance is unity. Hear then and understand.' Moira picked up the wand from the altar and continued: 'The wand that I hold is the symbol of Air. Know and remember, that this is the element of Life, of intelligence, of the inspiration which moves us onwards. By this wand of Air, we bring to your handfasting the power of Mind.'

Dan said: 'The sword that I hold is the symbol of Fire. Know and remember that this is the element of Light, of energy, of the vigour which runs through our veins. By this sword of Fire, we bring to your handfasting the power of Will.'

Moira said: 'The chalice that I hold is the symbol of Water. Know and remember that this is the element of Love, of growth, of the fruitfulness of the Great Mother. By this chalice of Water, we bring to your handfasting the power of Desire.'

Dan said: 'The pentacle that I hold is the symbol of Earth. Know and remember that this is the element of Law, of endurance, of the understanding which cannot be shaken. By this pentacle of Earth, we bring to your handfasting the power of the Steadfast . . .'

'How long will you be away, do you think?' Rosemary asked. It was past three in the morning, with the sky already lightening for the dawn and the pale full moon sliding to bed beyond the western hills. But the embers of the big Sabbat fire were hot enough for the four of them still to be skyclad, lingering after almost everybody else had gone to bed.

'Not more than a couple of weeks,' Dan said. 'It'll take the helicopters about three days to get all the representatives to Windsor and three to get us all home again. A week in between for the discussions.'

'How long will the fuel stocks last, ferrying people back and forth to Parliament?' Greg wondered.

'That's one of the items for discussion – how to use the helicopters best in the public interest, for as long as the stocks *do* last. There'll be people there who know how much Beehive had stockpiled. . . . Anyway, it's not a Parliament. It's a Constitutional Conference under the King's chairmanship, to arrange the rules for a Constituent Assembly, which'll decide the basis for a Parliament, which will then have to be elected. It's a long process and we've got to get it right.'

'The King's certainly thrown his hat in the ring,' Greg said, 'announcing that he'll offer his abdication to Parliament once it's elected.'

'Yes, but he did make it clear why – and he had to do it well in advance, to give people time to chew it over. It's so that we can start with a clean slate, politically – and that includes deciding whether we want a republic or a monarchy. My guess is that Parliament will hang on to the King *as* King – or even if they plump for a republic, they'll elect him President. He'd be the obvious choice.'

'I'm glad you and Moira have been called to the Conference,' Rosemary said, 'but I'm not sure I'd want either of you to be an MP. Camp Cerridwen needs you both. And *I* think Camp Cerridwen's important. Not just for the two hundred of us.'

Moira smiled. 'Anyway, that'll be out of the question for me for a few years – so I doubt if you could drag Dan away.'

'You're pregnant!' Rosemary cried.

'Two months.'

Greg laughed delightedly and Rosemary said: 'Well, that's marvellous. I'm about six weeks. We were going to tell you when we were absolutely sure – but I am, really.'

That ended the political discussion.

There were rather more people coming and going in the echoing corridors of Beehive these days, following the necessarily rough-and-ready decisions of the Constitutional Conference.

The guardhouses at the entrances were manned, for private looting had to be replaced by public salvaging; but the guards had little to do but keep an eye open for brigand groups attempting an organized raid – for such groups still existed, though their number was rapidly diminishing.

Then there was the Mint. Few people, even in Beehive, had known of the heavily protected 'Fort Mini-Knox' under Finsbury Park, in which the nation's gold reserves and much silver had been stored. After the Conference, it had been officially breeched and coining machinery, salvaged from the ruined Royal Mint by Tower Bridge, moved in beside it. The plan for getting a workable currency in circulation again was also rough-and-ready but practical. As soon as enough gold, cupro-nickel and bronze had been coined, distribution would start, as simultaneously as possible; £100 to each man, woman, and child in Britain, against a thumb-printed and signed receipt (parents or guardians signing for children under sixteen). That should be enough to start the replacement of clumsy barter by cash trade, though it might mean a certain temporary revival of brigandage, but district posses were being organized to deal with that. The funding of government, special allowances, loans to capitalize cooperatives, paper currency once confidence was established

– all these could be decided upon in due course by Parliament.

The power workers were very busy. The nuclear submarine-type generators at the London Beehive, and at each of the regional hives, were being rehabilitated as fast as the few available experts could deal with them, for linking to the National Grid which other gangs were working hard to restore on Surface. Generation by oil or coal was out of the question, probably for many years ahead; but it looked as though it might be possible to restore one or two of the hydro-electric stations.

Any rehabilitation of the Mohowatt couples, even if it had been practicable, was rejected out of hand.

Brenda and Gareth had returned to London, to organize the removal of her library to a suitable building near Bedford, as the nucleus of a conveniently central National Library. Both the British Museum Reading Room and the Bodleian at Oxford were unusable, but guards had been placed on their ruins against the day when manpower could be enlisted to salvage what remained of their contents.

Philip, too, had been briefly recalled to Beehive to inspect the ventilation system and ensure that it would remain adequate for the people who were having to work there. Betty had been unable to go with him, for they now had a month-old baby, but he had gone to their old cubicle and brought her back one or two of their personal belongings.

Among them was a poster which now hung on their cabin wall: a Zodiac painting by Johfra, a winged Virgo carrying a stem of barley in one hand and a flame-enclosing crystal egg in the other. Behind her were tilled fields and an open sky and she was surrounded by numinous symbols which Philip felt he was beginning to understand.

On her face was a secret smile.

Other Arrow Books of interest:

THE DANCE OF BLOOD

Stewart Farrar

For beautiful young model Louise Benson, marriage to Robert Page was her passport to the life of elegance and comfort she had always dreamed of. But before long the dream turned nightmare.

The sophisticated world of Robert and his friends hid a secret hell ruled by dark, primeval lusts . . . and Louise was to be their plaything.

Around her had closed a circle of evil – malevolent beyond belief, rooted deep in cruel rituals as old as man – evil which fed upon the very essence of life.

75p

THE SWORD OF ORLEY

Stewart Farrar

The dream . . . every detail of it had burst through into her consciousness, after its unreachable years below the threshold. She could see the chapel, see herself-not-herself spreadeagled naked on the stone altar, see the remorseless Gadd bending over her with the desecrated Host in his fingers. . . .

The psychic research team had gone to Orley Grange to investigate a ghost. What they found was a legacy of sacrilege, death and Satanism.

For Jane Blair in particular, the Grange's sinister chapel became a battleground as she fought for her sanity – for her life – against an evil so malevolent that its poison spread across the centuries. . . .

85p

DEATH DREAMS

William Katz

On a sleepy Saturday afternoon, Crista Spalding was playing by the garden lake with her daughter. After a life full of tragedy she had found love and security with a new husband and an adorable child. She had no idea that these were her last hours of happiness. At 6 p.m. her daughter, Jennie, drowned.

And then the nightmares began – the dreadful death dreams.

Jennie's ghost returned, night after night, voicelessly tormenting her mother, tugging at her dress and trying desperately to lead her towards the lake.

Are Crista's terrible experiences simply bad dreams? She has positive proof that they are not, but only one person will listen to her – nobody else dares believe the horrifying truth.

95p

MIST OVER PENDLE

Robert Neill

The forest of Pendle during the early seventeenth century: a wild inaccessible corner of Lancashire where the ancient fear of demons and witches is still part of life – and death.

When several local people die in mysterious circumstances, Squire Roger Nowell dismisses talk of witchcraft as superstition. But soon a series of hideous desecrations takes place, and there are unmistakable signs that a black coven is assembling to plot a campaign of evil and destruction.

Taking arms against the Devil, Nowell embarks upon a relentless hunt among the moorland farms for the witches and their sinister protector.

£1·25

BESTSELLERS FROM ARROW

All these books are available from your bookshop or newsagent or you can order them direct. Just tick the titles you want and complete the form below.

☐	BRUACH BLEND	Lillian Beckwith	90p
☐	THE HISTORY MAN	Malcolm Bradbury	90p
☐	A RUMOUR OF WAR	Philip Caputo	£1.25
☐	2001: A SPACE ODYSSEY	Arthur C. Clarke	£1.10
☐	THE GIRL WITH THE GOLDEN HAIR	Leslie Deane	£1.60
☐	BILLION DOLLAR KILLING	Paul Erdman	95p
☐	ZULU DAWN	Cy Endfield	95p
☐	FALLING ANGEL	William Hjortsberg	95p
☐	AT ONE WITH THE SEA	Naomi James	£1.25
☐	HITLER'S SPIES	David Kahn	£2.50
☐	IN GALLANT COMPANY	Alexander Kent	85p
☐	METROPOLITAN LIFE	Fran Lebowitz	95p
☐	THE CLIMATE OF HELL	Herbert Lieberman	£1.25
☐	THE MEMOIRS OF RICHARD NIXON	Richard Nixon	£4.95
☐	THE VALHALLA EXCHANGE	Harry Patterson	80p
☐	DANGEROUS OBSESSION	Natasha Peters	£1.85
☐	STRUMPET CITY	James Plunkett	£1.75
☐	SURFACE WITH DARING	Douglas Reeman	£1.00
☐	A DEMON IN MY VIEW	Ruth Rendell	85p

Postage _____

Total _____

ARROW BOOKS, BOOKSERVICE BY POST, PO BOX 29, DOUGLAS, ISLE OF MAN, BRITISH ISLES

Please enclose a cheque or postal order made out to Arrow Books Limited for the amount due including 8p per book for postage and packing for orders within the UK and 10p for overseas orders.

Please print clearly

NAME ....

ADDRESS ....

....

Whilst every effort is made to keep prices down and to keep popular books in print, Arrow Books cannot guarantee that prices will be the same as those advertised here or that the books will be available.